OASES

David A. Weiss

This book is a work of fiction. The events and characters are a product of the author's imagination, and any resemblance to actual incidents or persons, living or dead, is purely coincidental.

"Oases" by David A. Weiss, ISBN 978-1-949756-35-7.

Library of Congress Number on file with Publisher.

Manufactured in the United States of America.

Acknowledgements

I gratefully acknowledge those who have assisted me in this endeavor: Joyce McCormick who, as a long-time member of the Schenectady Fiction Writer's Club, has critiqued all eight of my published novels; Linda Hoxie, a friend from my tennis group, who critiqued and proofread this work and offered many excellent suggestions, including the addition of an invaluable character; my daughter-in-law Adrienne Weiss who proofread and critiqued this work and provided numerous valuable ideas; my daughter Lori Weiss who, as she has for my last six books, designed the cover; and my dear wife Joyce, who proofread and critiqued this work and continues to support me in my writing passion.

Quite apart from their abundant assistance, a common thread connects those whom I have acknowledged above. They are all kind, compassionate and steadfast, and exhibit the utmost character. Each has earned and enjoys my highest esteem.

Cover

The cover of "Oases" incorporates the center of a stunning sunset photograph of the J. N. Ding Darling National Wildlife Refuge on Sanibel Island, Florida, taken by and credited to Al Hoffacker. The full breadth of the photograph, which was posted on Tumbler by the U.S. Dept. of the Interior, 1/23/15, appeared on the cover of MowryJournal.com, posting 1/24/15 <https://mowryjournal.com/2015/01/24j-n-ding-darling-national-wildlife-refuge/>. The photograph can also be seen at <https://mowryjournal.files.wordpress.com/2015/01/ding-nwr.jpg>. Additional photographs of native wildlife of South Florida taken by Al Hoffacker may be seen on his Facebook page at <https://www.facebook.com/al.hoffacker>.

Lori A. Weiss, my wonderful and talented daughter, designed the cover of "Oases."

Contents

vi

CHAPTER I

EVERY ENDING IS A BEGINNING. Even death. But whether the cessation of a beating heart is merely the inception of vapid incarceration in a wooden box or the start of a spiritual rebirth in the realm of angels or some other unfathomable outcome, remains a mystery. Many deny the conundrum, certain what lies on the nether side of death's door. Perhaps they're right. Maybe not.

Armed with sad news, such were the ruminations of Kyle Gordon as he dialed the telephone number of his old college buddy Don Burns.

"Wonders never cease. Kyle Gordon actually knows how to call me."

Kyle would have countered Don's good-natured jab by saying he had called the wrong number, but given the reason for his call, such typical repartee needed to be skipped. He grabbed a quick breath. "I...uh...have some bad news. Bill Young passed away yesterday."

"You gotta be kidding."

"I wish I was." Kyle voiced the response despite knowing the reaction had been rhetorical.

"How? Was he ill or—"

"A drunk driver in a big SUV ran a red light and T-boned him. Eyewitnesses indicate the guy was flying like a stock car on a straightaway at Daytona. Turned Bill's Corolla into a mangled mass of crumpled metal. Bill didn't stand a chance." Kyle waited several seconds. "You still there, Don?"

"Yeah, just too stunned to react."

"I understand…and sorry to be the bearer of bad tidings, but I knew you'd want to know."

"Absolutely. When's the funeral?"

"Not sure. The exact date is yet to be fixed. I'm guessing it'll be in Provo, Utah, where Bill grew up, rather than his home in Florida."

"Do you plan to make the trip?"

"Definitely." With the answer to the obvious question not forthcoming, Kyle posed it. "What about you?"

"I…I doubt it. It's not that I…uh…don't want to, but I doubt that Bill would want me there."

"C'mon, as a member of the Inseparables, you can't say that."

"I wish you were right, but as far as Bill was concerned, I was *persona non grata.*"

"You're selling yourself short," said Kyle, aware not only of the circumstances behind Don's reluctance to attend the funeral, but facts to which Don was not privy. Disclosing what he knew was arguably unwise. Once the information crossed his lips, he could not pull it back. Discretion counseled silence, at least for the time being. Regardless, he had no doubt that he should encourage Don to attend. "Whatever transpired between you and Bill, I'm sure he'd want you there."

A doubting groan echoed from the other end of the line.

"Believe me. I know what I'm saying."

"You think Eric will come?" Eric Johanson was the last member of the Inseparables, four pals who had bonded during their days at Williams College.

"I'm sure he will. He's the one who called me with the bad news, though at the time he was yet to get the lowdown on the funeral, where and when it would be held."

"Well, I have to admit it would be great to see you guys, even if the occasion is a sad one."

"So, that means you'll come?"

"I didn't say that."

"True…but you'll come. Right?"

"Well…let's just say I'll think about it."

The progress, a lessening of Don's reluctance, cajoled Kyle to let the matter be, at least for the moment. "How's Linda?"

"Good, thanks."

"Lovely as ever, no doubt." The reference conjured a vivid image of the shapely, hazel-eyed brunette. Don and Linda, who had become sweethearts their freshman year at Williams College, had eloped the day after graduation. "Can you believe it…more than six freakin' years since we graduated?"

"Scary, isn't it? If statistics are right, roughly a third of our lives is behind us."

"Yeah…and we don't even get a break at half-time." Kyle heaved a sigh. "And thanks to that goddamn drunk driver, Bill didn't even make it through the second quarter."

"Not fair."

Kyle stemmed the urge to voice the cliché that life's unfair. "Of all people, Bill falls victim to a tanked asshole, one with a prior DUI, along with a prison record for burglary. And to make matters worse, the bastard walked away from the crash with only a few scratches."

"I hope they throw the book at the creep."

"Lot of good that'll do Bill."

A beleaguered sigh from the other end of the line underscored the assessment.

"Not to change the subject," said Kyle, "but all that stuff about Clinton Horstmeyer, it's really amazing, isn't it?" Horstmeyer, who had graduated with them in the Williams class of 2011, was Don's boss at the investment firm of Quigley and Watkins. The relationship had been in limbo ever since Horstmeyer had been arrested. "I was wondering—and tell me to shut up if I'm out of line—you hoping Clint never comes back to the office?"

"Well…"

Kyle read between the lines of the prolonged silence. Expensive suits may have replaced Horstmeyer's tattered jeans, but Clint was intolerable. "I understand. You'd rather not badmouth your boss, even if his days with the firm may be numbered. As my mom always said, 'If you can't say

3

something nice, don't say anything.'" Even before he finished the hackneyed saw, Kyle chided himself with a paraphrased version: *If your words are trite, shut-up.*

"Well...Clint isn't *all* bad."

"Now there's a ringing endorsement."

"I didn't mean it quite the way it sounded."

Maybe so, but it's a fair assessment.

"Unlike some, back at Williams, I managed to get along with Clint."

The thinly veiled reminder that Clint despised Kyle did not escape him. It all began freshman year when Clint had gotten an *F* in Philosophy. Half of his grade was based on a term paper. The morning it was due, having yet to write a word, he asked to photocopy one Kyle had written a semester before for another professor. Clint claimed he had been counting on the twenty-page essay on Descartes' *Social Contract* to earn a good grade. Kyle had gotten an A. Knowing that plagiarism, if discovered, would jeopardize his college career, along with Clint's, Kyle refused to give Clint a copy. From that day forth, Clint had it in for Kyle, not that Kyle cared. The animosity grew into a permanent grudge at the end of senior year when Clint was dating a girl by the name of Carla Pender. Kyle encouraged Carla to take a hard look at what her life would be, married to Clint. Soon after, Carla dumped Clint. Clint blamed Kyle for the breakup and vowed to get even. Kyle assumed it was an idle threat. He said, "You remember the day Clint made his acrobatic catch in the final minute against Wesleyan?"

"Who could forget it? Vintage Clint."

"The catch...or the dance and ill-fated flip he did in the end zone?"

"The latter, of course."

Clint's handspring, which sent him head over heels before he crashed into the band and ripped up his knee on a bassoon, played in Kyle's mind as if it were a television instant replay, complete with slow motion. Much as Clint might have preferred to forget the inglorious scene, a three-inch scar, shaped like a capital "T," provided a visible souvenir of his post-touchdown celebration. The disfigurement, like a big

4

tattoo of a heart circumscribing the name of a despised former girlfriend, guaranteed that the memory would remain vivid. "You have to admit it was a helluva catch…the leap in the air, fingertip deflection and snatch of the the ball while tumbling to the ground."

"Yeah, but so what. It made the score 45 – 10, and not in our favor."

Were the celebration a team leader's way of bolstering his teammates, Kyle might have defended the display, but not when it was an egotistical showman's attempt at self-promotion, albeit it permanently disfiguring. "You're right. It was all about Clint."

"You think he'll attend Bill's funeral, what with criminal charges pending against him?"

For an instant Kyle tried to put himself into Clint's shoes. If he were out on bail facing felony charges, he would be reluctant to make public appearances, knowing he would be the subject of whispers. An instant later, he realized the analysis was faulty. Whispers would not deter a peacock like Clint. He said, "Whether Clint goes to the funeral will probably depend on you."

"Me?"

That Kyle's obtuse assessment evoked a quizzical reaction was no surprise. "Chances are Clint won't know about the funeral until after the fact unless you alert him. Him being your boss, the ball's in your court…So, you plan to tell him?"

"All depends."

"On what?"

"Whether I decide to go. It wouldn't seem right for me, a member of the Inseparables, to skip it if Clint were going."

"Good point. But Clint may be pissed when he finds out you didn't tell him. In case you've forgotten, he's still your boss."

"Technically. But he won't be if they send him to the slammer."

"You prepared to take the risk, especially with a guy like Clint?"

"What if I didn't know about the funeral beforehand?"

"You think he'd believe that a member of the Inseparables wasn't notified about Bill's funeral? Anyway, I know you well enough. You're not going to lie." Kyle waited a moment. "So, the way I see it, you'll have to tell Clint, and that means you have to attend."

"Damn it, Gordon. You're twisting my arm."

"So, I can count on you?"

"I didn't say that."

"No, but..." Kyle let the matter be. He had all but gotten the commitment he sought. "About time we both get back to work. You take care." As he hung up the receiver, Kyle closed his eyes, his mind drifting back more than a half-decade to fond memories of bygone days when he and his buddies were students at Williams.

CHAPTER II

IN THE EONS OF TIME, four years is a fleeting, inconsequential moment. To a college freshman, still three weeks from his eighteenth birthday, having just arrived for orientation, it borders on eternity. Life beyond college is as distant as the outer reaches of the universe, billions of light years away. Its connection to campus life is tantamount to a parallel universe existing only in incomprehensible dimensions numbering more than our earthly three, even four, allowing a coordinate for time. Indeed, the beginning of college is not merely the start of a new life, it is the commencement of a lifetime within a lifetime.

That was how Kyle Gordon had regarded his upcoming college years when he had arrived at Williams for freshman orientation. But with the advent of graduation, the forever that had stood before him four years earlier had transmuted, its totality a brief moment. Such were his thoughts as he sat with his three college pals, Don Burns, Bill Young and Eric Johanson in a booth at the rear corner of the Irish Mist, their favorite hangout. Ever since they had met four years earlier as freshman roommates with diverse backgrounds from different parts of America, the storied watering hole had been their place for pizza, bull sessions and, thanks to Kelly, a petite, look-the-other-way barmaid, brews. But with graduation less than twenty-four hours away, the ales that filled their mugs were legal.

"Where the hell did it go?"

"Where did what go?" Bill, the fair-skinned Mormon, stocky, but solid, gave Kyle a look.

"You mean to tell me you don't know what he is referring to?" A shake of Eric's head underscored the shocked disdain in his voice.

"Uh...not really," said Bill, appearing to regret his show of ignorance.

"Well...guess what—neither do I." The 6'2" Eric, blond, blue-eyed and of Swedish descent, displayed a smirk before turning to Kyle, who sat diagonally across in the back corner of the booth. "But let me take a shot in the dark. You were looking for the fried leprechaun panini you didn't order."

With all eyes directed his way, Kyle was on the spot. His buddies, having all consumed a couple of brews, were primed to put him through the ringer. Four years earlier Kyle would have been ill-equipped to extricate himself from the good-natured gauntlet, but repeated practice had armed him with ample defenses. He waved to Kelly. "When you do the check, Johanson pays for the panini."

Kelly rolled her eyes...heaved a sigh...and went about her business.

Kyle, of medium build, not handsome, but arguably cute, with wavy hair and dimples, refocused on his friends. "For your information, *gentlemen*—and I use the term all too loosely—I was reflecting upon the fact that our college years have passed us by. They're over."

"Not until tomorrow."

"Yeah," said Kyle, looking directly at Bill. "You've made my point."

Glances, somber ones, exchanged around the table, underscored the point.

"C'mon...it's not like we've died and gone to...wherever." Eric moved his gaze over his three friends. "We'll still get together."

"Maybe so," said Kyle, "but it won't be all that often. Touch football in the quad, hanging out here at the Irish Mist and never-ending bull sessions are pretty much history. Whether we like it or not, the real world...reality...awaits."

"Gordon—you of all people, are hardly the one to make the point. And don't give me one of your quizzical looks." Don leaned back. "Unlike the rest of us who will be joining the nine-to-five working world—"

"Nine-to-five...don't I wish?" said Eric. "From what I hear, Granite Insurance makes rookies like me work fifty or even sixty hours per week. And because we're on the management track, paid an annual salary, rather than hourly, we don't get overtime."

"My point was not how many hours we'll be working, but that unlike Kyle, our school days are ending. He, on the other hand, is off to graduate school. His party continues."

"Sure." Kyle drew out the word, accentuating his sarcastic message. "The MBA program at NYU will be a real vacation."

Bill grabbed several napkins from the holder and distributed them to all but Kyle.

"What's this for?" said Don.

"To wipe our tears for our poor, suffering friend who will have to endure two more years relaxing in school while we toil for slave-driving bosses."

Kyle looked around the table. The possibility he could garner sympathy was out of the question. "Are we ever gonna take our trip out West?"

Eric put his hand to the side of his mouth, pretending to whisper to Don and Bill. "Seems someone wants to change the subject."

"You're damn straight!" said Kyle. "So, is our trip an extinguished pipe dream?"

"Eric and I were ready to go last summer. If you and Young weren't such party poopers, it would have happened."

"Some of us had summer jobs," said Bill, "a minor necessity, assuming we wanted to eat during the school year."

Kyle was glad that Bill had taken up the defense. Though his Mormon friend came from a comfortable middle-class family, with two brothers and two sisters, Bill had to shoulder a portion of the expense of his college education. Like Kyle, he would graduate with unpaid loans.

"Not all of our fathers own a liquor distributorship and belong to a country club." Though Bill's jab was good-natured,

9

its message reflected the sentiments that had governed the group ever since freshman year. If anything, there was reverse snobbery. Financial status could not be flaunted. More than anyone else, Eric had been responsible. The son of a Protestant minister for a large congregation, his family was relatively well off. Kyle suspected that Eric's family may have been as well-to-do as Don's. The difference was they didn't live as high. But with Eric, like the two of more modest means, inclined to downplay financial status, Don could ill-afford to act the big shot, lest he become odd man out.

"So," said Kyle, whose mother was a substitute English teacher and father, a social worker, "are we ever gonna take that trip?" Starting in their freshman year, the four had talked about driving west and tenting their way from national park to national park. Each fall plans for the upcoming summer, at least a month of travel, had been bandied about. And each summer it had been put off to the next.

"Sometime," said Eric.

Don rolled his eyes. "Sure...when the day from that old Johnny Mathis song, the one my dad loves to sing, comes around." Four years earlier the line would have left the other three puzzled, but Don had referenced "The Twelfth of Never" too many times to fool anyone. "C'mon, face it—we'll never see the West, what with three of us headed into the working world."

"Gordon will still have the summer off."

Kyle let the irony of Bill's point pass. The fact that his MBA program at NYU did not commence until the end of August was of little consequence. He would need to work during the summer. Don was probably right. Their oft repeated plans of a big cross-country trip would probably never come to fruition. It was nothing more than a quixotic dream of youth. Like the idealism that had been so often voiced in their bull sessions, the visions of a great excursion through the Rockies, Grand Tetons, Yosemite, Zion, Bryce and the Grand Canyon would fade amidst the realities of life beyond the ivied walls of college. Kyle imbibed an extended gulp of his tall brew. Alcohol's dulling effects failed to blunt sobering thoughts. "Do you think this might be our last visit to the Irish Mist? I mean all four of us together."

"Nah," said Eric. "We'll be back for reunions and...whatever."

"Maybe so, but this could be the last time we share a brew."

The seeming inconsistency of Bill's remark drew all eyes his way.

"Starting tomorrow, the rules of my Mormon upbringing...no alcohol...not even stimulants like coffee and tea, go back into effect." Bill heaved a sigh. "After four hedonistic years, it's gonna be hard. Damn hard."

"So, why do it?" said Don.

Bill shrugged.

Sensing the message behind the ambiguous reaction, Kyle let it pass without question, his thoughts drifting in a sea of analysis, projection and introspection. Roommates since their first day freshman year, each had felt the influence of the others. Like four corners of a quadrilateral, they had been drawn together along both the sides and the diagonals. No doubt ample differences remained, but the dimensions of the four-sided polygon had decreased, its area far less. But once they went their separate ways, influences, each on the others, were bound to mitigate. Lessons and values inculcated in earlier days would re-emerge, even as new influences came into play. Bill's Mormon upbringing would likely return. Out in the working world, Don, like his parents, would seek life in suburbia with a fine home, complete with neat-trimmed lawn and a Mercedes in the garage and, of course, a membership in the country club. And tall and handsome Eric, the son of a Protestant minister, would be a paradigm of good citizenship, honest, hard-working and modest. In some respects, Eric and Bill, perhaps owing to their strong religious backgrounds, were a lot alike, at least when it came to their values. But the similarity ended there. Three inches short of six feet and stocky, though not fat, the gregarious Bill contrasted with the quiet, almost shy and very private Eric. People meeting them for the first time were apt to view them as total opposites. The anomaly had struck Kyle many times. It had also made him aware of his secular background, and that awareness occasioned another oddity. At times he was thankful to be free of the seeming burdens, most prominently guilt, that invaded Bill and Eric's lives owing to their pious roots. How often Bill had chastised himself for consuming alcohol, and Eric frequently agonized over his failure to attend Sunday services. Both worried how their godless behavior would play when ultimately judgment day arrived. Might entrance into the heavenly afterlife be denied? Yet other times, Kyle envied the duo. When faced with difficulties, their faith bolstered them. Their unshakable belief in a greater, inexplicable plan helped them roll with the punches. Where Kyle, relying on reason, felt empty, Bill and Eric found solace in their religious convictions.

It was not as though Kyle had been raised in a home devoid of religion. His mother, Protestant, and father, Jewish, had joined a Unitarian Church. But like many others, they had chosen it for its humanism, values that they had made part of Kyle's upbringing. God, on the other hand, played little role in their lives. Though certainly not atheists, they were hardly believers. Agnostic, arguably, best described them, not that they classified themselves as such. Was there a God? Maybe…but maybe not. Kyle didn't know, and that was fine. His rational approach worked well, most of the time. But now and then when life's inequitable side reverberated, when nothing seemed to make sense, he coveted Eric and Bill's faith. Hypocritical though it was, he had tried turning to the very God whose existence he doubted. Lack of conviction rendered the gesture futile.

"Johanson, I assume that's your green and purple Dodge Omni parked out front."

The comment from fellow graduating senior Gary Parker, as he approached the booth, drew Kyle from his ruminations.

"Is there another car like it on the planet?" Bill surveyed the group, as if confirming that no one disagreed.

"Yeah, that's my car," said Eric. "What about it?"

"I found this note on the windshield." Gary held up a piece of paper. "It says: 'I just put a huge dent in the side of your heap. I'm leaving this note, since several people saw me do it. Naturally they think I'm writing my name, phone number, car registration and insurance information. Have a nice day, sucker.'"

Even before Gary had read the final sentence, Eric had leaped from his seat and was racing to the door.

"Was the damage really bad?" said Kyle.

Gary laughed hysterically.

Were it someone other than Gary, Kyle would have found the reaction bizarre, but knowing Gary, ever the joker, the likelihood of a prank was high.

"Johanson's car is fine." Gary garbled the words amidst continuing laughter. "When I saw his car parked out there, I assumed he'd be in here and decided to write the note."

"Parker, you're a piece of work," said Bill.

"Maybe, but you know you love it. And for that matter, you'll miss it once we all go our separate ways."

"Yeah, about as much as we'll miss—" The sight of Eric hurrying back to the booth prompted Kyle to cut himself off.

"Parker, I oughta wring your ever-loving neck." Eric raised his hands as if ready to strangle the prankster.

"Wring my neck? You should be thanking me."

"Thanking you? For what!"

"Your car is fine, isn't it?"

"Through no help of yours."

Gary shook his head and then directed himself to the trio seated in the booth. "Sad how unappreciative some people are." He glanced at his watch. "I'd like to stay longer, but I've got things to do. For that matter, I really didn't have the time for this little diversion. But I made time. Unfortunately, not everyone shows appreciation. Well...whatever." Gary turned and walked out of the Irish Mist.

"Can you believe that guy?" said Eric.

"I like him," said Don. "And I'll miss his humor."

Eric gave Don a look.

"If you were honest," said Don, "you'd admit that you'll miss him too."

Eric shrugged and slipped himself back into the booth.

"Do you know what today is?" said Bill.

Nothing that distinguished the day popped out at Kyle.

"The day before graduation," said Eric, a sarcastic tone suggesting he lacked the sought-after answer and, still miffed at Gary's antics, didn't care what that answer was.

"Yeah, but do you know what day it is?" Bill waited a moment, before turning to Don. "It's Friday, the 13th of May."

The mention of the date alerted Kyle what was behind the inquiry and why Bill's focus had been directed at Don. Don had several phobias, among them claustrophobia and triskaidikaphobia, the latter relevant to the current subject.

A hint of tension showed on Don's face, whom some said resembled Clark Gable, especially when he sported a mustache. "Go ahead. Make fun of me. See if I care."

Bill shot Don a look before focusing on the other two. "After four years of a liberal arts education, one would think our triskaidikaphobic pal could put his idle superstition to bed."

"Look who is talking, Brigham Young himself."

A stranger overhearing the exchange might have taken offense to the politically incorrect jab, but such exchanges, standard fare among the college buddies, were part and parcel of their mutual affection.

"Anyway, folks a lot wiser than I have recognized the perils of the number thirteen."

"Agreed," said Eric. "Of course, none of them had an IQ over sixty."

The quip drew laughter from the others.

"Very funny." Don rapped his half-raised mug on the table. "Historical proof of the dangers would fill volumes. And by the way, if you dunderheads need to spout off, at least use the proper term. For your information, fear of Friday the 13th is paraskevidekatriaphobia. But before you tumble down from your high horse, let me give you a few examples. Jacques de Molay, the last known Grand Master of the Knights Templar, was burned at the stake at Notre Dame on Friday the 13th, and the HMS Friday was launched on Friday the 13th, never to be heard from again. And here are a couple of special ones for you God-fearing fellows. Cain slew Abel on Friday the 13th, and, best of all, Judas, the thirteenth guest at the Last Supper, betrayed Jesus on none other than Friday the 13th. Those my friends are the facts." Don smirked before gulping his brew.

14

"Well, whoopie-do," said Eric. "Bad things happened on Friday the 13th...So what. With all the thousands of horrible events and atrocities throughout history, one could pick any date and get the same outcome. I'm sure Monday the 4th or Thursday the 27th would yield the same results."

"Wait a second," said Bill. "Don has a point."

The sudden defense of the superstition took Kyle by surprise.

"No, think about it," said Bill. "I don't believe there have been any bad happenings on Wednesday the 59th...or the seventh Tuesday of December." Bill smiled. Eric and Kyle roared.

"Funny...funny." Don folded his arms. "The next time you're in a tall building, check and see if the elevator has a button for the 13th floor. Seems that lots of people agree with me."

"You mean they're just as superstitious," said Eric.

Don shook his head.

"What's the matter now?"

"Just this. When you and your other God-fearing friend, Brigham Young, spout your religious dogma, it's unassailable—It's the word of God—but when I espouse views, even ones well-documented throughout history, you treat them as mere superstitions. The truth is: rather than being right, the only thing you have going for you is that others at this table agree with you."

"No quarrel that numbers don't make us right," said Eric. "And as for my beliefs, I admit, I take them on faith. But never...ever do I try to impose them on you. Therein lies a big difference between the two of us. You insist your superstitions are right."

"On the contrary, I simply try to free you from misguided ignorance."

Eric nodded slowly. "I rest my case."

Kyle chuckled to himself. The exchange summed up the difference in his friends. It also underscored an irony. Bill and Eric were conservative, politically right of center, whereas Don, like Kyle, was a bit to the left. While no one was near either end of the spectrum, there was never a doubt that two were on one side and two on the other. Though Kyle agreed with Don more than the other two, Don frustrated him more frequently. Unlike Don, who was generally inflexible, Eric and Bill were open minded. That's not to say that they bought into Kyle's more liberal views, but they respected them. Don, on the other hand, insisted he was right.

"Gordon, I understand that the two religious fanatics outnumber me, but how about a little support?"

Kyle preferred to distance himself from the issue. He grabbed his mug and took a drink.

"Sure, bury yourself in your beer while I'm left to defend the truth."

Kyle might have let the remark pass, but the degrading look that punctuated the words was more than he could take. "Burns, you're unbelievable. You mouth off, take yourself out on a limb and then expect me to bail you out."

"You telling me you disagree with my position?"

"As a matter of fact, yes!"

"So, since time immemorial, the many people who suffered bad consequences in the face of black cats or broken mirrors were all crazy?"

"Well...I can't speak for all of them, but in your case...the description fits."

Bill and Eric laughed raucously.

"And by the way, when it comes to broken mirrors, I suspect a fair number do get cut."

"That doesn't explain why they suffer seven years of bad luck."

The lack of logic had Kyle shaking his head. "You're making your point with circular reasoning. You've assumed that people who break mirrors actually endure seven years of bad luck."

Don shook his head. "Gordon, you're a gadfly."

"Me?"

"Yeah, you. Whenever I challenge our faith-based pals, you, the one who accepts nothing on faith, disagree with whatever I say."

"You know," said Eric, "Don has a point."

Kyle bristled. "What! You think I'm a gadfly too."

"Not that. Just that you always disagree with Don…and who can blame you? He's always wrong."

Kyle, Eric and Bill guffawed. Don seemingly sulked, though likely it was more show than pique.

"C'mon guys, we'd better tread carefully," said Bill, "lest our buddy pulls out his handy-dandy Swiss knife and gives us what for."

"Damn, don't remind me of that so-called lucky piece," said Kyle. "Last month Don almost got us tossed from the *Maroon 5* concert, even before we got in. I had to twist his arm to convince him to let the security people hold it until the concert was over."

"Hey, it's not my fault if you guys can't appreciate a lucky charm."

Bill threw up his hands. "But do you have to take it everywhere?"

"As a matter of fact, yes!" Don drew the red knife out of his pocket and displayed it proudly before putting it away.

"A lot of good it would have done us at the concert if some jerk had started shooting with an AR-15."

"You've missed the point, Gordon. The knife is a lucky piece. It brings me good karma, and it helps—"

"Enough," said Bill. "Our last time here before graduation shouldn't be filled with rancor."

"Why should today be any different from those of the past four years?" The raspy voice of Clinton Horstmeyer, as he approached the table, drew their attention.

"Grab a chair and join us," said Eric.

Clint took one from a nearby table and stationed it at the end of the booth. "Good news. I'll be joining you for tomorrow's festivities. I managed a *D* in poly sci. Woodard gave me a hook on my paper, god-awful piece of crap that it was. Enough to pull my 59 average on the tests up to a *D*. You're looking at a fellow who's graduating tomorrow…top 98% of the class."

"Some folks might call that bottom 2%," said Bill.

"They'd be wrong…cause I'm no worse than the bottom three."

17

"The last time I checked basic arithmetic, 100 minus 98 equaled 2, not 3." Don smirked.

"That may be," said Clint, "but someone in the top 98%, is not in the bottom 2%."

Kyle, whose first reaction was the same as Don's, realized Clint was right. The wide-receiver, who had found his place in the class with a full scholarship owing to football skills, not cerebral capacity, had outwitted them. More likely than not, someone else had clued Clint into the clever nicety.

"You guys realize this is your last visit to this wonderful oasis before you hit the real world?"

"We were talking about that just a few minutes ago," said Bill.

"You recall who designated this joint, 'The Oasis?'" Clint pushed out his chest. "Yours truly."

Kyle thought back to the day nearly four years earlier. "And if memory serves me, roughly two hours of existential gibberish followed."

"You casting aspersions on a Clinton Horstmeyer inspired philosophical discussion?"

"I would *never* do that." Kyle slowed his cadence, endeavoring to make his sarcasm evident. "Not even to such a vacuous incursion into the world of meaningless semantics."

"It wasn't meaningless." Bill's folding arms defiantly banged his chest. "Debating my point, that 'there are oases, and *there are oases*,' was the height of cerebral...baloney." A broad smile supplanted feigned indignation.

"Well, now that we're graduating and...*so much wiser* (Kyle rolled his eyes), anybody's view change?"

"As if I could recall mine," said Don.

"Loaded as you were, that's no surprise," said Bill. "Fortunately, I was not so indulgent, and my memory is better. You called this place, the Irish Mist, your oasis."

"No offense to this wonderful establishment," said Eric. "It's great. But for me, the ultimate spot, the one where I can most easily escape the world, is just a few blocks away...the Clark Institute."

"Apparently Johanson thinks he can impress us with his high-brow taste for art." The imprimatur of Clint's patented smirk punctuated the gibe. "Regardless, I'm glad that my well-chosen name for this joint is still stirring you boys with intellectual inspiration."

Checking the urge to slam the jock's pretention, Kyle asked him, "You still dating Carla Pender?"

"Yup."

"Can't imagine what a sweet person like Carla sees in a lug like you." A smile on Bill's face made it hard to discern whether he was serious. He signaled Kelly to bring Clint a beer.

"Hey, you know what that old song says: 'You gotta be a football hero to get along with a beautiful girl.'"

"Then according to the song," said Eric, "that lets you out."

Puzzlement etched itself across Clint's face.

"Player, member of the team, hardly equates to hero. Of course, bottom three percent, not surprising that an obscure word like *hero*, all fours letters of it, transcends your verbal mastery."

Clint bristled, but only for an instant. "Ooh...Sounds like someone is jealous."

Kyle suspected the same thing. Eric had dated Carla for about six months, right up until the beginning of March when she had begun dating Clint. According to Eric, he and Carla remained the dearest of friends following a mutual split. Kyle had no doubt about their friendship. Whether the split had been mutual was far less clear. That Eric might still have a thing for Carla, or perhaps even vice versa, was a distinct possibility.

"I'm not jealous. But I am concerned for her. Carla's a wonderful person, and I don't want to see her hurt."

"Then you've got nothing to worry about." Clint hoisted his mug that had just arrived. "Let me propose a toast. To the Inseparables. That's what you fellows call yourselves. Right?"

Though no one confirmed the designation—it was a title they didn't advertise—their silence was tantamount to an admission.

"May the friendship that you fellows have forged these past four years continue all through your lives."

As mugs clinked, Kyle weighed the possibility of adding words that would in some way include Clint. The idea was nice but had no chance. Even if the clique were not closed, Clint would have been among the last people they would have welcomed. Having to endure a greater dose of the jock's braggadocio was unthinkable.

"We appreciate the kind words," said Eric, the last to tap Clint's mug.

"Think nothing of it." Clint took a swig. "Good thing you fellows have your own little fraternity…seeing as how none of the real ones would have you."

The comment bore all the earmarks of affable ribbing, but Kyle could not rule out the possibility that it was spiced with malice.

"So, following graduation, what are your plans?" said Eric.

"My uncle down in Memphis has a Cadillac dealership. I'm gonna try my hand at sales."

A sheepskin from Williams generally opened better doors than a salesman's job at an automotive distributorship, but Clint, bottom three percent, was hardly the typical graduate.

"The reason I'm taking the job is cause my uncle is friends with the owner of the *Memphis Xplorers*. They play in the Arena Football League. He thinks I can land a spot on their roster. And naturally my uncle will work my hours so I can practice and play with the team." Clint raised his hands feigning a move as if he were catching a pass. "Hey, you never know, once the scouts see my talents, it might pave my way to the big time."

"The NFL?" Bill's eyes were wide.

"Why? Did you think I meant Pop Warner?"

Admittedly Clint was one of the best players on the Williams football team, but that was a far cry from a big-time, Division I program. At one hundred sixty pounds, timed at 5.1 seconds in the forty-yard dash, Clint was as likely to make it to the National Football League, as Bill, whose Achilles heel was math, was to prove Fermat's Last Theorem. Kyle kept the thought to himself. If Clint wanted to live in a fantasyland as farfetched as Greek mythology, no need to stick a pin into his balloon. And too, there was a good chance that deep down Clint knew his visions of playing in the National Football League were delusional. Regardless, he relished the opportunity to puff himself up. The thought reminded Kyle of the days when he played on his high school golf team. Their top player, Jerry Shor, a five handicapper, often talked about playing on the PGA Tour. Jerry was a fine golfer, certainly better than Kyle, but his blather about competing against the Tiger Woods of the world, gave the word *absurd*, new meaning. The preceding summer, while back home, Kyle had bumped into Jerry. He was working as a grease monkey at a local service station. His golf career, which included a weekend job as a ranger at the local municipal course, had highlighted with a second-place finish in the county amateur. But to listen to Jerry, one would think he had won the Green Jacket at Augusta.

Clint gulped the last of his beer. "I'd love to spend more time with you fellows, but the pool table is open, and Charlie Ruggers just walked in." Clint gestured toward the door. "A fish like him is too good to miss." He stood up, and as he started to walk away, glanced back. "If you want me to leave a couple bucks for my brew, just say the word."

Following a moment's silence, Bill said, "That's okay Clint. We've got it."

Clint sauntered to the pool table.

Ordinarily Kyle would have been fine covering the cost of a friend's drink, especially when it was divided four ways, but this one stuck in his craw. Someone else would have put his money on the table, rather than asking for a free ride. And what really irked Kyle, was that Clint had pulled the identical stunt numerous times before. He said, "I won't miss that guy one bit."

"Understandable," said Don. "He hates your guts."

"And lest there be any doubt, the feeling is mutual." Kyle looked around the table. "I don't know how you guys tolerate him. And as for you, Young, somehow you've managed to not only stay in his good graces, but for some unimaginable reason he thinks you're the best thing to come down the pike since Guttenberg invented the printing press."

"Oh, it dates back to a favor I did for him freshman year. Clint was already on academic and disciplinary probation when he spray-painted the wall of Morgan Hall. Dean Haskell suspected Clint was responsible, and with a little proof would have given Clint the boot. I saved Clint's ass when I refused to rat on him. Of course, the move got me a place on Haskell's shit list."

"Too bad you didn't throw the jerk in. The campus would have been better off without him."

"You got that right, Gordon," said Eric. "If you ask me, the guy is a psychopath."

His brew nearing his lips, Don halted. "C'mon, you don't mean that literally?"

"Oh, don't I?" Eric looked around the booth. "Anyone else disagree?"

"Admittedly, Clint's a braggart and prone to crazy antics, a stereotypical, over-testosteronated jock," said Bill, "but labeling him a psychopath is way over the top."

"Over-testoster…whatever," said Kyle. "That's a new addition to the English language."

"Maybe so," said Bill, "but you get my point. He's not a psychopath."

Temptation cajoled Kyle to lend support to Eric's allegation. But much as Kyle wanted to, much as he despised Clint, and much as he deemed Clint a louse, in his heart of hearts, Kyle did not believe that Clint was a psychopath. Regardless, Kyle refused to help Bill defend Clint. He said, "However you label Clint, anyone think he'll change?"

The question drew no takers, merely an exchange of looks.

Kyle welcomed the silence. Psychopath or not, no one deemed Clint worthy of defense. The leopard wouldn't change his spots. No sooner did the frivolous saw come to mind than the voice of his freshman composition professor rang in Kyle's head. Dr. Stoddard would have chastised Kyle for the banality. Kyle gazed in the direction of the pool table where Clint, some thirty feet away, was lining up a shot. Though predicting the future was a fool's errand, in Clint's case, the outcome seemed inevitable. But maybe…just maybe, the louse would mature.

Perhaps Clint would be the most successful of them. And perhaps he would, with time, even become modest...perhaps.

CHAPTER III

POMP AND CIRCUMSTANCE, the age-old music, symbolic of the anomaly where the finish line coincides with the starting gate, had begun to play. Notes familiar to all echoed a tradition that had played out thousands and thousands of times before. Graduation ceremonies, commencement, had concluded. Life was beginning. Yet slates were far from clean. Roughly twenty-two years, seventeen of schooling, had created footprints, an irrevocable past. Those footprints would influence the future, but influence is far from a charted course. Countless forks and detours, some serendipitous, others self-begotten, would lie ahead.

Kyle snatched the tasseled cap that he had tossed high into the air a moment before. He started to stick it back atop his head, but stopped and stared at the odd-shaped hat. How had it become standard graduation attire? Why? He gazed up at the stage where the pedagogues proudly bore their sartorially splendid velvet hoods. What was the purpose? Admittedly every culture had its ceremonies, complete with ritualistic dress. Often the attire, the rites, helped define a society and enable its members to find their places in it. Some such traditions even fed and enriched the masses. But what of the many customs that were little more than the imprimatur of those in power, a reinforcement of their sway? Kyle again eyed the robed throng on the stage. Chances were they represented a mixed bag. Some had come to celebrate the successes of those they had mentored; others welcomed the excuse to parade themselves in self-congratulatory, pompous display. On second thought, most were not so one-dimensional. They did both, but in varying degrees.

From his seat on the west lawn fronting Chapin Hall, Kyle circled out back the hundred-plus yards to Haystack Monument where, in 1806, five Williams students, in the landmark progenitor of Protestant missions, had met to consider the well-being of people in Asia. As pre-arranged, Kyle's parents were waiting near the monument eager to congratulate him. What moments earlier had seemed an anticlimactic ceremony acquired new meaning. Moisture in his parents' eyes, excitement in their words, evidenced their pride. With the financial sacrifices they had made in order that he could attend the esteemed, but expensive institution, they had more than earned the right. Graduation, an event Kyle could have done without, took on unexpected import.

The joy in the faces of his parents was unmistakable. But it was more than joy. The Yiddish word *kvell*, one of only about thirty that Kyle knew, all products of his father's Jewish roots, popped into his head. From time to time, especially when the English language lacked a sufficient counterpart, Kyle's father would resort to his Yiddish vocabulary. Indeed, his parents were *kvelling*.

"Thank you both for all you've done for me, forgoing trips to California and the Caribbean and newer cars and so much else, just so I could have a future."

"You are our future." His mother's eyes dotted with tears.

"Trips and cars...material rewards pale compared to the happiness you bring us. Your..." His father's cracking voice trailed off.

Almost never had Kyle seen the stoic man misty eyed, unable to voice his thoughts. Kyle spread his arms wide, embracing both his parents. Just as emotions had seconds earlier crippled his father's tongue, so too they impeded Kyle. Regardless, words were unnecessary.

Their group hug, one sustained for the best part of a half-minute, underscored something Kyle had known for years. He was fortunate to have such loving parents, to have grown up, along with his younger sister, in a caring home. So many of his college friends whined about nagging parents...parents to whom they often lied. They spoke of households filled with bickering and shouting, where dysfunction was the norm. From what Kyle had observed, it made no difference whether the homes were religious or secular. Kyle's own upbringing lay somewhere in the middle. With religion never a centerpiece, he felt free to decide for himself what role it would play in his life. On the other hand, values, such as the Golden Rule, hallmarks in the Gordon home, were indelibly ingrained.

The extended family hug had just broken up when Bill Young approached. After greeting Kyle's parents, Bill directed his attention to Kyle. "Can I talk to you for a minute...alone?"

Kyle glanced at his parents. "I'll be right back."

Bill led the way to the shade of a big elm, about thirty yards away.

"What's up?"

"Carla...Carla Pender is pregnant."

The disclosure sent Kyle's brain into high gear. A bit more than three months had elapsed since Carla's lengthy relationship with Eric had ended. Even amidst the romantic split, they had continued to maintain a close friendship. At the time, Carla had begun dating Clinton Horstmeyer. "Who's the father?"

"Not sure, but my guess is Eric."

"What about Clint? He's her current boyfriend."

Bill shrugged. "Yeah, he's a possibility, but..."

"So, what makes you think it's Eric?"

"Well, Megan Kilmer—she's the one who told me about the situation—suspected it might be Eric, not that she knew."

"You plan to ask Eric directly?"

Bill shook his head. "Private as Eric is, I think it's best to let him raise the issue, if and when he wants to."

Curiosity notwithstanding, Kyle silently concurred. "You think an abortion is a possibility?"

"Hard to say since I have no idea how Carla views the subject."

"Damn, I hope it isn't Eric." Kyle heaved a sigh.

"If it is, you think he might marry Carla?"

For a moment, Kyle weighed the permutations. "I don't know, but unfortunately it's a possibility."

26

"You say that as if it would be awful. You have to admit that Carla is smart and has a wonderful personality, not to mention a great body and mighty pretty face."

"Yeah, I suppose."

"So, why the long face?"

"Put yourself in Eric's shoes. Would you want to marry a girl you just broke up with because she's pregnant?"

"When you put it that way...I guess not." Bill looked off into space. "But given all her attributes and the fact they're still good friends, it could be worse."

"Could be worse." Kyle dragged out the repeated words. "That what you wanna tell yourself when you take a bride?"

"I get your point." A slow nod yielded to an odd expression. "Any guesses whether Carla might opt for an abortion?"

"Seems I asked you the same question a minute ago, and I didn't get much of an answer."

"Yeah...So what?" Bill smiled.

"Well, if it's up to Eric, we both know she'll have the baby." Of the Inseparables, none, even Bill, with his Mormon background, had stronger religious convictions than Eric. Having grown up in a home where his father was a minister, biblical teachings were not taken lightly. Views about abortion among the four friends were very clear. There were few issues they had debated as much. Don and Kyle, the liberals, supported a woman's right to choose, while Bill and Eric, the conservatives, viewed abortion as stealing the inalienable right to life. Though their positions were a clear dichotomy, for Kyle the issue was uniquely complex. And too, it provided the quintessential example of the difficulty he often experienced with Don's views. For Don the matter was simple. Third parties, religious zealots, should not be dictating to a woman what to do with her body. While Kyle agreed with Don that government should not impose itself on a woman's medical decision, he distanced himself from Don's categorical, closed-ear position. At times he even felt compelled to defend the view with which he disagreed. The point at which life merited protection was at best vague. Don's cavalier dismissal of the concern that Eric and Bill had for the unborn was infuriating, even more so because they never used the cloak of murder to close off discussion. Like Kyle, they viewed the matter as a difficult balance. They respected his position, and he respected theirs.

"It seems you've begged my question."

Amidst his ruminations, Kyle had lost track of the question. "Refresh my recollection, and maybe I'll do better."

"Will Carla opt to have the baby? And this time, rather than answering the question based upon what Eric would do, try it from Carla's viewpoint, keeping in mind that *Roe v. Wade,* not the *Bible,* is the law."

Kyle thought for a moment. "I have no idea what Carla will do."

"Any idea how Clint feels about abortion, not that it would be his decision?"

Kyle shrugged. "Don't know that I ever heard him discuss the issue. But knowing Clint, I suspect he opposes it, except in cases where he'd be asked to pay support."

Bill nodded. "That sounds like Clint. He always wants to do what's right...for Clint."

Illusion is a tapestry of similar but disparate weaves. Smoke and mirrors and slight of hand, silky veils, are the stock and trade of the magician. Makeup and costumes cloak the actor in a world of fantasy. Knavery and deceit, clever synthetics, are the cloths of the con artist. Bright colored plastics and cardboards are the fabrics with which Madison Avenue lures unsuspecting consumers. Denial, an impenetrable textile, masks the compulsive alcoholic, gambler or smoker from the truth. Artists, particularly many of the most renown, decry illusion. Their facility for capturing the three-dimensional world, even minute details, on a two-dimensional canvas stupefies ordinary mortals. But some, like con artists and magicians, cause eyes to see that which is not there. Like Madison Avenue's most adept advertisers, they trade on image, much of which rests in the phantasm of the beholder. Such is the skill with which the impressionist coats his canvas. Stand back at a distance and seemingly detailed buildings and windows and trees and even people are manifest. Step close and they prove to be nothing more than an adept brushstroke or two. Step back again, and denial, like that of the self-indulgent alcoholic, gambler or smoker, will insist the details are there. Such is the nature of impressionism. Such are its tapestries of illusion.

Just one day removed from graduation, Eric Johanson strolled from the Williams College campus down South Street to the Sterling and Francine Clark Institute. He climbed the broad stone stairs and entered the acclaimed art museum. Nowhere, not even New York or Boston, was there a gallery he liked more. He relished all the Clark's collections. Winslow Homer's seascapes, with their harsh Atlantic waves, sent his mind adrift on exciting voyages. John Sargent's portraits of America's Founding Fathers stirred memories of all-but-forgotten facts learned in middle-school social studies. However, the bulk of Eric's time was reserved for the Clark's huge collection of oils by the French impressionists. The dotted touch of Seurat, the vertical-line brushstrokes of van Gogh, the dancers of Degas, the scenes of Monet, Manet, Corot and Courbet, and so many more...Eric loved them all. But best among them, he adored the masterpieces of Renoir, and topping those were the red-haired beauties that decorated the master's canvases. Wall by entrancing wall, Eric viewed the paintings. Standing back, he marveled at their details. Inching closer, he watched the same minutiae disappear, only to be restored as once again his distance from the work increased. For more than an hour he exulted in the magnificence that filled his eyes. Only when his appetite was sated did he wend his way back to the hall that housed his favorite painting, Renoir's *Woman with a Fan*. He seated himself on the end of a bench about fifteen feet from the work. His gaze remained transfixed for more than a minute. He closed his eyes, the after-image of the work still visible. He could see her flowered straw hat and feel the soft fabric of her blue dress and silky red locks. The fragrance of her perfume, a breath of spring, spread through the air, as she waved the Japanese fan she held in her right hand.

An uncanny sense that he was not alone caused him to open his eyes. He observed a young woman seated about five feet away at the opposite end of the bench. Silky red hair hung down to her shoulders. That alone gave her a striking resemblance to the woman in the painting. But the similarity went further. The profile of her cute, turned-up nose duplicated that which decorated the masterpiece. Eric turned back toward the painting, if only to avoid staring. He knew the details of his favorite Renoir lady without the need to re-examine them. The lovely woman on the bench was another matter. Out of the corner of his eye, he viewed her perfectly postured, well-endowed curvaceous figure. Though his sideward glance focused on her for no more than a second before drifting to the floor below, his mind unbuttoned her white silk blouse. The alluring breasts of a Renoir nude flashed vividly into his imagination. A pang of conscience kept his eyes focused on the floor.

He felt the urge to say something, but tension tied his tongue. He again raised his head and stared blankly at the masterpiece he loved. Still the image of the young woman off to his right was all he saw. For another five...ten...fifteen seconds, he remained frozen, his mind catatonic.

"That's a wonderful painting, isn't it?"

Her voice, albeit melodious, launched shock waves throughout his body.

"Sorry, I didn't mean to startle you and, worse yet, interrupt your reflection."

"Uh...no, you...uh...didn't disrupt me at all." The words rattled from his mouth like a dirty corduroy scrubbing over the corrugated surface of a rusty washboard. Her face...her beautiful face...testified that she put little credence in his white lie. "I...I guess I was engrossed in the painting." Eric gestured toward the wall. "It has a way of doing that to me. It's my favorite."

"And I disrupted your peace."

Repeating his failed denial was foolhardy. Admitting his thoughts had, in truth, been shifted to her was out of the question. He wanted to tell her how beautiful she was. Judgment kept the rash declaration from his lips. "You bear a striking resemblance to the woman in the painting." He took note of his bench-mate's high cheekbones and blue eyes. They mirrored that which adorned the canvas. He gestured toward the painting again. "She's exquisite...wouldn't you say?"

The high cheekbones he had taken note of a moment earlier reddened her otherwise abashed countenance.

By indirection he had delivered the type of message that discretion dictated he avoid. "I...I'm sorry. I've managed to embarrass you."

"A bit...but please, don't apologize. Being compared to Renoir's depiction of feminine pulchritude is hardly the height of insults. And the truth be known, the resemblance—a friend pointed it out last year when first I visited the Clark—is what brings me back to this bench, not that I'm nearly so beautiful as the woman in the painting."

"I beg to differ...If anything, you're prettier." He eyed her soft, inviting lips. He didn't believe in love at first sight. But he was in love. The seeming paradox gave him pause, but only for an instant. This was far from first sight. Over the past four years, he had viewed her, indeed studied her, many times before. He had eyed her from a distance, and he had examined her up close. And he was staring at her again, only this time she was not mounted on the wall. "I...I apologize...the...uh...way I'm gawking at you. But it's as if my favorite painting has come to life."

Her face hinted that his words had rekindled discomfort.

"I have an awful knack for making you uncomfortable. I...I don't generally resort to the polymerized lines delivered by half-drunk boors at the barstools of smoky joints." He might have basked in his ability to deliver such cleverness were he not afraid she recognized that like the boors he had referenced, he had employed the wordy phrase before.

"I'd hardly compare your comments to what I hear from smashed jocks eager for some fast action." She smiled warmly.

"Do you come here often?"

"About once a year...I come down from Bennington."

31

"Are you a student there?" The college with the artsy reputation lay in the southwest corner of Vermont, a mere thirty miles from Williamstown.

"I'll be a junior in the fall. You a student?"

"I was...until yesterday, when I graduated from Williams."

"Great school. Ought to open some nice doors for your future."

Eric shrugged. "One never knows, but I hope." He gazed briefly at the painting before refocusing on its incarnation. "It really is my favorite painting, and you do look so much like her."

"I take that as an exceptional compliment. By the way, my name is Glenna...Glenna Snow."

Eric silently repeated the name. *Such a pretty name.* He would have voiced the thought were he not afraid of sounding disingenuous. "I'm Eric Johanson. It's a pleasure to meet you, Glenna."

"The pleasure is mutual."

"I take it you like the Clark."

She nodded. "I love art museums, but I'm not the big-city type. Being able to enjoy so many masterpieces in a quaint New England town is much more my thing."

"My sentiments exactly. Places like New York City and Boston are fine for a visit, but I'll take green grass and open spaces over high rises any day. That's not to say that I'd want to be a hermit out in the sticks, but traffic, honking horns and people pushing and shoving don't do it for me."

"A man after my own heart."

Though her words were plainly nothing more than concurrence, the urge to read more into them was tempting. Like him, perhaps she was seized by a fluttering heart. "What are you majoring in?"

"Psychology...at least for the time being."

"The time being?"

"I had to choose something, and psychology seemed as good as anything. What I'll do with it remains to be seen. Social work...maybe teach or...something." Her break in eye contact evidenced diffidence.

32

Eric welcomed the reaction, not that he wished her discomfort; simply because it made her seem less intimidating.

"I know. That's hardly a satisfactory response for one about to start her junior year of college. But the truth is: I don't know what I want to do with my life." She looked him in the eye. "You probably know exactly what you want to do."

Eric hesitated before nodding slowly.

"Just as I thought." She eyed him for a moment, as if expecting a further explanation. "So, you plan to tell me?"

"Travel the globe on a huge private yacht. Play golf...relax on a sunny beach, an icy drink in hand, gazing at the emerald green waters of a tropical isle..."

"Sounds like you're headed for a tough life. Must be rough being born with a silver spoon...or should I say diamond-encrusted gold?"

"That's hardly how I'd describe my upbringing. My father's a minister, and my mom, a housewife."

A puzzled look appeared on Glenna's face. "So, how do you plan to support that fancy lifestyle? Maybe you won the lottery?"

"Almost...except I didn't buy a ticket. But before you get confused, understand that I won't be living that high life. I was just answering your question...what I want to do. Given that I've got student loans and a desire to eat, I've taken a job as a claims adjuster for an insurance company."

Her face bore a definite reaction. Exactly what it meant was impossible to discern.

"You're impressed...perhaps? Or maybe that's a look of nausea?"

"Neither specifically, though it reminded me of the hard time my insurance company gave me last year after a hit-and-run driver sideswiped my car while I was sitting parked along the curb." She looked him in the eye. "You gonna be like the pompous suit who chiseled me out of a fair settlement? Told me I could take the matter to arbitration if I didn't like the check he had in his hand." Her lips grew briefly taut. "The guy was really nice, the first time I talked to him. He promised to take good care of me. Of course, once I signed a written statement confirming that I wasn't injured and only looking to recover my property damage, he played hardball." She studied Eric once again. "I'm a pretty good judge of character. You strike me as the kind who will give your customers a fair shake."

Back when Eric had gone through the application and interview process for his job, his sole focus had been on landing the position. The dilemmas he would regularly face as a claims adjuster had been far from his thoughts. Her comments brought them to the forefront. He said, "If you were my insured, I definitely would give you a fair shake." His cheap, flirtatious line reverberated with a hollow echo. Taking advantage of people who suffered losses was also unappealing. He said, "I'd like to believe that I'll be fair with people."

"I'm confident you will. I have faith in you."

Though the compliment was delivered with seeming sincerity, the possibility it was a white lie was undeniable. Regardless, Eric couldn't resist buying into it, not when he was so taken with her. He gazed at the wall and Renoir's masterpiece. Splendid though it was, its two-dimensional, inanimate image paled in the presence of Glenna Snow. She was the real thing. Unlike the untouchable canvases that lined the Clark's walls, her velvety smooth, flawless cheeks begged a tender caress. And too, Glenna was better endowed than the *Woman with a Fan*. Eric's imagination again reached beyond Glenna's silk blouse. Libido-driven lust eclipsed art's magnificence. He turned back to Glenna. "Would you...uh...like to get some coffee and a pastry perhaps?" The words came from his mouth almost as if his tongue had a mind of its own. His brain, confronted with the risks of rejection, stirred with anxiety.

For a moment, Glenna was silently pensive. "Yes. That would be nice."

Like a high school senior opening a letter of acceptance from the one college he longed to attend, exuberance supplanted tension. "Great!...How 'bout we head over to Tunnel City Coffee?"

"Don't know it, but okay."

"It's a cute little place over on Spring Street, about a ten-minute walk. Nothing fancy, but nice. And with most of the

34

students gone, it should be relatively quiet." He got up from the bench, and she did likewise. He was tempted to take her hand—he definitely wanted to—but unsure how she might react, avoided the move. Together they walked through the Clark's halls and out the front entrance.

As they stepped out into the glorious late-May sunshine, she paused gazing upward. The move caused him to do so as well. Cottony white clouds floated beneath an azure canopy. The silhouette of a large bird casually circling overhead caught Eric's eye. He pointed. "Boy, it must be nice to float through the sky like that eagle."

"It's a red-shouldered hawk."

"Sure." Eric gave Glenna a look. "I'm known to be gullible, but give me a break. Not only are its shoulders, be they red or otherwise, invisible from down here, but looking up, it's little more than a shadowy profile."

"Raptors are generally easy to identify when they circle that way."

Eric checked the temptation to roll his eyes. He looked skyward again as the bird gracefully drifted higher in an updraft. A spark of brilliance ignited as he noted the jagged shape of the ends of its wings. "Let me guess," he said. "The wing tips of a red-shouldered hawk are like fingers."

She nodded.

He sensed the self-satisfied smile that decorated his face.

"Of course, turkey vultures, bald eagles and ospreys, among others, have similar wing tips."

His shoulders sank, as he once again eyed the circling bird. "Well, at least I knew it wasn't a plane or Superman." He glanced her way. Her furrowed brow suggested that unlike him she was probably never a fan of the Man of Steel's re-runs. "So, tell me, how do you know that's a red-tailed hawk?"

"Red-*shouldered* hawk."

"Okay, shouldered."

She pointed upward. "Rather than straight across, the rear portion of its wings have a slight v-shape, flattened to about one hundred fifty degrees. There are some other differences, but that's the one I focus on."

Eric studied the large bird. "I guess I see what you're saying, but how do you tell them from the other birds?"

"Well...with the bald eagle, the leading edge of the spanned wing is almost a straight line. The bend of the edge is also very small, maybe ten degrees. The osprey, on the other hand, has a wing whose leading edge is an inverted-v, flattened to maybe one hundred fifty degrees, and the turkey vulture—"

"Wow...you know your birds."

A sheepish expression draped her face.

"I wasn't making fun. On the contrary, I'm impressed."

She studied him, seemingly assessing his sincerity.

"Really...I mean it."

"Well...okay, even if I did get carried away."

He smiled and led the way from the Clark, up South Street. His analytic propensities focused on the ironic benefits of the conversation that had immediately preceded. When first they had begun to talk while seated on the museum's bench, intimidation had put him ill at ease. Her self-conscious moments had made her seem more vulnerable. That was good.

Once they arrived at Tunnel City Coffee, they ordered two coffees and two doughnuts, jelly for her and maple frosted for him. She told him how she had grown up an only child in South Carolina and how her grandfather's stories of a youth spent in the rural mountains of Vermont had led her to apply to Bennington College. He detailed his days in Johnstown, Pennsylvania where he was the middle child of a close-knit family led by his father, a Protestant minister and his mother, a homemaker. Much to his surprise, he acknowledged the inner conflict occasioned by his secular college life, one that rarely included visits to church. Ordinarily he made no mention of the subject with strangers. Even with his Inseparable buddies, it was a subject he generally avoided. As he downed his second cup of java, flavored with two sugars and plenty of cream, he recited the rationalizations with which he minimized any guilt. College was a time to explore life, challenge preconceived notions and experience that which was unfamiliar. He no sooner voiced the excuses than he took himself to task, noting that principles were not water spigots to be turned on and off as convenience dictated. The ease with which he expressed the self-recriminations was unexpected; even more surprising was his willingness to forego propensities toward privacy.

On and on they talked. Their conversation flowed as effortlessly as a meandering stream in a bucolic countryside. Eric glanced at his watch. The five o'clock hour was but a minute away. They had been sitting together for two hours. "Would you like some dinner?"

Her eyes went wide.

"I know. It does sound crazy, but those doughnuts were small and..." He held his watch out for her to see. "It's just about supper time."

"Well..."

He reached for menus that were braced between the condiments and the wall and handed her one. "Give it a look. You've got nothing to lose."

"True...Of course, what I might gain (her hand went to her stomach) is another matter."

"C'mon, you've got a great figure."

"Flattery will get you...everywhere." She smiled. A moment later, she opened the menu, and before long Glenna was ordering a house salad with grilled chicken. Eric went for a cheeseburger and curly fries.

"It's Happy Hour," said their server, as she approached the table. "Two-for-one drinks."

Eric looked at Glenna. Her face showed nothing. "What the hell," he said. "Let's go for it."

Glenna shrugged.

"A glass of white zinfandel sound okay?" During his days at Williams, Eric had consumed a fair amount of beer, though far less than most. Wine, however, was foreign. In all his years, no more than a couple of liters had traveled his throat.

"Well...okay, I guess."

He turned to the server. "Two white zinfandels."

As soon as the server was out of earshot, Glenna leaned forward and whispered. "I'm not legal. Still five months short of my twenty-first birthday."

Eric feigned shock. "And I thought a woman never reveals her age."

"Only if she's carded."

"You weren't. So, how come you disclosed your years?" Were the booth's wall a mirror, rather than stained walnut, Eric would have checked out the smirk he sent her way.

"Hey…when you get to be old and senile, over twenty, you do and say things you never would have back in your younger days."

The ease with which she danced her way around her preceding verbal misstep confirmed what he had already concluded. Glenna had a quick mind. Several hours earlier with the intimidation factor at play, her quick comeback might have unnerved him, but in a single afternoon he had grown more comfortable. They had learned a great deal about one another. It was as if he had known her for a long time. He said, "I turned twenty-two back in March."

"Well…for a guy in his golden years, an old codger, and for that matter, a curmudgeon, I have to admit you're remarkably well preserved." She smiled broadly.

The arms he folded across his chest with pretended indignation felt the rapid beating of his heart. The affection conveyed by her good-natured taunt was patent. Still he was determined to outdo her. He doubled over, forcing a mien of pain. He moaned in a voice befitting the most prodigious of nursing-home whiners. "My heart bleeds from the verbal knife you have thrust into it."

"Oh…and I thought it was your stomach rumbling …Indigestion. Old folks like you should stay away from burgers and fries." She pointed at his plate that, along with hers, had just arrived. Her expression made it clear that she would extend him neither sympathy, nor quarter.

"You know…you're tough."

Her innocent smile demonstrated that she could playact as well as he…maybe better. It also turned him on. He wanted to jump across the table, take her in his arms and kiss her. Indeed, he wanted to do a helluva lot more. The young woman seated on the opposite side of the booth, the beauty he had beheld so many times before on the wall of the Clark, had come to life. Fantasy had turned into reality. Eric Johanson was smitten.

CHAPTER IV

MONEY IS THE ROOT OF ALL EVIL.

Donald Burns laughed at the absurdity of the hackneyed adage. The lack of money caused far more evil than money itself. Junkies wouldn't put knives to people's throats if they had the cash to buy drugs. Shoplifters wouldn't resort to five-finger discounts if they had the bucks with which to shop. And those in business wouldn't cheat on their taxes as long as they could make a decent living. On second thought, they might, provided they could get away with it. And who could blame them when big-spending politicians were taxing them blind, only to deliver pork to their contributors. But don't blame money. Along with capitalism, it had built the greatest economy ever. Men like John D. Rockefeller and Henry Ford proved Don's point. Women like Oprah Winfrey were proving it as well. A man bearing his own name, *The Donald*, king of the birthers, who had risen to the most powerful position on Earth, popped into Don's head. Sure, he was arrogant, bombastic, egotistical, narcissistic, not to mention prevaricating and obnoxious, but who could argue with success? Not Donald Burns.

He leaned back in his commodious high-back leather chair. His office, nine-by-nine, was small, but it was his office, and it felt damn good. It was his first day on the job at Kingman & Woodhill, a top-drawer brokerage firm in midtown Manhattan on the thirty-second floor of what was once called the Pan Am building. No longer a college kid in frayed jeans and a tee-shirt, Donald Burns was a man of the world, a vision of sartorial splendor, wearing a classy pinstripe suit, starched Ralph Lauren white shirt and a red power tie with black stripes.

Williamstown, the sleepy hamlet, about two hundred miles to the north, seemed as distant as the moon. Psychologically it was closer to Aberdeen, Maryland, his childhood home, than New York City, even though the Big Apple lay in between, not far from the midpoint. Time also seemed to be warping. He had been living a whirlwind. In the confines of less than two weeks, he had graduated Williams; eloped with Linda, with the blessing of their parents; spent five days honeymooning in Nantucket; and begun his working life. College felt almost as far removed as his boyhood days in a four-bedroom colonial in suburban Aberdeen. Childhood, high school and college were nothing more than past lives. His professional life was underway. He was upwardly mobile. Evidence thereof was already manifest. Seated at his desk, more than three hundred feet above the bustling streets of Manhattan, he had risen to rarified air. He was thrilled to be in New York City. The old cliché, "Make it there, and you can make it anywhere," had more truth than bunk, at least that's how Don saw it. Linda would have preferred a less metropolitan location, but she willingly acceded to the needs of his career.

Temptation cajoling, Don put his feet up onto his desk. Years earlier when he had first seen an executive do it in a movie, he had imagined himself someday assuming the identical position. If the wall of his office—in truth, little more than a cubicle—were glass, rather than wood, no way would he have risked the cocksure posture, not on his very first morning.

Don closed his eyes, savoring the empowering moment. The time had come to reap the benefits of twenty-two years of labor, not that he had ever been the hardest worker. At Williams, the gentlemen "C" had been Don's most common grade. "B" came in a distant second, followed by a rare "A" or "D." His grade point average would have been lower but for his diligent avoidance of tough courses and professors. Of the four Inseparables, Don had done the least work. He also had the lowest marks, though he could have beaten out Eric had he worked as hard. Bill and Kyle were a different story. Not only were they conscientious, but also bright, particularly Kyle, for whom everything came easily. But much as grades were nice, *life* had a different scorecard. Power and money were the measuring sticks. Whom one knew, not what, counted. Don understood the concept. He had tried to convey this wisdom to his pals, but his advice had fallen on deaf ears. His three buddies had kept their noses to the grindstone. And what had it gotten them? Bill had lined up a job teaching English at a private girls' school in Fort Myers, Florida. He would earn a pittance. Eric had taken a job as a claims adjuster for an insurance company. His pay would be decent when one included benefits, but it was the first rung on a ladder to mediocrity. As for Kyle, the MBA he was pursuing might open some well-paying doors down the road, but in the meantime, he would be piling up a mountain of debt owing to graduate-school loans. Don would not have traded places with any of his buddies. He was earning a good salary; his job as a broker on Wall Street had huge potential; and what he had lacked in grades, he more than made up for in intangibles. Simply put, he was the best equipped for the future, the odds-on favorite for big-time success.

Make no mistake. Don loved his three friends. They were terrific guys. Though he disagreed with them about the need to study hard, on most matters his views were similar to theirs. They were all into sports, and not merely as fans. Baseball, basketball, touch football—they played most anything. They were all athletic. None was a star. But Don was a little faster, a bit more agile, a shade better than the other three. He was also a better salesman. Not to brag, but he had charisma. Simply put, he was the coolest, the proverbial tall, dark and handsome man. Politics, with its aphrodisiac of power, was not beyond the realm of his future. But for the moment, money was his goal.

A knock at Don's door roused him from his musing. His feet immediately came off the desk. He flipped open a folder, if only to give the appearance of working. "Come in," he said.

Charles Bascomb, a senior partner, stepped through the door.

Don leaped from his chair. A newcomer, even a confident one, face to face with a big boss, experienced anxiety, especially the first day on the job.

"Don't get up." Bascomb took a seat on the opposite side of the desk.

"Uh...thank you, Mr. Bascomb," said Don, nervously slipping back down into his seat.

"Please, it's Chuck." He looked Don in the eye, seemingly confirming his desire for the informality. "As I told you when we hired you, I plan to be your mentor, and to my mind, a good mentor doesn't stand on ceremony."

The rubber band of Don's mind, stretched taut a moment earlier, eased back toward neutral.

"So...how's it feel, now that you're actually here?"

"Exciting!" Unlike his job interview where his responses were carefully planned and measured, the word popped from Don's mouth. It accurately assessed his feelings. He was excited to be out in the real world, and especially so, having a position at a prestigious firm in the heart of the Big Apple.

"Just how I felt my first day here twenty-nine years ago. Like you, I was fresh out of college, eager to take on the world."

"From what I can tell, you've retained that enthusiasm."

Bascomb leaned back, folding his arms across the dark blue breast of what was likely a hand-tailored suit. On the short side, stocky, with ruddy complexion and little hair atop his head, were it not for his impressive attire, he easily could have been taken for a blue-collar worker. Although in such case, one would have to assume the gold *Rolex* that became visible once he folded his arms was a street-corner knockoff.

"Well...to tell the truth..."

As Bascomb paused in seeming pensive analysis, a recollection from first-semester freshman year streamed from Don's brain. Professor Walker in English 101 deplored the use of expressions such as "to tell the truth," "to be candid," and "frankly." Since one was presumably being honest, the words were nothing more than vacuous surplusage. Worse yet, Dr. Walker warned that all too often their utterance was a prelude

42

to veiled misrepresentation. That admonition in mind, Don awaited what followed.

"To say that I'm as excited about my job as the day I started would be misleading, but that's only because something new is more exciting than that which is familiar. That said, however, I've got a great job. I pull down seven figures, and without working all that hard. Much of my time is spent schmoozing about football, golf or hockey, making clients feel comfortable, so they invest their money. Once they do, commissions start rolling in. A round or two at the country club, hardly life in the salt mines, helps cement the relationship. And as your clientele grows, you make more while hustling less." Bascomb shrugged. "What's not to like?"

"Nothing," said Don, though presumably the question was rhetorical. His mind reverted to Professors Walker's admonition. The clever-sounding warning rang hollow. Rather than pretend that every day was as exciting as his first, Bascomb had been up front. Unlike the Williams pedagogue who, from his ivory-towered perch, a low-paying one at that, was adept at talking about life, the Wall Street expert knew how to live it.

Bascomb looked Don in the eye. "You've got something on your mind."

"You're very observant."

With his index finger, Bascomb made a mark in the air.

"What does that mean?"

"I was chalking up a point for you. In this business, flattery is a valuable tool. Wealthy clients have big egos. Feeding those egos helps to fill your pockets."

Don made a mental note of the lesson. With each passing minute, he was getting to like his mentor more, all the while learning from him.

"Seems you managed to sidestep my earlier observation."

The comment left Don puzzled.

"A minute ago, I noted that you had something on your mind. You complimented me for being observant...without ever disclosing your thoughts."

Don made another mental note. Bascomb was nobody's fool. Fortunately, Don's earlier thought was one he was glad to share. There was no need to manufacture a quick disguise. "Earlier when listening to you, I was thinking about the picture you had painted, a potentially rich financial future, but one that grows without the burden of ever-increasing demands."

Bascomb nodded slowly. "Yeah, that's a pretty fair assessment." A smile, a self-satisfied one, appeared on his face. "Not a bad deal, is it?"

"Not bad at all." When Don had accepted the position at Kingman & Woodhill, he was certain it was an excellent opportunity. Just a single hour into his first day, he had ample proof of that conviction.

A botanical paradise. Plants from all around the globe thrive amidst the magnificent subtropical ecosystem known as the Everglades. Birds, large and small, of countless species sing their dulcet melodies. Nature's amazing harmony, a seemingly inconceivable masterpiece, dares one to deny the hand of God.

Bill Young sat on a bench along the banks of the Caloosahatchee River, on what was once the winter estates of Thomas Edison and Henry Ford. Despite the eighty-five-degree, mid-morning temperature, thanks to the shade of a Mysore fig tree and a breeze spawned by the adjacent waters, he felt comfortable. Unlike most who decried the late-June Florida heat, Bill had no complaints. Admittedly, a few degrees cooler would have been preferable, but compared to the bitter Massachusetts winters he had endured on the campus of Williams, it was Heaven.

Several weeks had passed since he had arrived in Southern Florida, Fort Myers to be precise, and it was exceeding expectations. His nine-hundred square foot, one-bedroom, one-bath apartment, with kitchen, living room and dining area, at eleven hundred dollars per month, was a step up from the digs the Inseparables had shared at Williams. The twenty-year-old beige stucco complex, consisting of four two-story buildings, each with twelve apartments, was only two miles from the beach. In the center courtyard was a large swimming pool, surrounded by umbrella tables, chairs and loungers. From the living room window of Bill's second-floor apartment, he enjoyed a great view of the pool's soothing, aquamarine water. Occasional bikini-clad feminine pulchritude was a bonus, though admittedly such beauty was the exception. At twenty-two, he was more than two decades younger than the average resident.

Roughly two months, July and most of August, remained before he would begin his duties teaching English at Fordison, a small private girls' school on the southeastern outskirts of Fort Myers. At thirty-six thousand dollars per year, he was hardly at the upper end of the pay scale of his fellow Williams' graduates. But with just himself to support, the salary was fine. And the job came with an added perk. Fordison had referred four students to him for tutoring. Over the summer, he was seeing each twice per week. At sixty dollars per hour, a mere pittance to the wealthy families whose children he taught, the tutoring added about five thousand dollars to his income. And it still left time to pursue his avocation, writing his first novel.

Bill pounded the keys of his laptop, sending his protagonist, a would-be inventor, loosely inspired by a young Thomas Edison, down the twists and turns of the Ausable River in New York's Adirondacks. By the time the climax ensued, the protagonist, having survived false accusations of arson, would have his first patent, and Bill, his first book. Admittedly, one was a paltry number, especially in the context of Edison who, by the time he had died, had a mind-boggling 1093 United States patents. Bill closed his eyes as he tried to calculate how long it would take him to write that many novels. Fifty…a hundred…two hundred lifetimes. With only a fraction of a chapter under his belt, and only the scant beginning of a story in his head, there was no guarantee he would finish his first. Eyes still closed, he turned his head to the right in the direction of the Edison Pier. He could see the great inventor standing there with Henry Ford, along with presidents, such as Harding and Coolidge, who traveled there for visits. Bill breathed in the pleasing Caloosahatchee air. The manifold fragrances that graced the estate were welcome, even if Bill could not identify them, except by reading the signs that dotted the grounds where Edison, in a later-life pursuit of a financially advantageous source of rubber, had planted countless exotic flowers and trees.

Bill opened his eyes. Atop the keys of his laptop, his fingers begged to resume their dance. Nary a one moved. The splendor, the history and the awe-inspiring wonder of the place was a double-edged sword. As readily as it stimulated the flow of his creative juices, it distracted him. Regardless, he viewed it as a win-win. Even on days when his writing failed to advance, he savored the serenity, the spiritual sustenance. It drew him closer to God, even closer than did the many biblical readings of his Mormon upbringing.

Bill gazed across the wide expanse of the river, upward at the cobalt sky. A pair of puffy white clouds stood face to face. Were he back in his childhood, he would have identified each as something from the animal kingdom. Expanded horizons, new interests, altered his perspective. Protrusions on each of the nebulous formations were enough to imagine noses. In one he saw Edison and the other, Westinghouse, two men who had engaged in a titanic battle to determine whether America would be powered by direct or alternating current. The story was electric, but it spun Bill's brain into a quandary. Edison, the great inventor, seemed right for the role of protagonist, leaving Westinghouse to play the antagonist. But history had proved otherwise. Edison, in a no-holds-barred battle, had ruthlessly endeavored to paint alternating current as a vile tool of the devil. Ultimately, the position of the more gentlemanly Westinghouse had prevailed. Transmitting direct current over long distances was impractical. The energy loss was far too great. Alternating current won out. Westinghouse was one of the few to best the intensely competitive Edison, though the latter won the financial war even while losing the theoretical one. But Bill was writing fiction. If need be, history could be modified, even ignored.

Bill gave the clouds another look. They had begun to coalesce. The battle was joined. They were a metaphor for his novel. Westinghouse, though less of a businessman, but also free of guile, became the model for his protagonist. Edison would be the antagonist. Far from cool, at times a nerd, Bill's protagonist had acquired a personality. He had come to life. His struggles would be many, but when the dust settled, he would win his patent and damages from the huge corporate monster that had tried to steal his brilliant invention. Bill's fingers pranced about the keys, though hardly with the creative genius of Thomas Edison or the remarkable efficiency of Henry Ford's mass production line. Regardless, words flowed with unexpected ease. Bill's first novel was drawing its initial breaths.

Violence...chaos...calamity...disaster. War...holocaust... volcanic eruption...disease. Both man and nature wreak havoc. The spinning Earth, a raging molten mass beneath an asymmetric surface, hurtles through space in ever-decaying ellipses, its destiny to ultimately crash into the sun. Draped by an atmosphere, an invisible realm capable of spawning hurricanes and tornadoes and forces that boggle the mind, roams man, pre-eminent defiler of his planet and those who share it. Yet amidst such pervasive havoc, an anomaly, magical and enchanting, emerges. Love, the ultimate aphrodisiac, supersedes affliction. Infatuation silences cacophony. And beating hearts spawn ineffable joy.

Whatever the state of the world, Eric Johanson was in paradise. Hand in hand with Glenna Snow, he strolled across the Bennington College campus. In the past he had dated attractive females, but none, not one, compared to Glenna. From time to time there had been crushes, but for the first time, Eric was in love.

Ever since he had met Glenna at the Clark Institute, they had spent every weekend together, five of them to be precise. Three times he had traveled from Hartford, Connecticut, where he had begun his career as a claims adjuster for the Granite Insurance Company, to Bennington College, and twice she had made the trip the other way. The day before had been a crescendo, the notes of its magnificent night still reverberating.

47

Together they had strolled the quaint streets of Connecticut's Mystic Seaport, imbibing the pleasant breeze of the Long Island Sound. At a bakery, they had shared the sweet taste of a scrumptious pecan turtle, rich with chocolate and caramel. At the Olde Ice Cream Shop they had savored waffle cones stuffed with freshly churned peppermint-fudge ice cream. And aboard the Charles Morgan, the big-masted vestige of the great American whaling fleet, they had savored innumerable kisses, each sweeter than the delectable treats they had devoured earlier. In the evening, they had enjoyed a candlelit dinner on the waterfront patio of the Pewter House. The charming inn, its servers nattily costumed in revolutionary period attire, had draped them in history dating back well over two centuries. High above, a canopy of stars, with footprints stepping across billions of years, obligingly twinkled, but none with the sparkle that Eric saw in Glenna's beautiful blue eyes. Nor too did the flaming orbs with scorching temperatures measured in the thousands of degrees burn with the fiery passion that Glenna and Eric had enjoyed that night. Emotion...Intimacy... Ecstasy. Together, they had shared their bodies with a glory as old as time, but as nascent as that which was yet to be conceived. And amidst the intimacy, with trepidation abounding, Eric had taken a fateful leap. He had uttered the momentous three-word phrase, a brief declaration that had him teetering on the brink of Heaven and Hell. A moment later, when the identical phrase, *I love you*, had crossed Glenna's lips, Eric, an angel in his arms, had passed through Heaven's parted gates.

Golden necklaces bedecked with rubies, emeralds and diamonds. But beware. Such chains can fetter; worse yet, around the neck, strangle.

"Wow!"

"Make that double wow!" said Linda, as Don pulled their Honda CRV into the long, semi-circular driveway of Charles

48

Bascomb's Westchester estate, bringing the eight-thousand square foot colonial with adjoining guest house into full view.

Don took his foot off the gas, allowing the vehicle to idle slowly forward. He needed a moment to collect himself before pulling up to the valet who was waiting beneath the canopy that fronted the mansion. "Not bad."

"You can say that again."

Don might have, were the impressive digs not impeding his tongue. He drew his vehicle to a halt underneath the stone-pillared overhang. Even before he could reach for the door handle, the valet opened his door, after which he hurried to the other side and did the same for Linda. Together they started toward the huge double doors that opened to the house.

"Excuse me, Sir," said the valet. He gestured at Don's right hand that held the keys to the car.

"Uh...sorry," said Don, conscious that customary aplomb had deserted him. He handed the keys to the valet.

Once the valet climbed into the vehicle, Linda whispered, "You didn't tell me we'd be partying at the Vanderbilts." She pointed toward the large pentagonal garden with multi-tiered fountain that stood about halfway between the home and the perfectly manicured privet hedges bordering the front of the property.

"I assumed he had a nice place, but something like this...you gotta be kidding." Don took a deep breath and prepared to lead the way to the door. "You ready?"

Linda flashed a wry smile, one that said more than words could express.

Don paused a second, just long enough to reset his compass. "Hey...you never know...if I play my cards right, we might have a spread like this someday. Well...maybe not this big, but a far cry from our current haunt." With confidence buoyed, though admittedly short of that which prevailed his first day at work when he had put his feet onto the desk, he slipped an arm over Linda's shoulder and led the way to the door. He was about to ring the bell when the portal opened.

"Greetings," said Bascomb, shaking Don's hand. "And you must be Linda. Don told me you were lovely, but his description fails to do you justice."

Don glanced at his wife. Some said she resembled Princess Kate. Attired in her little black dress, the slim brunette with high cheek bones and button nose had the English royal's paradoxical beauty, classical and understated, but nonetheless hot.

Bascomb leaned forward and pecked Linda on the cheek. "I'm Charlie Bascomb."

"It's a pleasure to meet you, Mr. Bascomb."

"Mr. Bascomb?…That was my father." He chuckled briefly. "Please, call me Chuck."

Despite Linda's nod, Don doubted his wife would follow the direction, at least for the time being. More likely, she would avoid saying the boss's name when talking to him.

"Your home is magnificent," said Linda.

Bascomb peeked over his shoulder where a huge crystal chandelier hung above a pink marble arcing staircase. "We find it comfortable." He led them into a large living room where he motioned to a server who provided Don and Linda with flutes of champagne, a strawberry adorning each. "Catch me later and I'll take you on a tour, but for now (he motioned toward the front door where more guests were arriving) duty calls."

As Bascomb disappeared into the entrance hall, Don ran his eyes over the finely carved foot-wide, crown moldings that traced their way around the tops of the four walls. He estimated the length of the room to be more than forty feet. "Amazing place, isn't it?"

"Quite," said Linda.

"And he's quite the guy."

Linda sipped her champagne.

"What—you disagree?"

She shrugged.

"What's that supposed to mean?"

She looked around to make sure no one was listening and, in a lowered voice, said, "I'm not all that impressed."

"You can't be serious."

She sipped her champagne again.

"C'mon, the man graciously welcomes you into his incredible mansion and you're—"

"I have my opinions, but let's leave them for later."

Judgment superseding pique, Don silently conceded it was not a good time or place to debate the merits of his boss and his home. Don polished off his champagne, but not before he took in the mural of a castle in a lush green setting atop a cliff overlooking the sea. *Not bad to come home to each night. Not bad at all.*

Another server approached with a tray of stuffed mushrooms. Don took one. He downed it in a single bite, following it with the strawberry from his flute. He had no sooner finished the fruited delight when the server who had provided the drink took his glass and encouraged him to take another. Don obliged.

In the ensuing hour, he consumed two vodkas, both his favorite, Grey Goose. He drifted here and there, exchanging easy conversation with the guys from the office, as well as strangers. He slapped a few backs. Feeling very good, he again headed to the bar where the bartender was fixing a martini for another guest. An animated fellow in the corner who was talking in a raised voice drew Don's attention, along with that of at least another half dozen.

"You can keep your goddamn baseball. Duller than a frigid witch in January. Especially with the goddamn Yankees always buyin' the freakin' pennant. Ya ask me, the whole thing is bullshit!" Gesticulations accompanying the loud mouth's rant spilled spirits from his highball glass.

"Another Grey Goose?" said the bartender.

The old adage, albeit with minor modification, *Discretion is the better part of stupidity*, echoed in Don's head. The effect of the drinks he had already consumed, more than he was used to, could not be denied. A display like the buffoon in the corner was the last thing Don needed. "A diet Coke will do just fine, thanks."

Don took a moment to check on Linda. She was seated on a couch in the living room, comfortably conversing with another woman he did not recognize. He availed himself of the opportunity to take in the remainder of the sprawling two-story home's first floor. All the while he admired the furnishings. In the dining room a large china cabinet displayed a wide collection of Venetian glass, painted with colorful enamels and etched in gold. Across the way, a second cabinet housed a collection of trays, chaffing dishes, candlesticks and bowls, all of polished silver. Whether they were sterling or merely plated, Don had no idea. Regardless, they were impressive. Equally impressive was the artwork that adorned the various rooms. Paintings in ornate frames, Grecian urns that reached to his waist and even a pair of life-sized, fig-leafed statues were but some of the adornments. But what most impressed Don were the three rooms at the far end of the mansion. The first, large and paneled, sported a pool table with finely carved legs well over a foot in diameter, the kind one might find supporting a humungous bed in a medieval castle. At the other end were leather chairs and couches, a green felt-topped, hexagonal card table and a well-stocked bar twice the length of the one being used for the party. A bear's head hung from the wall behind the bar. A door adjacent to the bar led into a theater of about thirty seats with graduated rows for perfect viewing. At the far end of the house was a marble and glass sun room bearing fifteen-foot Doric columns in each corner.

As Don headed back through the den to find Linda, a fellow holding a pool cue tugged his arm.

"You play pool?"

"A little," said Don.

"How 'bout a game?"

Don eyed the table. "Oh…what the hell. Why not?"

As the fellow handed Don a cue, he gestured at himself. "I'm Sanford, one of Chuck's golfing buddies at Twisted Creek."

"Nice to meet you. I'm Don. I work—"

"Nine Ball. I'll break. Okay?"

"Uh…sure," said Don, not expecting the game to be so businesslike.

Twenty minutes later, with two games completed, both in favor of Sanford, the shark started to rack the balls again.

"You sure are good," said Don.

The fellow gave Don a look. "Let me guess. You're about to propose a little wager."

"A wager?"

"Yeah, I've seen hustlers like you. Lose a few games and then turn on the heat for dough."

Don nodded slowly. "Gotta hand it to you, Sandford. You got a keen eye."

A puzzled look replaced the cocksure mien that Sandford had been sporting.

Don started toward the wall to hang up his cue.

"Where you goin'?"

Don shrugged. "Either you recognized me from ESPN...or you're just a master at sizing up the competition. Regardless, what can I say? You caught me with my pants down."

"You mean you really were hustling me?"

"You said it. Not me." Don hung up his cue. "Thanks for the game." He took delight in the befuddled look on Sanford's face. The fifty-something executive may have whipped his ass at pool, but when it came to matching wits, Don had put the shark to shame. Don headed out to find Linda. The crowd in the living room had thinned, and she was standing alone nursing what was likely ginger ale.

"How you doing, Sweetie?"

"Surviving." She glanced at her watch. "Quite a few people have left. What do you think?"

Don had mixed emotions, but knowing her preference, acceded to Linda's wishes. After thanking the Bascombs, they went outside where the valet brought their car. Linda went around to the driver's side. Though the effects of his earlier alcoholic consumption had largely worn off, Don climbed in on the passenger side. He was always glad to know that when they went out at night, he was free to imbibe without the risk of a DUI. Linda's blood alcohol was always well within the legal limit.

As they drove off, he said, "So, did you have a good time?"

"It was nice."

Her less than enthusiastic tone told Don her answer was a polite response to a call of duty. "Sorry, I shouldn't have wandered off the way I did."

"No, I was fine."

Don gave her a look.

"No...really. I met this lovely woman. She grew up on a farm about thirty miles west of Portland, Maine."

"Sounds exciting."

"I enjoyed talking with her. She was a history major, just like me."

"Let me guess. You talked about the Napoleonic Wars."

This time Linda gave the look. Hers was much quicker, as she quickly refocused on the highway.

"Isn't the Bascombs' home amazing?"

"In a manner of speaking...I guess." Linda kept her eyes on the road.

"C'mon, you had to be impressed."

"Well...it certainly is big, and admittedly it made an impression."

"An impression? Is that all you can say?"

"Showy...lack of taste. Perhaps those help clarify."

Don glared at her, not that she could see his expression amidst what had become the darkness of a country road. "I think you're jealous, not that I can blame you."

"Jealous!" She glanced his way. "You must be kidding. The place is gauche."

Don disbelieved his ears. Apart from the castle in San Simeon, California and the Biltmore Estate in Ashville, North Carolina, both of which required a hefty fee to be toured, the Bascombs' mansion outdid any home he had ever seen. "You telling me you wouldn't genuflect every day of your natural life for a place like that?"

"I wouldn't. But if by chance I had a huge home like that—not that I would want anything so big—I'd certainly decorate it with a lot more taste."

"Oh really. And just how would you do that?"

"For starters, I would remove the bear's head that hangs in the billiard room."

"It's a man cave!"

"Fine...Neanderthal room."

Don felt his blood pressure spike. It wasn't his home, but the attack was personal. Linda was putting down the home of his dreams. "What else about the place didn't you like?" His raised voice dared her to utter more criticisms.

"The Parthenon or whatever you call that monstrosity at the end of the house."

"What! There's something wrong with having a sun room with a southern exposure…one that's perfect for reading Steinbeck or Lewis or one of Shakespeare's masterpieces on a bright December afternoon?" The scene he had painted was as vivid in Don's mind as the freshly visited room. Self-satisfaction owing to the masterful touches of his verbal brush was impossible to deny.

"Reading classics in a cozy room with a wintry chill outside is wonderful. But cold, gray marble and garish pillars only detract from that ambiance. And I'd lay dollars to dirt that none of the authors you named, indeed none of the classics, have ever been read in that tacky hall of stone…least of all by Charles Bascomb."

Don had been ready to snap back, but her last phrase fettered his tongue. Imagining his boss reading great literature in the imposing lyceum was too great a stretch.

"In fairness, I…I have to concede the house does have a surprising consistency."

"You think so?" The apparent concession was pleasing, especially given the facts. The living room, with its Greek urns and statues, conformed to the Doric style of the sun room, but the den with its bear's head was Teddy Roosevelt.

"Take the kitchen, for example."

"I never got to see it."

"That's too bad. It's the color of pottery, along with turquoise. With its Southwest motif, it has three ovens, one a beehive. It also has two dishwashers, two refrigerators and two you-name-its."

The description, a sharp contrast to what Don had been envisioning a moment earlier, unveiled Linda's sarcasm, and Don knew he had taken the bait.

"The kitchen is the ideal complement to the home's theme." A few seconds later, Linda peeked at Don. "Aren't you going to ask?"

He pressed his lips together and folded his arms, though with her eyes already back on the road, likely she missed the reaction.

"That's okay. I'll tell you anyway. Your boss has a home whose theme is a paradigm of what I would term, 'classic gaudy eclectic.' And while far be it from me to attempt to improve upon such magnificence, I believe a Victorian turret in the center of the roof, a moat around the exterior, several gothic arches, complete with flying buttresses…oh, and just to round it out some baroque—"

"Fine, I get your message. You think it's overdone—and maybe it is—but, regardless, it's an impressive place. And more important, you have to give him credit. Like his house or not, there's no denying he's damn successful."

Linda nodded as she stopped for a red light.

"If I play my cards right, I can be successful too. And when the time is right, we can build ourselves a really fine home." He extended his left arm so his hand rested on Linda's shoulder. "And we'll make sure it's tasteful, not gaudy whatever."

Linda smiled.

Don leaned over and pecked her on the cheek.

CHAPTER V

TRUTH IS STRANGER THAN FICTION. The hackneyed saw can be inherently illogical. Fiction can stretch the imagination far beyond the bounds of reality. With minimal effort the imagination can embellish any occurrence, however implausible, with fantastic, mind-blowing adornments. Why then was Bill unable to deny the merit of the untenable maxim?

Comfortably relaxing on a chaise lounge, pool side at Palm Shadows where he rented his apartment, Bill Young closed his eyes, along with the paperback he had been reading. The content of the page he had just completed had largely escaped him. His mind had been wandering, focused on the television special about Philo Farnsworth he had watched the night before on *PBS*. The very idea that a fourteen-year-old farm boy could outdo the greatest engineering minds of the early twentieth century and invent television was preposterous. But that was exactly what Philo Farnsworth had done with his all-electronic image dissector, a device capable of breaking an image down into rows of magnetically deflected electrons that were transmitted through space and then reconstructed into the original image. Incredible as the accomplishment was, writing fiction, Bill could readily create a character whose achievements dwarfed those of Farnsworth. A deaf and blind eight-year-old who never attended school could fashion a human transporter that not merely sent an image but also conveyed people to distant times and places, turning them into superheroes at the same time. The potential for the incredible was boundless. Why then did his ideas fail to measure up to the accomplishment of Farnsworth?

Some children splashing one another in the pool drew Bill's attention. A teenage girl did a beautiful dive with a flip. Impressive, no doubt, but Bill could write about a dive with two, three, four...or even ten flips. But it would not compare to the real thing. Words meant nothing when stacked up against actual exploits. Science fiction was fun. Philo Farnsworth was the real deal.

His mind on his own manuscript, Bill leaned back on his lounger, eyeing the cover of the book he held. Whatever his protagonist invented would be window dressing. His manuscript would rise or fall on the strength of the characters he created. He reclosed his eyes, asking himself what it was he wanted to say about the human condition; what story and messages did he wish to communicate; and how could he create oases where readers could imbibe the fresh waters of self-insight.

A tap on his shoulder drew Bill from his reverie. Standing alongside was...what's her name...one of about ten people at the complex he had met.

"Must be nice, Bill, to have teachers' hours. Summers off, and even when school is in session, get out at two-thirty and vegetate by the pool."

Bill restrained the urge to point out that once classes commenced, his day would begin before eight and, with extracurricular responsibilities, a facet of his private-school job, rarely end before five. And many an evening would include time preparing lessons and grading papers. He tried to remain cool as he searched his mind for her name. His inability to do so, and worse yet its transparency, was disconcerting. His eyes stole a quick glance at her shapely figure, all of which, apart from the cover of her iridescent pink bikini, was readily visible. With flowing blond hair, she was a stunner. Except for noting that she wore sunglasses and was very pretty, other curvaceous aspects had him too preoccupied to detail the features of her face.

She eyed his book. "Whatcha reading?"

"'Ubiquitous Conundrum'...It's by Colin Walker Hendry."

She shrugged. "Can't say that I've heard of it...or him."

"Don't feel bad. Not many have. And the truth be known, they haven't missed much."

"If that's how you feel, why you reading it?"

No way was he about to admit that he had picked it up for a buck at a Dollar Tree when his eye caught the cover, a glossy shot of a goofy-looking oaf ogling a sexy babe from behind a dinosaur skeleton in a science museum. "Supposed to be a captivating adventure in which reality blurs in a world of the fantastic." The description, a decent paraphrase of one of several tantalizing characterizations from the back cover, rolled off Bill's tongue with remarkable ease.

"Sounds interesting."

"I assure you—it wouldn't be worth your time." The last thing he wanted was for her to borrow the book. Chances were she would discover he had parroted the words from the cover. His mind darted as he tried to find a good way to suggest they spend some time together. He could propose cooking her dinner at his apartment, but might that be too forward? Perhaps an invite to a restaurant would be wiser. Or he could offer to bring a lounger for her next to his.

"Well...I'll let you get back to your reading." She started to walk away but stopped and looked back. "By the way, for future reference, my name is Andrea." She winked, though certainly not provocatively.

The flushing Bill felt was no doubt visible. Unless she thought he had suffered an instantaneous facial sunburn, his embarrassment was patent. He watched her as she headed off. Silently he recited her named several times, making certain the next time their paths crossed he would not look as stupid. His eyes returned to the pages of his book. He read a paragraph. He was about to start the next but realized the lines just traversed had not been absorbed. His brain had remained fixated on Andrea. Discretely he stole a glance down near the other end of the pool where she was applying suntan lotion. His eyes returned to the book. His stare was blank. The image of Andrea's voluptuous body was still fresh. He shut his eyes.

Like the oaf on the cover of Ubiquitous Conundrum, Bill envisioned himself peeking from behind a museum dinosaur. But unlike the oaf who ogled a woman in a suit, Bill pictured Andrea, scantily clad in her pink bikini. The lines between fiction and reality intersected. Scenarios woven from titillating threads abounded. Bill basked in the rays of the warm sun and the even warmer glow of his thoughts until he finally emerged from his reverie. He glanced once again at Andrea. His own novel's protagonist had just acquired a love interest. Her name was *Andi*. Her image, pink bikini and all, was deeply ensconced in Bill's mind. And with a little luck—well, maybe more than just a little—truth would be stranger than fiction. Perhaps the beautiful image he would put to words in his manuscript would find her way into his arms.

Echoes resound...but only briefly. Soon enough their reverberations grow silent, blurred into the huge oblivion of the past. Yet now and then the past insinuates itself into the future, often in strange and unexpected ways.

As Eric Johanson, a mere four months clear of his college days, reviewed a homeowner's casualty claim for hail damage, mixed emotions competed. Growing up the son of a Protestant minister and a stay-at-home mother, integrity, compassion and fairness were stressed. His experience at Williams had reiterated those values, at least inside the classroom. But outside, the lines were foggy. Students were known to take shortcuts. Copies of old tests provided some with advantage. A few had submitted papers purchased over the Internet. High in academia's ivory towers, virtuous words were spoken. Down in the dorms, pragmatics, the push for grades, was known to drown out their faint echoes.

Through his four years at Williams, Eric had refused to compromise. The values from his childhood had prevailed, though not without considerable resentment. Watching a classmate shortcut his way through a course was galling; getting a lower grade than the classmate, infuriating.

Having left the cloistered confines of the classroom behind, issues, formerly clear, blurred. As a claims adjuster for Granite Casualty and Life, he had a duty to his employer's bottom line. That responsibility didn't require him to screw policyholders out of legitimate claims. On the other hand, approving a claim was only the first step. Assessing the amount of the payment was another. He eyed the file on which he had been working. The roof was ten years old when the hail had struck. A new roof would run seven thousand dollars. Sure, the roof was badly pitted, but it wasn't leaking. The policy had a thousand-dollar deductible. He could approve a payment anywhere from nuisance value, five hundred dollars, up to six thousand. Based upon depreciation owing to the roof's age, four thousand would be a fair award. But conversations with the claimant had convinced Eric there would be no litigation. Choosing a lower number, perhaps two thousand, would be safe. It would also be good for his career. Rumor had it that adjusters who settled claims more cheaply enjoyed bigger bonuses and quicker promotions. Common sense dictated a low number. Echoes from his childhood demurred.

Eric leaned back and stared up at the ceiling, unable to pick a figure. His mind drifted to a more palatable subject, Glenna. She was constantly interrupting his thoughts. Infatuated as he was, ordinarily he welcomed the interruptions. But unlike most occasions, the distraction kindled consternation. Several weeks earlier while visiting her at Bennington, he had shared the dilemma he constantly faced when adjusting claims. Glenna, much like the ivory-towered lecturers who were guiding her education, minimized the problem. She argued that policyholders, having paid their premiums, were entitled to a fair shake. Affording such treatment only to the squeaky wheels was shameful. Eric looked back at his file. He flipped the folder closed and pushed it aside. Being an adjuster was harder than he had anticipated.

Las Vegas has it down to a statistical certainty. Roulette is a prime example. Thirty-six numbers, half red and half black, paying even money for a bet on either color, is the perfect formula to break even. Throw in two extra green numbers, zero and double-zero, and the scale tips neatly to the house. To the average bettor, the extra duo bears little consequence, but to the house, it's everything. Over the long haul, red comes up 18/38's of the time; black, 18/38's; and zero or double-zero, 2/38's. Over many spins the house takes 2/38's, a hefty 5.263 percent, of all the bets. The casino needs only to draw people to its tables. More players generate more bets, and more bets mean more money.

Wall Street Journal in hand, Donald Burns leaned back in his fine leather chair. Just months after embarking on his Kingman & Woodhill employment, he had discovered that being a broker had far more in common with Las Vegas than he had ever imagined. It was all about the house's percentage. Even a small percentage of a big number produced a big take.

Mutual funds offered a prime example. A client buys shares of XYZ fund. Incorporated into XYZ's annual prospectus is the fee, perhaps one percent, for managing the fund. XYZ pays the broker named on the account one-half of that fee. Five-tenths of one percent may sound small, but, like Las Vegas, when multiplied by large numbers, it generates a big payoff. And better yet, the fee keeps coming, year after year after year, often with no work, except maybe to reassure a nervous client during down times.

Much like Las Vegas gamblers, clients yearn for higher returns. As a member of Kingman & Woodhill, Don willingly obliged. Clients were encouraged to place their funds into managed accounts where they would benefit from the firm's expertise. Of course, managed accounts meant higher fees; i.e., the house's percentage was higher than for a mutual fund. And too, there were added bonuses for the house, though not necessarily the client. No longer were fees split with a mutual fund. And buying and selling for the account generated commissions. Cynics termed it churning; Don's mentor, Charles Bascomb, called it good business.

Even before Don had graduated Williams, his professors had prepared him for the disadvantages that *kids* fresh out of college often faced. Though aspects of the admonition were proving true, in the real world, Don was discovering that his fledgling status was a double-edged sword. Individuals beginning their careers in other fields were apt to sign on as clients. When they did, it was generally for the long haul. Retirement was decades away. Their accounts would grow, and so too, the concomitant fees. The possibility those fees would continue into retirement when the client began to draw down on the account was a bonus.

Don stared into space as he contemplated his next contact. Unlike most junior associates who had called their best prospects the first two weeks on the job, he went to that well infrequently, saving his best opportunities for moments when recent successes had been few. The approach enabled him to maintain a steadier flow of new business. Where other jack-rabbits watched new business grind to a disheartening halt, Don continued to march forward. Though his pace was often far from torrid, he was hardly the proverbial turtle.

It was late August, and Don had endured an inordinately slow week. It was time to dip the bucket into his well of best prospects. He flipped his Rolodex (a stubborn streak, though he preferred to call it independence, kept the antiquated device on his desk). After pulling up the needed number, he dialed. For the first time, he would solicit a fellow member of the Inseparables.

Moments later, a voice at the other end answered, "Granite Casualty and Life. Johanson speaking."

"Hi Eric. It's Don. How've you been?"

"Good...And you?"

"No complaints. Am I interrupting anything?"

"Not at all. As a matter of fact, I can use a break. Looking at file after file has me bleary eyed."

"I understand...but it could be worse. You could be in my shoes, cold calling folks who are less receptive than pit bulls."

"Well, unlike you who can choose whom you call, I can't pick my files."

Were they back in Williamstown at the Irish Mist, Don would have continued the debate, but winning the meaningless argument had nothing to do with the purpose of his call. If anything, it would undermine his goal. He said, "I hear what you're saying. And you're probably right, though each of us feels the cross that comes with our job is tougher than the next."

"Not our good pal Bill."

"What makes you say that?"

"I talked with him just last week. While you and I have begun absorbing the lashes of the working world, Bill is hanging out at the pool, not to mention the banks of the Caloosa...Caloosahonic or something like that, working on his tan. Classes at that girls' school where he'll be teaching won't begin for another two weeks. Just like our days at Williams, he still gets the summer off."

Don felt a pang of envy, but only for an instant. A couple months free was appealing, but a teacher's salary was hardly the mechanism for acquiring a second home by the shore, exotic vacations, weekends at the country club and the countless other trappings of the high life. He said, "Summers may be nice, but admit it—no way would you trade places with Bill."

"What makes you so sure?"

"You could have taught rather than taking the job at Granite."

A moment of silence ensued before Eric finally responded. "I like your argument, even though it proves me wrong. Last week, after I spoke with Bill, I was envious, but looking at the big picture, you're right—I wouldn't trade places with him."

And I wouldn't trade places with you or Bill or, for that matter, Kyle. Don embraced the thought, not with hubris, but joy that he had made the right decision when choosing an occupation. He said, "Besides calling to say hello, I wanted to see if you might be interested in opening an account. You know...it's never too early to plan your financial future."

"Nice cliché." A slow drawl coated the quip with sarcasm.

"Cliché...maybe. Regardless, that's no excuse to ignore your financial future."

"Fair enough, but here at Granite, we have a retirement plan."

64

"That's all well and good, as a starting point."

"Well…there's always Social Security."

Don laughed, arguably more for effect than humor.

"What's that supposed to mean?"

"You willing to bet your sweet golden years on the promises of politicians?"

"You really think we won't get our benefits?"

"Oh…we'll get them. The question, however, is how much? And for that matter, when? Hell, by the time our day comes, eligibility will probably start north of a hundred."

"C'mon, you're exaggerating."

"Sure, but you get my point." Don waited a moment, satisfied that the ensuing hiatus sufficiently blessed his argument. "Assuming for the moment that you build a decent retirement account at Granite…and get Social Security too—and at this juncture those are big assumptions—you still should be saving for retirement, whether or not you do it through me. Private accounts are the final leg of the renowned three-legged retirement stool. And in case you haven't noticed, stools with only two legs aren't too stable."

"Damn, you sound like you're lecturing me."

"I am." A month earlier Don would have denied the insinuation, but brief experience had already taught him that the concession would be disarming. And too, it avoided the risk of being sidetracked with a debate whether he was sermonizing.

"Well…much as I hate to admit it, you have a point. But don't get a swelled head thinking you convinced me. It just so happens my dad sold me on your argument long before I graduated college. He repeatedly urged me to start saving for retirement as soon as I entered the working world. As he put it, an early start will reap the amazing benefits of compounding, especially with a Roth IRA where benefits paid on the back end are entirely tax free. He warned that procrastination, more often than not, becomes a pattern. Before you know it, the years left to accumulate for retirement are all too few. My dad also emphasized that having money put away allows one to sleep better. If by chance a rainy day comes, you've got an umbrella."

65

"Your dad was a wise man." Not only had Eric's father made Don's pitch for him, but the last point about sleeping better and money for a rainy day provided Don with new ammunition when peddling his wares. He jotted the word "sleep," a reminder to incorporate the notion into his spiel. "So, you ready to open an account?"

"Yeah...tell me how to go about it."

"Very simple. I'll send you the forms."

"Any suggestions about a number?"

The bigger the better. Discretion counseled that greed be contained. Getting the account was enough for one day. "For now, I'd say start with something small. Think about it for a few days. Pick an amount you won't miss...something that won't wipe out your bank account. Keeping a few bucks liquid in case of an emergency is important. Down the road, if you can contribute more, great. The important thing is to get started...And with that done, let's move on to more appealing subjects. Tell me about your love life."

"It couldn't be better. I met this girl—her name is Glenna—at of all places, my favorite museum, the Clark. Remember that painting, the Renoir, *Woman with a Fan*, that I used to rave about?"

"Not really...but let me guess. She came to life, stepped right off the canvas into your arms."

"You're making fun of me...but that's basically what happened."

"Now who's making fun of whom?"

"No, really. I was sitting there gazing at the painting, when this stunning redhead, the spitting image of Renoir's masterpiece, appeared at the other end of the bench. One thing led to another, and to make a long story short, we've spent most every weekend together since then."

"Does she live in Williamstown or, perhaps down your way, in Hartford?"

"Neither. She's a student at Bennington College. And she's...she's incredible. Amazing, and that's with a capital A."

In the several years that Don had known Eric, he had never heard his pal gush as much over any woman. Even Carla did not demand that level of praise. The characterizations

66

always seemed mixed. The women with great faces and figures had annoying personalities. Those with great personalities were generally physically unattractive. Junior year there had been an exception, Peggy. She had personality, brains, face and figure. After two dates, with Eric's interest rapidly growing, she informed him that she was a lesbian. In an instant, almost smitten turned into *Oh my God*. It wasn't that Eric disapproved of the gay lifestyle; only that finding someone who lived it had no chance of fulfilling his dreams. "So, this sounds like the real thing."

"I think so. It's the—Oh, I've gotta go. One of the secretaries just motioned. My boss wants to see me. Take care."

"You too." As Don hung up the receiver, he leaned back, recalling the magic that had come into his life four years earlier when he had first met Linda. He felt a warm feeling. He was happy for Eric. And too, he was pleased he had landed another account. With a little luck, maybe Eric would refer some of his friends and associates as future clients.

Rocky walls rise from the depths of a chasm. Whether narrow twisting corridors, like those carved by the Adirondack's Ausable River, or wide, like the prodigious expanses of the Grand Canyon, their clefts abide.

As far back as Bill Young could remember, work and recreation had always been separated by an undeniable divide. As a kid, he had chores: taking out the garbage, tidying his room and mowing the lawn. They were work, a required inconvenience. They bore no resemblance to playing ball or having a yo-yo contest with his pal Bucky. His mother tried to convince him his chores could be fun if only he approached them with the right attitude. Attempts to heed her advice proved otherwise. A burden was still a burden.

At fifteen Bill had even tried Tom Sawyer's ploy. Exercising rare guile, he endeavored to cajole a naïve thirteen-year-old neighbor into believing that operating a lawn mower was a big thrill. Bill was certain the kid would all but beg to do his work. The plan backfired. The young pigeon feigned eagerness to do the job, but begged off claiming his conscience prevented him from depriving Bill of the pleasure. A smug grin, proof that the would-be sucker had outsmarted Bill, made Bill resent the task even more.

When he arrived at Williams, Bill studied hard. He diligently wrote his papers and earned good grades. It was work, but knowing it would benefit his future, he did it, and generally without whining. His conscientious approach left plenty of time for recreation, hurling a Frisbee or playing touch football in the quad and partying. The pattern conformed to what he had learned as a child: Both work and recreation played active roles in a full life, but those roles were separate and distinct.

Following college graduation, when he moved to Fort Myers, an anomaly developed. By the midpoint of the summer, the irreparable fissure dividing work and recreation seemingly vanished. Bridging it would have been remarkable enough, but drawing the walls together like a neat-fitting puzzle was unfathomable. It was as if the Atlantic Ocean had been swallowed up and Europe and Africa had reconnected to North and South America. With the summer months off until his teaching assignment commenced, Bill was free to hang out at the pool and swim or play golf at the local municipal course. Evenings provided sufficient opportunity to work on his novel. That would have conformed to the dichotomy he had known for over two decades. Instead, most days he opted to write, not owing to the dictates of conscience, but because writing was even more fun than swimming or golf.

Armed with an annual pass to the Edison and Ford Estates, three, four or even five days a week he sat on the same bench along the margin of the Caloosahatchee River pounding the keys of his laptop. The purchase of an extra battery, along with a packed lunch, most times a peanut butter and jelly sandwich, enabled him to write for hours. Back in college he had hopes of one day becoming a published author, perhaps even earning a living at the craft. But knowing the goal might be pie in the sky, he had accepted the teaching job, an insurance policy in case his plan did not pan out. Regardless, he had always assumed that writing would be work. Life always required work. The axiom was inviolate, at least until he had begun his novel. Suddenly the principle crumbled. Writing, a voyage over an imaginative expanse, pulverized a flat earth into a round sphere. Theretofore unknown continents linked to familiar terrain. So-called *work* became a passion. Far from labor, it was hard to even label it an avocation. It was recreation. His fingers danced over the keys of his laptop. Lines of text appeared one after another on the screen. Pages of his manuscript accumulated with remarkable alacrity and, even more remarkable, joy. Passion had not merely erased a narrow chasm. It had swallowed the whole of the Atlantic Ocean.

You can't go back. Life moves inexorably forward. These are wise phrases...so wise that their sagacity is exceeded only by their banality.

Kyle Gordon sat on the three-sided steps of Chapin Hall on the campus of Williams College. He leaned back, gazing upward at the towering Corinthian columns that supported the isosceles triangular pediment above. Following his junior year in high school, his parents had taken him on a week-long, summer tour of the magnificent college campuses that dotted New England. Amherst, Bowdoin, Wesleyan, Dartmouth—he loved them all. But Williams topped his list. The quaint college town in the northern Berkshire Mountains was his kind of place, and typifying its allure was the neo-classical brick structure known as Chapin Hall.

Perhaps it was the influence of Miss Elliott, his eleventh-grade English teacher. Under her tutelage, the class spent several weeks reading and analyzing Sophocles' "Oedipus Rex." Interspersed with their study of the tragic play were discussions of ancient Greek democracy, culture and architecture. Kyle marveled at photographs of the Parthenon. When he visited Williams after junior year, Chapin Hall, the embodiment of the renowned centerpiece of the Acropolis, captivated him. It was as if the noblest of the ancient Greeks—Aristotle, Homer, Demosthenes, and, of course, Sophocles—were luring him from the sky above. As an impressionable high school student, the inveigling bait was irresistible. He was hooked. Five years hence, upon graduating the esteemed institution of higher learning, his decision to attend was irrevocably validated.

Five months had elapsed since graduation. It was Kyle's first visit to the campus as an alumnus. He had arranged to meet Bill, Eric and Don in front of Chapin Hall at two o'clock. He had been waiting on the steps for several minutes when he glanced at his cell phone—2:03. His buddies, except maybe Don, were always punctual. The possibility that he had been stood up crossed his mind. He immediately dismissed the idea. His pals would never leave him in the lurch. That's what he told himself. Still, denying the improbability that all three would be late was difficult. Not once in his college years could he recall that happenstance. He asked himself whether he might have confused the plans. The purported explanation was absurd. They had agreed to meet at the appointed time on Homecoming Weekend. Banners on the campus confirmed it was indeed Homecoming Weekend. And the appointed time had been confirmed with texts.

It would be the first time since setting off on diverse paths that the Inseparables would be re-united. Roughly one hundred fifty days had passed since graduation. In the great scheme of time, it was hardly a lot, but for a quartet that had been so close for four years, it was substantial. And more than anything else, the scheduled reunion was symbolic. During the final days of their college years, assurances that they would regularly get together had been rampant. In the back of his mind, Kyle had harbored doubts. Though far from obliterated, the planned return had tempered his skepticism. However, as the seconds ticked by, the doubts were beginning to re-emerge. If he did not hear from his buddies within five minutes, he would text them for an explanation.

"Make a move, and it'll be your last!"

The gravelly snarl, coupled with the jab of what felt like the barrel of a gun in his back, launched a chill down Kyle's spine. His stomach knotted. Panic supplanted ruminations. "You...uh...want my money, you got it. I'm carrying well over a hundred dollars." The sum was paltry compared to his life.

"Nah...I want you!"

The threatening voice from seconds before had vanished, replaced by a familiar one. Kyle looked back over his shoulder and gazed at a laughing Bill Young. "Damn, you really know how to scare a guy."

As Bill continued to chortle, Don Burns and Eric Johanson stepped around the corner from the near façade. "How the hell are you?" said Don.

"Stone-dead petrified...but apart from that, fine."

"We figured your life could use a little spice, and so, to surprise you, we circled around to the back of the building. It was our way of suggesting that in the future you may want to think twice about being the last to arrive." The display of Eric's bright white teeth left no doubt his smirk was contrived.

Kyle longed to give his buddies a taste of their own medicine, but on the short end of a three-on-one and armed with no retaliatory plan, revenge needed to await another day. He stood up and hugged his pals. "Can you believe it? We really made it back."

"You thought otherwise?" said Bill.

"What, and you didn't, at least a little?"

"Well...maybe. But let me tell you, after I came all the way from Florida, Southwest Florida at that, I would have been pissed if any of you hadn't showed." Bill stepped down one stair and gazed across Chapin Hall Drive at the grassy expanse that lay between the L-shaped Sage Hall and Williams Hall. "We're really here. All of us. The Inseparables." He turned back to the others. "Anybody wish we could return for another four years?"

The question took Kyle by surprise. He loved Williams and his years there. Months earlier he had hated to see them end, but still he didn't want to go back. Not really. He was eager to get on with his life.

"Would I have to take Murker's course again?" said Eric.

"Of course not," said Bill. "It's barred by the Constitution."

The puzzled looks Kyle observed on Don and Eric's faces suggested he was not the only one confused by the remark.

"Damn. Are you guys senile already?" Bill waited a moment, seemingly allowing his pals a second chance to analyze his comment. He shook his head. "You know—the constitutional ban against cruel and unusual punishment."

Don gave him a friendly shove.

"He's got a point." Eric focused on Don. "If you had endured Murker's misery, you'd understand."

"Hey, the only cruel and unusual punishment around here (Don pointed a finger at Bill) is Young's warped sense of humor."

Kyle laid a hand on one of the monstrous stone pillars. Philosophers, the kind who had orated from the steps of the great Greek edifices, had said one couldn't go back. Not only had the Inseparables returned, but they had picked up right where they had left off. Others might have termed their banter frivolous and sophomoric, but others didn't understand. As outsiders, never privy to the camaraderie of the Inseparables, they couldn't.

"What's first on the agenda?" said Don.

"I'm starved." Bill pressed his hand to his stomach.

"Young, you're always starved." Eric gestured at Bill's mid-section. "Based upon your waistline, I can't imagine why."

Bill shot Eric a look. "Apparently four years of Donald's caustic tongue rubbed off on you."

"Hey, what do you want from me?" said Don. "Johanson made the dig. Give him the flak." He tapped the back of his hand against Bill's stomach. "Of course, he has a point. But gentleman that I am, I was too polite to say anything." A wink of his eye, and he added, "What say we head over to the Irish Mist?"

Moments later the quartet was on the way to their favorite haunt, and soon enough they were seated in their favorite booth in the rear corner.

"Like old times," said Don, as Kelly delivered four ales.

"To the Inseparables," said Bill. They clinked their mugs.

Kyle restrained the urge to remind Bill of his avowed intention to re-adhere to his Mormon ban on alcoholic

72

beverages. Usually a sipper, Kyle took a gulp. He nearly choked, but no mind. He was back in his element. Time had been traversed with nary a skipped beat.

Fueled by their brews, the jocularity continued until Eric, needing to relieve himself, got up. Once he was out of earshot, Kyle seized the opportunity, though in a decidedly soft voice. "Any word about Carla…what she did…whether she decided to keep the baby?"

"She did," said Don. "I got it from Joey Peterkin, who got it straight from her. He said she dropped out of Williams. Too bad, with two years to go."

"Did Peterkin say who the father is?" Kyle kept an eye out, making sure that Eric was nowhere to be seen.

"Nah. He didn't know." Don eyed his pals. "Has Eric said anything to either of you about the situation?"

Kyle shook his head. "Not a word. I was afraid to say anything unless he brought it up."

"Same with me," said Bill. "But my guess, Eric has to be the father."

"What about Horstmeyer?" said Kyle. "Or maybe it's someone we haven't even considered."

"Horse's Ass may be a possibility," said Don. "But other than that, no way. Carla isn't the type to sleep around."

"Yeah, I guess you're right." Kyle silently chided himself for posing the possibility that someone other than the two guys Carla had dated might be the father. "But what makes you so sure it's Eric's?"

His ale about to reach his lips, Don halted. "What?—You think otherwise?"

Not really. Kyle stole a glance at Bill. His stone face confirmed what he had already said: His money was on Eric. Kyle was about to pursue the matter further, but the sight of Eric coming back toward the booth prevented the inquiry.

"You guys are awfully quiet." Eric eyed them, one by one, before sitting down.

"Us?" said Bill with the aplomb of a double dipper caught plunging a half-eaten tortilla chip into the dip.

Eric studied the others again. "Something is going on that I should know about."

Shoulders slumping, Don heaved a woeful sigh. "Okay, I'll spill the beans."

Kyle found it hard to believe that Don was about to confront Eric about Carla's pregnancy. Still, with curiosity abounding, he was not altogether disappointed.

Don pointed at Bill. "Young, your blessed Mormon buddy, is hopin' to score. He slipped Rohypnol into your brew when you went to the head."

Bill held up his three middle fingers in front of Don's face. "Read between the lines!"

Eric chuckled as he turned toward Don. "You gonna take that?"

Don, a broad smile across his face, shrugged.

Kyle quietly took in the exchange. When it came to academics, Don ranked fourth in their little group, but he was far and away the smoothest salesman. With seemingly no effort he had deflected Eric's inquiry as to what was going on. Even Dicken's Artful Dodger would have been impressed. Kyle certainly was, especially knowing that had he been on the hot seat, he would have fared no better than Bill. He said, "So, tell me, what's it like for everyone, now that we've moved beyond the cocoon of ivy-covered walls into the real world?"

"You think falling down the big hole into Wonderland is the real world?"

"You dislike teaching that much?" said Kyle.

"Actually, I'm enjoying it."

"You start that great novel you always talked about?" said Eric.

"No, as to great...but as to writing, I spend some time most every day. And over the summer, before the school year started, I was putting in a whole lot more."

Don put his hand to the side of his mouth as if he were shielding Bill from his words. "Unlike the rest of us, our buddy still resides in the fabled world of academia. He simply climbed across the desk to the other side. In his spare time, he fashions tales about the non-existent adventures of fictional folks. No wonder he's in Wonderland."

Bill leaned forward and, to the extent his seat in the booth allowed, bowed. "By the way," he said, "you're apt to find

74

those fictional folks you referred to a whole lot more real than you think."

"Just what does that mean?" said Eric.

"What better characters could I create than the weirdos sharing this booth with me?"

"We in your novel?"

Kyle found it hard to tell whether Don's raised voice was a product of excitement or indignation. Equally hard to discern was whether Bill was serious.

"Hey, you'll just have to wait and see." A self-satisfied smile on his face, Bill leaned back. "In the meantime, tell me, how goes it with you guys?" When the inquiry drew nothing more than meaningless non-verbal reactions, Bill motioned to Eric. "Let's hear from the nine-to-fiver."

"You make it sound like I've been sentenced."

"Is that how you view it?" said Don.

Eric shook his head. "It's got its pluses, along with some minuses. The pay and benefits are pretty good. On the other hand, chiseling a decent person out of a fair settlement is no picnic. Of course, all too often the claims are for phony neck and back injuries."

"Sure," said Bill. "We know how it is, now that you're a claims adjuster. Everyone who walks through the door is presumed to be a scammer."

"Think what you will, but if you saw my files, you'd sing a different tune." Eric sat up taller. "But rather than wasting my breath trying to convince you guys, let's hear from our two business tycoons, Mr. MBA and Mr. Wall Street."

"Wait a second," said Kyle. "Starting a graduate program en route to an MBA hardly qualifies me as a tycoon. You'd better confine your inquiry to our buddy from Kingman & Woodhill." Kyle gestured at Don, as if to give him the floor, whether he wanted it or not.

"What can I say? Life is good. But don't get me wrong. Cold calling people is no cruise on the Mediterranean. On the other hand, it's not a bad price." Don grew briefly pensive. "Take my boss, Charlie—"

"No way," said Bill. "He's all yours...not that I know him or anything about him."

Don ignored Bill's jocularity. "Well, let me fill you in. He's got a knack for know-how. Admittedly, if you gave him an IQ test, odds are he'd come up short against our Williams professors, but when it comes to the real world and making money, it's no contest. Next to those puppies, Charlie is a bulldog."

"What he means," said Bill, "is that his boss is vicious." He focused on Don. "By any chance, you following in his footsteps?"

"As I was saying before our impertinent author put his two cents in (Don paused long enough to flash Bill a look), my boss Charlie Bascomb has a home...make that an estate...to die for. According to him, if I play my cards right, I too could be living the high life. Sure, I'm working hard...let me rephrase that...I'm working long hours, though so much of it is nothing more than gabbing with clients about sports and politics...whatever ingratiates me to their good side...but in the long run, it could have a huge payoff."

"Is it better than our days at Williams?"

"Better?" Don stared off into the vacuous space of the Irish Mist as he seemingly contemplated the question. "No, I can't say it's better, but..."

"So, you'd rather be back here at Williams?" said Bill.

"No." The glib reply fired off Don's tongue with a bullwhip's snap.

"Hardly what I'd term a model of logical parlance."

Convinced that Bill was about to put the smooth talker through the wringer, Kyle leaned back in preparation for the show.

"On the contrary," said Don, plainly unruffled. "Williams was more fun, but I'm past the high jinx of college days. I'm eager to get on with my life, along with the opportunity for success. Even if it takes some long hours, I'm willing to pay that price."

The reply was punctuated with uncomfortable seconds of silence. Whether it was the seeming arrogance with which the message had been delivered or the unexpected quiet, its echo made Kyle uneasy.

"So, what about you guys?" said Don. "Would you rather be here amidst the ivy-covered walls of Williams or out there in the real world?"

"When you put it that way," said Eric, "I guess I feel the same as you."

"Not me," said Bill. "Hell, if someone was willing to pay me to keep studying and, of course, playing here on campus, I'd jump at the chance."

Kyle might have voiced his feelings on the issue, except he wasn't sure how he felt. Yes, he wanted to move on with his life, but given the chance, would he turn down the scenario that Bill had outlined? Hard to say. Regardless, coming from a middle-class family, gold spoons were not the way he had been fed. He had loans to repay. Once he finished his graduate program, he would need to earn a living.

"Gordon," said Eric, "you're the only one who hasn't answered the question. What say you?"

Kyle shrugged. "I don't know. I've got mixed emotions, but...does it really matter? Hell, we all know we can't turn the clock back."

"True," said Bill, "but that doesn't mean we can't meet here from time to time. Case in point—right now."

"Let's drink to that," said Don.

Mugs clinked.

"And come hell or high water," said Don, "someday we're gonna take that trip out West...all four of us."

Mugs clinked yet another time, more decisively than before.

Kyle eyed his buddies, wondering about their thoughts. Did they really believe the great venture would come to fruition? Or perhaps, like him, camaraderie and brews were fueling false hopes. Making their way back to campus for Homecoming Weekend or a class reunion was one thing; packing up and heading off to the Grand Canyon, Yosemite, Yellowstone and Rocky Mountain National Park, another. Curiosity wheedled Kyle to press the issue. Reluctance to throw a damper on enthusiasm, whether real or not, silenced him. They had made it back, and for the moment, that was enough.

CHAPTER VI

PRIVATE EQUITY. WITHIN THE FOUR WALLS of a classroom, the esoteric term is a fascinating concept, a means to attract capital for what, more often than not, are ailing companies and to bring them back to life. From a purely theoretical standpoint, private equity is virtuous. It is capitalism, free enterprise, at its best. Prior to 2012 the American public was no more familiar with private equity than the Aboriginal musical instrument the digeridoo. With the advent of the 2012 presidential election, people came to know the concept, not necessarily its meaning, but as a symbol reminiscent of the cold-blooded robber barons of the nineteenth century. Mitt Romney had made his money from private equity. At a time when the nation was reeling from recession, companies on the verge of bankruptcy, desperate for an infusion of cash, were ripe for the taking. Existing management had virtually no bargaining power. Vultures from without could dictate terms. Axes slashed through work forces, terminating employees and cutting pay for those who stayed. Such was the nasty shadow that became associated with private equity.

High in ivory-colored towers, office buildings far taller and far more splendid than the edifices that decorated a college campus, the masters of private equity painted their enterprises with a different brush. They rescued companies; they saved jobs; and they invigorated what otherwise would have been wastepipes of the economy.

As with so many things, the truth lay somewhere in the middle. Private equity aided many a company, but often ruthlessly. At times, it created jobs. Unfortunately, all too many were in China, Indonesia, Singapore, Mexico and the Philippines, places where employees earned a small fraction of the pink-slipped American workers they replaced. And all too often the private-equity managers made out regardless whether a successful turnaround or sale of the company ensued. Many had no skin in the game. Win, lose or draw for the company and its workers, the private-equity managers raked in hefty fees.

Several months into his MBA program, Kyle Gordon sat reading a private-equity case study. Revenues at the Silicon-Valley start-up were slow to grow, and the burn rate of capital was far too high. For the company to survive until orders were sufficient for a turnaround, not only did the burn rate need to be reduced, but also a substantial and immediate influx of capital was required. The likely source of that capital was private equity. The funds were sure to be accompanied by no-holds-barred conditions. That was how the case had been framed. Back when Kyle was at Williams and preparing to pursue his MBA, he might have viewed the case through a different lens, one of win-win. Back then, with the little he knew about private equity, it sounded exciting. Wheeling and dealing, negotiating multi-million-dollar deals was action. A good head for numbers was imperative. He had that. For a time at Williams, he had even toyed with majoring in mathematics. He took Calculus I, II and III and Differential Equations. But as the courses began to increasingly focus on the abstract theoretical facets of mathematics, his interest waned. A more practical use of mathematics had greater appeal, and so he leaned toward an MBA. In the back of his mind was the world of private equity. He chose economics as his major, convinced that he would have all the necessary tools for the field. However, graduate school, with its countless case studies, shed a new light. He discovered that he lacked one prerequisite. He wasn't ruthless. He had a heart. Slashing to the bone, firing people, many of whom were sole breadwinners for their families, all in the name of maximizing investors' profits, left him empty. He understood that private equity was a dog-eat-dog business. The more coal one stuffed into the stockings of decent folks, the greater the private-equity investors' return. Arguably that return was merited because it carried the risk associated with a failing company. As much as the point had merit, Kyle knew it was rife with rationalizations. Private-equity investors focused on their own bottom line. If that meant dismantling the company and selling off its assets and leaving dedicated workers to suffer in the wake, so be it!

Early on in his MBA program, Kyle listened to the arguments pro and con for private equity. Several of his closest classmates set their sights on its fast action and huge dollars. Not Kyle. To him private equity felt like a pact with the devil, one whose cutthroat demands would put knots in his stomach while leaving him vacuous. That is not to suggest that Kyle was a bleeding heart. Fields such as social work or health care were never for him. By nature, he was a businessman, but not the ruthless type. An MBA was what he wanted. Self-assessment, an analysis of his strengths, needs and aspirations, superimposed upon classroom experience, convinced him that the degree could enable him to achieve financial security and self-actualization, and that he could do so without becoming a vulture, without sacrificing his conscience.

Stalking prey is an art. With a heart, in proportion to size, twice that of a lion, a hyena can stalk a target for miles until the victim, worn from exhaustion, has nothing left. When that moment arrives, the hyena, having paced itself at a mere six miles per hour, attacks at five times that speed. The exhausted victim quickly succumbs to the hyena's powerful jaws. Though rewarding, the chase is arduous. Others in the animal kingdom have developed less taxing methods. Spiders, driven by instinct, weave webs and wait for their prey to come to them. If the webs are well placed, the rewards are ample.

A young broker looking to build a clientele is put to the task of stalking prey. Initially sheltered with the free ride of a salary, he/she soon goes onto commission. Zero percent of nothing is nothing. The young broker must become a predator.

Cold calling is the method. Unfortunately, the technique lacks the inevitability that accompanies a hyena's pursuit. Victims, or should one say would-be clients, simply hang up the telephone.

Don Burns understood the dilemma he faced as a young broker. While other neophytes at Kingman & Woodhill diligently, but with limited success, tried to emulate the hyena, Don cast his lot with the spider. He didn't have the huge heart of a hyena, but unlike the spider that was relegated to instinct, he had a sizeable brain. Admittedly not huge, but a penchant for shrewdness, coupled with a keen wit, taught him to network. Let the clients come to him, and when they did, his glib tongue could seal the deal. He joined the racquetball club. He volunteered at the Methodist Church where he and Linda belonged. He became a member of the Rotary and the Chamber of Commerce. He was active on Facebook. He took a page from the century-old character "George Babbitt." That his uncle, a town supervisor in northern New Jersey, steered loads of connected people his way, didn't hurt. Yes, Don Burns put in long hours stalking his prey, but he never chased them, at least it never appeared so. But come they did to his sticky web.

Don had just hung up the receiver after talking to a fellow Williams' alumnus when Charlie Bascomb stepped through the door of his office. Unlike so many firms where newcomers worked from desks and cubicles in a big room, at Kingman & Woodhill junior salesmen had offices, though undeniably miniscule.

"How's it going?" said Bascomb.

"Good." Even if it were otherwise, Don would not have said so. With senior members of the firm loath to hear their underlings whine, discretion dictated that any complaints be reserved for Linda's ear and the confines of their home.

"Amazing how time flies. Hard to believe you've been here six months." Bascomb eased into a chair on the far side of Don's desk. "I've been looking over the firm's numbers. Among the new hires, you know who brought in the most money for the firm?"

"Not really." Don knew he was near the head of the class, but exactly where everyone ranked, he wasn't sure.

A smile on his face, Bascomb gestured at Don. "You, my friend, are top dog. Even guys like Holt and Bigley who came on board a month or so ahead of you have lower numbers."

"Well, I've had some good fortune along the way."

"You're too modest. Getting clients to put their money with you is not like roulette...spin and wish. It takes talent."

Don shrugged, the outward reaction veiling satisfaction.

"Your numbers, the income you've generated, put your salary to shame. Had you been on commission, you would have earned considerably more than we're paying you. I plan to recommend to the partners that we give you something extra."

Don shook his head. With his eyes on bigger prizes down the road, foregoing the offer was easy.

"I can't believe you're telling me *no*."

"I have to. It's only fair."

A puzzled look showed on Bascomb's face.

"The way I see it, newcomers such as myself are like investments. By guaranteeing us a salary regardless whether we produce, the firm assumes the risk. With any investment, the party who takes the risk is entitled to the big return. Take, for example, an entrepreneur securing a loan from a bank. Normal protocol requires him to assume the risk of the venture. The bank, to protect itself, demands security, perhaps a cosigner or mortgage on the businessman's home. The bank gets a fixed return, the interest rate on the loan, while the businessman, who faces the consequences of a failed enterprise, is entitled to the fruits of big success. Since I didn't take the risk, I shouldn't reap the fruits of success."

Bascomb nodded slowly. "That's a damn good analogy, the kind reflecting a keen understanding of this business. Still, it's hard to argue that all the salaried newcomers, whether they're non-producers or stars, should be treated the same. Regardless, with Christmas just a few weeks away, your bonus will reflect the difference. Of that, there is no doubt."

Passion is a pleasing paradise. Obsession can be an all-consuming black hole. They are as distant as Heaven and Hell.

Yet at times their borders draw so close as to seemingly overlap. Such is the paradoxical realm of motivating forces.

"My God! Don't you ever go home?"

Bill looked up from his desk in his classroom at the Fordison Girls' School where he taught English. Standing in the doorway was Herman Culver, who had worked there as a custodian for nearly forty years. Everyone knew Herman, and he knew everyone. Though his rank in the pecking order bordered on the bottom, no one was better liked or more respected by both faculty and students.

Herman pointed at the clock. "It's after five. School let out for Christmas vacation more than two hours ago. Don't you think it's time you leave? Or maybe you're waitin' until after Santa comes down the chimney?"

"I'll leave soon...well, as soon as I finish reading my students' stories."

"You realize that you and I are the only ones left in the building? Me—I got an excuse. I'm supposed to be here until I finish cleanin' up. But you...you should be on vacation."

"I will...in another half-hour or so."

Herman rolled his eyes.

"What's that for?"

"If you say a half-hour, two is a good bet."

With the comment bearing too much truth for Bill to argue, he shrugged.

"Any special plans for Christmas?"

"I'm flying home to my parents' place in Provo, Utah. All my siblings will be there. More than two years have slipped by since our whole family has been together. How 'bout you?"

"My wife and I are going to our daughter's home just twenty miles north of here. It'll be the first time in over thirty years we haven't celebrated Christmas at our place. Guess it's a sign that old age is creepin' up on us. Of course, at your age— twenty-three?"

"Twenty-two."

"Better yet...You have no idea what I'm talkin' about when I refer to old age."

Bill guessed that Herman was in his mid-sixties, and indeed that seemed about as far off as eternity.

"You'll be surprised how fast it sneaks up on you." Herman eyed Bill closely. "I can see you don't believe me. Can't blame you. When I was your age, I was immortal, at least so I thought. Now that I'm a senior, it's another story."

Easy as it was for Bill to understand the philosophical nicety, it nevertheless remained a distant abstraction. Still he suspected that far down the road when he reached Herman's age, his perspective would change.

"How's that novel of yours coming?"

If the question had come from someone else, it would have surprised Bill, but Herman was one of a few people, the only one in Fort Myers, with whom he had spoken about his writing. Several times when Bill had stayed well into the evening, occasionally past eight, Herman had chided him for being a workaholic. After several such scoldings, Bill explained that it wasn't all schoolwork; that he was penning a novel. "It's moving along."

"Good. 'Cause like I told you. Once it's published, I'm gonna buy one, and you're gonna sign it for me. Right?"

"Not quite....and don't get excited. I will definitely sign a copy for you, but it'll be one I give to you, not one you buy."

"That's mighty nice of you."

"Not really."

The puzzled look on Herman's face was predictable.

Bill flashed a wry smile before explaining. "Cows have about as much chance of flying as I have of getting my novel published. So, the truth be known, you'll never get that signed copy."

Bridges provide invaluable links. Often they enable one to cross that which is otherwise impassable. But some bridges are better left uncrossed. Adversity may lie on the opposite side.

Hand in hand with Glenna, Eric had strolled the roughly one mile from the center of the Bennington College campus down College Drive across Route 67A onto Silk Road. Less than two hundred yards ahead stood the Silk Road Covered Bridge, an eighty-eight-foot span across the Walloomsac River.

"You're right," said Eric. "It is beautiful."

"See, I knew you'd love it."

During his college days at Williams, Eric had seen a couple of the many covered bridges that dotted the New England landscape. They were nice...but that was as far as it went. With Glenna close, her hand in his, the structure, dating from the mid-nineteenth century, was inspiring.

Glenna glanced his way. Her lovely smile gleamed like the snow crystals that covered the grassy areas adjoining the road.

Eric squeezed her hand as they drew close and stepped into the red-stained span. The tightening of her fingers sent his heart racing. He drew in a deep breath, savoring the bucolic setting. He reached out and touched the lattice truss beams that supported the side. He gazed through the three-foot wide latticed opening that ran nearly the full length of the bridge. "It's as if we've been transported back two centuries."

Glenna nodded ever so slightly, her smile again reflecting sentiments.

Eric slipped his arm over Glenna's shoulder and pecked her twice on the cheek. Silence, serene perfection, abounded. He shut his eyes, luxuriating amidst the uncommon haven.

The sound of a vehicle approaching drew Eric's attention. He gestured at the oncoming car. "We best get out of here." He pulled Glenna along, as they hastened toward the near entrance. "Wouldn't want to be standing against this side wall with a car coming through."

Once they had stepped out of the bridge and onto the road's edge, the vehicle, which had already slowed, pulled up alongside and stopped. The driver lowered his window. "Sorry to interrupt." He pointed at the structure. "She's a beauty." He drove into and across the span.

"That guy has good taste, but damn, he ought to mind his manners."

Glenna displayed a confused looked. "He slowed down, and he even stopped, once he saw us."

"I'm not talking about his driving. I was referring to the pass he made at you…his flirtatious comment."

"What flirtatious comment?"

"He called you a 'beauty.'"

"He was referring to the bridge."

Eric was aware of that. "The guy said *she*, not *it*…I rest my case."

Glenna rolled her eyes, those beguiling blues.

Eric shrugged. He had already pushed his absurd pretense too far. "C'mon, let's go back in and enjoy the bridge." He took Glenna's hand and led the way.

Once they traversed about two-thirds of the span, they stopped, again gazing through the lattice work. Down below, the sparkling waters of the Walloomsac meandered.

"It's like a picture from a Currier and Ives card," said Glenna.

Eric shook his head.

"You disagree?"

"Absolutely. It puts those cards to shame. Three-D, with the sounds of gurgling water, and you can touch it." He ran his hand over the timeworn timbers. "It's the real thing."

"Good point…for a change." Glenna cuddled closer. A curious expression spread across her face. "Any dark secrets hidden in your past?"

"You back on that kick?" said Eric, recalling that she had made a similar inquiry two weeks earlier.

"Well…yeah…but only because you didn't answer my question last time." She looked him the eye. "It's important for a couple when they're getting serious to make sure they know one another. You agree, don't you?"

"Yeah."

"So, tell me, what's the worst thing you've ever done?"

"Not sure." Eric disliked the question but sensed that dismissing it would only amplify her probing. "Maybe the time I took Jimmie Palmer's pencil in fifth grade and then denied it when he confronted me."

"That's the worst?"

"Well, technically it was stealing."

"So, there are no skeletons in your closet, the kind that would cause a girl concern?"

"Not really." Eric observed a strange, disquieting, scrutinizing stare emanating from Glenna's eyes. Eager to extricate himself from the unsettling probe, he said, "And...uh...while we're on the subject, any skeletons in your closet?"

"Me?"

"Hey, what's good for the gander, is good for—"

"Quick, another car is approaching the bridge, and this one's coming faster." As she spoke, Glenna tugged him toward the nearer end, the one opposite from which they had previously exited.

The vehicle slowed as it entered the bridge.

"Damn, that's two in a row that made a pass at you."

Glenna shot Eric a look. "The driver was a woman!"

"So I noticed...A lesbian no doubt." Eric displayed a smug smile. "C'mon, you can't deny she looked."

"Yeah, at both of us."

Eric drew back histrionically. "You think she's one of those...the kinky kind? Into threesomes? Let's get out of here." As they headed back toward the Bennington campus, it crossed his mind that Glenna had never addressed the question about skeletons. He might have raised the point were he not just as happy to let the entire subject be.

Standing on one's property, gazing over the proverbial fence, the grass is greener. Walking about one's lawn, staring directly at one's feet, ugly weeds and bare spots are patent. Peering at a more distant expanse, clover, chick weed, purslane and crabgrass blend nicely with fine fescues in a seemingly verdant carpet. Such is the illusion that leads one to seek the apparent bounties of other pastures.

Kyle Gordon plopped himself down onto a stone bench in Washington Square Park. He was into his second semester of the two-year Masters-in-Business program at New York

University. The course work was interesting, but he was eager to get on with his life. Unlike his days at Williams where, despite working hard, there was always plenty of time for women, sports and frivolity, graduate school was all business. Even when he wasn't studying, his free time lacked the laidback spontaneity of his college days. Evidence that he had left his carefree youth behind and embarked on the road to professionalism was omnipresent.

He sunk his teeth into a hot dog, laden with mustard and sauerkraut. The pedestrian meal, a substitute for the pizza and burgers that had dominated his college days, had become all too common. It was not a matter that he couldn't afford more time to eat; simply that he was too lazy to cook, and the alternative on a bun was easy. With his free hand, he hooked the uppermost button of his topcoat. The temperature, about forty-five degrees, was warm for February, but the breeze, albeit light, cast a chill. Whether it was the way he was dressed or a trick of his mind, thirty degrees back at Williams never seemed as cold. Perhaps the dampness attributable to the waters surrounding the island of Manhattan helped explain the anomaly.

Kyle glanced down at the economics book that sat at his side. Back in high school when he had taken advanced placement mathematics, he had learned a lot about calculus. More than once he had questioned his teacher, Mr. Simpson, why he needed to learn the mathematical concepts. Being told that it would help in college seemed a meaningless answer. The idea that it would improve his problem-solving ability no matter what course his life took, though more convincing, was still unsatisfactory. Back then Kyle never imagined that he would pursue an MBA. He had no idea that mathematical devices enabling him to understand the change of one variable with respect to another would prove invaluable. He owed Mr. Simpson a note of appreciation. Whether he would get around to writing it was another matter. Inertia, a concept he had learned about in high school physics, helped explain the stumbling block.

"Mind if I join you?"

"Company would be more than welcome," said Kyle, his attention drawn to Elaine Walker, a classmate from South Carolina.

"I see you also opted for the Big Apple's Epicurean delight." Elaine held out her vendor-purchased hot dog, as she seated herself next to Kyle.

"Hell—who wants a hundred-dollar Kobe steak when you can have one of these?" Kyle dug his teeth into his fat-laden frankfurter. Once he had finished chewing, he said, "How do you like living in New York City?"

"Suits me really well. Theaters, museums...bright lights and action. It's a whole lot better than Wellford, South Carolina, where I grew up. Back there, come Saturday night, you had a choice. You could either go to Tasti-Cone for a soft ice cream or watch dew collect on the grass."

"Was it really that bad?"

"From my perspective—yes, though lots of folks there seemed to like it." She paused, gazing briefly into space. "Why? I never could fathom."

"Wasn't there anything there?"

"Hollywild Park."

"An amusement park?"

Elaine took a moment to swallow a mouthful. "No, a wild animal park with about two hundred animals. Come Christmas time, they decorated the place with a zillion lights. It was pretty, but compared to the glow of Times Square, it was nothing."

Kyle gestured around the busy confines of Washington Square, the grounds of which included an ample supply of cement, along with an uncommon share of individuals ranging from the eccentric to the downright weird. "You prefer this land of *Oz* to the peaceful surroundings of wide-open green spaces?"

"As a matter of fact, it's part of what I love about New York. You've got the whole nine yards. Greenwich Village...quaint and kooky; fashionable uptown; Times Square with all its glitz; and places like 34th Street, with the Empire State Building and Macy's screaming excitement. And then there's Wall Street, the center of the financial world. Throw in

89

Broadway with its theaters, Central Park, the museums, the Yankees, Mets, Knicks, Rangers, Giants and...I could go on and on, but I think you get the picture. Anyway, comparing Wellford to the Big Apple is like..." Elaine hesitated just long enough for a mini-skirted woman with purple hair walking a Bedlington Terrier to pass. "...like comparing the stuff in that bimbo's pooper-scooper bag to a fine steak."

Though the analogy was over the top, Kyle found it hard to disagree. Nevertheless, he leaned toward Wellford. "I understand what you're saying, but given the option, I'd pick your South Carolina hometown over New York."

Elaine shook her head. "So, come the end of next year when we graduate, you won't shoot for a high-paying job downtown?"

"I won't even apply." Recollections of the days around his graduation from Williams flashed into Kyle's mind. Back then he was excited about heading to the big city. Hindsight had altered his perspective. The enticing metropolis with its skyscrapers of steel and stone had grown far less appealing. The grass of a more rural or suburban setting was far greener.

"If that's how you feel, why'd you come here for your MBA?"

Kyle was reluctant to concede that he had made a mistake. "Not everybody who goes to Harvard is looking for a job in Boston."

"True. But in most cases, that's because they want to come here or Washington DC or Los Angeles."

Her point was well taken. His attempt to hide his mistake had failed. On the bright side, it was better that he had discovered that New York City was not the place for him while he was still in school, rather than after he had landed a job there paying big bucks. Trading the latter for a less prestigious position at a far lower salary would be a tough pill to swallow.

According to John Bartlett, the icon of familiar quotations, Maréchal Villars, when going forth from Louis

90

XIV, said: "Defend me from my friends; I can defend myself from my enemies."

Just back from lunch, Eric pressed the message-play button on his telephone's answering machine.

"Hi Eric. It's Clinton Horstmeyer. Hope all is well at your end. Please give me a call at 413-555-1917. Take care."

Eric jotted the number. As he did, he tried to imagine why Horstmeyer would be calling. Back at Williams the insufferable clown occasionally hung out with the Inseparables. Those occasions were generally by special invitation, one Horstmeyer had given himself. At times it seemed he had designs on turning the group into a five-some, but the idea was a non-starter. The four pals had no use for the braggart. Eric debated whether to return the call; his deliberations framed around speculations regarding its purpose. A contribution to their alma mater was a possibility. There was even the chance that Horstmeyer was looking to borrow money. Arguably that was farfetched, but with Horstmeyer anything was possible. Or maybe he was calling about Carla Pender, the one female they had in common. The touchy subject made Eric uncomfortable. He was tempted to ignore the message, and he might have, had intuition not convinced him that Horstmeyer would call again. If so, not only would his dodge prove fruitless, but he would owe an apology. Opting for the lesser evil, Eric dialed the number.

Moments later, a familiar raspy voice responded. "Horstmeyer here."

"Hello Clint. Eric Johanson returning your call. How've you been?"

"Good...and you?"

"No complaints. We missed you at Homecoming this past fall." The white lie rolled off Eric's tongue more easily than it might have in the past. Ten months in the business world merited credit for the skill. An older colleague referred to it as *tact,* which in Eric's mind was a euphemism for duplicity.

"Yeah, I had hoped to go, but a busy life...demands, demands...killed my plans. The reason I'm calling is that here at Quigley and Watkins, the brokerage firm where I'm working—"

"I thought you planned to sell cars at your uncle's dealership down in Tennessee."

"I did, but it didn't work out. The coach of the Memphis Xplorers—they're in the Arena Football League—was a half-brained prick. Rather than naming me starting wide receiver, he stuck me on the taxi squad. The bastard never gave me a shot. Cut me even before the season started."

Eric read between the lines. Clint lacked the talent, and given what a pain in the ass he was, the coach got rid of him fast. "What about the car sales job?"

"Hell, I only took that because it was blocks from where the Xplorers play. That plus I thought my uncle had an in with the coach. But enough about bad history. The reason I'm calling is that here at Quigley and Watkins we have these great annuities. They have a guaranteed return with all the benefits of tax deferral. And unlike some of the second-rate policies that others peddle, ours can be dressed up with loads of great bells and whistles. They're—"

"I'm sure they're excellent, but I've got a 401-K that includes matching employer contributions."

"Well, that's good. Anytime you can get matching employer contributions, you want to take advantage. But our annuities are top notch. And the more you put away now, the quicker your road to early retirement."

Though hardly an expert, Eric knew that the Internal Revenue Code restricted the amount one could defer. Whether its provisions would come into play was neither here nor there. "I'm sure you have a great product (white lies were flowing as easily as a post-thunderstorm waterfall), but my student loans have to be paid off first." The truth be known, between his parents' generosity and an excellent financial-aid package, the paltry amount he had to borrow to fund his days at Williams would be repaid in a couple of years.

"I hear you. Those sheepskins we got are mighty nice, but too bad they leave us with a mountain of debt."

"You got that right." No way was Eric about to let on that his was more like a toddler's sand pile at the beach.

"Well, there's always *domani.*"

"The money?"

"No, *domani.* It's *tomorrow* in Italian. I spent a week in Rome this past July. Man, do they have some fine women there. But anyway, down the road...*domani*...once you've paid off those loans...maybe sooner, I'll check with you again. As I said, you never can plan too early for retirement."

Eric was certain he would never buy any of Horstmeyer's products. If he wanted to make any new investments, Don Burns was his man. Indeed, he had already established an account with Don. But that was none of Horstmeyer's business. On the other hand, forgoing his privacy was a lesser evil than having Horstmeyer hock him again. "Not to turn your champagne flat, but just so you know, I'm doing my investing with Don Burns. He's with Kingman & Woodhill in New York City."

"So I know."

The tone, even more sarcastic than the words, suggested Horstmeyer may have already been beaten out by Burns when soliciting other Williams' graduates. Eric had no intention of exploring whether the surmise was correct. Another subject, Carla Pender, popped into Eric's head. Much as the subject intrigued him, judgment suppressed curiosity. The conversation was better ended, and apparently, Eric was not the only one of that mind.

"It's been really nice talking to you," said Horstmeyer.

"You too." As he hung up the receiver, Eric chided himself for delivering another white lie. However, quick analysis forced him to reconsider. The hat trick of fibs, a first for him, had to be canceled. A part of him, albeit small, had enjoyed talking to his fellow Williams' alumnus.

CHAPTER VII

LIFE PATHS DIVERGE. Friends are driven in different directions. Promises to meet again, however well intentioned, never come to fruition. Relationships fade in the wake of new roles and responsibilities. Seemingly immutable bonds evanesce into the all-but-forgotten past. Such is life...but not always.

"Damn, can you believe it?" said Bill. "With graduation growing more distant, the Inseparables are back together on campus for the second consecutive year."

"You expected otherwise?" said Eric.

Bill shrugged, as he popped the top of a new can of Wilson tennis balls.

Kyle understood the reaction. Sure, they had all promised to return, but experience suggested the vows might be empty. Back in fourth grade after his elementary school pal Rusty had moved to Oregon, there was never a telephone call. Not even a card at Christmas. Just because Rusty hadn't kept his end of the bargain, did that excuse Kyle's failure? And too, how quickly contact with long-time high school friends had ceased with the advent of college.

"You think we'll pull this off every year?" The doubt in Don's voice was palpable.

"Of course," said Eric. "It's—"

"Easy for you to say. Hartford is only sixty or seventy miles from here...an hour or so drive. Try flying all the way from southern Florida just for a weekend, and you'd sing a different tune."

"He has a point," said Kyle.

Eric shot Kyle a look. "Don't tell me New York City is too far for you and Burns, especially when you can ride together."

"It's not that. But if mid-terms had been this coming week, rather than last, no way would I have made it. Last weekend I was studying eight, nine hours a day."

"Fine. But come June, you'll have your MBA. Excuse gone." He gestured at Don. "You're working. You have no excuse."

"I didn't make one."

"I saw your look earlier."

"Damn! When did you get so touchy, Johanson?"

"I'm not touchy!"

Kyle spurned the urge to add a jab of his own. Good-natured sarcasm was one thing, a caustic dig another. He slipped off the cover of his tennis racquet.

Eric gazed at his three friends. "Sorry, I didn't mean to jump down your throats. It's…it's just that listening to you guys, I get the distinct impression these get-togethers are destined to become fewer and farther between." A sigh punctuated the assessment. "Does that mean our trip out West, always a plan for the future, has become never-to-be pie in the sky?"

"No way," said Bill. "The trip will happen."

"And when will that be?" said Don.

"I don't know…But mark my words, we're gonna do it."

"Great," said Kyle. "But for now, you mind if we play some tennis?"

"We could, if I could tear the metal top off this damn can of balls." Bill held out the container for all to see. "The pull tab separated from the top when I tried to open it."

"No problem," said Don. He pulled out his little Swiss Army knife from his racquet cover and pried the top off. "Now, after all these years, maybe you guys will finally understand the benefits of always carrying my lucky Boy Scout treasure."

"Yeah, about as much as we understand your crazy superstitions." Bill put an arm over Kyle's shoulder. "C'mon, we'll take these hotshots on." He pointed at Don and Eric. "I hope you boys brought your wallets because losers buy at the Irish Mist."

Don turned to Eric. "It appears our friend spent a few too many hours in the sun down in Fort Myers. Apparently he thinks they have a chance to win."

"Hey, whad'ya expect? I write fiction. I live in a fantasy world."

Kyle noted the smile on Bill's face. The good-natured trash talk was welcome. The Inseparables had their mojo back; well, at least three of them. Along with Bill, Kyle headed for the far baseline. "You want to play the net? I'll stay back."

"Fine by me."

Kyle looked to the other end of the court where Eric and Don were huddled. He whispered, "What's up with Eric?"

Bill's reaction said something, but what—was hard to discern.

"C'mon, that peevish guy a minute ago was like an imposter, not the easygoing Eric we know."

"Well, right now, his life is on two distant borders. One is Heaven, and the other, Hell."

"What the hell does that mean?"

"That he's totally smitten with Glenna. No girl ever hit him like this. He says she's the one."

"I take it she doesn't feel the same about him."

Bill shook his head. "From what I understand, it's just the opposite. The attraction is mutual and equally strong."

"Wait a second. A moment ago, you said his life was a mixture of Heaven and Hell. All I hear is Heaven."

"Remember, the picture includes another woman…Carla."

The name provided more than a clue, but Kyle wanted something more definitive, and when it was not forthcoming, he said, "She giving him a hard time?"

"I doubt it. She probably doesn't have to. When it comes to doing the right thing, we both know there's nobody better than Eric. He's been giving her money for her baby."

"How do you know that?"

"It doesn't matter. Anyway, I assure you it's the case."

Bill's source left Kyle curious. On the other hand, it provided a seemingly definitive answer to another question.

Eric, not Clint, must be the father of Carla's baby. "Between you, me and our tennis racquets, where'd you—" A tennis ball whizzing over his shoulder halted Kyle's tongue.

"You two plan to gab all day?" yelled Eric. "Or are we gonna play some tennis?"

Kyle peered down the court to the far baseline. "In a moment...as soon as the good guys plot a little strategy."

"You want strategy?" said Don, who was closer to the net. "I'll give you some. Once we whip your asses, you two split the tab at the Irish Mist. Fifty-fifty...no arguments."

A monarch butterfly, its orange wings striped with black, gently glides through the air alighting on a milkweed flower. A sip of sweet nectar, a moment's pause and on to another flower. Flitting and floating from here to there, off to wherever, it basks in the sunshine of nature's brightly hued palette. Boundaries, the butterfly knows none. Guided by instinct, time is inconsequential. Freedom, unencumbered, prevails.

Saturday morning, and Bill Young peddled his way over the Sanibel Causeway onto Periwinkle Way, continuing westerly on Sanibel-Captiva Road to the "Ding Darling Wildlife Refuge." He had biked fifteen miles from his apartment in Fort Myers. Add on the four-plus miles of the estuary's Wildlife Drive and the distance back home later in the day, and his trip, once completed, would total nearly forty miles. He was an experienced biker, not that he was especially fast, but the day's outing would equal his longest.

The preceding day an unexpected letter had greeted him upon his arrival home from school. The *Rochester Star* had offered him a job as a reporter. Six weeks earlier Bill had submitted his résumé on a lark. Even as he had interviewed there during a school vacation, he had made no effort to hide mixed emotions. At the time, he had assumed his transparency would result in a rejection. Much to his surprise, the offer had come, and with it, the need for a decision. There were moments when the possibility of being a reporter had tantalized him.

Other times he had questioned why he had ever begun the process. Normally decisive, his thoughts and feelings about the opportunity were *Jello*.

A few days after his interview, he had called his old high school friend Tina Mackler. Back at Willburne High, with journalism her favorite subject, she had dreams of becoming a newspaperwoman. Following college, she had landed a position as a staff reporter for a local daily in Scranton, Pennsylvania. Bill had contacted her, hoping to get a picture of life as a reporter. Much as he wanted it to be unvarnished, he anticipated hers would come with unbridled enthusiasm, a landscape bright with sunshine and fragrant flowers. Contrary to expectations, the picture she painted bore a striking likeness to the gray shade that so often dominated the Scranton skies. Tina loved to write, but not in the vapid framework of her job. Day after day, she churned out the *who, what, where, when and how* of this and that, never smelling the roses, though frequently feeling their thorns. It was as unrewarding as spitting out romance novels under a publisher's incarcerating formula that included not only a specified number of lurid sex scenes, but also the exact pages on which they would take place. With reduced staffing, the ever-growing Internet and fewer and fewer people buying newspapers, speed and quantity had become the measures of her work. Thoughtful analysis was all but irrelevant. Masterful metaphors were trifling wastes of time. And as for Tina's opinion, she could keep that to herself. The editorial staff of the paper, a reflection of its owner's political views, frowned on any such expressions by staff.

A bike ride to Sanibel Island's Ding Darling Wildlife Refuge was a chance for Bill to think. Amidst nature's solitude he could weigh the pros and cons of his job offer. He wended his way about half the length of Wildlife Drive to the Cross Dike Trail, where he turned off to escape from any motor vehicle traffic. He followed the narrow, paved trail through mangrove-lined saltwater marshes to a spot not far from the observation tower. There he seated himself on a bench. Close by, amidst the wildflowers, butterflies fluttered. His mind did likewise, but hardly with the unfettered ease of his winged neighbors. He leaned back, closed his eyes and breathed in the fresh air. Chirps, trills and tweets filled his ears. He had no clue as to the identity of the birds providing the music. It didn't matter. Their dulcet notes were calming. They were welcoming as well, a seeming invitation for him to share the carolers' glorious refuge.

He opened his eyes and gazed across the watery expanse. On a nearby sandbar a snowy egret bathed itself in the golden sunshine. Bill delighted in his ability to identify the bird. Since arriving in Florida, he had learned to recognize a few of the larger species, among them anhingas, pelicans and herons, not that he could generally distinguish their different varieties. For well over a minute he remained focused on the snowy egret. Devoid of cares, the regal bird exalted.

Bill closed his eyes once again. His brain conjured an image of the busy press room at the *Rochester Star*. It had an air of excitement. On second thought, excitement was a euphemism for stress. Earlier expectations that a job as a newspaper reporter would allow him to earn a living doing what he loved—writing—were fatuous. Deadlines that all but preceded assignments—that's how Tina had described her work—painted a stark scene. And how much starker that scene would be in the long, icy winters of Rochester, New York. In place of the pure white of the snowy egret would be the white of snow. Bill's years at Williams had educated him about Northeast winters. All too quickly, delicate flakes and pristine powder transformed into blackened slush. Roads, mined with potholes, deteriorated into treacherous skating rinks. And bathing suits donned in the warm days of summer were stowed amidst cold, gray days with long, dark nights.

Accepting the Rochester offer would require him to give up his position teaching. Admittedly its demands were large. But the rewards, non-monetary, were great. His students were conscientious and bright, and, most important, their enthusiastic responses to his classes were priceless. With more than two months off in the summer, plus weekends and vacations, he had time to pursue his passion, his novel. And because it was an avocation, not a job for a daily newspaper struggling to stay afloat, what he penned was dictated by his heart, not pragmatic business concerns.

Bill re-opened his eyes. The egret was still basking in the tropical warmth. No way would the fowl abandon its paradise for the likes of Northeast winters. No way would Bill do it either. In less than ten minutes he had made his decision. There was even the possibility the decision had been made three hours earlier when he had left his apartment and headed for Ding Darling. Though not consciously professed, a part of him may have suspected how the trip to the refuge would influence his thinking.

The snowy egret spread its wings and took flight.

Bill watched the graceful bird soar over the salty marsh, up and over the mangroves, quickly vanishing from view. "Thank you, my fine-feathered friend." A supreme calm, an unparalleled peace, gripped him. He drew in a deep breath of pure Gulf-of-Mexico air. Like the birds and butterflies, Bill basked in the tranquil oasis.

The End of the World. From the ancient Mayans to Nostradamus to modern clerics begging attention, predictions of doomsday have echoed. But the end of the world, Armageddon, is not always as it seems. Far from any metropolis, in Vermont's idyllic environs, on the campus of Bennington College, stands an impressive, symmetric federal-style building with double chimneys at either end and another on either side of a square tower from which rises a domed cupola with a weather vane pointing skyward. The structure's broad, two-story portico looks out over The End of the World, the label given by Bennington students to the quad fronting their commons building. Distant as the edifice's location is from urban centers, that gap pales when compared to its psychological distance from metropolitan bustle. Amidst its pastoral landscape, conformity holds no sway. Doors remain unlocked. Traditional rules and conventions crumble.

A picnic basket and a bottle of wine at their side, Eric lay on a blanket, his arm draped around Glenna. With her head on his chest, she lay perpendicular to him. The sun's full flame, along with a southerly zephyr, drove the inordinately warm April temperature well up into the seventies. An even warmer glow filled Eric's heart. He closed his eyes, giving credence to the apt name Bennington students had given the grassy expanse. It was light years from the steel-framed, cement building where Eric worked as a claims adjuster. So far, that, on second thought, it lay beyond The End of the World. Indeed, it was Heaven.

Eric ran his hand over Glenna's silky blouse. His forearm brushing her breast stirred images of her magnificent contours and the passions shared the night before. "I love you," he whispered.

She turned her head enough to momentarily press her lips to his chest. "I love you too."

Well over a year had passed since they had begun dating. Glenna was definitely *the one*. Eric had no doubt. Come Monday, back in Hartford, after work, he would pay a visit to Woodford Jewelers. The time had come to purchase a diamond. Eric closed his eyes. He pictured himself on one knee. The scene bore no background. The time and place where he would give Glenna the ring were yet to be determined. And too, the way he would pop the question still needed to be thought out. Regardless, where…when…how he did it…perhaps alone at an intimate dinner…maybe in a rowboat on a Berkshire lake…or there on the quad of the Bennington campus, he would be in a heavenly place, far beyond The End of the World.

———

Sew a seed in, of all things, dirt, and amazing vegetation burgeons. From time to time the planting may even yield a beanstalk, one that stretches forth into skies laden with gold.

Don Burns eyed a list of twenty-five prospective new clients. They all had been in his Williams' graduating class two years earlier. The list included a couple of friends, several acquaintances, a few for whom he could only match a face to the name and over a dozen that were nothing more than names he had pulled from the most recent issue of the alumni magazine. Each represented a potential new account. While most days he started with cold calls, seeing as how it was a Monday and a mulish rain had spoiled his late-June weekend with Linda in the Catskills, he needed a lift. The time had come to once again draw from his dependable well. He flipped his Rolodex to the letter *Y*. He would have called Bill Young far sooner had he not concluded that the likelihood of success would be enhanced by delaying his pitch until after Bill had a chance to accumulate some savings. The delay was also a product of the harsh Halloween lesson he had learned at the age of seven when he had eaten all his favorite candies immediately after arriving home from *Trick or Treating*. The gluttonous orgy had left him with a horrible stomach ache. And for two long weeks thereafter, with nothing more than sour tarts, hard candies and raisins remaining, he had to watch his frugal older sister blissfully consume Milky Ways, Charleston Chews, Hershey Bars and other sumptuous delights. The experience had taught him that rapid consumption was tempting, but patience had its rewards. With the lesson in mind and forbearance duly exercised, Don dialed Bill's number. Long gone was the need to rehearse that had preceded calls when first he had begun his job. Patter and confidence developed through many repetitions had rendered such dilatory preparation unnecessary.

"Hello."

"Hi Bill. It's Don Burns. How are things in the world of teaching?"

"Good from my side of the desk. As for the students, you'd have to ask them."

"I can just imagine...all those teeny-bopping girls swooning over you."

The groan that filled the receiver was protracted.

"You denying that the lasses at that girls' school where you teach have a crush on you?"

"I am, but be that as it may, tell me—how's the tycoon of Wall Street?"

"I wouldn't know, but I'll ask him...if and when I meet him." The failed attempt to duplicate the clever repartee of their college days persuaded Don to move forward. "The reason I'm calling is that I thought you might consider opening an account."

"What?—with you?"

Whether Bill was merely engaging in fatuous banter or being serious was impossible for Don to discern. "Assuming you're interested, we have some excellent products."

"Well...I could do with a decent form of investment, not that I have a lot to invest."

Landing big accounts was always nice, but pulling in small ones was very worthwhile. As with a tiny seed, there was growth potential. A small investor might become a big one or, perhaps, a source of new clients. "We have an easy minimum, one thousand dollars."

"That's within my budget...and I have a bank CD, a little over two grand, coming due in a couple of weeks. The current rate sucks, and the renewal numbers are worse yet."

"I think we can help you. At your age, you belong in equities."

"Much as I'd love a better return, I don't want to lose my principal."

Having heard the identical refrain countless times, Don was well prepared. "I understand. What I suggest is an index fund. Historically they grow at about seven percent...and that's compounded."

"That's a helluva lot more than what I'm getting. But what exactly is it?"

"It's a huge fund of stocks carefully selected. Often it replicates an entire market. For example, a fund indexed to the Dow Jones average would move exactly like the Dow."

"Which, if I understand, means it can go down as well as up."

"Absolutely. But if you plan to leave your money in for the long haul—let's say three or four decades when you decide to retire—an index fund is a damn good bet. It minimizes the downside risk associated with a single stock. Despite short-term fluctuations, historically it grows over time with higher yields than fixed income investments. And to quote your earlier assessment, your CD's 'current rate sucks.'"

"You've convinced me."

103

"I think your cheapskate bank deserves most of the credit, but regardless, I'm glad you've decided to come on board. I'll send you a prospectus, along with the forms to open your account. Once your CD comes due, just have your miserly bank issue a check, and we'll deposit it into your new account. Sound okay?"

"Good enough…but…uh…while we're on the phone, I might as well cover another base. I…I doubt I'll make homecoming this fall. I hate to be the first of the Inseparables to go AWOL, but unlike you guys who can easily drive to Williams in a few hours, for me the weekend schlep from the southern end of the Sunshine State is a tough go."

Under other circumstances Don might have given Bill a hard time, but he was not about to sting the ear of a new client. "I understand. Traveling a thousand miles—"

"More like fourteen hundred each way. Hardly a leisurely stroll at the seaside. But maybe we could all get together sometime, down here in Florida. In the depths of winter, it would be a great opportunity for the three of you to escape the arctic Northeast."

"Sounds like an excellent idea." Even as Don endorsed the suggestion, he doubted it would happen. Getting all four together in a distant place was far from easy. Their continued inability to take their long-planned western jaunt had proved that. "So, on a more important note, tell me— how's your love life?"

"Eh…a couple of dates here and a couple there, but no one special."

"What about that girl Andrea you met at your apartment complex a while back?"

"We dated for a time. She was *really* nice. Unfortunately, she took a job with one of those wonderful multi-nationals. The company transferred her to Australia."

"I hear that's a beautiful country. Maybe it's worth a trip. Where else can…" Judgment guided Don to keep an inane remark about kangaroos and koala bears to himself. "Yeah, I guess a long-distance relationship, especially one to the other side of the world, is tough. Though I must admit, I'd love to get down under someday." An intrusive thought accompanied the glib comment. Their lives had drifted in different directions. For the moment, there was little more to talk about. With the exchange of a few pleasantries, the call ended.

Don gazed at his list. He sipped his coffee as he put a check mark next to Bill's name. The inked demarcation arguably perked him more than his caffeinated beverage. He ran his finger down the list stopping at Kyle's name. His pal had just completed his MBA. Don crossed out Kyle's name. A BMW salesman didn't call an Audi counterpart to sell him a car. That left only one other member of the Inseparables, Eric, as a possible candidate. With a good job and already on board as a client, he might be ready to enlarge his account. Don stared at Eric's name but decided to skip it for the time being. Perhaps at the end of the day or maybe at the start of the next, he would make the call. The device, a way to improve his chance of beginning or finishing a day on a high note, was part of Don's *modus operandi*.

Through the balance of the morning and, after a leisurely lunch, he otherwise went alphabetically through his list. Don managed to reach seventeen. Eleven were flat-out *no's*. Either they already had accounts with other firms or were just not interested. Five others were *maybes*, though Don could tell that two of them were simply giving him the slow brush off. The lone *yes* was a very nice account. Jordan Deland was sending him forty thousand dollars, half to be invested in a tax-exempt municipal bond fund and the remainder in an aggressive equity growth fund. Better yet was the possibility that Jordan, a successful entrepreneur, might send him a whole lot more in the future.

It was four-thirty in the afternoon when Don finished what could have been his last call. With hours of schmoozing under his belt, talk about baseball, football, politics and, of course, days at Williams, he considered packing it in. A new strategy, a relatively painless technique to induce existing clients to up their ante, seduced him to make one more call. He entered Eric Johanson's number.

"Granite Casualty and Life...Johanson speaking."

"Hi Eric. It's Don Burns. How've you been?"

"Okay. And you?"

The lack of enthusiasm in Eric's voice was undeniable. The possibility loomed that he surmised the purpose of the call. An immediate solicitation was unwise, especially with a long-time friend. "I'm good. You'll be at Homecoming Weekend in October…Right?"

"It's on my calendar. And you?"

"Definitely. But apparently Bill Young won't make it. I spoke with him earlier today, and he says the trip is too long for a weekend."

A brief sigh ensued. "Well…I guess it's hard to blame him. If I were in Florida, I'm not sure I'd be willing to make the trip, especially with the cost."

"Flights from Florida are pretty reasonable."

"Maybe for Wall Street stockbrokers, but not necessarily for a school teacher like Bill. Plus he has to come from Fort Myers. That's not like Orlando where they have flights up the wazoo. And even then, once he lands, be it Hartford or Albany or wherever, he has to rent a car."

"Good point." Back when Don was in college, professors had taught him to question most everything. By nature, a cynic, the approach came naturally. When Don arrived at Kingman & Woodhill, he was already gregarious, but it took a little time before he became a schmoozer. To do so, first he had to learn the niceties. Right from the get-go, Charlie Bascomb, his boss and mentor, had taught him: Clients, even those who voice the ridiculous, are always right. Proving them wrong may feel good at the time, but it's bad for the pocketbook. Laugh, but only silently, at their ignorance. In the beginning, Don found it hard to follow the advice, but once he saw the payoff, ego stroking became easier. A few complimentary or agreeable words, and he would move on, often to another subject. "Do you know whether Kyle plans to make Homecoming?"

"The last I spoke with him—it's been a few months—he was a *yes*."

"Well, according to 'Meatloaf,' that can't be bad."

"Come again?"

"You know, the Meatloaf oldie, 'Two Out of Three Ain't Bad.'"

106

"Sorry, the song is before my time, not to mention that your math is off."

Don was aware that three-quarters of their group planned to attend. He disregarded the chance to point out that was even better than two-thirds. He said, "My reason for calling is not just social. I want to make sure that the monthly statements for your account are clear. With all the numbers and abbreviations, they can be confusing."

"I suppose, assuming one has a huge, complicated portfolio. But with my one little mutual fund, it's easy. Each month I look at the bottom line. One month it's up a little, and the next, it's down."

"Overall it's done well." Don eyed the account which was front and center on his computer. "In the short time you've had it, it's grown by more than five percent."

"So I've noticed. Just hope it can continue for the next thirty years."

"The good thing is: You were smart enough to start early. Most people wait until they're fifty or older to begin thinking about retirement. By then, it's generally too late. And while we're on the subject, I would be remiss if I failed to mention there's another strategy you might want to consider." Don had finally reached the real purpose of his call. The previously avowed reason, concern about account statements, was contrived to make his sales pitch appear like an afterthought. "One of the best ways to grow your retirement nest egg is to set up a payroll deduction from your salary. Just a small amount with each paycheck not only adds up, but it has the added benefit of dollar-cost averaging."

"I suppose it does."

The blasé reaction, though hardly shocking, hinted that Eric was less than enthusiastic. Judgment dictated another dose of patience, not that it was a panacea. On the other hand, pressing hard was a recipe for immediate refusal. "As I said, it's just an idea, not something you need to jump into today. Perhaps we can talk about it down the road. In the meantime, can I send you a pamphlet with more information?"

"Well—okay, I guess."

The negative tone with which the reluctant acquiescence was delivered caught Don off guard. Ordinarily people he called were satisfied with the easy way out. "You don't sound all that enthusiastic." Thinking back over their conversation, Eric's usual enthusiasm had been absent throughout. "Would you rather I don't send the pamphlet?"

"Oh, no. In fact, I'm really interested."

Sure. Don kept the sarcasm from his lips. "Then why the reaction?"

"It's…it's nothing."

The uninspired tone belied the words. "Is it anything I've said or done?"

"No, no. It's not you."

Don waited a moment. "Then what?"

An uncomfortable silence ensued.

"C'mon, maybe I can help."

"Don't I wish!"

Discretion kept Don from uttering, *Try me.* Business, the original purpose of the call, had yielded to a more important issue, concern for a friend.

"Glenna…Glenna dumped me the day before yesterday."

The news knocked Don for a loop. Months earlier, he and Linda had met Eric and Glenna for dinner halfway between New York City and Hartford. At the time, Glenna had told Linda that she was crazy about Eric; that he was a fabulous person; and that she had never felt so strongly about any guy. Don struggled to find some comforting words. "Maybe it's just something that will blow over…Did you two have a spat?"

"No. Out of the blue she called and said we should stop seeing one another."

"She didn't say why?" The question, one that already seemed answered, was voiced for lack of something better.

"Nope…no explanation, not even when I pressed her."

With Eric in Hartford and Glenna in Bennington, a possibility crossed Don's mind. He kept it to himself.

"I'm glad you called. These past two days I've been in the dumps. I've needed to talk to someone."

"Is there anything I can do?" Sincere though the offer was, Don knew the answer.

"Can you cast a spell on Glenna and change her mind?"

Resorting to one of their sophomoric retorts was out of bounds. Silence was the best Don could offer.

"I...I keep wondering if maybe she met another guy. It's the only explanation that makes any sense."

That was exactly what Don had been thinking a moment before. "It doesn't sound like Glenna." Indeed, it didn't, but with affairs of the heart, one never knew.

"Can you think of another reason?"

Even if Don could have, unlikely he would have expressed it.

"Yeah...I can read between the lines of your diplomatic dodge." Eric sighed. "There's only one person who can bring joy back into my life, and she's not about to. And that said, I might as well get back to work. It's an escape from my nightmare, not that I can escape myself."

"Perhaps it would help if you come down here to the City for the weekend. Linda and I would love to have you."

"Appreciate the offer, but I'm going to pass."

"Wouldn't it be better to be here with company?"

"No offense, but for now, watching a happy couple would do nothing for my spirits. You know the old phrase: 'Misery loves company.' For now, I need a little *misery* to share mine."

The point, unlike some earlier ones, was well taken. Unfortunately, Don's forte was stroking egos, not providing misery. An exchange of good-byes, and the disheartening call ended.

CHAPTER VIII

DARKNESS IS RELATIVE, a function of one's perspective. The brightest sunlight cannot penetrate walls, even invisible ones.

Eric Johanson sat in the big easy chair of his two-bedroom Windsor Locks apartment. Friday evenings had become special. They marked the start of a weekend with Glenna, half the time at Bennington College and the other half at his apartment. Even on those rare weekends when they didn't get together, they would spend several hours talking on the telephone. But all that was in the past. Visits had ceased, and conversations had grown short. To make matters worse, one day earlier when Eric had telephoned, Glenna had made it emphatically clear that she preferred to sever all contact. Why—she had refused to say, but there was no equivocation.

The early evening setting sun shone through the west-facing window of Eric's living room. His freezer was stocked with several frozen entrees. When he had arrived home from the office, he had considered nuking one in the microwave, but with no appetite, he instead took a bottle of Heineken from the refrigerator and flopped himself down in his big lounger. He pressed the television remote and surfed through a dozen channels before turning the flat-screened wizard off. Ordinarily Eric was a news and sports junkie, but he was in no mood for either. He was in no mood for anything.

Just weeks earlier, Eric had been ready to buy Glenna an engagement ring. He was certain she would be thrilled. How did his world turn upside down? Over and over he asked the same question, one he had pondered a hundred times before.

Why had Glenna dumped him? Perhaps when she had teased him about his tapered-back, short haircut, she was serious. Maybe she no longer found him attractive. She had spoken about a career in social work or teaching, something that would help people. She had no desire to enter the corporate world. Perhaps his job as an insurance company claims adjuster turned her off. Or maybe she preferred a man with a high-powered job. The conjecture made no sense. Glenna was not demanding. She was not a gold-digger. Her tastes were simple. A big house, fancy cars, designer labels and a spouse with a humongous income were not what she valued. Repeated analysis eliminated every explanation, save one. Off in the pastoral Vermont hills on the campus of Bennington College, Glenna had found another man. Eric didn't want to believe it, but nothing else added up. Glenna Snow must have found a new beau.

Eric gazed out the window. His world was dark. His thoughts spiraled him downward. He took another sip of Heineken. The brew did nothing to alleviate his pain. A six pack wouldn't do the job. Even if it could, soon enough the alcohol's mind-numbing powers would wear off. Reality, its devastation, would return.

The inevitable and that which eventuates without cause or design seemingly lie at the far ends of a wide linear spectrum. Yet that which separates these diametric opposites may border on nothing more than interpretation. What one terms fate, another labels coincidence. Could it be that kismet and chance are poles of an ellipse? Travel far enough from one pole and the path leads back to the starting point. Heresy? Perhaps. But Christopher Columbus did not fall off the edge of the Earth.

Kyle Gordon stood alongside his bride Katelyn Reed in the living room of a Deerfield, Massachusetts, Justice of the Peace. The couple had met only six months earlier in Washington Square Park in the Big Apple. Katelyn, who never wore hats—well, almost never—had been sporting a yellow bonnet. A strong spring breeze launched her chapeau, sending it hopscotching down the park's cement walkways. As she chased the windblown topper, Kyle leaped from a bench and snatched it. And so, he met the lovely third-year law student. A whirlwind romance followed as he completed the final months of his MBA and she, law school at New York University. Katelyn was first to line up a job. It was with a top-notch firm in Springfield, Massachusetts. For Kyle, who was eager to leave the bustle of New York City, Springfield bore no special attraction, but once Katelyn and her job were added to the equation, nowhere else came close.

Katelyn, an only child, had lost her mother, a single parent, the preceding summer. She had not seen or heard from her father for more than a decade. To the best of her knowledge, he had gone off to New Zealand with a nineteen-year-old hottie. Katelyn had no desire for a big wedding, and that suited Kyle just fine. Owing to costly educations, both had loans to repay. Neither wished to compound their burden for the sake of a big party. Such was the reasoned pragmatism that had guided them to the home of the Deerfield Justice of the Peace. Joined only by Kyle's parents, his sister and the wife of the Justice of the Peace, they were there to exchange their vows.

Kyle gazed into the green eyes of his slim, auburn-haired bride. Joyfully, he uttered the tiny, but monumental, three-letter sentence that memorialized their marital bond. Reservations, he had none. Graduate school had been fine, though admittedly a weak second to his years at Williams. But great as those days had been, they paled in comparison to this new pinnacle. With his many successful years of schooling behind him, he was eager to begin his life as an adult in earnest. The road ahead was freshly paved and clear. Less than a month before, he had lined up a position as a broker with Larry Rockland, a man in his early seventies who, with an established clientele, was expecting to retire from his Springfield office in about eighteen months. While Kyle might have explored the corporate world, once he and Katelyn had decided to tie the knot and she had landed her job with the Springfield law firm, he confined his search to that area. The more he had gotten to know Larry

Rockland, the more enthusiastic he had become about the opportunity.

Kyle, ever the rational type, put little stock in fate. Though hardly a goody-goody, he had never been wild and crazy. In high school, rather than diving twenty-five feet off the rocks into the billowing waters of Grandy Gorge, he had endured the verbal abuse of the more intrepid—from Kyle's perspective, more foolhardy—who, armed with youthful invincibility, had taken the leap. Their claims that disaster would only strike if it was their time held no water for Kyle.

Standing before the Justice of the Peace, a thought he had entertained dozens of times before flashed into his mind. Were it not for that fortuitous breeze in New York City's Washington Square Park, Katelyn, who almost never wore a hat, would not have lost hers. Kyle would never have rescued it, and they would never have met. He would not be standing at the altar with the love of his life. His entire future would have been different. There would have been no move to Springfield, no position with Larry Rockland and, most of all, no marriage to Katelyn. In the face of the facts, it was hard to call it all a coincidence. Were Kyle to claim so, those who believed in fate could hurl his own circumstances back into his face. Perhaps they were right. At that moment, Kyle didn't care. Whether it was fate or coincidence was of no matter. Whatever the explanation, Kyle was sublimely happy.

Life is replete with moral dilemmas. Even a toddler confronts them. Caught in a minor transgression, he/she oscillates between denial and admission. Desire to escape punishment wheedles a lie. But a skeptical, cross-examining adult provokes the truth. Amidst inner conflict the child develops a conscience, one certain to be tested many times in the years that follow.

Charles Bascomb, as he was wont to do, plopped himself down in a chair fronting Don Burns' desk. The mentor's visits were rarely substantive, but Don was always glad to shoot the breeze with the high-powered senior partner. A rehash of the Giants' gridiron battle from the preceding afternoon, typical Monday confab, was a good bet.

"Friday's meeting was a real downer. Those numbers for the last quarter were dreadful. Worst we've seen in a decade. Accounts have been disappearing faster than a scantily clad femme at a magic show. Not good."

The anticipated rehash of Sunday's football game had suddenly become a longshot. But unsure where Bascomb was headed, Don, far from a rookie, had mastered the art of punting. "You got that right." The diplomatically vacuous response slid off his tongue as if it were Teflon sprayed with canola oil.

"Friday afternoon on the golf course—damn, it's sad when business spoils a relaxing day on the links. Anyway, on the second tee, Dick Conners from Information Systems—you'd think he could have waited until the back nine—started yapping how we gotta get more mileage from our existing accounts."

Suspicions about the direction of the conversation mounted, but Don stuck to his playbook, lest he get blindsided.

"Far too much money is sitting in mutual funds, be it bonds or equities. What do we get? An annual administrative fee of three or four-tenths of a percent, a damn pittance." Bascomb looked Don in the eye. "Conners has a point. I'm sure you agree."

Whatever his view, Don felt little choice. "I hear what you're saying."

"Good, because we can do a whole lot more for our clients, not to mention the coffers of Kingman & Woodhill. There are some great opportunities out there, investments like the Silver Sky Fund. It returned eleven percent last year. Did you know that?"

"I knew it had done well, but not the exact number." Don also knew that over the past five years the highly aggressive fund had yielded a negative return. Its success the preceding year was not the result of a sparkling bright future, but being oversold in what was then a rising market. He assumed

Bascomb was aware of that fact. He was equally sure the senior partner did not want to be reminded of it.

"We have clients who are making less than one percent in money markets. It's a damn shame. It's our job as financial advisors to help them do better, and the best way to accomplish that is to encourage them to put more of their funds into managed accounts."

The strategy, like the *flea flicker*, a play invoked when old reliables failed, was becoming eminently clear. A managed account could yield fees of three or four percent, ten times what many mundane investments produced. The ability to buy and sell for the account could also generate commissions, the amounts of which could be enhanced with a little *churning*. Don had no intention of using the word, sure it would stir the ire of his mentor. Still he needed to at least voice some concern. "In their investment profiles, many of our clients marked 'preservation of capital' as their primary goal. They want to avoid high-risk, growth investments."

"Good point."

Don was pleased his mention of the conservative objective had not been met with an all-out blitz.

"But you know as well as I, most of our clients are naïve. They look to us for guidance. Sitting on our hands while they get nothing more than a paltry return, one less than inflation and nevertheless taxed, would be unthinkable. I'm sure you agree."

The senior partner's last sentence, a declaration, not a question, left no doubt who was selecting the plays. Don was not about to call an *audible*. "Oh…uh…you're absolutely right. We have to look out for our clients' interests." The inconsistency of his reply was not lost on Don. On the one hand, he had emphatically agreed; on the other, he had spoken like a fiduciary. The good news—Bascomb's earlier comments had demonstrated a willingness to gloss over the distinction.

"I knew you'd be on board." Bascomb leaned back in a seemingly more relaxed posture. "What I want you to do, like the rest of us, is to contact your clients and encourage them to shift their funds to managed accounts, encourage them to consider Silver Sky. Remind them that inflation and taxes are beating them up."

"What if they're reluctant?"

"Good question," said Bascomb, himself an aficionado of football metaphors. You can only chart the X's and O's; you can't carry the ball for them. But having said that, you can still encourage them to invest their money using a playbook which will give them a better return...and, at the same time, yield more fees for Kingman & Woodhill." Bascomb extended his arms and motioned with both hands. "It's a win-win approach."

The game plan was elegant, a blueprint that generated the best of all worlds, except it neglected a huge factor—risk. In exchange for a potentially higher return, an investor's principal would be exposed to increased danger. The still, small voice in the distant reaches of Don's brain urged him to make the argument. Judgment, the instinct of self-preservation, counseled otherwise. Bascomb was well aware of the point, and, more important, he had no desire to hear it.

"It's a terrific approach. You concur, don't you?"

"Yes...although it does—"

"What's especially nice is that it gives fellows like yourself whose production has recently begun to sag, an opportunity to find redemption." Bascomb looked Don straight in the eye. "You know I'm in your corner, one hundred percent, but when the time comes to determine whether you make partner or get sent on your way, I'm just one vote. The remaining partners will have their says, and before they accept an associate into their club, they need assurance he plays the game their way."

Bascomb's words said one thing; his message, another. If Don was unwilling to do it Bascomb's way, then Bascomb didn't want Don on his team. And while Bascomb was only one vote, he was Don's mentor, and if your mentor failed to give you a *yea*, you were a guaranteed *nay*. "The plan makes good sense. As you aptly put it, 'It's a win-win.'"

"I knew you'd see it that way." Bascomb pumped a fist, though not nearly so high as a week earlier when he had holed a ten-footer on the eighteenth green giving himself and Don the win on a twenty-dollar Nassau at Bascomb's club. "I'm always glad to have you on my team." He smiled broadly and headed out of Don's office.

Don wasn't sure he could say the same, definitely not the day on the links. On the sixteenth hole, with their match tied, Bascomb drew a thick lie in the rough. With water looming between him and the green, his only avenue seemed a pitch out into the fairway. But a little nudge with his club head, and his ball sat nicely on a tuft of grass. A moment later, his finely struck shot onto the green kept the match even. When it finally ended on the eighteenth, Don hated to take their opponents' money. The alternative, calling his boss a cheater, was suicide. Afterwards at lunch, Don tried to share the check, but Bascomb simply signed the tab for the entire foursome. He even refused to let Don put his winnings on the table for the tip. Once the two were alone, Bascomb said, "I don't like to lose, but I owed those pigeons. Fair is fair."

With all the drinks that had been consumed at lunch, from a purely financial standpoint, Bascomb was the big loser. But fair? On the way out of the club, Don stuffed his winnings into a charity box to provide a scholarship for a deserving caddie. The gesture helped ease his conscience...a little. He told himself that Bascomb, not he, had cheated. Expecting him to kill his career in order to expose an ill-begotten golf bet was absurd. Unfortunately, the need to compromise himself was turning into a common theme. Recent financial trends, the bears, out of hibernation, clawing the bulls, had clients pulling money from their accounts. Kingman & Woodhill, a firm with a century-old tradition, enjoyed the finest of New York City digs. The overhead was huge. Everyone had to pull his weight. That included Don Burns.

Amidst America's densely populated, high-rise metropolises, desperately needed oases provide an escape from the dirt, cacophony, odors and incivility that plague the streets. How fortunate that the colonists of Boston, nearly a century and a-half before the nation was founded, had the sense and foresight to set aside the Commons in the center of their newly developing city; that William Penn preserved three squares for the people when founding Philadelphia; and that the Victorian moguls of the nineteenth century, pretentious and mercenary though they were, had a love of nature sufficient to adorn the heart of Manhattan with its singular masterpiece, Central Park. Had the task of preserving these once pristine lands been left to the devices of subsequent greedy developers and perfidious politicians, the havens that grace America's most historic cities might not exist.

Seated in the center of the rowboat that Linda and he had rented at Loeb Boathouse, Don Burns stroked through the waters of Central Park Lake. Rising among the trees that draped the shore was the impressive Manhattan skyline, its tallest buildings endeavoring to touch the puffy cumulus dotting the azure October sky. Still air allowed the glorious view to duplicate itself, albeit inverted, beneath the surface of the mirror-like lake. Don drew the oars from the water, allowing the boat to serendipitously drift according to nature's whim. He inhaled the cool, fresh, early Sunday morning air. He gazed at Linda who sat facing him in the stern. Her silky hair gleamed beneath the bedazzling coronet of the sun's rays. Her soft, rosy cheeks beckoned his caress. "God, you're beautiful."

"Flattery will get you everywhere." She smiled.

The urge to make love to her, out in the open, in the center of Manhattan, was powerful. Don looked around. Some people were strolling the shore. Several rowboats, one no farther away than fifty yards, cruised the placid waters. Don redirected his gaze to Linda. Desire was undeniable. Circumstances were prohibitive. Reluctantly carnal instincts yielded to discretion. He lowered the oars back into the water, pushing with the right and pulling with the left. The boat rotated clockwise. Off in the distance, the flag atop the witch's cap on the grand turret of the legendary Gothic and Romanesque Belvedere Castle drew his attention. The structure, reminiscent of the medieval fortress that decorated a lakeside cliff in northern Slovenia, transported him across the ocean to the area of Eastern Europe he had visited while spending a semester abroad his junior year in college. He closed his eyes. His mind transformed into a world of virtual reality. He was back amidst the magnificent, alien landscape, where countless Karst-region caves with prehistoric remnants revealed tales of people dating back to the Neolithic Age. When finally he re-opened his eyes, the rowboat had rotated, nearly re-orienting to its earlier position. A cloud temporarily blocking the sun cast an expansive shadow. Without the warm rays of Earth's great benefactor, a chill draped the landscape. The hint of autumn and the winter that lay beyond was undeniable. Shaded by the cloud, the bar-graph skyline of Manhattan was drabber than earlier. In less than twenty-four hours, Don would be back in his thirty-seventh-floor office at Kingman & Woodhill. Clients would have to be contacted. Nettling matters regarding their accounts would need to be addressed.

"You've got something on your mind."

The remark might have come as a surprise were Don not familiar with his wife's uncanny knack for reading him. "Pardon me?" he said, despite having heard her words.

"You have that familiar look. You can't fool me."

He shrugged, knowing the gesture was tantamount to an admission.

"So, what is it?"

Don heaved a sigh. "As I've told you, the past six months in the office have differed from those that preceded. The accounts of numerous clients have declined. Lots of them are unhappy. A few have moved their money elsewhere. The bottom line—the firm is facing tough times."

"And?"

"Bascomb paid me a visit on Friday. Like others in the firm, I've been encouraged to recommend vehicles that will enable clients to get a better return."

Linda shook her head.

"What's the matter?" His question was rhetorical. Camouflaging second-rate fish legs as king crab had not fooled Linda.

"I can guess what these new vehicles entail…a whole lot more risk and much larger fees for Kingman & Woodhill."

Her ability to absorb past lessons about the aspects of his business, normally a valued characteristic, was suddenly

119

unwelcome. Don glanced in the direction of Belvedere Castle. Its impenetrable granite parapets were far more effective than the stone face he endeavored to display.

"So, what are you going to do?"

"C'mon...what can I do?" His instinctive effort to dodge her question rang hollow. Even as he focused on the watery expanse, he could feel her chiding stare trying to engage him. "Okay, you're right. There is additional risk, but that's the price of a potentially higher return." The explanation, nearly as bogus as its predecessor, had him swallowing hard. Her silence confirmed the analysis. "Fine...you tell me what I should do."

She shook her head slowly, but demonstratively. "Don't think for a moment you can push the problem off onto me."

"You're right. It's my dilemma, and I have to deal with it."

She nodded. "Now that you're talking sense, I'm glad to be a sounding board."

He laughed.

"What's so funny?"

"Me...Thinking I could cleverly duck the issue. By now I ought to know that you'd wait me out, force me to face it straight on."

A smile, a demure one, greeted his concession.

The look, every bit as seductive as the one that had him hot and bothered earlier, rekindled amorous designs. Judgment had already proscribed their prompt fulfillment. He reached out and took her hand. "I move we spend a quiet afternoon alone in our apartment."

She leaned forward and kissed him. "Your motion is seconded and carried."

He that repeateth a matter separateth his friends. So says the Bible in the Book of Proverbs, Chapter XVII, Verse 9. But wise though the Bible may be, repetition is not without merit. Knowledge often flows from such. And too, a difficult task may grow easier. As for friendships...much like the consequences of war, collateral damage.

For the better part of two days, Don had been calling clients. The first had involved considerable delay. Even with ample rehearsals, he had hung up the receiver twice before finally entering the entire number. When at last the call connected, the client, eager for an improved return, was enthusiastic. The element of risk never came up. The next call was more challenging. The client immediately voiced a question about the dreaded issue. But Don, though far from comfortable, had prepared his response. He took his cue from countless television pharmaceutical commercials, where honey-tongued barkers, backed by soothing music, delineated side effects such as heart attacks, strokes and death as if they were blessings. Warnings about risks, a shield from lawsuits, were given to consumers, but not without masterful camouflage.

"I'm glad you asked," said Don. "Naturally there's increased risk. That's the fundamental concept underlying all investing. The greater the potential return, the higher the risk. The two go hand in hand."

"But do you believe this new product is worth the risk?"

"Rather than offering my humble opinion, I refer you to the position of our firm's investment research analysts, as fine as any in the industry. They're encouraging our clients to go with the Silver Sky Fund." The response was masterful, not for its prose, but its content. It was entirely accurate. Kingman & Woodhill did have a top-notch research team, and the firm was recommending the product to all their clients. The reason for the recommendation was left unsaid. What Don especially liked about his response was that it circumvented the need for him to give a personal endorsement.

"The recent decline in my account reflected in my monthly statements has me concerned. It's reassuring to know your firm keeps an eye on things."

"That's our job. We're always concerned about our clients." Again the statement was truthful. Building a client's assets was a goal of the firm. Not only was it important in order to retain accounts, but also to encourage the investment of additional funds. What Don failed to mention was that the firm's number one concern was its bottom line, not its clients.

"Well, okay. Move my moneys into Silver Sky."

"Glad to see you've decided to take the plunge." With a quick exchange of final pleasantries, the call ended. Don leaned back. Though a tiny pang persisted, he felt far more relaxed than when he had prepared to make the call. Potential rancor had not materialized. The task had been completed without a single lie. Omissions, perhaps, but no overtly false representations.

Unlike the day when he had solicited fellow graduates from Williams to open new accounts, his first call had not been to a friend. Instead he had contacted clients with whom his relationship was purely business. All through that workday and into the next he continued with more calls. The vast majority, nearly two-thirds, opted for Silver Sky. The success rate lessened the need to pressure those who were reluctant. Indeed, he avoided the use of any high-pressure salesmanship. Don was nearly at the end of his list when he pulled up Bill Young's information on his computer. The account, originally small, had grown, not from performance, but from an additional deposit Bill had made.

After a quick perusal of the data, he dialed Bill's number. Upon hearing the familiar voice, Don said, "Hi Bill. It's Don Burns. How've you been?"

"Can't complain. What's new in the big town?"

"Same old...same old." Back in his freshman English course at Williams, Don had learned to minimize the use of clichés. But as a stockbroker, where gab was a way of life, they came in handy. "Let me guess—you're lying on a Gulf Coast beach?"

"No, but just as good. I'm sitting on a bench at the Edison Estate along the Caloosahatchee River...doing my writing."

"Man, you've got it made. And probably no sympathy for us poor slobs who toil in the sweat shops of Manhattan's cement edifices."

A protracted groan preceded a more articulate response. "If I had a violin, I'd play 'Hearts and Flowers.'"

"Off tune, no doubt." The quip's failure to evoke anticipated repartee compelled Don to press forward. "The reason I'm calling has to do with your account."

"You mean that thing that's like a block of ice in the sunshine—always shrinking?"

"I know...returns have been less than stellar."

"That's an understatement."

"Well, that's why I'm calling. Perhaps we can improve the trend. Our firm is recommending a new product, the Silver Sky Fund."

"What is it?"

"An equity fund...comprised of relatively aggressive growth stocks." Don surprised himself when he uttered the second phase. His conscience had cajoled him to give Bill, a fellow Inseparable, a better picture of the offering.

"Aggressive...that means more speculative. Right?"

"Speculative is not really fair. Admittedly, it entails more risk, but its upside potential far exceeds what you have now." Though the analysis was accurate, it ignored the key issue, whether the upside potential justified the risk.

"You think it's good?"

Would I be calling you? Don shunned the glib reply, one that he had used in a couple of earlier calls. "Well, as I said, it's less conservative than your current fund, but it will open the door to a much better return." The need to please his boss, to produce good results, was face to face with a desire to be up front. Unfortunately, the two goals were anything but consistent. "A good way to do it is with diversification: Move part of your account."

"Well...I could use more diversification. What say we put fifty percent in...what's the name of that fund you're touting?"

"Silver Sky."

"Fine. Put fifty percent in Silver Sky."

You won't regret it. The phrase, another of Don's favorite clichés, was too hard to voice. Instead he said, "Diversifying is a sound strategy. I like it." As he concluded the call, he silently assessed the result. He did indeed like it, though admittedly it was far from perfect. He eyed his list. There was only one call left...Eric Johanson. The distasteful chore was almost done.

Thus far, it had gone well, and the consternation he had felt when he had begun his calls had all but dissipated. Even the remaining call to Eric, as difficult as any, seemed less onerous. His conversation with Bill had provided an excellent model.

He pulled up the account on his computer. It showed a balance of slightly more than thirteen thousand dollars. If this were his first call, rather than his last, triskaidekaphobia would have spooked him sufficiently to push it aside in favor of another client. Still he was not ready to ignore the omen. He checked his calendar. Fortunately, it was the eleventh of the month. Had it been the thirteenth, an exacta, he would have postponed the call to the following morning.

Moments after he had pressed the final digit, a voice rife with lethargy answered.

"Granite Casualty and Life…Eric Johanson speaking."

"Hello Eric. It's Don Burns. How've you been?"

"Okay…And you?"

Don had planned to engage in considerable small talk before turning to business. The need for such an approach had become more pronounced. "I'm doing pretty well, at least well enough that I can't complain. How are things at the insurance company?"

"Okay." The lifeless voice said otherwise.

Don wondered if Eric might be sending a not-so-subtle message that he knew the call during business hours was not social and that he had no desire to be solicited. With the rest of his calls completed and his success rate more than satisfactory and a foreboding number displayed on his computer screen, Don decided not to press his luck. "Sounds like I caught you at a bad time. I can—"

"No, it's not that…and sorry, it's…it's just that I'm not myself."

Don waited a moment. "Is something the matter?"

A languid moan seemed to confirm the speculation.

"Anything I can do to help?"

"Perhaps…if you're skilled at casting spells on a reluctant angel."

The comment jogged Don's memory. He had all but forgotten that when last they had spoken, Eric was gloomy, a consequence of Glenna having dumped him. "Is it Glenna?"

"What else?"

Don waited a moment, hoping a fuller explanation might be forthcoming without the need for additional questions. "Has she at least explained why she broke up with you?"

"She has refused to discuss it. And yesterday, she made it final. She asked that I not call her anymore, and her tone suggested it was an order, not a request."

Unable to summon appropriate words of comfort, Don opted for a patient ear.

"I just don't understand. The breakup was so sudden and now, so final. I've tried a hundred times to figure it out, but it makes no sense. The only logical possibility is another guy. It's hard to accept, but for want of anything else, I must. Hell—if she had simply decided that I wasn't the right guy for her, she would have let me down easier. I'd bet on that. On the other hand, if she found another guy, he may have insisted that she cut off all ties with me. And to think, I was ready to give her a ring."

"I'm really sorry." Don wished he could offer more comforting words, but he didn't know what to say.

"Thanks...but anyway, I imagine your call had a purpose other than to hear my whining."

From the moment Eric had begun discussing his misfortune, Don had decided to leave Silver Sky for another time. "You've got enough on your plate. No need for me to bother you with mundane nothings."

"Just the opposite. Much as I may not be eager, I have to get on with my life. The more I wallow, the worse it gets. So, good, bad or indifferent, whatever the reason for your call, lay it on me."

Don hemmed and hawed. With his friend in pain, he preferred to put business on the back burner.

"If you close down now, you'll only make me feel worse. So, let's have it."

"Well..." The oily rehearsed patter that had flowed so easily during many calls suddenly turned viscous. "The firm

125

is...uh...recommending that our clients shift moneys into a new vehicle. It's the...uh...Silver Sky Fund. It's a—"

"If your firm likes it, then do it."

"It's a more aggressive growth fund...uh...a little riskier than what—"

"You guys are the experts. And especially given my current state, outside guidance is particularly important."

Don suspected that the element of risk had flown over Eric's head. Even if he had heard it, and that was dubious, in his state of mind, he certainly hadn't weighed the issue. "You're sure?"

"Absolutely. So, do it. I'm—Oh, our Administrative Assistant just signaled that my boss wants to see me immediately. If you don't mind, I'll say goodbye."

"No problem. You take care."

"You too."

An instant later the telephone clicked. Don stared at the receiver, yet to be returned to its cradle. The arduous task, something he had dreaded all weekend, was finally complete. An impressive percentage, higher than he had anticipated, had signed on to Silver Sky. The partners, his mentor Charlie Bascomb included, were bound to be pleased. Don was as well, though he would have preferred a product that left him more confident that he had put his clients' interests at the forefront. But Silver Sky was a reasonable collection of equities. There was potential for significant growth. It would do well...he hoped.

Put a child in an environment where integrity is lauded in speech but compromised in practice, and confusion is possible. Far more likely, however, example will supersede rhetoric. In some respects, adults are like children. Place an adult under the tutelage of a shark, and razor-like teeth are apt to gnaw away at earlier inculcated principles.

"Something smells awfully good," said Don, as he opened the door to his uptown apartment. He stepped into the kitchen and pecked Linda on the cheek. "You smell very good too."

"Like flounder?"

"Uh…more like clams." The askance look that greeted his words gave him pause. "Only teasing."

"How'd your day go? Is the ordeal *finis*?"

"Yup."

"And…what's the verdict?"

"It went well. Unlike many of the other associates, the majority of my clients made the move to Silver Sky."

"That's great. Appears your worries that the increased risk would outweigh the opportunity for a better return were unjustified."

Don reached for the newspaper.

"Wait a second. Your response, or should I say lack thereof, was ambiguous."

Don focused on the front-page headline, ignoring his wife's overture.

"Did you tell your clients they were taking on greater risk?"

"Whenever they asked."

"Whenever they asked!" Linda flipped a pot holder onto the counter. "Is that all you told them?"

"I told them the fund was more aggressive, that it entailed added risk."

"But did you detail the level of that risk and to what extent it increased their upside potential, both the likelihood and the extent? In other words, did you explain it in a way that they could make an informed decision?" Linda stood stone-faced with folded arms.

"Jeez, whad'ya expect me to do? Tell them that I think it's a bad idea?"

"Yes, if that's what you thought." Linda looked Don in the eye. "If it was your money, would you have switched to Silver Sky?"

"C'mon, that's not fair. You know I had Bascomb and the rest of the partners breathing down my neck. I didn't have a choice."

"Didn't have a choice?"

Don hated when Linda repeated his statements, especially when it came in the form of a question. Her incredulous tone chopped his glib remarks to shreds. "You can't expect me to commit career hara-kiri."

She shook her head. "How do you expect me to react—praise you for putting your interests ahead of your clients?" She gave him a look. "Let me guess. Any mention of increased fees was also skipped...unless the clients asked?"

In an effort to gain refuge from the question, Don focused on the newspaper, not that his brain could process the printed words.

"Just as I thought."

The need to defend himself had become imperative. "You're ignoring the fact that my clients have an excellent opportunity for a better return."

"True."

The possibility that he had turned the tide had him breathing a sigh of relief, but a short-lived one.

"But they also have a better chance of losing their shirts." Linda waited a moment. "What about your friends? Were you at least up front with them?"

Don's last call of the day to Eric flashed into his mind. In his depressed state, Eric would have done anything Don suggested. He was depending upon Don. The scenario underscored the merit of Linda's comments. He said, "This entire discussion assumes a bad outcome. The Silver Sky Fund has a lot of potential. There's a good chance it will do very well, and my clients will be thanking me."

Linda brought him a plate bedecked with breaded flounder, cheese-coated broccoli and a sweet potato laced with cinnamon butter. "For your sake, as well as theirs, I hope so."

CHAPTER IX

IN THE AUTUMN OF THE YEAR, when crisp leaves turn gold and red and orange, to stroll over the lush green rolling fairways of a manicured mountain golf course is to commune with the enigmatic realm that stretches far beyond earthly boundaries. At every turn, another summit touching its lips to the Heavens beckons one to paradise. No matter the strokes needed for the dimpled sphere to descend into the abyss, uplifted spirits soar.

Kyle Gordon sat in the pristine white clubhouse of the Taconic Country Club, along with the other three Inseparables. Over three years had slipped by since they had graduated, and far more than a year had passed since all four had been together. It had taken considerable arm-twisting to get Bill up from Florida. Even though they had only a weekend, with the fall spectacular in full display, they were happy to allot five hours for a trip around the glorious layout. Carved from the rolling Berkshire Mountains, the course, owned by their alma mater, had been rated the most beautiful in Massachusetts by the *Boston Globe*. The faithful claimed the seventeenth hole, a part of the original nineteenth-century layout, was the oldest in America.

With the scorecard's final tallies added, Bill turned to Kyle. "You didn't even break a hundred."

"And the amazing part," said Don, "he managed to maintain a smile the entire time."

Ordinarily Kyle would have met the banter with sarcasm, a barb armed with the full force of a sand wedge exploding a ball from a bunker. But a glance out the big picture window prompted a far more delicate shot. "Hey, with such an incredible setting, how could anyone complain?" He looked around the table. Old habits, spurred by fond memories, triggered irresistible temptation. He adopted a theatrically thoughtful mien. "On second thought, some better company to share the day would have been nice."

Eric nodded. "Yeah the three of us spent the entire round saying exactly that about you."

Kyle happily swallowed the gibe. Slipping back into the daftness of their college days was fun; seeing Eric bounce back from his doldrums, a huge bonus. "Sure, you guys are all ganging up on the poor stockbroker from Springfield." He took a moment to eye both Bill and Eric. "No doubt our buddy from the Big Apple wined and dined you for your business, just so he'd have a three against one when we gathered here."

"As a matter of fact," said Bill, "he got my account without even buying me a *Coke*."

"Make that two of us," said Eric. "But let's say we start rectifying that immediately." He gestured at Don. "Guess what, my friend, the check for lunch today is all yours."

"Even for Gordon?"

"For the whole foursome," said Bill. "After all, you got our business, so you get the check."

"I'd say you guys are giving me *the business*…right now. But sport that I am, okay." Don smiled.

Kyle did likewise, though only inwardly. A moment earlier he had been the target. Now Don was getting a turn. They all got theirs, and they welcomed it because the seeming taunts bore affection.

"By the way," said Eric, "that Silver Sky Fund you got Bill and me into is looking pretty good. It's nice to see my monthly account balance head north, rather than south."

"I'm glad it's working out," said Don.

Kyle was familiar with the aggressive growth fund. It was not one he recommended to his clients. Knowing Eric and Bill were hardly the Las Vegas type, he was surprised they hadn't opted for something more conservative. Curious though he was, because they were not his clients, he kept the thought to himself.

"You guys all remember Gary Parker?" said Eric.

"Of course," said Don. "No one could forget the King of Pranks."

"Remember the time he made caramel apples for Halloween," said Bill. "But instead of apples, the clown used onions."

"Typical Gary," said Eric. "Anyway, it just so happens he's moved to Hartford, taken a job at Travelers. He and I have lunch together about once a month."

"Is he still playing his jokes?" said Kyle.

Eric's brow furrowed. "Presumably that was a rhetorical question. Why just last month, when we had lunch, he put clear plastic tape over both the ear piece and the speaker of my cell phone. I had left it on the table when I went to the rest room. It wasn't until just before I went to bed that I discovered his stunt, why I could barely hear anything on the device all day."

"I bet you wanted to wring his neck," said Kyle.

Eric shook his head. "Matter of fact, I laughed when I realized what he had done."

"There's something about Gary," said Don. "Even when he infuriates you, it's hard to be mad at him. And before any of you dis me for my last comment's lack of logic, I'm changing the subject." He directed himself to Kyle. "When you going to introduce us to Katelyn?"

"I met her three months ago," said Eric. "Can't imagine what a peach like her sees in our buddy." He heaved a sigh. "Wish I could find one like her. Then again, I did. Unfortunately, she dumped me."

Kyle had been poised to return the dig, but his pal's pain altered his approach. "Well, the truth be known, it's Glenna's loss."

"Yeah…sure."

"Have you been dating since?" said Don.

Eric shrugged. "Now and then, but nothing to write home about. This guy at work fixed me up with his cousin. Told me she was a ten. Turned out she was more like a twelve…on a scale of fifty. There was this one girl I dated a couple of times. She was attractive and intelligent, and she had a nice personality, but…"

"But what?" said Bill.

"She wasn't Glenna." Eric heaved a sigh. "I know. I need to move on."

Kyle had no intention of giving advice. He silently let the comment stand. Don and Bill did so too.

"In some respects, I've done that. I'm not down in the dumps anymore...well nothing like the first few months after she gave me the heave-ho. But I have to admit I'm not doing all that well when it comes to the dating scene. Anyone I go out with, I compare to Glenna. And yes, I know, now that I'm seeing her with hindsight, I've put her on a pedestal, one so high that Aphrodite couldn't measure up."

Another silent hiatus greeted Eric's assessment.

"C'mon, can't you guys say anything?"

Kyle exchanged blank looks with Don and Bill. Finally, Bill said, "Not much to add. You said it all yourself."

"I suppose that's true."

"Well...if it's any consolation," said Bill, "my love life is pretty much on par with yours."

"Any predictions by the two old married men," said Eric, "who's destined to be the curmudgeon bachelor? Will Bill grab the honor, or will it be me?"

"As for the bachelor part, I've got no clue," said Don. "But married or not, when it comes to curmudgeon, you're both sure things. And don't give me a look because you know I'm right." He turned to Kyle. "Tell them."

"Don't expect me to get you out of the rough." A furrowing brow added depth to Kyle's jab. "By the way, did you fellows hear that Clint Horstmeyer has taken a job as a stockbroker here in Springfield? He's with a firm by the name of Quigley and Watkins."

"Their misfortune," said Don. He looked at Kyle. "How come *you* didn't hire him?"

Were Kyle with someone other than his college buddies, he would have simply dismissed the question with a laugh. "As a matter of fact, Clint sent us a resumé."

"Really?" Don's eyes were sunny-side eggs.

"Of course, I'm kidding. But given that you asked the ridiculous question, I thought it merited an equally ridiculous answer. Truth is: Clint would never want to work with me. Chop me into little pieces and fry me in a blast furnace is more likely. Regardless, my boss, who's on the verge of retirement, isn't looking to add anyone new. Even if he were, the devil himself would be a more likely choice than Clint."

"Once your boss retires, assuming he does," said Bill, "will you take over the firm?"

"Well…it's not cast in stone, and not something I would share with most people, certainly not folks around Springfield, but just between us, Larry and I have already worked out the details. It's all but a *fait accompli*."

Alligators have roamed the Earth for eons, far longer than man. Thick skin shields the leathery amphibians from trauma. An elfin brain incapable of creating memories of complex misfortunes enables them to escape life's emotional vicissitudes. Such are the anomalies of nature.

Bill Young, just home from a day of teaching, turned the key to his mailbox. The open door revealed three items: an advertisement offering a Chevrolet Malibu for an astoundingly low price; an envelope from his doctor, no doubt a bill; and a letter from Spellbinders, Inc.

Briefcase in one hand, his mail in the other, he headed to his second-floor apartment. He dropped his briefcase by the door and went into the kitchen where he tossed the mail onto the table. Rather than open it, he went to the refrigerator for a bottle of Four-Buck Chuck from Trader Joe's. Wine was rarely part of his afternoon. Indeed Chuck, half-empty following a friend's visit, had been in the refrigerator for the best part of three weeks. Bill's Mormon roots, its rules against alcohol, had regained a foothold, but beliefs developed during a liberal education were yet to yield to conservative principles learned in childhood. He rationalized that a drink now and then did no harm. And in the face of all-but-inevitable bad news, perhaps it could mitigate disappointment. He poured a glass and sat down at the kitchen table. He folded the Malibu offer into a paper airplane and sailed it in the direction of the garbage can, not that it was possible to land it in the tightly sealed container. He tore open the letter from his doctor. The charge of $18.27 after insurance was more than acceptable. A quick swig of Chuck, final preparation for the inevitable, and he reached for Spellbinders' letter. The skinny envelope bore all the earmarks with which colleges sent bad tidings to applicants. He held it up to the light. The technique revealed nothing. He slit open the envelope. Inside was a printed card that read:

> *We regret to inform you that your manuscript does not fit our needs. Our best wishes for future success with your writing career.*

Bill eyed the card a second time. It was his fifth rejection and, with the exception of one, fit the pattern, a missile as thoughtful as a tiny, blank cement gravestone. He leaned back and guzzled the remaining few ounces of Chuck. People had warned him that like an alligator, writing required a thick skin. Bill had that. But the similarity to the big-toothed reptiles that roamed his Everglades environs ended there. Bill was more like an elephant. He had a memory…and, for that matter, feelings. He gazed blankly at the ceiling for more than a minute before reading the card one more time. He folded it into another paper airplane and sailed it in the direction of the garbage can. With a perfect landing, it came to rest atop the lid of the big dumper. From all indications, his writing career was headed there too.

Free means free. Not always. Sometimes there are invisible strings. They may not be measured in dollars and cents, but the cost is there. And sometimes that cost, be it in the form of indebtedness, frustration, guilt or vexation, dwarfs the value of that which was supposedly free.

"Can I buy you a drink?"

As he heard the words and felt a hand on his shoulder, Kyle Gordon, just a few feet from the bar at the monthly meeting of the Springfield Brokers' Association, turned and saw Clinton Horstmeyer, who had approached from behind. "Uh...okay...a white zinfandel, thanks." Had he not been caught by surprise, Kyle might have refused the offer. There was even the possibility that Clint's overture was a sadistic device to make Kyle uncomfortable, rather than an act of generosity. Admittedly the view was cynical, but it was indeed possible, given their past at Williams, the *F* that Clint had received on his philosophy paper and his claim that Kyle's meddling had ruined his relationship with Carla Pender.

Clint squeezed his way to the bar and soon returned with two glasses, one a white zinfandel that he handed to Kyle and the other a mixed drink for himself.

"Thanks...and I've got the next round." Kyle would have been happy with a single drink, but being indebted to Clint, even for a measly libation, was unacceptable. "So, how do you like being a broker here in Springfield?"

"Early returns indicate it's right up my alley. Gaffney, a top dog at the firm, has taken a shine to me. Says I have big potential. Called me executive material. Even encouraged me to join the Springfield Golf and Country Club. Sure, it costs a few shekels, but already it's starting to pay off. Just last week I teamed up with Woody Jensen, the owner of Holland Lumber. I knocked in a birdie on eighteen to win our match against a couple of hotshot contractors. During lunch at the nineteenth, I convinced Jensen to open an account. Not bad—play golf, beat the suckers and line up an income stream, all in the sunshine. But hey, when you got what it takes, you..."

As Clint droned, Kyle kept his eyes trained on the self-important salesman. His brain, however, tuned out the words. He could only endure brief doses of Clint, at most ten nanoseconds. Then again, even that was too long. No doubt there were some from their graduating class whose personalities would transform, but equally sure, a few like Clint would be as constant as Old Faithful. Bragging, the showboat's quintessence, was an eternal given, at least that's how Kyle saw it.

"You agree, don'tcha?"

"Uh…pardon me."

Clint's brow furrowed, perhaps a reflection he sensed his monologue had been ignored. "I asked whether Rockland plans to pack it in soon."

Though his boss's plans to retire seemed firm, Kyle preferred to be circumspect, especially with a character like Clint. "If you really want an answer, you'd have to ask Larry."

"You mean to say you took a job with the guy, and you've got no clue about your future?"

Kyle struggled to bite his tongue.

"If he decides to stick around, does he plan to make you a partner?"

"Tell you what," said Kyle, mustering maximum sarcasm. "Once I find out, I'll make sure you're the first to know."

"Hey, it's your future. If you don't care about it, why should I?"

Kyle gulped the final swig of his wine, the act a device to stifle a snarl. The momentary hiatus enabled him to adopt a more prudent strategy. "I'm sure our paths will cross from time to time, now that we're both here in Springfield. Enjoy the rest of the meeting."

"Excuse me."

The sardonic tone slowed Kyle's planned departure.

"I thought you promised to buy the next round."

Kyle swallowed hard. No way would he give Clint a reason to call him a cheapskate. "What are you drinking?"

"Seven and Seven…on the rocks."

"Wait here. I'll be right back." A minute later, Kyle returned with a single glass that he handed to Clint.

"Where's yours?"

"I'm driving."

Clint's wide eyes were riddled with derision. "You can't handle a second white zinfandel?"

Not when it includes your company. "These days you can't be too careful." Kyle ignored the groan that greeted his words. "Enjoy your drink." He walked away.

Be it a day or two or many, sooner or later, clouds, gray and ominous, darken even the bluest of skies.

Seated at his desk, Don Burns took an extra sip of his coffee before examining the quarterly report of the Silver Sky Fund. He needed a boost in advance of facing the numbers. It wasn't a matter of bracing for a huge surprise. The data would merely put an exclamation point on the information he already had. Silver Sky was tanking.

He flipped to the third page and the fund performance. It was down thirty-one percent. If the entire equity market had suffered a similar downturn, it could be largely explained away. But the Standard and Poor's Index had risen two percent over the same period. Silver Sky*'s* precipitous drop was attributable to its own portfolio. As with many venture capital portfolios, the aggressive fund had its share of losers. That was to be expected. Prior to the preceding quarter, among Silver Sky's fifteen investments, it had a seeming home run and three others that looked extremely good. In the world of venture capital, that was the kind of batting average that would enable it to easily surpass the broader markets.

Don moved to the section of the report that updated the status of the individual investments. A patent infringement lawsuit suggested that one of the potential stars was nothing more than a second-rate minor leaguer. Another was looking bad because the scouts had failed to do due diligence. The business model on which the company had obtained financing from Silver Sky was based upon spurious data. And the sure-fired home run had curved foul. A competitor had not only built the proverbial better mousetrap, but it had done so at a lower cost.

Don checked the summaries for the rest of the line-up. Three months earlier none appeared as though it was destined for the Hall of Fame. Another quarter reinforced that conclusion. Don gazed up at the ceiling. The stadium where he worked, his little office, had a roof, but the ominous skies were palpable. The game was past the fifth inning. Once the downpour came, and it was all but certain, the results would go into the books with Silver Sky on the short end. He reached for his coffee mug and took another swig. He needed some sustenance before responding to a message that Eric Johanson had left on his voicemail. With the quarterly report in his clients' hands, it was a safe bet that more of them would be calling. Exactly how he would field their questions was less clear. He dialed Eric's number.

"Granite Casualty and Life. Johanson here."

"Hi Eric. It's Don, returning your call. How've you been?"

"Pretty good. And you?"

"No complaints." Don would have continued the empty small talk were he not convinced that it would merely delay the inevitable. "What can I do for you?"

"This morning I received the quarterly report for Silver Sky. Not too rosy."

Disputing the obvious was futile. "I hear what you're saying."

"Any suggestions?"

"Well…it may not be as bad as it looks."

"If I translate that correctly, you agree it's bad."

Applauding a batting average that was down near one hundred and still declining was absurd. "On its face, it's not great, but…" Don felt himself pushed back into a corner. Bascomb had made it clear what needed to be done. "Very often a bad patch is a golden opportunity."

"Just how do you figure that?" An edge slipped into Eric's voice.

"For someone like you who's buying with a regular payroll deduction, the decrease in price means you're getting more shares for the same dollars. In the long run, that could really pay off."

"C'mon, don't treat me like a naïve kid."

"What's that supposed to mean?" Don understood where Eric was coming from, but for lack of a better comeback, resorted to the pretense of confusion.

"It's one thing when a security with great fundamentals drops because the whole market is taking a dip. Buying low, taking advantage of dollar-cost averaging is great, but throwing more dough into a sinking ship is a different matter."

"Who says Silver Sky is a sinking ship?"

"Based upon the quarterly report, it has all the earmarks of the Titanic."

The assessment bore too much truth to simply dismiss it. "If that's how you feel, then perhaps you shouldn't buy any more shares."

"Yeah...and maybe sell the ones I have."

"Damn, if you do that, you'll take a big hit." *And Kingman & Woodhill will stop getting commissions, and my chances to become a partner will suffer.*

"But at least I'll get something for my investment. On the other hand, if I wait, I might get zilch."

"With any investment, that's always a risk." The cliché triggered a pang. Eric was a friend, and Don had led him into the chancy fund.

"What do you think? Is Silver Sky likely to turn around?"

The echo of Bascomb's voice had Don wanting to say *yes*, but evidence the other way was compelling. "To be honest...I don't have a crystal ball."

"I understand, but as my advisor...and a friend...what do you think?"

"Given the current state of affairs, a turn-around may be tough." Don made the concession in part from moral obligation, but as much because an argument to the contrary would come across as disingenuous.

"It's what I figured, not that it was rocket science given the report." Eric heaved a sigh. "Let's stop my payroll deduction purchases. No sense throwing more good money after bad. As for my current holdings in Silver Sky..."

Rather than interrupting the inordinately long pause, Don simply waited for the verdict.

"...leave them as they are, at least for now."

"Sounds like a good strategy." The platitude dripped from Don's tongue as if it were a badly leaking faucet. An instant later, its annoying impact reverberated in his ears. Bad enough he had induced his pal to invest in what had turned out to be a loser. His apparent lack of concern in that outcome had been laid bare.

"I've got a call on the other line. Gotta go."

"You take care." The almost simultaneous click of the telephone suggested that Eric may not have heard those final words. Don stared briefly at the receiver before hanging up. Dissatisfied clients and an unhappy boss, both a product of diminishing returns, were stripping the fun from work. Back when investments were flying high, it was schmooze, laugh and reap the benefits. With his number one offering, Silver Sky, tanking, stress and frustration had crept in. An ominous dark cloud hung low over what once had been a ball game in the sunshine. From all indications, a cacophonous thunderstorm loomed large.

Alas, when the ordeals of life wreak havoc, what better source of strength and solace than home and loved ones.

"How'd your day go, Hon?" Linda set a glass of Merlot alongside the *New York Times* that lay waiting on the kitchen table.

Don pecked her on the cheek. "Pretty good." Understanding his two-word answer, one that he used on most days, required focus on inflection, rather than content. Most times it bore enthusiasm with an emphasis on the *good*. Recently there had been a trend toward a more somber tone, and the heavy sigh that followed on that evening belied the convenient phrase.

"What happened?"

He seated himself and sipped his wine. "I spent most of the day absorbing the grumbles of clients, who, like me, had just received Silver Sky's quarterly report."

"Well…at least it didn't come as a surprise. I mean their reactions. All along you knew they'd be upset."

"I know, but that's hardly a great consolation. Kinda like when you were a kid and knew you were gonna catch hell for misbehaving. Advance knowledge of the wrath did nothing to lessen the pain."

Linda, who was making a salad, halted her chopping of a carrot and directed her full attention to Don. "So, did many of your clients pull their accounts?"

"Only a couple. But a bunch sold their shares in Silver Sky. And a few others ended their payroll deduction purchases. Eric Johanson was among those in the last category." Technically Don was supposed to keep information about his clients' files confidential, but he always shared everything with Linda. He needed a place outside the office to vent. He suspected that most of his colleagues did so too, though few admitted it. Back in the office, Don never did.

"What about Bill Young? Did he pull the plug...either on his account or Silver Sky?"

"Nope."

"He didn't?"

Out of the corner of his eye, Don, who was seeking refuge in his *New York Times*, caught a glimpse of Linda turning his way. Rather than engage her, he maintained his focus on the newspaper.

"So, Bill is satisfied with Silver Sky?"

"I guess so." The terse reply floated from Don's lips.

"What do you mean? You guess so."

Don finally looked up. "Just what I said."

Linda, hands on hips, was glaring. Her silence suggested she expected a more substantive response.

"Well...he didn't voice any objection."

"Did you talk to him about it?"

"No, but I'd be glad to."

"Very kind of you."

"Don't be sarcastic." Even as he voiced the reaction, Don questioned its prudence.

Linda shook her head. "Don't you think Bill is entitled to your guidance?"

"I'm always ready to provide it." Thoughts of the assessment of Silver Sky he had given Eric stirred pangs. "It's not like he's in the dark. It's all laid out in the quarterly report."

"Where—on page twenty-seven in the nethermost reaches of an arcane piece of mumbo jumbo? And just to put matters into perspective, what percentage of your clients read anything beyond the opening summary, if they even read that?"

"How should I know?"

She shook her head again.

"What's the matter now?"

"The point is—and you know it—most of your clients don't read the voluminous gobbledygook that fills those reports."

Discretion kept Don from claiming that clients could only blame themselves for such inattention. The excuse would only amplify Linda's ire. And too, it didn't fly; certainly not in Bill's case. He had invested in Silver Sky relying on Don's advice. Supposedly Don was looking out for his friend's interests. Little did Bill realize that Don was peddling that which Kingman & Woodhill was pushing; that which would yield far bigger commissions for the firm; and that which would enhance Don's career. But telling that to Bill was unthinkable. Once again, Don sought sanctuary in his *New York Times*. He gulped the remainder of his Merlot, hoping to blunt an echoing conscience. The several ounces of alcohol were of no help. In all likelihood, a liter would have been ineffective.

CHAPTER X

AN EXCELLENT ADMINISTRATIVE ASSISTANT can be a boss's greatest asset. Some bosses recognize this. Others do not.

"Nice to meet you, Rachel." Her handshake was firm. "Okay if I call you by your first name? And please, call me Kyle." He ushered the attractive brunette into his office. As he gestured her to a seat, she handed him a résumé. He seated himself behind his desk and perused the document. "Very nice. I see you completed a Clerical Certificate Program at Quinsigamond Community College. What exactly did that entail?"

"It was a yearlong program with a total of nine courses."

"And what were some of the more important ones?"

"Keyboarding Applications, Business Office Procedures and English Composition. It also included a course in web-page development."

"That's good because we've been talking about creating a web page for our firm." He eyed Rachel Wallace's résumé. "I see that you keyboard eighty words per minute."

"Yes, and in high school I was one of three business students awarded a commendation for my keyboarding."

"Excellent...You're currently working at Quigley and Watkins. Right?"

"Yes, I've been there for nearly four years. During that time, I've had all sorts of clerical duties...preparing documents, photocopying, entering data, filing, reception, you name it. I'm even licensed to execute trades."

"That's excellent experience. Pretty much what we're looking for. Of course, we're a smaller firm, just Larry Rockland, our current Administrative Assistant and me. And Larry will be retiring in a few months." Kyle would not have made the disclosure, but for the fact that Rockland, just a week before, had publicly announced his departure. "Down the road I may bring in an associate, but for the foreseeable future, I'll be the only broker. Our Administrative Assistant's husband, an engineer, was recently transferred to California. They'll be leaving in a month. That's the reason for the opening for which you've applied." Kyle hesitated, trying to ensure his next question did not sound impertinent. Over the years, he had interviewed for various jobs. Most involved nothing more than summer employment. The interviews had been brief, almost perfunctory. This was his first time on the opposite side of the desk. "Tell me a little more about yourself." Though the question was far too general to elicit the information he was seeking, he reasoned it was preferable to sticking his foot into his mouth.

"I'm not sure what you're asking."

"Well..." For an instant, it was as if he were back on the other side of the table. "Uh...anything that would help me know you better...or anything you'd like me to know."

"Let's see...I was born an only child in Sandusky, Ohio. Mom was a single parent. She died of a heart attack right after my eighteenth birthday." Rachel heaved a sigh. "Ever since, I've been on my own. I didn't have any family, not even an aunt or an uncle. All during my days at Quinsigamond, I waitressed part time to get by. That, plus a partial scholarship and a tiny insurance policy Mom had purchased, got me through."

Kyle scribbled a note: *diligent, self-starter*. "What prompted you to answer our ad?"

"It sounded interesting."

Discretion had enabled Kyle to avoid the risk of embarrassment. It had even yielded some useful information. But it had left unanswered the question still uppermost in his mind. If he wanted a response, he needed to risk impertinence. He would have to be direct. "Is there a particular reason you're looking to leave your present position?" Just a few days before, Kyle had seen an advertisement in the *Springfield Republican* indicating that Quigley and Watkins was looking to add two more associates. With that prestigious firm expanding, why would Rachel Wallace want to move to the office of Larry Rockland? Kyle said, "Given Quigley and Watkins' size, they must have a nice fringe benefits package, presumably better than what you'll get here."

"I suppose so, but..." Rachel fidgeted with the arm of her chair.

The poise she had consistently displayed seemed to evaporate.

"I didn't mean to make you uncomfortable. I assure you that's not my purpose."

"That's okay. It's...it's just that the subject is touchy. My...uh...current boss can be difficult."

"How so?"

The eye contact she had maintained throughout the early stages of the interview was absent. "Well...when it comes to himself, he's very forgiving, but heaven forbid we office staff make a mistake."

"May I ask his name?" With virtually all of Springfield's brokers participating in the local brokers' association, odds were if Kyle didn't know him personally, Larry did.

"You won't tell him what I say? I don't even want him to know I've applied for this job."

"You needn't worry. It will remain our secret...that is, unless I hire you. In that case your cat will be out of the bag." Kyle chuckled, though arguably more from unease than humor.

"I appreciate that because I'm afraid there'd be a price to pay if he found out. And unless and until I land a new job, I need the one I have."

Kyle glanced at the bottom of the résumé. "I see that you've listed Professor Herbert Willis from Quinsigamond, along with Thurmond Atkins of Evlend, Inc., as references. Any problem with me contacting them?"

"None at all. In fact, I was hoping you might. I had Professor Willis for two courses while I was in school, and I worked for Mr. Atkins for about eighteen months after I graduated."

"Any particular reason you left Evlend?"

"There was no possibility for advancement, and Quigley and Watkins offered me five thousand dollars more than I was making."

Kyle jotted a couple of fast notes. "Returning to the subject of your current boss, I'd appreciate you telling me his name, and before you respond, once again, rest assured, your answer, as well as the fact you've applied, will be in confidence."

"I appreciate that." Rachel took a deep breath. "My boss is…Clinton Horstmeyer."

With Quigley and Watkins having nearly a dozen brokers, including both partners and associates, the possibility had already crossed Kyle's mind. "Good old Clint."

"Uh…sounds like you know him well." Her voice was filled with trepidation.

"All too well. We were in the same class at Williams." Kyle rocked his chair back. "I can only imagine what it must be like having to answer to an ego the size of Clint's." The comment forked Kyle's mind in two directions. Thoughts of being saddled with Clint as a boss juxtaposed with self-recriminations for voicing the negative feelings, especially to a stranger. "I shouldn't be badmouthing him, but suffice it to say that I understand why you're looking for a change." Kyle gazed at Rachel's résumé once again. "What salary are you looking for?"

"If I could match my current pay, forty-two thousand per year, that would be fine. Mainly, I'm looking for a change."

In a moment of contemplation, Kyle gazed briefly into space. "Assuming your recommendations are positive—and I expect they'll bear out nicely—you've got the job."

"Wow…That's great. Thank you so much."

"And thank you." Kyle got up from his seat and guided her out of his office. She had no sooner left than he contacted Willis and Atkins. Both confirmed she was extremely capable, conscientious and well-organized. Kyle had found himself a new Administrative Assistant.

Every human being possesses a self-image, which in varying degrees is shaped by others. Praise enhances it. Rejection scars it. Many times the positive and negative influences are justified. But often they're not.

Briefcase in one hand, his car keys and a shopping bag full of gifts in the other, Bill Young approached his mailbox. He laid his briefcase on the ground and unlocked the tiny portal. The compartment revealed a sales promotion from Geico, a monthly statement for his Visa card, a quarterly summary of his Kingman & Woodhill account and a letter from Amber Oak Publishing. He eyed the last item for a moment before stuffing it, along with the other mail, into his shopping bag.

He glanced in the direction of the Palm Shadows community pool. Now that the school year was over, there would be lots of time to hang out in the sunshine, albeit with Florida's characteristically hot and humid tropical environment. Bill was especially looking forward to the end of the month when he would travel to Vancouver in advance of a week's cruise to Alaska. He headed to the stairs that led to his second-floor apartment. Except when loaded down with groceries or the rare occasion when he purchased a large item for his apartment, his fifty-inch flat screen television the quintessential example, he passed up the ease of the elevator.

Once in his apartment, Bill laded a tall glass with ice and filled it with orange juice from the refrigerator. He seated himself in his big easy chair and began opening presents from his students. There was a gift card to the Lobster Shanty, a red metal apple, a Cross pen, Godiva chocolates, a silk tie, a tiny bonsai tree and several packages of home-baked goods. Much as he enjoyed the gifts, he appreciated his students' notes even more. A number said he was their favorite teacher. The praise justified his dedication. It validated his choice of profession. Back in his first year of teaching, things had gone well, but at times he had felt unsure. All too often, preparation for the succeeding day had found him working well past midnight.

147

The following year, armed with experience, plus the benefit of a full set of lesson plans, his job grew easier. In the two that ensued, his confidence increased and his workload lessened. Though he still spent time on class preparations most every day, stress declined, while opportunities for creativity rose. A good job became an excellent one. An unsure rookie matured into a seasoned veteran. And the notes from his students, positive feedback, put an exclamation point on another successful year.

With all his year-end gifts and notes opened, Bill leaned back and took stock of his life in Southwest Florida. The assessment was overwhelmingly positive, though admittedly his love life needed a boost. Ever since his three-month fling with Andi had fallen victim to her new job in Canberra, Australia, anything resembling a serious relationship had been non-existent. While he had dated a number of women, they were mostly one and done; occasionally, two and adieu; and just once, three and *finis*. Still there was reason for optimism. The computer dating service he had recently joined had a surprising number of attractive prospects.

Bill sipped his juice and reached for the mail. He pushed the Geico advertisement aside before quickly scanning his Visa-card statement. Everything appeared to be in order. He opened the envelope from Kingman & Woodhill. Several months had elapsed since he had last reviewed his account. Most times he deposited the statements, still in their envelopes, in his file cabinet. The ensuing month was always soon enough to check the status of funds whose use lay well over three decades in the future. He felt his eyes widen as he stared at the bottom line. His account had lost over thirty percent of its book value. The reason became clear once he directed his attention to the details of the report. His investment in Silver Sky, the largest portion of his portfolio, had tanked. The eight thousand dollars he had invested in the fund had a market value of just over four thousand dollars.

"Damn it," he barked. He gave the document a second look. The ugly numbers failed to magically change. "That son of a bitch." The epithet no sooner crossed his lips than second thoughts stirred. He found it hard to deny that he shouldered a share of the blame. Sure, Don had recommended Silver Sky, but all along Bill had doubts about the investment. Common sense had urged him to investigate the fund, evaluate both its risk and potential. Inertia, or more accurately laziness, had enabled him to convince himself that the folks at Kingman & Woodhill would look out for his interests. Bill reached for his glass, leaned back and dumped a couple swallows down his gullet. Melted ice had watered it down.

He eyed the last piece of mail, the letter from Amber Oak. With the right contents, it could instantly erase the off taste the bland drink had left in his mouth. He held the envelope up to the light, not that he anticipated the gesture would yield any insight. He gulped the last of the nearly clear liquid at the bottom of his glass. A distant memory surged from the recesses of his brain. It was déjà vu...almost. In the fall of his senior year in high school, having applied to Williams for early decision, the letter holding his fate arrived. In the two weeks before it had come, every day he had raced to the mailbox to see if it was there. All along he had assumed he would tear it open the moment he got his hands on it. When it finally came, he balked. The possibility he might be denied admission was too hard to face. Ever since the preceding spring when he had decided to go the early decision route, his heart had been set on Williams. Anywhere else had become a disappointing consolation prize. For the better part of an hour, with the unopened envelope in his back pocket, he jogged up and down the streets of his suburban teenage locale. At long last, after seating himself on the doorstep of his house, he summoned the courage to learn his fate. Upon seeing an acceptance letter, his shrieks of joy reverberated throughout the neighborhood.

The recollection stirred momentary debate in Bill's head. Perhaps with the letter unopened he should go for a jog. After all, it had history on its side. He might have followed the intuition, except it ran counter to his nature. He was not superstitious. Back at Williams he had often chastised Don for yielding to such fatuous irrationality. He gave the envelope one more look. He took a deep breath and slit it open. He drew out the contents, a single tri-folded sheet of paper. He unfolded it and gazed at the lone paragraph. In a fraction of a second, just long enough to view the first two words, *We regret*, the verdict was patent. His query letter for his manuscript had been rejected. In nothing more than a lousy. two-sentence form letter, Amber Oak had told him to get lost. Seconds later, he finished reading the remainder of the missile, a sledgehammer candy-coated with a disingenuous wish for a successful writing career.

Shoulders slumped, Bill stared at the paper, trying to discern something beyond the perfunctory message. Did it mean the publisher viewed his effort unworthy of comment? Did someone toss his proposal into a slush pile without even reading the first sentence? Was it rejected because he was unpublished and had no agent? Bill longed for answers. All he could do was guess, and his best surmise was hardly uplifting. His eyes moved to the stack of gifts and cards from his students. They, along with Fordison's administration, said he was an excellent teacher. Their adulation should have put him in great spirits. It didn't. His finances had taken a hit, and far worse, his ego, his aspirations for his first novel, had been crushed again.

What goes around, comes around.

Don Burns stood in the middle of his office and stared blankly at the brown cardboard box parked atop his desk. He reached for the container's cutaway handles but halted midstream and circled around to the other side of the desk, where he sank back into his commodious leather high back. He eyed the box once more as he tried to comprehend what was taking place. Just fourteen days earlier, on July 13th, he had been given his notice. It had come on high-quality, twenty-four pound, 98-bright, premium-white, Kingman & Woodhill watermarked letterhead, not on a thin, tacky pink slip. The message had been cordial. In fact, it had been more than that. It had wished him great success in his future endeavors. With all the agility and grace of a sugar plum fairy—Don and Linda had already purchased seats for the upcoming December production of *The Nutcracker*—the letter had danced around its nasty consequence. Don had been fired. Of course, the letter had phrased it differently. Hard times had hit. Kingman & Woodhill needed to downsize. After careful deliberation, the partners had determined it would be unfair to ask associates, like Don, to toil long and hard for what was certain to be inadequate remuneration. Rather than placing them in an unenviable dilemma where they would need to weigh their loyalties to the firm, the partners were taking the affirmative step of downsizing. Said another associate who, like Don, had been excessed, "Such benevolence, no doubt, deserves a thank-you note."

In conjunction with his termination, Don found perverse proof of a long-held belief, the devilish power of the number thirteen. Not only was his termination notice dated the thirteenth, but Kingman & Woodhill's profits for the first six months, year-over-year, had dropped thirteen percent. No doubt his Inseparables buddies, ever the non-believers, would have dismissed the facts as mere coincidence. Such was the universal device that skeptics invoked to ignore mountains of compelling proof. But triskaidekaphobia was no idle superstition. When the number thirteen came up, bad things happened.

Over the preceding two weeks, Don had felt as if he were an assistant to the clerical staff. Codes and passwords had been changed. Like the others who had received termination notices, his access to files and information was nil. His days had been idle, except to provide occasional bits of information needed by the clerical staff to ensure a smooth transition once he and his counterparts departed. A fellow pink-slipped broker had urged those who had been excessed to refuse to cooperate. All others, Don included, rejected the mutinous plan. Its futility was exceeded only by its stupidity. Without access to files, it would have had negligible impact. Would-be employers were certain to contact Kingman & Woodhill for recommendations. Revelations of the attempted sabotage, albeit vain, were certain to kill any prospects of being hired. Men walking the plank hardly needed to don an iron ball and chain before they leaped.

Don spun his chair one-hundred-eighty degrees, so it faced his office's rear wall. He gazed at the picture of the Manhattan skyline that hung in the center. The many high rises that filled the photograph were rife with elevators. Don was about to take a ride on one, perhaps all the way down to the bottom floor, perhaps even to the sub-basement. He closed his eyes. Anger, the kind that raged when first he had received his termination notice, stirred. His emotions, however, were mixed. Stock taken in recent days had forced him to re-evaluate initial fury, even to the point of guilt. Ample warning regarding the devices that guided Kingman & Woodhill had been provided. When traditional conservative investments had failed to generate sufficient income, the firm had pushed Silver Sky. Greater fees and commissions outweighed the risks of exposing clients to speculative perils. The interests of the firm trumped those of clients. And too, those interests, as reflected in the financial well-being of the senior partners, trumped those of the associates.

The fact that Don had long been aware of the firm's propensities would not, by itself, have quelled his ire. What did, however, was the ugly realty of self-reflection, the knowledge that he was complicit. Rather than resist the culture of greed, Don, like those above him, had pushed Silver Sky, even with his closest friends. When Linda had confronted him with the error of his ways, he had rationalized that the security of his job necessitated it. Don had become a tintype of his mentor, Charlie Bascomb. He had put his own financial interests ahead of his clients. Like the old saw, *what had gone around, had come around.*

Don checked his watch. It was 5:07. The clerical staff was gone. The time for a dash to the exit, an effort to avoid last embarrassing face-to-face contacts, was ripe. He picked up the box with his personal items and headed for the elevator. The box, close to thirty pounds, was heavy, but compared to the weight of his own opprobrious conduct, it was light.

Hopes and dreams have always shaped the human condition. The possible and the impossible compete in decision-making processes. Some reach for the stars; most do not. To settle or not to settle, that is the question.

The day's edition of the *Hartford Courant* and a plate of scrambled eggs and sausage in front of him, Eric Johanson sat at the kitchen table of his Windsor Locks residence. The comfortable, two-bedroom garden apartment, located off Old Country Road, not far from Bradley International Airport, was an easy, dozen-mile ride down Interstate 91 to the Hartford headquarters of Granite Casualty and Life. But on that morning, a Saturday, there was no need to make the trip.

It had been a hectic week at the office, and, having slept in past nine, Eric was happy to relax. Bite by bite, he consumed his breakfast; and page by page, he did the same with the *Courant.* He brewed a large mug of southern roast pecan coffee, took a moment to put a stamp on an envelope and, after grabbing his checkbook, returned to his seat at the hard-rock maple kitchen table. He took several sips of his hot beverage and stared briefly into space. He proceeded to write a check to Carla Pender. He stuffed the check into the envelope. He raised the envelope close to his lips but halted before he licked it. Perhaps he should include a note. The idea was good, but he opted for the easy way and ran his tongue over the gummed border. He sealed the envelope.

He leaned back, stretching his arms to full extension. A familiar debate stirred in his head. Carla Pender remained a very dear friend. Several years earlier when they had stopped dating, there had been no rancor. On the contrary, they had remained extremely close. Their split by mutual consent had rendered them pals, not lovers. But their relationship, excellent though it was, lacked a spark. Why then did he fear he might be missing a wonderful opportunity? The rumination cajoled him to re-think his relationship with Carla. When he was in need, she was there for him, just as he was for her. He thought back to his senior year at Williams when, after their break-up and despite his protestations, she had insisted upon driving him to Johnstown, Pennsylvania so he could see his gravely ill

153

grandmother before she passed. Only months later did he discover that the trip forced her to part with a cherished ticket to a James Taylor concert at Tanglewood. The information came from a third party. Carla never mentioned the sacrifice she had made. And there was the time before she moved to California when he had a devastating case of the flu and she had brought him chicken soup and orange juice and nursed him back to health. Carla was the sister Eric never had. And wonderful as that was, it was also the problem. Much as Eric loved Carla, he was not in love with her. Even assuming his feelings might change, would he want a long-distance relationship? With Carla and her son having moved to California, roughly three thousand miles away, getting together would be difficult. Struggling as she was, a single mom who was forced to leave college without a degree, she could hardly afford to make the trip east. Eric stared at the sealed envelope. Who was he kidding? Carla was a wonderful friend, but she was exactly that. She was not the woman he wanted for his wife. She was not Glenna Snow.

Beggars can't be choosy.

Seated in his favorite living-room easy chair, Don Burns shifted his position. Despite the seat's perfect fit, solid lumbar support and wonderfully soft feel, he was anything but comfortable. A review of his assets had indicated that he and Linda could survive for roughly three months before he would be compelled to invade his retirement account. After several discussions with Linda, he had concluded that the time to leave the Big Apple had arrived. Linda was anxious to escape from the large metropolis to a smaller setting. Don was less enthusiastic about the idea, but with layoffs rampant and Wall Street not hiring, there were lots of lookers competing for virtually non-existent jobs. Add to the equation, a baby on the way, and the need to explore other locales was undeniable.

After ample procrastination, largely a product of pride, Don dialed. Moments later, a voice at the other end responded.

"Kyle Gordon speaking."

"Hi Kyle. It's Don...Don Burns. How you doing?"

"Good...and how are things in the Big Apple?"

Don had anticipated a lengthy, small-talk-laden prelude, but the question, an excellent segue, obviated the need to dance his way to the issue. "It's been a blood bath here, particularly at Kingman & Woodhill. Pink slips have been dealt faster than cards at a Vegas Blackjack table. And sad to say, I got one of those slips. To put it simply, I've joined the ranks of the unemployed."

The disclosure drew unexpected silence.

"Did you hear what I said?"

"Unfortunately, all too well, but it...uh...put me at a loss for words. I don't know what to say."

"That was kinda my reaction when I got my notice."

"What do you plan to do?"

"Find another job...I hope." Don swallowed hard. "I thought maybe you could help me."

"Gosh, I'd like to, but...my own situation is in flux. My boss is retiring, and I'm taking over the business. Just how many of his clients will stay, remains to be seen. There's no way I can think about expanding. Not now. I...uh...hope you understand."

"Absolutely." Don made a conscious effort to conceal his disappointment. Low expectations made it easier. "Well, maybe you know of an opening in the Springfield area or, for that matter, anywhere."

There was another silence. Don waited patiently.

"There is one position that I know of, but I...I doubt you'd like it."

Images of something low paying, bordering on clerical, flashed into Don's head. "Hey, whatever it is, run it by me."

"Okay, but understand, I'm not recommending it, merely saying it's available."

"Fair enough. Shoot."

"There's a firm here in Springfield, Quigley and Watkins, that's expanding. I understand they're looking for a couple of new brokers."

The opportunity, especially with multiple openings, was a welcome surprise. "Gosh. That sounds good. Linda wants to move to a smaller city, one where we could have a home in the suburbs. And she loves the nearby Berkshires."

"Yes, but..."

The instant Kyle hesitated, Don sensed there was a huge kicker. "Let me guess, the devil himself is doing the hiring. I have to trade my soul to get the job."

"I wish it were only that."

What a minute earlier had sounded like an excellent opportunity was taking on a different tone. "Alas, now that I'm forewarned, give me the horrific news."

"Our dear friend and fellow Williams' alumnus, Clinton Horstmeyer, is a broker at Quigley and Watkins."

Don waited a second, anticipating there might be more. "And?"

"Isn't that enough?"

"If that's the whole of the bad news, I'm ready to apply."

"I'm glad you feel that way. 'Cause if I were in your shoes, I'd probably say, 'Forget it!'"

The assessment forced Don to rethink the matter, but history quickly banished second thoughts. "I hear what you're saying. If I were you, no way would I step into the den of the Horse's Ass. No offense intended, but he hated you. Given a chance to screw you, I'm sure he would."

"No arguments, but you sure you could tolerate the jerk, especially when he'd be senior to you, at least in tenure, if not in title."

The message was food for thought, but in need of a job, Don could ill afford to kick a gift horse in the mouth, even one by the name of Clinton Horstmeyer. "How big is Quigley and Watkins?"

"About a dozen brokers, and roughly that many more in clerical staff. With their new hires, including some additional clerical people, I imagine they'll total close to thirty."

"Not bad odds."

"Pardon me?"

"Oh, I was just thinking out loud. One goon out of thirty. Less than four percent. I can live with that."

"You're assuming there aren't any others."

"You know of more?"

"Uh…not really. And when you put it that way, I have to concede that the other men and women of the firm, and I know most of them, are good people."

"Anything else you can tell me about the job?"

"Not really, but I'll fax you a copy of their advertisement from *Business West*. It's central Massachusetts' business journal."

"I appreciate that."

"No problem…but just remember, if you land the job, count your fingers after shaking hands with Clint."

Don laughed heartily. "I'll do that." With good-byes exchanged, he hung up the receiver. Admittedly, working alongside Clinton Horstmeyer would be far from nirvana, but given the situation, he could not be choosy.

Friends do favors for one another. Assistance is begotten less easily from others. A prior indebtedness can alter the landscape.

The moment Kyle hung up the receiver, he accessed his telephone's alphabetical list of speed dial numbers. He moved down to the letter *Y* and, after spotting the desired name, clicked. Following four rings, he heard the familiar recording inviting him to leave a voicemail at the tone. Much as he preferred to put the unpleasant task behind him, reality forced him to yield to the directive. "Hi Bill. It's Kyle Gordon. Hope all is well there. Give me a call at your earliest convenience. Talk to you soon. Thanks."

Kyle hung up the receiver and returned to a prospectus he had been reading just before his conversation with Don. No more than five minutes elapsed until his telephone rang. "Kyle Gordon speaking."

"Hi Kyle. It's Bill returning your call."

"Wow…that was quick."

"I just got out of the pool here at my apartment, and I saw your message on my cell phone. I hope everything is okay. Your voice had a hint of concern."

"I'm fine...but I need a favor."

"Tell me what."

Kyle took a couple seconds to collect his thoughts. "It's Don...Don Burns. He's been laid off from his job in New York City."

"Gosh, I'm sorry to hear that. But apart from a recommendation, and mine as a friend would carry virtually no weight, I can't imagine how I could help. I'm sure he's not looking for a low-paying job down here teaching at a private school...not that I'd have the influence to get him one."

"Agreed." Kyle spoke the word with casual inflection.

"Hey, merely because I'm low on the totem pole, no need for you to concur."

"Well, just call me...Mister Darcy." Kyle had no doubt that Bill, the English teacher, would understand the literary reference to the *agreeable* character. "But just to set the record straight, I was referring to Don's lack of interest in a teaching job, not your dearth of influence."

"Sure, tell me another. On second thought, tell me what Don wants."

"Well, there's this brokerage firm, Quigley and Watkins, here in Springfield."

"Never heard of them. And that said, now I really can't imagine how I can help."

As one who detested asking for a favor, even one to benefit a friend, Kyle found it hard to be direct. "Our fellow alumnus, Clint Horstmeyer, is employed at Quigley and Watkins."

"So?"

The interrogative reply did nothing to simplify the task. "I was hoping, uh...maybe, you could talk to Clint, get him to intervene on Don's behalf. It could make a huge difference." Kyle waited a moment hoping Bill would step up to the plate. The silence pressed him to resume his sell. "Hey, you know as well as I that employers are more apt to hire someone who's been endorsed by one of their own."

"Being a broker yourself, why don't you give Clint a call?"

"C'mon, we both know that Clint hates me. Anything I ask for, Clint would do the opposite." Kyle avoided mentioning that in a short time Clint's Administrative Assistant, Rachel Wallace, would be working for him. The circumstance compounded the mountain of reasons why he could not ask Clint for a favor.

"So, you want *me* to do the dirty work?"

"C'mon, it's help for a pal, not dirty work. And you're the only person I know whom Clint might listen to. He owes you for the heat you took, covering for him freshman year when he cherry-bombed that desk."

"It was an end table…in the dorm lounge."

"Desk…end table…whatever. You get my point."

Bill mumbled in a barely audible voice. "The guy sucks me in, has me invest my hard-earned money in the Silver Sky sewer, and now I'm supposed to help get him a job."

With no effective response, Kyle pretended not to hear the comment, though he assumed the pretense was transparent. "It's the Inseparables. You know, *All for one and one for all.* Like "The Three Musketeers," not that I need to tell you, literary maven that you are."

"Spare me your unctuous flattery. And before you resort to some other equally conniving routine (Bill breathed a protracted sigh), fine…I'll call Clint."

"Thanks. I owe you one."

"You're welcome, but no, you don't owe me. You're getting nothing out of this, and asking me was certainly no pleasure. But before we get ahead of ourselves, my willingness to make the call is subject to one condition."

Kyle froze, afraid the seemingly done deal was still iffy. "What's the condition?"

"You promise not to tell Don that I called Horstmeyer on his behalf."

"You've got my word." The commitment could not have been easier. Kyle had no intention of telling Don that he solicited Bill's assistance. With an exchange of some brief small talk and goodbyes, Kyle hung up the receiver, the unappealing chore done.

CHAPTER XI

IRRESPECTIVE OF THE SEXES OF THE PARTIES, the relationship between an administrative assistant and a boss bears striking similarities to a marriage. A good one, in which mutual appreciation and respect reign, is invaluable. A bad one can be a nightmare.

A month had passed since Larry Rockland had retired. He was still coming into the office for a few hours each week, but just to clean up a few final odds and ends. His Administrative Assistant of two decades had left with her husband for his new position in California, and Clinton Horstmeyer's former Administrative Assistant, Rachel Wallace, had come on board. Kyle reached into his in-box for a letter and spreadsheet that Rachel had put there. A quick perusal confirmed the documents, which had been completed with remarkable speed, were highly professional. It was no surprise. In the preceding days, samples of her work had already proved her competence. With the letter and spreadsheet in hand, Kyle headed out of his office to Rachel's desk in the reception area.

"Great job!" He held out the papers so she could see them. "I'm very impressed with your skills, as well as the way you handle yourself with clients."

"That's really nice to hear." A sheepish smile painted her face. "I'm not used to having my work complimented."

"That's unfortunate. High quality merits recognition." As he spoke, Kyle again waved the papers. "So, what do you think?"

Her expression was blank. "Pardon me?"

"Oh—I meant about the job. How do you like it so far?"

"Excellent. Having a boss that appreciates what I do is a big step up from toiling for a nitpicker."

Kyle suppressed an impulse to badmouth Clint. Down the road when he knew Rachel better, it might be different. He said, "I'm glad you're pleased. I know I am."

Nothing ventured, nothing gained. So goes the old cliché. But like most clichés, it tells only part of the story. With something ventured, comes risk of pain.

Rather than having lunch with his cohorts from Granite Casualty, Eric Johanson went out for a walk at the nearby park. On the way, he picked up an oversized slice of pepperoni pizza and a bottle of honey-sweetened green tea. About a hundred yards into the park, he seated himself on a bench beneath a sprawling live oak, one whose huge trunk suggested it might date back to the nation's founding. As he devoured the pizza, he briefly contemplated his productive morning. It had included the settlement of two claims, both of which had the earmarks of costly litigation. His thoughts, however, were mostly elsewhere. Internal debate raged. He gazed upward where the canopy of the oak's branches blocked the view of the bright, August sky. He inhaled the fresh summer air. A chipmunk scurrying along the surface of a gnarly limb caught his eye. Its pace suggested conviction far more certain than Eric's.

He reached into his back pocket and pulled out his cell phone. He went into his contact list where he highlighted the appropriate number. After briefly eyeing the familiar numerals, he closed his eyes. Images of magical moments emerged from the archives of his mind. An agreeably warm zephyr caressed his face. It was akin to the glorious stroke of her fingers on his cheek. He sipped his tea. The sweet libation was the nectar of her kiss. Temptation, a hope-springs-eternal mentality, overcame reluctance. He tapped his phone causing the selected number to be called. Seconds later, the distant ring echoed in his ear. Inertia, coupled with knowledge that her caller-ID would give him away, counteracted an urge to terminate the call before she answered. Three more rings ensued before a recording, her lovely voice, invited him to leave a message at the tone. A moment later, he heard the beep.

"Hello Glenna. This is Eric Johanson. It's…uh…been a long time since last we spoke. I'd love to talk to you…catch up on what's happening. If nothing else, perhaps you could…uh…explain to me why you refused to see me anymore. I hope all is well with you, and…uh…that you'll return my call. Take care." Eric again stared upward through the branches of the oak. Pride, the possibility his ego would suffer another beating, stirred doubts…undeniable doubts, but not regrets. On balance, he was glad he had taken the risk. Maybe…just maybe, he could resurrect his relationship with Glenna. Admittedly, it was a long shot, but it was worth the chance.

Superstitions can enslave the mind. Rational wisdom says disdain them. A sage mind heeds the wisdom. But now and then, even a sage mind yields. And what harm? If by chance a superstition proves true, one benefits from its counsel. On the other hand, if it turns out wrong, one has additional evidence to refute the foolish guide. Of course, anecdotal evidence disproving a superstition is no better than that which purports to prove it. That said, in the interest of safety, might the sage mind be wiser to give superstitions greater credence?

Armed with a lox and bagel sandwich, a container of pineapple coleslaw and a *Pepsi,* all stuffed into a small cooler pack, Bill Young, clad in navy spandex, a light blue tee bearing the image of the Monterey Peninsula and his bicycle helmet, headed from his apartment, ready for another twenty-mile ride to the Ding Darling Wildlife Refuge. Halfway down the walkway that led to his Schwinn Volare Road Bike, he spotted the postman climbing back into his truck. As if a halfback feinting to avoid a would-be tackler, Bill shifted left and right debating whether to let the mail await the return from his bike ride. Compromise, one of his hallmarks, led him to the box, but only for a cursory check of the contents. A turn of the repository's key revealed a weekly flier from Supersaver; an envelope with what appeared to be a bogus check, likely for several thousand dollars, but doubtless non-negotiable, from Hakely Auto Sales; and a letter from Forever Publishing Company. The final item forced him to rethink his plan. Bill slipped the flier and the auto-sales advertisement back into his mailbox and locked the door. He eyed the letter from Forever, running his fingers over the ends of the envelope. It had some heft. It was definitely thicker than the numerous rejection letters he had previously received. If his experience years earlier when he had submitted college applications was any indication, it was an excellent sign. He glanced off in the direction of his bicycle and then stuffed the envelope into the zippered side pocket of his cooler pack. The solitude of Ding Darling was more apropos to learning the fate of his manuscript query letter.

With the days of August waning, in all likelihood, the ride to the refuge, his third of the season, might be his last for several months. Once summer vacation ended and school started, his teaching responsibilities would leave few opportunities, though weekends were still a possibility. He peddled across the Sanibel Causeway following Sanibel-Captiva Road to the sanctuary. All the while his mind remained focused on the contents of the zippered pocket. Might it contain a dream-fulfilling message?

He wended his way out Wildlife Drive. As he approached the Mangrove Overlook, he was tempted to stop, but an odd feeling cajoled him to push forward to the Cross-Dike Trail. He turned off and headed to an area not far from the Observation Tower, where mangroves lined the saltwater marsh. He went directly to his favorite bench. As he seated himself, a nervous optimism bubbled. Disquieting thoughts regarding his conduct over the preceding hour stirred as well. All through college he had scoffed at Don's dependence upon senseless superstitions. Why then was he refusing to open his potentially *lucky* seventh response until he had arrived at the chosen spot? Any suggestion that it could enhance his likelihood of a favorable reply was fatuous. The letter said what it said. Where he opened it, could not change its contents. He unzipped the pocket and drew out the envelope. Amidst his fingers, the beefy parcel had a great feel. Bill took a moment to survey the marshy estuary. One last glance at the envelope, and he slit it open. He no sooner unfolded the top sheet than the letter's terse message had been absorbed. Forever Publishing Company was sorry to inform him that his proposed manuscript did not fit within the company's plans. Bill flipped to the accompanying enclosures, four glossy sheets displaying books that Forever was looking to peddle to him. "Damn—What a nerve...What a damn nerve!" he snarled. "After giving me less than lip service, the creeps have the balls to hock me with their stinking wares."

Bill leaned back. A couple hundred feet away, atop a sand bar, a great white snowy egret bellowed several of its guttural croaks. "Shut up," barked Bill. Where ordinarily he loved the symphony of the many birds that inhabited the wonderful sanctuary, he was in no mood for their noise. He slumped back in his seat, and after one more quick reading of the rejection letter, closed his eyes. What stupidity had prompted him to latch onto absurd superstitions. Lucky seven was a moronic irrationality. Where he opened the envelope was of no consequence. Taking it to Ding Darling could not change one iota of its contents. Bill felt foolish. But much more than that, he was depressed.

It helps to have friends, especially in the right places. Of course, some friends are better than others.

Don Burns checked his watch—4:58. His first day at Quigley and Watkins had nearly ended. Like most first days in a new job, it had seemed inordinately long, much more than eight hours. Unfamiliarity with the setting and protocol, coupled with typical first-day nervousness, was responsible.

"Welcome aboard."

The voice drew Don's attention, just as he was putting a folder into the cabinet that adjoined his desk. In the doorway, he spotted Clint Horstmeyer. "Thanks. How've you been?"

"Good. But the bigger question, how are you doing, now that you've put day one behind you?"

"Pretty well...I think."

Clint's brow furrowed. "That's an apathetic response."

"Sorry, I didn't mean to sound unenthusiastic. It's...it's just first-day jitters. You know, it takes a little time to adjust."

"I guess. Although knowing you, ever poised and gregarious, I wouldn't have expected it, especially given your experience in the Big Apple."

The comment had Don doing an instant self-assessment. The image of his inaugural day at Kingman & Woodhill when he leaned back with feet on his desk flashed into his mind. Back then he was an inexperienced kid fresh out of college. Logic suggested that current confidence should be greater, not less than when his career had commenced. But logic in a vacuum, devoid of salient facts, could be grossly misleading. Like a guy on the rebound after being dumped, with his firing from Kingman & Woodhill still fresh, Don had lost his mojo. "Well...let's just say as the new guy on the block, I need to learn the ropes."

A smile, arguably a smirk, appeared on Clint's face. "Yeah, that makes sense. Unlike me who's carved myself a solid niche, a newcomer is...a newcomer."

Don read between the lines. Clint had sent a message. Technically they were both brokers with the title of Senior Specialist, but Don, the new guy on the block, was lower in the pecking order.

"Not to blow my own horn, but the good word I put in for you with the partners definitely helped you land the job." Clint looked Don squarely in the eye. "Who knows? Down the road, maybe you'll repay the favor."

Once again Don got the message. Clint expected recompense. "I appreciate what you did for me." Don gladly voiced the words of thanks; any willingness to commit to future obligations was another matter.

"Hey, you know what they say, purple runs deeper than red."

Don silently repeated the cryptic comment.

"Don't you get it? Just as blood is thicker than water, college colors, in this case our Alma Mater's purple, trumps the red of blood. College buddies are tighter than family."

Sure, when you're twisting a guy's arm to make him beholden to you. "Speaking of family, how's your brother doing?"

"My brother...what's he got to do with anything?"

"Hey, you mentioned blood and family...and I just wondered about your brother."

"Well, you can forget about him because I couldn't care less." Clint's jaw tightened as he gazed off into space. "Hell, he never cared about me. Back when we were both six and in a foster home—our parents had been killed in an auto accident before our first birthday—a rich uncle agreed to take one of us in. Just because Shelby was seven minutes older, he got picked. You think the son of a bitch, my dear twin, has ever written or called to see how I was doin'? 'Course not. He took his good fortune and said the hell with his brother." Clint pounded a fist into the palm of his other hand. "The only thing the bastard ever did for me was screw me out of a chance for a nice home. Thanks to him, I got stuck with a parade of foster parents, most of whom used me to grab a few bucks from the government." His gaze fixed squarely on Don. "You've got something on your mind."

Had he not been confronted with the question, Don might have contained curiosity. "If memory serves me, back at Williams, you spoke well of your foster family."

Clint chuckled briefly before responding. "Yeah, my sixth. I went to live with them when I was fourteen. As for the five that preceded, they got progressively worse, impossible as that seemed at the time. Number five was rock bottom. My so-called father was a drinker, a fucking impotent loser, who was hardly ever sober. His favorite pastime was whipping me with his belt. Looking back, I'd say it was his way to prove he had some power."

The surprising disclosures drew Don's sympathies, even as they left him searching for words. "Well, in spite of your beginnings, you've achieved a lot...I mean getting into Williams and all."

"Yeah...though football, more than grades, is what got me there. From the time I started playing football, I knew why I loved it. I could hit people...hit 'em hard, and no one yelled at me. Instead, for the first time they praised me. Football became my haven. Grades were a distant second. But I couldn't ignore them, or there would have been no football. But as far as being a great student, never. Like I said, football, coupled with my disadvantaged background, is what opened the door to Williams." Clint chucked. "I guess all that explains why I graduated at the bottom of the class."

Recollections of his own upbringing forced Don to acknowledge his good fortune. He suppressed the urge to voice the thought, lest he come across as gloating.

"Grades are nice, but guys like us got sheepskins the same as the ass-busting pals in your little clique."

Don, who graduated in the middle of the class, resented being lumped with Clint. By the same token, he could hardly compare himself to Kyle and Bill who were in the top echelons.

"And the truth is, now that we're out in the real world, our skills, glib tongues and personalities, count far more than smarts."

For years Don had expressed that exact sentiment, but fresh from being canned, he was far less sanguine about the claim. "Well...in some situations a smooth tongue is best, but a keen intellect and hard work are nothing to scoff at."

As if Don had said nothing, Clint eyed his watch. "God, it's well after five...Why the fuck are we sitting here?"

One person's co-worker from hell is another's colleague. One person's Simon Legree is another's mentor. On second thought, Simon Legree is Simon Legree.

168

"Can I get you a beer?"

"No thanks," said Eric Johanson, who was visiting Kyle and Katelyn Gordon at their suburban Springfield colonial.

"Don't tell me Bill Young's Mormon influence has rubbed off on you?"

"Oh, I forgot to mention. I made the conversion a few months back."

Kyle felt his eyes widen. An instant later, he kicked himself knowing that a quick comeback had one-upped his frivolous query. "How 'bout a *Coke*?"

"I could go for one."

A minute later, Kyle returned with a beer for himself and a tall glass of iced soda that he handed to Eric. "I'm really glad you finally took us up on our invitation. There's no reason we shouldn't get together more often. Hell, it's only what...maybe thirty miles from Hartford to Springfield."

"True, but in case you haven't noticed, I-91 has lanes running south as well as north. You could make the trip to Hartford just as easily. I do have a two-bedroom apartment. And for that matter, it's easily done as a day trip or just for an evening."

Several times Kyle had thought about traveling to Hartford, but good intentions had repeatedly gone by the wayside. "Both Kate and I have been on a merry-go-round lately, but once things quiet down a bit, we'll come down. That's a promise."

A tray of stuffed mushrooms in hand, Katelyn returned from the kitchen. As she offered Eric the hors d'oeuvre, she said, "Have you heard anything from Glenna recently?"

Eric shook his head, not that the gesture was needed. His pained look was a sufficient answer. "I called her several weeks ago and left a message, but she didn't respond."

"You sure you dialed the right number?" Out of the corner of his eye, Kyle caught Katelyn's frown. "Hey, you never know...or for that matter, she may have moved or..."

"No, it was definitely her voice inviting me to leave a message at the tone." Eric gazed blankly into his glass. "No matter how many times I've rehashed the facts, I can't fathom why she dumped me…unless…" His words yielded to a sip of his drink. "…she found someone she liked more."

"Knowing Glenna," said Kyle, "that's hard to imagine. You two were in a committed, exclusive relationship. Right?"

"So I assumed. But you tell me, if not another guy, then what?"

A woman maybe? Kyle kept the sarcasm from his tongue. Even in their college days, he would not have uttered such a quip. Their jabs were good-natured, not intended to strike at raw wounds or otherwise cause hurt. "By any chance did you hear that Don Burns recently moved here to Springfield? He hooked up with a local brokerage firm."

"I knew he had left Kingman & Woodhill in New York. Where he went, I didn't know, not that I…"

Kyle waited a moment until curiosity superseded judgment. "Not that what?"

"Back when he was in New York, he was my broker, and the truth be known, my interests took a back seat to—" Eric squeezed his lips together but then muttered loud enough to be heard, "Don't say something you'll regret." He breathed a sigh. "Anyway, it's water over the dam, and whatever that water may have contained, sewage included, friends best let it meander downstream. Who knows? Maybe the rocks there will make it sparkle again."

Kyle sensed what lay in Eric's unspoken words. Conversations with Bill had provided more than a clue. Amazingly Bill had gone to bat for Don and helped him get his new job. Much as curiosity cajoled Kyle to explore the matter further, he sensed that Eric preferred to leave it be. If that weren't enough, a glance from Katelyn stemmed his prying propensities. He said, "Don now works for a firm by the name of Quigley and Watkins. And you'll never guess who works there with him."

"O.J. Simpson's grandmother?"

"How'd you know?"

"Touché," said Eric, adding a sheepish smile. "I asked for that." He waited a moment. "So, you gonna tell me, or do I first get ten lashes?"

Kyle turned to the otherwise taciturn Katelyn. "That's his way to wangle down from the fifty he deserves."

She shook her head. "Enough of your inane talk."

Reluctantly Kyle contained the urge to counter that she had missed the point. Of course, their exchanges were inane, but that was part of the fun of getting together with old college buddies. Even if they couldn't turn the clock back, feelings from those great days could still be re-created.

"So, you plan to tell him?"

"Sorry, I got sidetracked with my thoughts." Kyle turned to Eric. "Clint Horstmeyer also works for Quigley and Watkins."

Eric rolled his eyes. "Boy, what more could you ask for?"

"If recollection serves me, unlike some of us, you could stomach Clint."

Eric fired a look. "Admittedly he despised you more than me, but stomach the jerk? You gotta be kidding. And regardless, living on the same campus with him was one thing; working alongside him everyday would be another. And is it just alongside?"

"Come again?"

"Well, I assume Clint has been there longer. Is he over Don?"

Kyle shrugged. "Not sure, though it seems a good possibility." The comment gave Kyle pause. The idea of working alongside Clint or, worse yet, with him as a boss was horrible. But Kyle was viewing it through his own eyes. Don would see it differently. Sure, he disliked the Horse's Ass, but not nearly so much as did Kyle. That said, however, Kyle's antipathy for Clint likely paled in comparison to the hate that ran the other way.

Size matters. But according to the adage, good things come in small packages. Of course, some contain bad things. Perhaps Forest Gump's mom had the right idea. Packages are like a box of chocolates. "You never know what you're gonna get."

Bill Young climbed out of his Honda Insight Hatchback with briefcase in hand. Though he had left school before four, considerably earlier than usual, he was exhausted. The first day of school, especially when juxtaposed with summer vacation and its lack of routine, was always enervating. His fatigue had nothing to do with his students or their behavior. On the contrary, if first observations of his flock had merit, he was in for another excellent year. He headed down the walkway of the Palm Shadows complex toward his apartment, along the way making his usual stop at the mailbox. He unlocked it and, after stuffing the two thin items it contained into his briefcase, headed to his second-floor apartment.

He went directly to his big recliner, where after laying his briefcase aside, he kicked back with feet on the footrest. A tall cold drink, especially with someone to serve it, would have been perfect, but for the moment he had to settle for several minutes of quiet relaxation. Very simply, he was too tired for anything.

He started to reach to the adjoining end table for the television remote but instead closed his eyes. Exactly how long it took him to doze off, he couldn't say, but when he awoke, it was nearly six. He dragged himself out of the chair and went to the kitchen where he took an Epic-Delight four-cheese frozen dinner from the freezer. While he generally avoided the sodium-laden, prepared entrees in favor of healthier choices, he kept one or two of the packaged meals on hand for days when no-fuss preparation was imperative. He loaded the cardboard-encased cuisine into the microwave and grabbed a can of Arnold Palmer iced tea from the refrigerator. He popped the top and imbibed. By the time the microwave's beep announced that his dinner was ready, the beverage was almost gone. He took the dinner, remaining drink and a fork to his recliner and, after turning on the local news, seated himself. Countless evenings juggling a meal while channel-surfing had enabled him to turn the process into an art. Within minutes, the dinner, all nine ounces of it, was history.

Bill reached down into his briefcase and pulled out the mail. A flier from Dorkin Furniture addressed to occupant stole several nanoseconds of his attention. The other item, a letter from Ocean Cliff Publishing Company, drew a momentary pause. As he was prone to do, he ran his fingers over the envelope. The thin piece of correspondence gave ample hint of its contents. His query letters had already drawn rejections from eight publishers. With stoic resignation he slit the envelope open with his finger. If nothing else, repeated rejection had educated him about the folly of hopes. Where earlier correspondence had sparked anticipation that perhaps his invitation into the literary world had arrived, recurrent turndowns had tempered such excitement. Indeed, they had all but negated it. Bill was conditioned. He was one of Pavlov's dogs.

With impassivity akin to that which the Dorkin Furniture flier had commanded moments before, he unfolded the one-page enclosure. He casually scanned the opening line. The words, quite different from the standard saccharine brush off, triggered a jolt. Bill did a double take. He sat up straighter and carefully ready the message.

> *Dear Mr. Young:*
> *Your query letter regarding your novel "Bits and Bytes of Love" caught my fancy. It strikes me as a uniquely modern and, might I say, anomalous combination of "Elmer Gantry" and "Cyrano de Bergerac." I would very much like to read your entire manuscript.*
> *If you wish to have the manuscript returned, please include a SASE.*
> *I look forward to hearing from you.*
> *Sincerely,*
> *Janet Carlston*
> *Assistant Editor*

Even before Bill had begun reading the second paragraph, a scream of "Holy shit!" poured from his mouth. The moment he finished reading the letter, he read it a second time, just to make sure he hadn't imagined its contents. He leaped from his seat sending the television remote bouncing onto the floor, not that he cared. Moisture welled up in his eyes as he war-whooped around the room.

He grabbed the letter and read it again. Unlike the previous reading, it was merely to savor the contents. He eased down into his recliner, leaned back and slowly consumed the last ounce of his iced tea. He closed his eyes, conscious of the smile that painted his face. The judicious part of his brain sounded a sage admonition. He had only received an invitation to submit his manuscript. It had not been accepted. The odds that Ocean Cliff would ultimately publish his novel were still against him. The dose of reality gave him pause, but nothing more. His query letter had intrigued someone, an Assistant Editor. She wanted to read his manuscript. That was a huge step forward. Whether she would recommend publication was a bridge to be crossed another day. Future hurdles were irrelevant. It was a time to celebrate, and nothing...absolutely nothing was about to dampen his joy.

———————

Every life has a beginning and an end. Along the way there are other beginnings. From crib to bed, starting school, college, a job, marriage...each, like graduation, is another commencement. Some are scheduled; others, such as a new diet or resolution, are mere decisions, even whim. All too often, the best of intentions falls by the wayside. Habits, character flaws or weakness prevail.

Don pulled his three-year old Honda Accord into the parking lot behind the offices of Quigley and Watkins. He drove past the first row. Those spaces, all reserved for the firm's partners, bore signs with their respective names. The spot on the left end, closest to the offices' front entrance, belonged to the most senior partner. The rest followed based upon seniority. Don continued back to the second row where general parking began. He pulled into a spot adjacent to a shiny BMW 540i. As he climbed from his car, he eyed the sleek, seventy-thousand-dollar piece of German engineering. How, he wondered, did Clint afford such pricey wheels? The fact that he was single certainly made a difference, but having grown up in foster homes, the vehicle seemed a stretch. Even most cars in the first row, an impressive array of Mercedes, Cadillacs, Infinities and the like, bore lower price tags.

Don headed into the two-story building and his first-floor office. The tiny space, arguably nothing more than a cubicle, was a far cry from the fancy digs the partners enjoyed one floor up. He circled behind his faux-wood desk and sank down into its fabric-cushioned desk chair. It was comfortable enough, but hardly the big leather he had enjoyed at Kingman & Woodhill. With a full week under his belt he was becoming acclimated, not that he had the enthusiasm that had marked the start of his career in the Big Apple. A familiar image popped into his head. He could see himself, first day at the Manhattan firm, with feet on the desk, ready to conquer the world. But equating that cocky, up-and-coming star with the grunt he had since become was like comparing a shiny new Rolex to a second-hand Timex. Still he was thankful to have a job. After many long talks with Linda and lots of soul searching, he was determined to put an over-ambitious, excessively materialistic past behind him. Fiduciary responsibility would no longer be a meaningless afterthought. Regard for his clients' interests would come first.

Don pulled up the "Value Line" report for the Nuveen Municipal Value Fund. Before recommending the tax-exempt municipal bond fund to clients, he needed confirmation it was a quality investment. A favorable *Morningstar* review had already provided ample evidence. Its 3.72% return, considerably higher when compared to a taxable counterpart, was very attractive. The fact that it consisted of bonds from virtually every state provided diversification. He jotted a note to remind clients that income from other than their home state would be subject to state income tax. He flipped to a five-year chart and began analyzing the fluctuations of the fund's net asset value and price.

"Anybody home?"

The gravelly voice drew Don's eyes from his computer screen. "Sorry, Clint. I didn't see you. You been there long?"

"Thirty seconds." He pointed at his watch. "It's not even nine yet. What the hell you doing?"

"Come again?"

"You wanna give the rest of us a bad name?" Clint leaned in closer and peered. "Not even a copy of the *Sports Illustrated* swimsuit issue tucked in there." He breathed a beleaguered groan. "That's not the Don Burns I knew back at Williams. Unlike grinds who did all the busywork their professors dished, he knew how to separate the caviar from the hard-boiled eggs."

Don shrugged, mainly from discomfiture.

"I don't get it. You've been outta school for four years. Surely you know that the ivory-towered shit from the walls of academia doesn't cut it in the real world." Eyes narrowed, Clint appeared to study Don. "Then again, that may explain why you got the boot from Wall Street...Aren't you gonna say anything?"

You're still the same asshole who roamed the campus at Williams. Don bit his tongue.

"Hey, don't take it personally. It's just a little friendly razzing. All the rookies get it."

Only difference is that your quips are malice-laden daggers. Once again, Don opted for discretion. He said, "Like the banter we exchanged in college?"

"Exactly." Clint glanced at his watch. "Gotta get me a cup of coffee." He started to leave but turned back. "Seriously, if I can ease your transition in any way, just let me know...I mean that. So, don't hesitate."

Don watched as Clint disappeared in the direction of the coffeepot. Despite the obnoxious encores of his college days, his last comment seemed sincere. Perhaps the annoying vestiges of bygone days were nothing more than that— vestiges. Time might prove that when the chips were down, Clint was a stand-up guy.

CHAPTER XII

LIFE IS WROUGHT WITH CHANGE. Change yields opportunity. Leopards don't change their spots, but people aren't leopards. On the other hand, scientists tell us that the DNA of people and leopards bear more similarities than differences.

Kyle poured himself a mug of coffee. The preceding Friday, Larry Rockland had cleaned out his office. No longer was he coming in several hours per week to wrap up his last odds and ends. No longer was Kyle the junior member of the firm. It was all his. He gazed around his office. He was free to move into Larry's. The sixteen by eighteen digs, an area roughly fifty percent larger than what Kyle was accustomed to, would be a great upgrade. A week or two down the road would be soon enough to make the move. Kyle breathed a deep sigh, one accompanied with mixed emotions. Having Larry alongside had distinct advantages, the greatest of which was security. The constant availability of a knowledgeable sounding board was also invaluable. Being on his own was certain to be a challenge. Nevertheless, Kyle welcomed it. Even when working on his MBA, he had imagined himself one day being his own boss, having his own firm. Little did he imagine that the opportunity would come so early in his career.

The ring of the telephone drew him from his musing. He reached for the receiver. "Kyle Gordon speaking."

"Hi Kyle. It's Bill Young. How've you been?"

"Good, thanks." Kyle quelled the urge to immediately expound on his new circumstances. Excitement in Bill's voice suggested the call involved more than a friendly hello. "What's up?"

"I've got some great news."

"Let me guess. You're engaged."

"No, but it ranks up there with that."

"You won seven-hundred million in the Power Ball Lottery?"

"C'mon, you're making fun of me."

Kyle might have debated the absurd point but for the fact that there had been no mega-size jackpots for months. "Okay, you win. I'm all ears. Give me the scoop."

"I just received a call today. My manuscript...it's been accepted for publication. I had to tell someone."

"Fabulous!" Kyle was not only thrilled for his buddy, but flattered that Bill had chosen to call him first. "Who's the publisher?"

"Ocean Cliff Publishing Company. I know, you've never heard of them. But they're a real publisher, not one of those vanity companies that charges several grand to turn any piece of garbage, however bad, into a book. Ocean Cliff actually reads a manuscript before putting it into print. In fact, three editors looked at mine before they gave the thumbs up. The woman there with whom I've been dealing said they get seven or eight hundred queries a year and only publish about fifteen."

"They only choose the worst?"

"Of course."

Much as Kyle anticipated that Bill would see through his good-natured ribbing, the rapidity of the droll response caught him off guard. "So, Bill Young, my pal from Williams, is about to become a household name, the next to land on the New York Times Best-Seller List."

"Hardly."

"Well, regardless, it'll be great to see your name in print." Kyle waited a moment, anticipating a response. "You still there?"

"Yeah...but I'm not sure you'll see my name in print."

"Come again?"

"I might use a pseudonym."

"A pseudonym? Why in God's creation would you do that?"

"Critics can be mighty tough. A pseudonym provides shelter. I can always go back to my real name if and when people like my stuff."

"Interesting." Kyle had never understood why authors hid behind a pen name, not that he had thought about it much. "Well, once it's published, whether it says Bill Young or Dudley Dickdong on the cover, I'll be looking forward to reading it. Any idea when it will debut?"

"Many months, I guess, what with revisions, editing, galleys and whatever. New as I am to the whole process, I'm not sure how long it'll take."

"What's the title?"

"Good question. I had one, but Ocean Cliff isn't crazy about it…not commercial enough, so it's up in the air for now. But enough about me. How are things on your end?"

"Good…I think."

"That's a decisive answer."

Even as he had uttered the response, Kyle had been conscious of its ambiguity. "My former boss, Larry Rockland, recently called it a career. Today is my first day completely on my own."

"Congratulations…and that explains your reaction a moment ago. New always comes with question marks."

"You got that right. And the biggest one for me is how many of Larry's clients will decide to ditch me."

"On that subject…clients, I have some experience, not that…"

"Not that what?"

"Oh, nothing."

"C'mon, that's not fair, starting and then leaving me hanging."

"Damn you, Young," muttered Bill, just loud enough to be audible. "Can't you think before you open your trap?"

Kyle opted for silent patience. If need be, he would twist his pal's arm.

"It has to do with my brokerage account, not that it's all that big. I'd prefer it was with you, but I...I haven't got the heart to take it away from Don."

"Stop right there. You have no reason to apologize. Just because we're friends, I don't expect—"

"No, it's not that way. As I may have told you, back when Don was working in New York, he got me into this aggressive fund, Silver Sky. A better name might be Nasty Clouds or Drenching Downpour. Anyway, I lost almost half of what I put in."

Kyle might have urged Bill to transfer his remaining account elsewhere were it not his policy to avoid sticking his nose into another broker's business. And too, he sensed that any such comment might come across as a solicitation on his own behalf.

"Logic tells me I have no obligation to stay with Don, especially after he led me astray, but emotion...maybe friendship...loyalty...inertia—I don't know just what—prevents me from making the move, especially after he lost his job."

"I understand. And as the guy who helped him get a new job, you're the last one who needs to explain."

"You didn't tell him that I contacted Clint, did you?"

"Of course not. I told you I wouldn't."

"Good..." Bill's voice trailed off. "Whad'ya think? Will Don turn over a new leaf?"

Kyle longed to answer in the affirmative, but with Bill's savings hanging in the balance, the inquiry demanded better. And too, Don was working alongside or, perhaps, junior to Clint. "I hope so." Even as the vacuous response echoed in Kyle's ears, he reiterated, "I really hope so."

Gravity once bounded mankind to terra firma. Acumen, ambition and ego, coupled with ineluctable determination, propelled people into space, seemingly defying the laws of nature. These same traits have also been known to lead many down a greedy road, one that violates manmade laws.

Don leaned back in his seat beside the passenger-side window as Clint pulled back on the wheel. The plane lifted off the runway and began climbing. "Wow, this is even better than a big jet."

"It's my definition of freedom." Clint glanced at the altimeter. "The moment I don my pilot's cap and begin soaring, I leave all my earthly cares behind." He eased back on the wheel and banked right, heading west from Barnes Municipal Airport in Westfield, Massachusetts toward the Berkshire Mountains.

"Spectacular view," said Linda, who was seated in the rear of the four-seater. "We really appreciate your taking us up."

"My pleasure."

"It's our first time in a small plane," said Don.

"Mine too." Clint glanced back over his shoulder at a wide-eyed Linda. "Only teasing. I've logged well over one hundred hours on this baby, and I had over forty before I got my private pilot's license."

"Are you limited how far from the airport you're allowed to fly?" Don checked his seat belt, making sure it was securely fastened.

"I would be—just fifty miles—if I only had a recreational pilot's license. With my few extra hours of training, like most, I qualified for a private license."

"How high are we?" said Linda.

"Close to three thousand feet. We'll be cruising at about ten."

Don gazed out over the expanse of farmland below. Unlike the view from commercial airliners that quickly climbed to altitudes exceeding six miles, details dotting the landscape remained vivid. Red barns, white houses, black roadways and even the aquamarine waters of an in-ground pool decorated the sun-drenched palette. "Flying a plane on your own must cost a pretty penny."

"It not cheap." Clint flashed a self-satisfied smile. "Of course, it's not like I'm picking up the whole tab. Belonging to a flying club spreads the cost over a large group."

"Does your group rent the plane?" said Linda.

"Nope. It's all ours. Cost us five-hundred-fifteen grand. A few in the club wanted to buy a little two-seater, a hand-me-down Piper Cub or some such thing. But the majority prevailed, and we got this 2013 Cesna Turbo 182T Skylane. It's a beautiful piece of machinery. Comes equipped with synthetic vision technology. Makes it easy to fly in darkness, rain, fog or other IFR conditions. Its screen has graphics that recreate the landscape even in zero visibility. And unlike some little can of beans, this baby can do over a hundred fifty miles an hour with a range of thirteen hundred sixty miles."

As Don soaked in Clint's monologue, one that he suspected had been recited before, he couldn't help but feel impressed. Denying a bit of envy was equally impossible. But even without looking back to check Linda's expression, he conjectured that her reaction differed.

"Going back to your question of cost," said Clint, "dues for our club are four hundred a month."

"Not bad," said Don. "I would have guessed more."

"Four hundred is the dues. Every time you use the plane, flight time—that excludes any time on the ground, even overnight—is one hundred fifty dollars an hour."

"Oh…" Don swallowed hard.

"Yeah, like I said, it ain't cheap." He turned and looked Don in the eye. "You think you might like to get a license and join?"

Don doubted the question was serious. New at the firm, with the recent birth of their son, flying a plane hardly fell within the family budget. Even if it did, convincing Linda would likely be a non-starter. "It's a great hobby, but not one I can think about, certainly not for the foreseeable future."

"It's not just a hobby. It's a great way to get from place to place without the hassle. Languishing in traffic is for the other half. If you ask me, the birds got it right. Flying is the only way to go."

Don could not dispute that it was a great way to travel. Whether it was the only way was another matter. He kept the thought to himself.

Clint looked back over his shoulder. "You'd encourage Don to get a pilot's license, wouldn't you?"

"Perhaps...if he wanted to."

Though Linda was adept at hedging when faced with an impertinent inquiry, Don suspected she resented being put on the spot. "Maybe a decade down the road, I'll get the itch to fly, but for now, I'd just as soon suffer along on the highways."

"Well, have it your way. But one day when you're in a hurry and you're stuck on I-90 because it's turned into a parking lot, don't come crying to me."

Much as Don was tempted to point out that weather frequently forced flight delays and cancellations, he let Clint have the last word. "We really appreciate your taking us up today."

"As I said before, it's my pleasure." Clint turned the wheel, banking to the right. "Coming up on your side is Williamstown. I'll go down a little lower, so you can get the best view."

"God, it always was a pretty campus, but from up here, it's spectacular." Don pointed. "Over to the right, I can see Chapin Hall. It looks like the Parthenon."

Clint continued to circle. Coming up at two o'clock out your window is the Clark Institute." He completed a one-eighty. "Straight ahead is the Taconic Country Club."

"Damn," said Don. "I should have brought my Nikon." He eyed the lush green fairways, dotted with bunkers and greens, carved from the mountain terrain. "Now I know why professional photographers take so many of their pictures from the air." He pulled out his cell phone. "It's not an SLR, but it's better than nothing." He snapped a shot.

Clint eyed his watch. "I'm going north to Bennington. It's only fourteen miles and well worth the view. We'll have just enough time to circle back to Barnes and still land within one hour of takeoff, not that it matters. In our club, fractional parts of an hour are charged exactly as such."

For the balance of the trip, about twenty minutes, conversation in the cockpit grew sparse. For the most part, Don took in the scenery, now and then admiring the ease with which Clint put the airplane through its paces. Just before landing, Don closed his eyes, not from fear, but merely to savor the ineffable freedom. Unlike flights that he had taken on commercial airlines, a predictable potpourri of airport hassles, crowded cabins and frequent delays, it had been an escape to the Heavens. Touchdown, a couple of minor bounces of the wheels, aroused him from his reverie. Once they taxied to the hangar, he climbed out of the cabin and, after helping Linda down, said, "Can we buy you lunch?"

Clint glanced at his watch. "Gotta take a rain check. An hour from now I'm meeting Pete Walker. He's the CEO of Walker Plastics. Landing his account would be a feather, a solid gold one, in my cap." Clint flashed a smirk. "When opportunity knocks, Clint rocks."

"Well, okay, but we'll hold you to that rain check."

"We really appreciate your taking us up today," said Linda. "It was a great experience. It's easy to see why you love flying."

"It's my aphrodisiac...and I'm happy to share it." Clint smiled and headed off.

Don took Linda's hand and led her in the opposite direction toward their car. "One glorious morning, wouldn't you say?"

"I have to admit it was something special, better than I expected. The view from up there puts one from a hilltop to shame."

"I knew you'd love it." Don caught a glint in Linda's eye. Picking up on his wife's non-verbal cues came easy. Interpreting them was another matter. "Something's buzzing in that head of yours."

"You're quite perceptive."

Don waited, on the chance that Linda might be forthcoming without further prodding. No such luck. "So, what is it?"

"Clint reminds me of someone else we know?"

"And just who might that be?"

For an instant Linda's mouth turned down. "Your former boss...Charlie Bascomb."

The possibility she was suggesting they looked alike was impossible. Where Bascomb was short, stocky and bald with a big nose, Clint, the one-time football player, sported a muscular physique, along with good looks. "I take it you don't care for Clint."

"Well...I hate to badmouth him after he was so nice to take us up..."

Don waited several seconds. "But..." He gestured at Linda. The sealed lips that greeted his eyes forced him to press her more. "You don't like him?"

"Not really."

Much as Don could not blame Linda, he felt the need to defend Clint. "Admittedly, he's brash."

"That's an understatement."

"Okay, he's narcissistic, and, for that matter, annoying. But you have to understand where he came from."

"Where...Mars?"

Don shot her a look. "For your information, he grew up in foster homes, most of which were abusive. One of his foster fathers beat him regularly. And to make matters worse, Clint has an identical twin who was taken in by a rich uncle. But the guy was only willing to take in one child. Because Clint's brother was a few minutes older, he was chosen. As for Clint, he got the shaft...So, it's understandable that he bears resentment."

"Fair enough...but now that he has gotten a good education and job, a fancy car and goes flying on weekends, his past can't be a permanent excuse to behave like a boor."

"He's not a—"

"I withdraw my last remark. But don't get me wrong. It's not that I've changed my mind; only that my assessment is premature. For now, I'll withhold judgment. And that said, understand that from what I've seen, he strikes me as the kind of person, like Bascomb, who looks out for himself. As for his clients, they take a back seat."

Instinct pressed Don to balk. Reason prevented him. Clint's history at Williams supported what Linda had said. Though she had only met Clint once before, and that encounter had been brief, good judge of character that she was, she had sized him up quite well.

"I hope your new job won't be a repeat of Kingman & Woodhill."

185

"What—You think I'm gonna get canned again?" Even as he posed the question, Don doubted that was what his wife was implying.

"C'mon, you know that's not what I was saying." She looked him in the eye, allowing time for him to disagree. "Just to set the record straight, I'm concerned you'll have another boss who will push you to ignore the interests of your clients."

"Clint's not my boss."

"I understand, but, unlike you, he's established at the firm, and he helped you land your job, something he's not likely to let you forget. Regardless, that begs the issue. Only time will reveal how the firm conducts business, whether the partners put their clients' interests first."

Don was unable to argue the point. It had crossed his mind more than once, and he could not deny it was a concern. Determined as he was to avoid a repetition of past mistakes, he understood that it might be difficult. With the inevitable ups and downs of the market, the firm's bottom line would not always square with fiduciary dictates. Tough choices were a distinct possibility. With a job on the line and a family to support, even one with good intentions could find it hard to travel the high road when faced with pressure from above.

A strong conscience is often the font of heavy burdens. It is also known to spawn good deeds, many of which go unrewarded. But now and again, exemplary acts bear unexpected, gratifying fruit.

Eric Johanson sat in the living room of his Windsor Locks apartment, eyeing his most recent pay stub, the first since his promotion to Senior Adjuster. He had become a member of management. He had the authority to approve settlements up to twenty-five thousand dollars without first consulting his superiors. Best of all, his promotion included a six-thousand-dollar raise.

He thought back to his days at Williams when, by mutual agreement, Carla and he went from lovers to friends. Carla

186

immediately began dating Clint Horstmeyer. Not long afterward, she discovered she was pregnant. Ever the riverboat gambler, Clint, who was smitten, wanted to marry her. Carla conceded the nuptial might be ill-advised, but given her circumstances, seriously considered the proposal. Eric, along with Kyle, advised her that the marriage would be a mistake, one she was bound to regret. The warning proved prophetic. Even as the infatuated Clint begged Carla to wed, he repeatedly cajoled her to abort the baby. To Carla that was out of the question. More than anything else, Clint's pressure regarding the baby convinced her to reject his marriage proposal.

Once the baby was born, Clint kept his distance from Carla. Wanting no part of the child and the obligations it represented, he vigorously denied paternity. But at the same time, he threatened, though never in writing, that if sued for support, he would use visitation, not that he actually wanted it, as a weapon to make her life and that of her child miserable. Alternatively, he offered to give up his rights, if any, regarding the child, provided she relinquished any claims for child support. The proposal, which, among other things, would free her son for adoption if someday she found the right man, was tantalizing.

Carla, whose mother, herself a single parent, had died several years before, once again turned to Eric for advice. Sensing the need to get Clint out of her life, Eric encouraged her to accept Clint's offer. And once she did, Eric, recalling how Carla had been there for him in his most difficult of times, felt a sense of obligation. Irrespective of whether he had fathered the child, Eric began sending her money. Though the sums may have been less than what a court would have provided in an order of support, for a single mother whose income as a waitress was reduced by day-care costs, they were a Godsend.

As time went on and Carla's son grew into a toddler, Eric developed a connection with little Ricky. That link, more than rectitude, became the motivating force behind his payments. Before long, Eric was Uncle Eric. Whenever they got together, albeit infrequently, Ricky effervesced. So too, did Eric. He relished the camaraderie of his young pal.

187

Eric reached for his checkbook. His new raise enabled him to be more generous. He wrote a check for six hundred dollars and, after affixing his signature, slipped it into an envelope, along with a picture of a brontosaurus and a note promising to take Ricky to Disneyland the next time he went west for a visit. When first he had begun sending money, little had he imagined the benefits. He had gained a nephew. Legally, no; but in reality, indeed. And in Carla he had a friend on whom he could always rely. Numerous times after Glenna had dumped him, Carla's patient ear had helped mitigate his pain. Erase it, no way, but lessen his burden, undoubtedly. At times he had contemplated renewing the amorous relationship he and Carla had shared at Williams. Judgment counseled against the idea. Whether, however, judgment was clouded by fatuous yearnings for Glenna, was a different question. Eric understood the nicety. Addressing it was another matter. In the face of emotions, logic flew no better than a kite in a vacuum.

At the ponies, hunches are free; so too, expert handicapping. You can find the latter in the newspaper every day. Inside information, the kind that produces winning results, is hard to come by and, in all likelihood, not kosher.

"You have a minute?" said Rachel, poking her head into Kyle's office.

"Anytime...You needn't ask."

"I...I've got some information that I...uh...thought you might find interesting."

Rachel's uncharacteristic hesitation aroused Kyle's curiosity. "Shoot."

"The stock of Diquour Drugs is gonna jump today."

Apart from having heard of the small company, Kyle knew nothing about the firm. "What makes you think so?"

Rachel shrugged.

"Let me guess." Kyle turned toward his credenza and gestured at his Magic Eight Ball, given to him by an eccentric client. "You shook the mystic sphere this morning, and it revealed this great investment opportunity."

"Not exactly."

"It came to you in a dream last night?"

"You're teasing me."

Kyle was about to protest, but second thoughts forced him to acknowledge her point. "Sorry, I didn't mean that the way it sounded."

"That's okay. I asked for it."

Kyle waited a moment, hoping Rachel would explain her curious prediction. "So, you plan to leave me in the dark?"

"Well...suppose we sit back and see what happens."

"Fair enough." Kyle chuckled to himself as Rachel left his office. Many a time he had hunches about stocks. Now and then they were right; unfortunately, no more than one could expect with random luck. He returned to his work, dismissing her prognostication as nothing more than fanciful speculation. Well...perhaps not entirely. Three times during the balance of the day, he checked the price of Diquor Drugs. As expected, it fluctuated, up and down, but nothing more than a fraction of a dollar. Like him, no doubt, Rachel enjoyed guessing about stocks.

CHAPTER XIII

WHEN IT COMES TO PREDICTING whether stocks will rise or fall, gurus abound. Studies suggest a youngster throwing darts at the stock page may be equally adept. But arm anyone, whether a guru, dart thrower or whatever, with advance knowledge of important news, and the odds of picking a winner become extremely favorable.

Before entering his office suite, Kyle paused long enough to read the brass lettering on the oak door. The better part of two months had passed since Larry Rockland had retired, but it was less than two weeks since a contractor had installed the new logo, one bearing only Kyle's name. The emblem, symbolic that he was the master of his own ship, was still sufficiently new to draw an ego-satisfying glance. Kyle stepped through the door into the reception area. Rachel was already at her desk.

"Either my watch is slow and I'm late, or you're here very early."

She shook her head. "You've ignored a third alternative. Perhaps your watch is right, but you can't read it correctly."

He forced an exaggerated scowl, one plainly feigned. That she already felt comfortable enough to engage him with such repartee evidenced how rapidly they were developing an excellent rapport.

"Did you happen to check the price of Diquor Drugs?"

"Yup, just before I closed up shop last night." That she would call attention to her erroneous prediction was a surprise.

"And?"

Was she a masochist, begging him to underscore her error?

"By any chance did you give it a look-see this morning?"

He shook his head.

She motioned him over. She punched the letters *DQDR*, the symbol for Diquor Drugs, into her computer.

Kyle did a double take. Sure enough, it was Diquor Drugs, but its price had rocketed up from 33.51 the day before to 42.25. He looked at Rachel. He opened his mouth, but not a word came forth.

"Something the matter?" A self-satisfied smile punctuated her question.

"What the hell is going on?"

She shrugged. "Hey, even a gassed, gawky golfer occasionally finds the bottom of the hole."

"That may be, but not with his tee shot on a long par five." Kyle waited, but hopes of an explanation remained unrealized. "C'mon, enough of this Hide and Seek. What's going on?"

"Borduan Industries tendered an offer to buy Diquor Drugs for $47 per share. It happened yesterday, after the close of trading."

The information shed light on the anomaly, but only half of it. "How did you know it was going to happen?"

She pointed in the direction of Kyle's office.

"What does that mean?"

"Your Magic Eight Ball, the one that sits on your credenza, told me."

"Yeah...and I'm Babe Ruth."

"May I have your autograph? My grandfather was a huge fan."

Kyle groaned. "Are you or are you not going to tell me how you knew?"

"I guess...provided you promise it will remain our secret."

"Agreed."

Rachel took a deep breath. She looked around the room and then shook her head ever so slightly.

Kyle sensed she was about to renege. "C'mon, you said you'd tell me."

"Yeah, unfortunately, I guess I did." She heaved a sigh before continuing. "As you probably know, Quigley and Watkins, my former employer, makes a market in a number of over-the-counter stocks, including Diquor Drugs."

"I knew they were a market maker, though not all the specifics."

"Anyway, when I worked there for Clint, I learned all the passwords and codes to his computer."

"He gave them to you?"

"Yes and no."

Kyle gave her a look.

"I know. That's no answer, but let me explain. One day he gave me a binder with information for a letter I was doing for him. Tucked in a compartment in the back cover was a sheet with all his passwords and codes. I...I photocopied it." She looked away, her face a guilt-ridden canvas. "I know. I shouldn't have done it...You probably think I'm a terrible person."

The assessment, though far harsher than Kyle's, bore an element of legitimacy. Rachel had the run of his office. Did he need to deal with her at arms length?

"Your silence confirms my speculation...but please, let me explain. It's not the kind of thing I would normally do. In fact, there had been many such opportunities for me to take advantage of my position, and I never did."

"So, what was different this time?"

"For more than a week, Clint had been stressed...crazy stressed, a god-forsaken, certifiable lunatic. Anyway, it seems he had made a terrible mistake, and the partners were on his back. Every day he took it out on me. His berating was incessant. On one occasion, he even implied that I was responsible for his mess. Supposedly I had asked him a question, something about his chicken-scratch handwriting I couldn't read. He claimed I distracted him, screwed up his work. All I could do was grin and bear it. Well, to make a long story short, when I saw the passwords and codes, I photocopied them. At the time, I wasn't sure why."

"I take it, you've since figured that out."

"Not really...though now and then I have accessed the files in his computer. That's how I got the inside scoop on Diquor. As the stock's market maker, Quigley and Watkins knew of the buy-out offer before it was made public."

"Did you, by any chance, buy any Diquor stock yesterday?"

"Absolutely not...and I never even considered it. As I said before, I've never used Clint's private information." Rachel hesitated, appearing to study Kyle. "You're judging me, aren't you?"

"No, not at all."

"Well, given your expression, you've got something on your mind."

"I was trying to figure out why you've told me all of this."

Her mien grew pensive. "The way I see it, we're in the same boat."

"Same boat? What are you talking about?"

Rachel remained mute.

Once again Kyle tried unsuccessfully to make sense of her comment. "This so-called boat we're in. Do we have a problem?"

"Well, not really, but..."

"But what?"

She shrugged, though seemingly more from diffidence than ambiguity. "I...I don't want to be the bearer of bad tidings, especially knowing you might decide to shoot the messenger, but Clint dislikes you even more than me. Based upon his comments, *a whole lot more*."

The disclosure was hardly a surprise. "Oh, no big deal. He's despised me for years. It dates to our days at Williams."

"So he told me. He said you caused him to get an *F* in some course freshman year. And worse yet, you helped convince the love of his life to dump him."

Kyle chuckled. "Ah yes, history...according to Clinton Horstmeyer. There's a germ of truth to what he told you. What he forgot to mention was that he wanted to plagiarize a paper I had written, a stunt that could have gotten not just him, but me as well, kicked out of Williams. As for the young woman who dumped him, I was among those who encouraged her to do so.

She was a class act, and I hated to see her ruin her life with a creep like him." A question that had been stirring in the back of Kyle's mind jumped to the forefront. "Why have you come to me with this information about Diquor?"

"I thought you might be interested."

"Why so?"

"Oh, I don't know."

Kyle derailed a gut reaction to challenge the non-answer. "So, did you ever use any inside information to your advantage?"

"The answer is *no*." Her tone was emphatic. "That you ask me again suggests you didn't believe me before."

"Sorry, it's not that at all." Any temptation Kyle had to pursue the matter further was stemmed by her umbrage.

"In the future I could give you some early scoops." She smiled.

Kyle laughed. Presumably the comment had been made in jest. He glanced at the clock. "Yikes. I promised Pete Towilliger that I would call him about his account first thing this morning, and it's well after nine."

"And I've got a bunch of filing that needs to get done."

Kyle headed into his office. Once he finished his call to Towilliger, his mind drifted back to his conversation with Rachel. Something about it didn't sit right. It was not that he didn't trust what she had said, but that wasn't the point. His Administrative Assistant had access to inside information from another firm. The fact she didn't use it, failed to make it okay. Unfortunately, Kyle had knowledge of these facts. If he ignored the situation, could he have culpability? The whole thing seemed farfetched, but as the afternoon wore on, concern increasingly gnawed. Near the end of the day, he made a decision. He would call his old friend and college classmate Denny Larson who worked in Washington at the Securities Exchange Commission. Kyle waited another twenty minutes until Rachel had left for the day before dialing Denny's number.

"Larson speaking. How can I help you?"

"Hi Denny. It's Kyle Gordon."

"Well, talk about a blast from the past. You here in D.C. by any chance?"

"No, Springfield, Mass."

"So, how've you been?"

"Good...and you?"

"No complaints. Let me guess, you're calling about our tenth reunion?"

Kyle did some quick math. "You've gotta be kidding. It's roughly four years away." He glanced at his *Seth Thomas* wall clock. "Five-twenty and you're still in the office. I thought government workers were strictly nine-to-five."

"Yeah, sure. That's the rumor that all the critics of government employees love to perpetuate. Truth is: I put in over fifty hours a week, and I don't get paid overtime. But enough of my gripes. No doubt you have a reason for calling."

"I...I've got a question. Strictly off the record."

"Sorry, I'm not a newspaperman. I can't do that, but you're free to ask a hypothetical—no names. One caveat: That doesn't mean I'll deny we had this conversation. That said—choose your poison."

Kyle quickly analyzed the ground rules. Were he aware of them before he dialed, he might not have made the call. But with Denny already on the line, he fired away. "What if a broker had an employee who had been with another firm and that employee had access to the computers of the prior firm, including information about stocks in which the prior firm was making a market?"

"Damn, that would be some sweet inside information."

Kyle, who thought he had been circumspect, recognized his naiveté. Investigators at the Securities Exchange Commission were watching for insider trading all the time.

"Does the broker have any reason to suspect that his employee is using the inside information?"

"No...not at all. In which case, the broker would be off the hook. Right?"

"Not necessarily, though it's certainly less problematic than if he knowingly ignored insider trading."

"So, what would you recommend the broker do to avoid any possible problem?"

"Actually, I'm not altogether sure. Suppose I give it a little thought and get back to you?"

The response seemed curious, but Kyle had little choice. "Whatever you say." They shared a few old memories before concluding the call. As Kyle hung up the receiver, he contemplated what he had been told. A Securities Exchange Commission investigator like Denny should have been able to easily answer the question. Why didn't he?

Love is blind. Ergo: A blind date is the ideal prescription for love. Reason counsels that the foregoing analysis is devoid of logic. But love is illogical. Therefore, blind dates make sense, at least in the realm of Wonderland.

Eric Johanson sipped his Merlot. Across the table sat Alice...Alice *what's her name*, his blind date. A colleague at work had helped arrange the get-together. He had described Alice as smart, pretty and shapely, with a quirky sense of humor. There was no denying she was all of that. A graduate of Boston University, the tall, slim, well-endowed blond with a cute turned-up nose and large cerulean eyes was a knockout.

"You know why I love wine?" Alice gazed pensively into her glass of Chardonnay, her second.

"I don't know...the taste maybe?"

"Yeah, I like the taste...but what I really love is the way it makes me feel. Life...the daily grind is a goddamn pain in the ass. Aggravation up the wazoo. You start your day driving to work, and sure enough, you get behind some idiot going thirty-five."

"On the main highway?"

"Nah, the half-mile from my apartment outta the complex."

"What's the speed limit there?"

Her jaw tightened momentarily. "Jesus...don't start with that. Goddamn signs saying twenty-five. It's nothing but bullshit."

Eric nodded. It was easier than debating the issue.

196

"Next thing, you get onto the expressway and jump into the passing lane. Sure enough, some moron in cruise at seventy is backing up a line of cars."

Pointing out that the speed limit was sixty-five seemed futile.

"And most days you run into an accident or something that turns the road into a freakin' parking lot." She guzzled her remaining half-glass of wine.

"Yeah," he said, trying to be agreeable, "commuting is no pleasure. Coming down I-91 into Hartford each morning, I find—"

"Then you finally get to the office. You're barely through the door...haven't gotten your coffee yet...and some flunky tells you that your boss, Gomer Assbrain, was looking for you ten minutes earlier. Wants you in his office yesterday. Then the real bullshit kicks in. You know what I'm saying?"

"Uh...I guess so."

With eyes narrowed, she peered across the table. "You're not very talkative."

Eric shrugged. "I guess not...at least not tonight."

"What the hell does that mean?"

Oh nothing. Eric barely managed to keep the sarcasm from his lips. Since entering the working world, talking with new acquaintances had grown easier. But youthful shyness wasn't the problem. The gorgeous blond with whom he was face to face was ugly, though not to look at. On second thought, given her personality, she was growing homelier by the minute.

She waved at their server who was taking an order at the adjoining table.

The server held up one digit. Though it was his index finger, as if to say, "One moment," Eric wondered if the man, having already endured more than enough of the demanding blond, might have preferred to use the adjacent one.

"Yo, Charlie. Another Chardonnay." She rapped her glass on the table. Remarkably the stemware remained intact.

"Be with you in a minute."

She rolled her eyes, the big blues, before training them on Eric. "When you pay the check, don't give the son of a bitch

197

more than ten percent. And if he gives us any more crap, stiff him!"

While Eric had planned to pay the check, he always appreciated when women offered to share, not that he ever allowed them on a first date. Any possibility of such an offer had just vanished.

"Where was I, when we were so rudely interrupted?...Oh yeah, my boss. A freakin' slave driver. You'd think this was the dark..."

A painting of a woman on the farthest wall caught Eric's eyes. Though the portrait was too distant to ascertain many of its details, the subject's red hair was enough to set his mind adrift with images of his favorite Renoir at the Clark Institute. Thoughts of Glenna Snow raced through Eric's brain. If only he were with her, rather than the witch with whom he sat.

"You gonna answer, or do I have to repeat myself a third time?"

The bark halted Eric's ruminations. "Uh...sorry, my...uh...mind went off for a moment." The glower that greeted his eyes forced him to up his apology. "I...uh...didn't mean to—" The sight of their server delivering another Chardonnay to his date provided a welcome excuse to clip his tongue.

"Are you ready to order?" said the server.

"I'll start with a shrimp cocktail...and I'll have the surf and turf, with the filet mignon, medium rare." Her tone was filled with condescension. "That's *medium rare*, not raw like sushi, and not medium like...whatever. And in place of the broccoli, fried onion rings...extra crisp. Oh...and another Chardonnay with the meal, and this time be sure it's properly chilled."

Eric ordered the halibut for himself. He would have opted for an appetizer to start, but his date had already served him more than enough to whet his appetite...for an early end to the evening.

The blond took a couple of swigs of her wine. "I like to be up front. Wasting time is not my style. No offense, but you're not my type." She held up a hand, almost as if an apologetic gesture. "Don't get me wrong. I'm not about to walk out on you. After we eat, we can go our separate ways."

"Fair enough." Eric's response contradicted his thoughts. Between her drinking and her choice of the most expensive items on the menu, fair was hardly part of the equation. On the other hand, an early end to the horrible evening was an undeniable blessing.

Conversation grew briefly sparse before the blond began carping about the countless imbeciles who resided at her apartment complex. She appeared satisfied to conduct her rant without further chastising Eric for obvious lapses in attention. She ordered an additional Chardonnay, plus a Crème Brûlée, of which she ate no more than a third. With that, their dinner was done. When the check came, she said, "You oughta give Schmucko Chucko the stiff job. Maybe then he'll learn how to serve a meal."

Eric shrugged before adding a tip of twenty-five percent. With what Charlie had endured, he had certainly earned it. Out of the corner of his eye, he saw Alice *what's her name* shake her head. Patent disdain painted her face. Eric's one consolation: His ordeal was over. Unlike the March Hare, Dormouse and Mad Hatter who had been relegated to a perpetual tea party, Eric was thankful he could escape the chimerical rabbit hole into which he had fallen.

A wise man avoids trouble, assiduously taking steps to steer clear of it. Yet all too often the wise man finds trouble...or perhaps vice versa...trouble finds the wise man.

Two days had elapsed since Kyle had talked to Denny Larson at the Securities Exchange Commission. While certainly not a perfectionist, Kyle, though rarely a procrastinator, could live with unfinished details, at least that was generally how he viewed himself. The issue at hand hardly proved the point. Only forced restraint had kept him from telephoning Larson, rather than waiting for a call. The investigator's oddly ambiguous response to what seemingly should have been a routine question had Kyle nervously waiting to hear.

Shortly before noon on the second day, Larson finally called. "Sorry I didn't get back to you sooner."

"Oh...no rush." Like a well-oiled ball bearing, the disingenuous reply rolled off Kyle's tongue. "So, whad'ya think?"

"Well, before responding, I need to ask a question, not that you have to answer it...By any chance did the hypothetical you threw at me the other day involve your employee, Rachel Wallace?"

"How did you know that Rachel Wallace works for me? Is she in trouble? Do I—"

"Relax. She's not in trouble, nor are you. And to answer your first question, I did some checking after we talked. And let me explain why...well, at least in part. We have an ongoing investigation related to circumstances in Springfield, and on the chance it might have a link to your call, not that you're involved—"

"Presumably I wasn't, but maybe I am now."

"Easy. As I said, it's not your problem, though I'd like to ask for your help."

Reluctant to get involved and not knowing what the request might be, Kyle was hardly ready to commit.

"Though I can't be specific, our agency is looking at some issues that involve Rachel Wallace's former firm. Just to put your mind at ease, let me reiterate—there's no indication that she's connected. Based upon the little you told me, if I read between the lines, she has access to inside information from her former firm, Quigley and Watkins."

Concern about the direction of the discussion, a hypothetical that had ceased to be such, inhibited a response.

"Your silence tends to confirm my assumption."

"Perhaps...but perhaps not." Kyle wanted to be circumspect, but it was apparent that Larson was steps ahead of him. "Before saying anything, I want to know where I fit in."

"Fair enough." Larson cleared his throat. "As you can well imagine, insider trading cases are sticky wickets. Often they're no more than circumstantial. Information is exchanged in person, leaving no traceable records. Even over the telephone, it can be in seemingly meaningless code. I had one where the supplier of information told his user, "The forecast for tomorrow is sunny." That was the signal to buy the stock in advance of breaking news. More often than not, suppliers of information get paid off in cash. Paper trails are few and far between. That said, it appears that Rachel Wallace might give us an inside track to whatever is going on at Quigley and Watkins."

"So, let me guess, you'd like me to ask her to work with you." Kyle had no idea whether that was what was about to be proposed but threw it out because it would minimize his involvement.

"Not exactly…at least for now. Not knowing whether she would help us or blow our investigation, we'd like you to monitor her use of Quigley and Watkins' information."

"You want me to spy on my own employee?"

"Well…in a manner of speaking, I guess you could call it that."

"And how do you expect me to do that?"

"We'd like to install a recording device in your office."

"You gotta be kidding! You plan to record everything I say and do. Sounds like you'll be watching me."

"No, nothing like that. Not only will you know about the recordings, but you'll determine what's recorded. There'll be a tiny switch underneath your desk that you'll activate with your knee. We're only asking you to turn it on if and when conversation with Wallace is relevant to Quigley and Watkins."

"Damn, you really do want me to spy on her."

"I wouldn't be asking if you hadn't called me first."

"So, it's my fault." Just loud enough to be heard, Kyle muttered, "No good deed goes unpunished."

"Calling us with a hypothetical was hardly a good deed."

"Maybe so, but it's being punished."

"Not really, though I'll admit my request is not all that appealing."

"That's an understatement."

"But you'll do it. Right?"

Kyle quickly debated the alternatives. For all he knew the SEC might wiretap his telephone. The scenario seemed unlikely, but it urged the need for abundant caution. Working with the SEC, as opposed to turning them down, appeared preferable. And by doing it Larson's way, Kyle would be the one deciding what conversations were recorded. He would be in the know, and down the road if something went awry, at least he could say he was cooperating with the good guys. "Okay, you've twisted my arm. I'll do it...or, let me rephrase that, I'll try it for a while."

"You understand, you can't let Wallace in on this."

"Yeah, I know." The acquiescence imposed no additional burden. Implicit in the entire discussion had been the assumption he could not tell her.

"We want to get the system in as soon as possible, but it has to be at an off hour. How about Sunday morning?"

"Sunday?" Kyle waited a moment before heaving a sigh. "Whatever."

"Good. You name the time."

Gee, thanks a bunch. Kyle contorted his face, not that Larson could see it. "How about ten a.m.?"

"Ten it is. Our guy, his name is Lionel Fisher—he'll have credentials—will meet you at your office. He'll install the equipment and show you how to use it. Okay?"

"I guess."

"Before you go, let me give you my cell-phone number. That way you'll be able to reach me whenever."

Kyle wrote down the ten digits that Larson rattled off.

"Any last questions?"

Kyle had a bunch, mainly about the details of the investigation. Confident Larson would not give him answers, he spurned the urge to ask. "I'll be here on Sunday."

CHAPTER XIV

THOSE WHO ARE CREDULOUS are doomed to disappointment. Yet children thrive in a world of fantasy. Might a man, if he be wise, partake of such anomaly, if only vicariously.

Breeze caressing his cheeks, Eric Johanson basked. The smile etched on little Ricky's face as they soared in circles in their big, blue flying Dumbo was an amazingly powerful, mind-altering drug. The spur-of-the-moment decision to travel to California for four days and keep his promise to take Ricky to Disneyland had been more than rewarded. Not since the distant days when he was dating Glenna had he felt so exhilarated.

Round and round, up and down, Dumbo soared and swooped. As Ricky gazed out over the expanse that floated below, Eric focused mainly on Ricky. The youngster giggled. His laughter, its unmitigated joy, was infectious. Eric began to chuckle, but within moments the guffaw magnified. The reaction drew Ricky's attention. Their eyes met. In an instant, both were roaring uncontrollably. Tears, rapturous tears, gloriously dripped from Eric's eyes.

All too soon the ride began to slow, and Dumbo dipped, hovering just off the ground. As they climbed down, Ricky said, "Can we go again, Uncle Eric...can we?"

"Wouldn't you rather do as many different things as possible?"

Ricky displayed an ambiguous gaze, but definitely not one of agreement.

Eric glanced at the nearby Storyland Canal Boats, what he had assumed would be their next venture. His eyes darted back and forth between the two attractions. With the delight from moments before still rife, consternation resolved. "You're right...Let's do it again!" A quick peek confirmed there was hardly a line to re-board. A minute later they were back on the ride; this time in a pink Dumbo.

The second time around was worth every second, though admittedly a notch below the incomparable predecessor. From there they moved on to numerous other attractions. By five o'clock, with more than seven hours of merriment under their belts, they were back on Main Street near the entrance to the park, making their final stop before heading home. Together they sat in the Gibson Girl Ice Cream Parlor. Ricky was savoring a Mickey-Mouse-shaped, red, yellow and green ice on a stick, while Eric was licking a moose tracks ice cream cone. The melodious refrain of "It's a Small World" repeatedly drifted through Eric's brain, just as it had for much of the two preceding hours since they had boarded the ride.

Ricky looked up at Eric, his smile as broad as that of the Mickey Mouse pop he was devouring. He leaned over and put his free arm around Eric and squeezed. "This has been the best day of my whole life. Uncle Eric, I love you."

A tingle raced through Eric's body. For a moment, he grew pensive. His experiences spanned far more years than Ricky's few, and over the course of them he had enjoyed many special days. But could he name one that was better? Maybe yes, but maybe not. "You know what: This is the best day of my life too. I love you."

They finished their treats and headed for the parking lot. Within minutes after they left Disneyland, Ricky was sound asleep in his car seat in the rear of Eric's rental. Coming to California, giving Carla a day of freedom from her challenging schedule and fulfilling his promise to take Ricky to Disneyland, had been anything but a sacrifice. Prior to coming, Eric had studied the map of the park and laid out a plan for the day. They had covered far less territory than he had anticipated, little more than a third. Eric was glad it had worked out that way. It gave him a good excuse to return, maybe more than once. In a single day, parenthood, an abstraction with vague appeal, had become remarkably enticing. He had discovered a new doorway to the joys of life. When shared with a youngster, especially the right one, the vicarious thrill of child-like adventures could equal anything one could experience directly. The anomalous observation was arguably as amazing as it was unremarkable. Eric had heard others express a similar view, but always it had passed through his ears, a seeming platitude laced with hyperbole. A trip to Disneyland, a day in the Magic Kingdom, had breathed meaning into the idea.

As he turned north toward Pomona and Carla's apartment, a thought crept into his head. Carla was a wonderful woman. She was intelligent and pretty, with a great personality. She was also a terrific friend. A son better than Ricky was hard to imagine. Living alone, going on frustrating dates with vapid women, was depressing. He could have the dream, a wife and family and even a picket fence. Tantalizing ruminations raced through his mind. Common sense cajoled him to seize the opportunity. To do otherwise would be folly. Yet a subtle, countervailing force from the depths of his brain demurred. Emotions stood in the way. Eric was not in love with Carla. Very simply, she was not Glenna Snow. His rational side reminded him that echoes of infatuation had placed Glenna on a pedestal so high that even the fairest mythological goddess could not compare. His heart refused to yield. Eric looked into the rearview mirror at the sleeping Ricky. The choice was hard, too hard for the busy freeways of Southern California. Another day, back in his Connecticut apartment, or somewhere, sometime, he would weigh the alternatives.

Knowledge is glorious. So much of one's life is devoted to its acquisition. But alas, there are times when ignorance is surely preferable.

Don Burns poured himself a mug of coffee, his second of the morning. Nearly two hours earlier, before seven, when he had arrived early to catch up on some paper work, the offices at

Quigley and Watkins had been deserted. He gazed out the window of the second-floor lounge toward the parking lot. Others were just beginning to arrive for the day. Out in the farthest corner, the better part of a football field away, Clint Horstmeyer, who normally came in his polished BMW, climbed out of the passenger side of an olive-green Nissan Sentra. Before exiting the parking lot, the Sentra circled closer to the building, near enough that Don could identify the driver as a woman. Who exactly, he couldn't say for sure, but the ugly colored car gave an unmistakable clue. Events in recent months, however, rendered the surmise dubious.

Rather than head back to his office, Don sipped his coffee by the window. Curiosity kept him in place. Clint always started his day at the coffeepot, and sure enough, less than two minutes later he arrived.

"Morning," said Don, holding his mug forth in salutation.

"Top of it to you." Clint, who only a week earlier had been promoted—his new position elevated him to a step below partner and made him Don's boss—reached for a Styrofoam cup and filled it. "You just arrive?"

"Actually, I came in early...had a few things that needed attention. And don't give me grief, because I'm not the eager beaver trying to impress."

"Sure." Clint took a sip.

"I noticed you got a ride into work today."

Clint's eyes widened. "Maybe you're not the eager beaver, but apparently, you're the proverbial owl."

"You mean wise?" Don doubted that was the allusion but tried the dodge anyway.

"I was referring to your vision...big keen eyes."

Don might have pointed out that the owl was renowned for nocturnal sight, but with one maneuver having already failed, discretion counseled against a second.

"Yeah...my car is in the shop, and I got a ride."

"Unless I'm mistaken, that was Rachel Wallace's car."

Clint eyed Don for a moment. "Let's go down to my office." Without waiting for a reply, he headed into the hallway. Don followed, and once they arrived, Clint closed the door behind them. He slipped into the chair behind his desk, gesturing Don to a seat on the opposite side.

"Yeah, Rachel drove me here, but that's strictly between us."

"I thought you broke up with her when you canned her."

Clint laughed.

Don waited.

"She and I are still an item."

"I don't get it. She's a crackerjack Administrative Assistant. One would be hard pressed to name any here as good. Why, if you like her, did you send her packing?"

Clint leaned back. A devilish grin stretched nearly to his ears. "Back at Williams, Gordon screwed me...screwed me royally. Got me an *F* freshman year, nearly enough to get me kicked outta school, and then senior year, along with Johanson, he convinced Carla to dump me. I told those bastards I'd get even. They may not have taken me seriously, but I meant it. When Clinton J. Horstmeyer makes a threat, it's a promise...Truth is, I didn't push Rachel out. She took the job over at Gordon's place to help me get him. You might say she's my mole."

"What do you plan to do?"

"That's for me to know, and Gordon to find out." Clint looked Don in the eye as he pointed a finger across the desk. "If I hadn't needed a ride—My car is being serviced—and you hadn't seen me get out of her car, this conversation would not have occurred. It's off the record...strictly off the record. Don't even think of repeating it." Clint folded his arms. "If anyone, especially Gordon, learns that Rachel and I are still linked, I'm holding you responsible."

"But suppose—"

"Don't suppose anything. If word gets out, your dick is a wick, and I've got the matches! One reason you got a job here was my say-so. One bad word from me, and you, my newcomer friend, will be out the door. I can guarantee that. And let me tell you, fresh from getting the boot at Kingman & Woodhill, you can ill-afford to get bounced here. You won't be able to get a job anywhere, especially if I tell prospective employers that you're a rotten, backstabbing conniver who'd screw his mother." Clint smiled before drawing in a deep breath. "Fortunately, I'm sure we understand one another, and such an unpleasant consequence will never ensue." Clint leaned forward against the desk. "I believe we're clear…eminently clear. Right?"

Don swallowed hard. He nodded.

Clint started to reach for his coffee but stopped. "By any chance did you watch the Red Sox last night?"

"Uh…no, but I…uh…heard they won."

"Yeah, it was a helluva game." Clint eyed his watch. "About time we get our noses to the grindstone." He got up from his seat and, as Don rose as well, he came around the desk and patted Don on the back before ushering him to the door. "Relax. You and I are in good shape."

Don forced a smile and headed to his office. All day the chilling conversation echoed. Where typically his day ended between five-thirty and six, the moment the clock struck five, he was out the door. The need for Linda's patient ear was undeniable. After pulling into the garage, he stepped through the mud room into the kitchen where Linda was preparing dinner.

"You're home early."

He pecked her on the cheek.

"Everything okay?"

He shrugged, though he suspected his face belied the gesture. "You might say Yogi Berra paid me a visit today."

"Excuse me?"

"It's *déjà vu…all over again*." The befuddled look that showed on Linda's face prompted Don to add, "That was one of Yogi's many curious sayings."

"And?"

"I know certain things that a friend needs to know. And just like Kingman & Woodhill, if I do what's right, I'm destined for walking papers."

Linda looked him in the eye. She said nothing.

She didn't need to. He had already addressed his predicament and what he had to do. The rationalizations he had used when he had tried to save his prior job had been all wrong. No way would he screw a friend again.

208

Linda put her arms around him and gave him a hug. "You'll tell me all about it over dinner. In the meantime, sit down and try to relax."

Don leaned his head back and forced a feeble smile. The warmth of Linda's arms, though hardly a panacea, was soothing. It was more than that. It was an oasis in what had been a day in a harsh desert.

In the decision-making process, one should always search for a win-win scenario. Alas, some decisions are Hobson choices. The lesser evil, not necessarily a minor one, is as well as one can do.

Don Burns picked up the receiver and reluctantly dialed Kyle Gordon's home number. He would have called sooner, if only to get the ordeal over, but he did not want to call during the dinner hour. Kyle's wife Katelyn answered, and, after a quick exchange of pleasantries, put Kyle on the line.

"What's up?"

"I've got some information that you need to know."

"Whoa...this sounds serious."

Whether Kyle's comment was in jest, Don was uncertain. Regardless, he needed to go directly to the issue. "Rachel Wallace, your office assistant, is still dating Clint Horstmeyer." The immediate reaction Don had anticipated was not forthcoming. "Did you hear what I said?"

"Yes."

"And?"

"And apparently, I've been had."

"That's probably a good assessment, not that I know what Clint has in mind. But one thing is sure, he's out to screw you. He still holds a grudge from back at Williams."

"No surprise. He vowed he'd get even someday."

"I know he threatened, but any reasonable person would have let it go."

"Maybe so, but who ever said that Clint was reasonable? And anyway, how can you be sure about his relationship with Rachel?"

"He told me, not that he had originally intended to. His car was in the shop, and Rachel drove him to the office. I happened to be looking out the window when she dropped him off. It was only after I asked him about it that he clued me in. He swore me to secrecy and warned of dire consequences if I blabbed."

"So, you're taking a big risk by telling me."

Don knew that all too well, but he was pleased Kyle recognized the point. "Whatever you do, please don't let Clint or Rachel know that I told you."

"Don't worry. My lips are sealed."

Though Don trusted his pal, he harbored concerns. If the information somehow leaked, whatever the source, he would get the blame. So too, if Kyle fired Rachel. "So, how do you plan to deal with the situation?"

Kyle had already begun contemplating the issue. "Great question...and for the moment, I have no idea."

Following some small talk, along with Kyle's thanks for the warning, the call concluded. As he hung up the receiver, Don worried that he had just committed career suicide. Nevertheless, he was glad he had taken the risk. Self-preservation at the expense of a friend, a path previously traveled, would have been worse.

When the FBI or the police or any government enforcement agency is involved with one's affairs, it is generally better to be working with them, rather than against them. But the benefit of their help comes at a cost. Most times they call the shots, and those shots may be unpleasant.

As soon as he finished talking to Don, Kyle dialed the number for Denny Larson's cell phone. Making the call the following day from the office when Rachel would be close by was a bad idea. Impatience, a need for immediate clarification as to what he was getting himself into, negated any possibility of waiting for a more opportune hour. A moment later, he heard a familiar voice on the other end.

"Larson speaking."

"Hi Denny. It's Kyle Gordon. Am I getting you at a bad time?"

"No. I'm just sitting in the office, working as usual."

"The response caught Kyle by surprise. A moment before dialing, he had checked his watch—8:27.

"Just teasing. I'm at home in my easy chair with a beer and the Nationals' game. So, what's up?"

"I just got off the phone with a friend who tipped me off that my Administrative Assistant, Rachel Wallace, is still dating her former boss, Clinton Horstmeyer. When I hired her a couple of months ago, she claimed she needed to leave Quigley and Watkins because Clint was an unbearable tyrant. My friend says Clint wants to settle scores with me from our days at Williams. Apparently, Wallace is part of his plan."

"Intriguing."

Kyle waited a moment, hoping he might get a more meaningful response. It was not forthcoming. "So, tell me— what am I getting myself into?"

"What do you mean?"

C'mon, I wasn't born on the seventh Thursday of April. "You folks at the SEC are doing some kind of investigation of Quigley and Watkins, and you've got me recording conversations with one of their former employees, who just happens to be in cahoots with one of their brokers that is trying to screw me. Am I getting mired in something that may blow up in my face?"

"I don't think so."

The glib reply frustrated Kyle. "You think I should confront Wallace, maybe even fire her or—"

"Whoa...slow down. Firing her will do neither of us any good. It won't get Clint off your back, and it will impede our investigation."

Kyle wondered if Denny was merely looking out for the SEC's interests. "Firing Wallace might get me out from the middle of whatever is going on between your offices and Quigley and Watkins."

"Possible, but you'll still have Clint to deal with. And that said, you'll be better off working with us than not."

Once again, the argument made perfect sense...from Denny's perspective. "So, what are you proposing?"

"That we go ahead exactly as planned. Look at it this way. The only difference from before is that you now know that Wallace, along with Clint, is out to get you. The new information puts you in a better position. You know to be wary when dealing with her."

The eminently logical point was hard to argue. Why, Kyle wondered, did it leave him anything but satisfied? The analysis underscored that he had never been comfortable with the original arrangement.

"You mind telling me who clued you in that Wallace is in cahoots with Horstmeyer?"

Kyle had promised not to let Wallace or Horstmeyer know that Don was his source. Telling Larson was different. Disclosure in no way violated his promise. And concerned as he was about his own situation, he was desperate to get as much information as possible. "Fine, I'll give you my source, provided you tell me if my source and/or Horstmeyer are part of your investigation."

"You drive a hard bargain, a two-for-one trade."

"Seems you've forgotten that you asked me to be your eyes and ears...to record my conversations with Wallace."

"Touché."

"Does that mean you'll answer my questions?"

"Provided you answer mine."

But for the fact that a bad answer from Larson could place him in a difficult position, Kyle would have been pleased with the bargain. "My source that Horstmeyer is still dating Wallace is Don Burns. You may remember him from Williams. He graduated with us, and he recently joined Quigley and Watkins."

"The name is vaguely familiar, not that I can attach a face. As for your questions, Horstmeyer is the primary target of our investigation. Whether others at Quigley and Watkins will be drawn into it is not completely clear, though at this point I have no reason to assume so. Regardless, you understand that all of our communications have to remain completely confidential."

"You mean I can't give Don Burns, the friend who warned me, the same courtesy?"

"Absolutely not. That could blow our investigation."

Even before he had posed the question, Kyle was certain he would get a *no*. "So, we all set?"

"Let's just say for the time being. If there's any change, I'll give you a heads-up in advance. Okay?"

"I guess so." As the conversation ended, Kyle's reply reverberated in his head. He had voiced acquiescence, but not without reservations.

The Book of Proverbs teaches that a virtuous woman is worth far more than rubies (Bible, Book of Proverbs, Chap. XXXI, Verse 6). If by chance she is wise as well, then perhaps her value exceeds diamonds...or maybe even stocks illegally purchased with inside information.

About fifteen minutes after Kyle had hung up the telephone following his conversation with Larson, Katelyn arrived home from grocery shopping. Kyle immediately filled her in on what had happened: his conversation with Don; that Rachel was apparently in cahoots with Clint; and his conversation with Denny Larson. Even as he had agreed to Larson's requirement of complete confidentiality, Kyle had planned to share the information with his wife. He shared everything with her, never doubting whether she would hold their confidence inviolate. Katelyn was both a needed outlet and sounding board. "Nice can of worms, isn't it?"

Katelyn nodded thoughtfully before reaching into her shopping bag. She drew out a large almond crescent cookie and handed it to Kyle. "Maybe this will help."

Kyle took a bite of the flavorful confectionary. He smiled before gesturing at the kitchen table. "So, what do you think?" he said, as he seated himself at the oval bear-claw.

Katelyn put some eggs and a container of milk into the refrigerator and then joined him at the table. "How well do you know this Denny fellow?"

"Denny Larson. He was in my dorm, one floor up, my freshman year at Williams. We spoke loads of times, not that he was one of my close friends. After freshman year, our paths only crossed occasionally. I think he was in my psych class junior year, but that's about it."

"You sure you can trust him?"

"I think so." Kyle's doubts were greater than his words. "Don't forget, he's with the SEC."

"Understood, but..."

"But what?"

Katelyn heaved a sigh. "I hate to see you dragged into some cloak and dagger investigation."

"Come on. It's hardly that."

Her brow knitted. "An SEC investigation which has you surreptitiously recording your employee, who is part of a scheme to screw you. I'd call that cloak and dagger."

Kyle found it hard to disagree. "So, what would you recommend?"

"Perhaps you could get a letter signed by Larson indicating that he asked you to work with the SEC and to record your conversations with Wallace. That way, if things become messy, you'll have evidence of how and why you got involved."

Why didn't I think of that? "Damn, now I know why I married you. You're beautiful...and smart." He leaned over and kissed Katelyn. He glanced up at the clock on the microwave. "I'm going to give Larson a call back right now." Kyle again dialed Larson's cell phone. Though the task spawned anxiety, the result justified the effort. By nine-thirty Kyle had acquired some peace of mind. He had a fax on Securities Exchange Commission letterhead, signed by Dennis Larson, citing their investigation of Quigley and Watkins and requesting Kyle's assistance, including the recording of conversations. The following morning Kyle stopped at the bank and stored the letter in his safe deposit box.

Masks come in many forms. Some, like those worn by robbers, the Lone Ranger and children on Halloween, are made of cloth or rubber or plastic. Others are little more than the product of misleading reactions: a smile hiding pain, a statement contrary to one's feelings or simple silence. Still others are mere labels. Such is the nature of an alias or nom de plume.

"Long time no hear from you." Telephone receiver in one hand, Kyle pressed the mute button on his television remote with the other. He leaned back in his family-room easy chair. "So, what's new in the Sunshine State?"

"No complaints. Things are going well at the school. I don't make big bucks like you financial wizards, but I do love it. This year I've got the best crop of students ever. They're enthusiastic, intelligent and a joy to teach. How are things at the brokerage firm, now that you're on your own?"

"Overall, I'd say better than expected." Kyle felt the need to be circumspect. Much as he would have liked to tell Bill that his recently hired Administrative Assistant was a plant in cahoots with Clint Horstmeyer, his promise to Denny Larson barred the disclosure. "How's that book of yours coming along?"

"Ocean Cliff, my publisher, expects it to hit the shelves in a few months."

"That will be cool, a book written by my pal, Bill Young."

"Written by me, but not under my name."

"So, you opted for a pseudonym. I remember some months back you mentioned that possibility—concern about tough critics, if I recall."

"Yeah, this way I can have it both ways, anonymity if my book bombs, and credit if it's a hit...though a part of me is leaning toward anonymity regardless how it fares."

"Ever the modest one."

"Private is more accurate."

215

Kyle chuckled, but only to himself. Bill's response had served to prove Kyle's point. He said, "Private is more Eric's style than yours."

"Yeah, I guess that's true."

"So, what's your pseudonym?"

"Not telling anyone, maybe not even my family."

"How the hell will I get your book?"

"If it bombs, you won't. But if it's even half-successful, not necessarily financially but in the minds of the critics, I'll send you a copy. That's a promise...Uh, while I've got you on the phone, I've...uh...been wondering, how is Don making out...you know, with his new job at Quigley and Watkins?"

Bill's hesitancy when asking the question paled in comparison to the discomfort Kyle felt about responding. Conflicting forces were at work. Larson's gag order limited what he could say. But Bill was entitled to an answer. He had been instrumental in helping Don get the job, not that Don knew it. Don was also unaware that Kyle had enlisted Bill to help, another reason Kyle felt compelled to give his buddy's inquiry more than lip service. He said, "From what I know, he's doing okay." The response echoed in Kyle's ears. It was the very lip service he had meant to avoid. But with the SEC investigation, his tongue was tied. "You might better ask Don. He can give you the lowdown much better than I."

"You telling me that two members of the Inseparables living in the same city and working in the same field aren't keeping track of one another?"

"Uh...no, it's not like that, but...you know how it is...when you get away from the office. You like to talk things other than shop."

"First, I don't know how it is; and second, it's hard to imagine that Don doesn't say anything about his new job?"

Kyle was glad he was on the telephone, rather than face to face. Eye contact would have been tough. "No, I didn't mean it that way. I suspect his job is going along okay, but folks in a new situation generally don't say too much."

"Are you suggesting that, like Eric, Don is a very private person?"

Determined to avoid digging a deeper hole, Kyle said, "Maybe, but enough of the mundane, tell me about your love life."

Laughter bubbled from the other end of the line.

"What kind of response is that?"

"What I'd call a fair description of my love life. I've had a few dates here and a few dates there, but nothing to write home about."

"What about that school where you teach or the apartment complex where you live? You must meet *some* attractive women there."

"Yup, and most are married or living with a significant other."

"Have you tried any dating web sites?"

This time a groan reverberated.

"Translation needed again."

"I tried *Connecting.com*. The first woman I linked up with said she was twenty-seven. Turned out, she was more like forty-five. Then there was the pretty brunette from Texas. We met at a bistro on a Sunday afternoon. She had a great figure and was really nice to talk to."

"So, what's the problem?"

"After our date, I checked her out on one of those background sites. She served more than a year in prison for embezzling over thirty thousand dollars from her employer. She also had a conviction for credit-card fraud. Whether she did time for that, I couldn't say…Hell, if I could find a peach like your Katelyn or Don's Linda, I'd be glad to commit. But enough about my love life. How's our fourth compatriot, Eric, making out in the world of women?"

Kyle chuckled. Even before he regained composure, Bill responded to his own question.

"Unlike you who requires explanations of odd-sounding reactions, I have highly sensitive antennae. Eric is still hung up on Glenna…Right?"

"As far as I know."

"A Renoir on the wall of the Clark. Damn, the guy's more screwed up than I."

"C'mon, we both know that's impossible. Of course, kind soul that I am, I'd never say."

"Sure…and on that kind note, I'll let you go, but on one condition: you don't let too many months go by until we talk again…with the next on your nickel."

"Deal." Kyle hung up the receiver. With his faint reflection in the family-room window staring back, he sat motionless in reflective contemplation. Staying in touch with his three college buddies was important. Disparate lives, as well as distance, didn't make it easy. But it was important…too important to be ignored.

CHAPTER XV

EVERY TIME A STOCK IS SOLD, it is also bought. Therefore, someone thinks it is going down, while someone else thinks it is headed up. Both the buyer and the seller have it figured out. Their flawless logic can't be wrong...or maybe not. On second thought, skip the maybe.

Fresh from Quigley and Watkins' regular Friday afternoon meeting, Don Burns headed for the parking lot with mixed emotions. As usual, the two-thirty meeting had wrapped up close to three, giving the weekend an early start. Unlike Monday through Thursday when employees, especially non-partners, like himself, were never discouraged from working late, on Fridays everyone left immediately after the meeting. The early TGIF lifted Don's spirits. However, the primary subject of the weekly get-together subtly gnawed in the back of his mind.

"Burns."

The sound of his name turned Don's head and brought him to a halt. Hurrying to catch up was Clint Horstmeyer.

"Looks like Wolldorn Manufacturing is the stock of the month."

The comment only served to amplify Don's concern. "What do you think Gene (Gene Watkins was one of the firm's founding senior partners) meant when he urged us to put Wolldorn's stock at the forefront when dealing with clients?"

"Hello?" Clint gave Don a look. "You really need an explanation?"

"No. I know he wants us to give it a little extra push, but..."

Clint shook his head.

Don searched for a delicate way to make his inquiry without sounding stupid. "One can push a stock and...one can *push* a stock. You know what I mean?"

Clint chuckled briefly. "If you're not sure, stop in Gene's office first thing Monday morning and ask him. Or better yet, give him a call at home tonight."

The sarcasm helped confirm Don's worst fear.

"In case you've forgotten, our firm makes a market in Wolldorn's stock. With three consecutive losing quarters and a balance sheet loaded with debt, resulting in a price drop from twenty-two down to just over eleven bucks, without a pick-me-up, it could be headed for the big dumper."

"Given those facts, how..." Don clipped his tongue before uttering the phrase *in good conscience.* "... how can we push it?"

Clint rolled his eyes. "Wolldorn has downside risk. No doubt about it. On the other hand, beaten down as it is, if things turn around, its upside potential is huge."

Whether Clint was as optimistic as his words or voicing the party line, Don had no idea. "What about the fact that our firm is making a market in the stock?"

"No problem. Anytime I recommend a stock in which we make a market, I include that in my letter that gives the lowdown, not that most clients have any clue what it means *to make a market.*" Clint laughed again.

"Do you plan to recommend Wolldorn to your clients whose investment profiles are conservative and/or geared to preserving principal?"

"Nope. I don't look for trouble." Clint winked. "Of course, when I bring new clients on board, I encourage them to fill out their profiles indicating a desire for growth, including some speculative opportunities. The way I put it: The best portfolio is a diversified portfolio. Allow room for everything." Clint glanced at his watch. "What the hell are we doing? Talking shop in the parking lot when our weekend should be underway. And speaking of that, I booked my club's Cesna

Turbo. I'm flying down to Lancaster, Pennsylvania tonight and coming back on Sunday. You take care, and have a good weekend."

"You too." Don turned and walked slowly to his Honda and climbed in. He slipped the key into the ignition, but rather than turning it, sat in silent reflection. Was he about to face the same unsavory scenario he had confronted at Kingman & Woodhill? Did it have to happen so soon? Was it pervasive throughout the brokerage business or just his good fortune to face a repeated diet? Or maybe he was making a mountain out of a molehill. Perhaps his worry was unfounded. Gene Watkins was hardly another Charlie Bascomb. From what he had seen, except for a couple of exceptions, Clint being one, the team at Quigley and Watkins looked out for clients, not that the interests of the firm were ever given short shrift. Don glanced in the direction of the building. With steadfast conviction, he gritted his teeth. Whatever others did, if and when he talked to a client about Wolldorn Manufacturing, he would be up front with all the facts, and in no event would he recommend it to any client who had either expressed a need to be conservative or who could ill-afford to take significant risk. Whatever the personal consequences, no way would he repeat the mistakes he had made at Kingman & Woodhill. Though hardly a panacea, the resolve mitigated the discomfort stirred at the afternoon meeting.

Man was never meant to fly. And yet he does. Amidst the seductive diversions of a theme park, aboard gravity-defying balloons, airplanes and rockets, or in the reverie and dreams of his mind, he soars far beyond the mundane locales of terra firma.

Having just purchased three tickets, one of which was a child's, Eric headed to the Guest Relations building on the right side of the main entrance to Disneyland. He checked his watch—8:55. He had arranged to meet Carla and Ricky there at 9:00. He would have come with them, presumably after staying

221

at Carla's place, twenty miles to the north in Pomona, but he had planned the outing in conjunction with a business trip to Granite's San Diego office, eighty miles south of Disneyland. Rather than fly out on Sunday for his Monday morning meeting, he made the trip on Saturday and arranged to meet Carla and Ricky on Sunday. Up at six, after a hot breakfast at the Hampton Inn where he was staying, he drove his rental car to the theme park.

Minutes after Eric had arrived at Guest Relations, he spotted Carla and Ricky coming his way. A wave of his arms drew a like response from Carla. Ricky began racing the fifty yards that separated them. Roughly a dozen seconds later, Ricky leaped into Eric's arms.

"Can we go to Adventure Land first? Can we, Uncle Eric?"

"Wherever you say, that's where we go…so long as your mom gives the okay." Eric doubted there would be any objections, and even if there were, he assumed they would be ineffectual.

A moment later Carla arrived, and after greeting Eric with a hug and a peck on the cheek, she focused on Ricky. "Rule number one: You don't run away from me."

"But I only ran to Uncle Eric."

"Maybe so, but from now on, stay right with us."

Eric held up the tickets. "Ground rules set, shall we begin the fun?"

"We're going to Adventure Land," said Ricky.

"Ricky voted, and I gave the *okay*, provided you didn't exercise a veto."

Carla chuckled before leading the way.

Through the turn styles at the entrance, down Main Street and then off to their left, they wended their way to Adventure Land. The moment they reached the area, Ricky pointed at a boat that was boarding. "Let's go on that."

"The Jungle Cruise?" said Eric, reading the sign at the boarding point.

"Yeah, the Jungle Cruise!" With one hand, Ricky grabbed Eric's hand, and with his other, his mother's. "Hurry, before we miss it."

A minute later, the trio was on board and soon winding along a river amidst a jungle filled with animatrons. Monkeys swinging from vines squealed. Hippos, their gigantic mouths opening wide, drew menacingly close. Left and right, a wide-eyed Ricky took in the action. Normally loquacious, the spellbound youngster remained silent.

Their boat rounded a bend in the river. From the rear, the voice of the Captain over the loud speaker bellowed: "Watch out! Wild elephants on the left!"

A huge pachyderm drew closer to the boat. From his trunk, a burst of spray doused those on the port side.

"He got me!" shouted Ricky.

"Me too," said Eric, who, on the outside, was wetter yet.

"Boy, this is cool," said Ricky.

A quick scan of the jungle-river scene had Eric concurring. The duplication of nature, animation and sounds were all amazing. He glanced at Ricky. The precocious youngster's face was a candlelit jack-o-lantern. Eric soaked it all in. Undeniably the Jungle Cruise was fun, but experiencing it vicariously through Ricky's eyes, sublime. Before long, the voyage, little more than five minutes, drew to halt along the dock, close to where they had boarded.

"For a second I thought those hippos were going to eat us," said Eric.

Ricky shot him a look. "C'mon, Uncle Eric, we both know they weren't real."

Carla jabbed a finger into Eric's hip.

He shrugged. "Okay...so maybe—"

"Let's go ride that one." Ricky pointed toward the nearby Pirates of the Caribbean.

Less than five minutes elapsed before they were aboard a boat winding through subterranean passages. From chamber to chamber they sailed until reaching the cavernous hall where cannon balls from a pirate ship on one side and a fort on the other crashed alongside their vessel. Eric closed his eyes, not from fear, but to indelibly stamp joyous emotions into his brain. A rare and glorious sense of harmony, the importance of family, gripped him. And too, he grew conscious of its anomaly. There in Disneyland, reality's ultimate escape into an unmitigated world of make-believe, with eyes locked tight, he was capturing magic, but magic that was real, magic that dwarfed the heights of fantasy.

So went the remainder of the day, its ebb and flow, transitions among various levels of delight. The ride back to San Diego and his meeting the next day were little more than blurs intermingled into a continued high. Soon he was back on board another ride, one seemingly as quixotic and chimerical as those at Disneyland. Thirty-eight thousand feet above middle America, Eric was seated next to the window of a United Airlines, Boeing 727. That a humongous mass of metal could soar through vacuous space was arguably harder to comprehend than the most bizarre of Disneyland's illusions. Recollections of a beach ball spinning above a column of air at the local science museum and his high school science teacher's explanation of Bernoulli's famed principle, the basis of lift, did little to quell the oddity.

Eric gazed out the window. Down below, puffy white clouds floated gently past. The world was upside down, and yet, it was perfect. He closed his eyes. He was walking down Main Street at Disneyland. Hand in hand, with Ricky in the middle and Carla and him on either side, they strolled, exactly as they had done less than forty-eight hours before. The image was inveigling. He could turn it into a lifetime reality. When compared to his current life…there was no comparison. Not that he was unhappy with his lot at Granite, but night after night, returning to his apartment alone, all too often his only company was ennui. Carla was a wonderful person. A better kid than Ricky was hard to imagine. Passing up the chance for the made-to-order family was a recipe for regret. But candor could not deny that Carla, however dear, was only a friend. Love her? He did, but like a sister, not amorously. Back at Williams when they had stopped dating, that had been established. But maybe…just maybe…

Ambivalence turned his brain into a hummingbird, a darting, stopping, starting instrument of indecision. Eric tilted his seat back, intermittently dozing. Both his mind and body drifted somewhere in the far-flung space midway between Disneyland and his apartment outside Hartford.

224

On rare occasions great acting earns one an Oscar. Most times the rewards are less. And now and then, even the finest performance becomes one's ticket to the slammer.

"You got a minute?"

Kyle, busy reading the Value Line analyses of several utilities, looked up from behind his desk. "Of course, anytime." He gestured to a chair on the opposite side.

Rachel, who was standing in the doorway, closed the portal and took a seat.

"What's up?"

"I've got some information that I think you'll find very interesting."

It had been about six weeks since Rachel had broached the subject of Diquor. With his right knee, Kyle pressed the button that turned on the recording device the Securities Exchange Commission had installed beneath his desk. He had done so a number of times before, a couple merely for practice, but all had been totally uneventful. "So, fill me in on this interesting information."

"This morning, as I occasionally do, I accessed Clint Horstmeyer's computer. Following the close of the market today, Tiqoud plans to offer twenty-five dollars per share to buy out Solstinergy. As of two minutes ago, Solstinergy was trading at 13.37. Quigley and Watkins makes a market in Solstinergy."

"Very interesting." Kyle tried to remain impassive.

"I thought you'd think so."

"A person could make a lot of money if he bought Solstinergy today."

"He certainly could." An arc nearly the size of a banana was etched on Rachel's face.

Ever since she had first come to him disclosing her access to inside information, Kyle had run countless scenarios through his head, planning an apropos reaction. "I assume you're telling me so I can make a killing."

225

"I want you to have the opportunity."

"I appreciate that." With the benefit of the rehearsals, Kyle was well armed. "You plan to take advantage of the information too?"

"I might, but for two reasons. The first, the important one, is that I lack the funds."

"People are known to buy on margin."

"My buying on margin when I'm fresh from a position at Quigley and Watkins would be a red flag. Regardless, when you have no money, you can't open a margin account."

Her point was well taken. "So, what's the second reason?"

"I'm saving my pennies. A year or two down the road, when my connection to Quigley and Watkins is much further in the rearview mirror, I should get my chance. In the meantime, this is yours."

Kyle nodded. Outwardly the gesture seemingly reflected agreement. His thoughts, however, revealed something quite different. Rachel Wallace had come well prepared, perhaps better than he.

"So, you gonna take advantage of the opportunity? You never know if another will come along, especially one this good."

Kyle checked his watch—11:53. "I might...but lunch will allow me time to mull it over. Regardless, I'd have to decide how much Solstinergy to buy."

"Well, the more you invest, the more you'll rake in." She got up from her seat and headed out to the reception area.

Kyle remained at his desk for about five minutes. He ran some numbers through his head, calculating potential profits. The activity was secondary to his primary purpose, killing a bit of time before heading out to lunch.

"I've got your back." Comforting words, not always confirmed by actions.

Once he was out the door, rather than going to one of his favorite restaurants, Kyle headed to a quiet park about a half-

226

mile from his office. On the way he picked up a couple of hot dogs and a *Pepsi* from a street vendor. He found a bench in a deserted area. After wolfing down his food, he pulled out his cell phone, scrolled down to the appropriate number and tapped on it. A moment later, a voice responded from the other end.

"Larson speaking."

"Hi, it's Kyle...Kyle Gordon. Am I getting you at a bad time?"

"Not at all. What's up?"

"Rachel Wallace, my Administrative Assistant, brought me an inside tip this morning. According to her, Tiqoud Industries plans to offer twenty-five dollars per share to buy out Solstinergy tomorrow. As of a little while ago, Solstinergy was trading just over thirteen dollars."

"What, if anything, did you do with the information?"

"Nothing yet. I left the office for lunch. I'm alone in a park."

"Good. When you go back to the office, I want you to buy it."

"Really?"

"Don't worry. It's fine."

Easy for you to say. "How much are we talking about?"

A protracted pause ensued. "Let's do three thousand shares. That'll make it about forty thousand dollars, enough to be serious money. If need be, I can wire the funds to your personal account."

"That's okay. I can use my money market."

"Good...but just remember, whatever the outcome, win or lose, it's on the SEC's dime. You can't keep the profits, and you won't bear the losses. That's a promise."

"If you were to bet, which do you think it'll be?"

"Well...my guess is they'll throw you a bone before they screw you. That way they might get you to go for a really big pay day, the kind that's likely to be on margin and leave you in serious debt."

Kyle leaned back and stared at the cumulus-dotted blue sky. *What the hell am I getting into?*

"You still there?"

"Unfortunately, yes."

227

"What does that mean?"

"Oh…just that I'm less than enthusiastic about the whole scenario."

"I understand. But as I've said all along, we've got you covered."

You may have said it, but it's still my neck.

"So, when you go back to the office, buy three thousand shares, and make sure Wallace knows about it."

Kyle heaved a sigh. "I'll do it, not that I'm eager." Moments later, with the call completed, he slipped his cell phone into his pocket. He headed back to the office where he instructed Rachel, who executed most of his trades, to buy three thousand shares of Solstinergy at the market for his personal account. He reached for a prospectus and began reading. He was halfway through the first page when he realized he had no clue what it said. His mind remained transfixed on his otherwise illegal purchase. It had been made at the direction and with the blessing of the SEC. Larson and his cohorts would protect him from any adverse consequences. Everything was hunky dory. Why then did he feel so tense?

———

When it comes to a horse race, there's nothing better than an inside tip from one who knows the outcome even before the jockeys board their mounts…unless, by chance, the tip is bogus.

Having just finished his dinner, rather than heading into the family room to watch the nightly national news as he normally did, Kyle went to the den and his desktop computer. He clicked on *Yahoo Finance* and punched in the symbol for Solstinergy. He scrolled down to the stock's headlines and clicked again. There it was: "Solstinergy lowers guidance for the quarter from a per-share profit of twelve cents to a loss of four cents." He checked for other news, namely an announcement that Tiquod Industries had tendered an offer to buy out Solstinergy. It was nowhere to be seen. Rather than doubling, Solstinergy was certain to take a big dive.

He headed back down to the kitchen and gave Katelyn the news.

"What do you plan to do?"

"First thing tomorrow, I'll confront Rachel."

Katelyn loaded the last of the dirty dishes into the dishwasher. "You're not going to let her know that you're working with the SEC, are you?"

"Of course not. Denny Larson would blow his top, not that I would think of upsetting his apple cart."

"What do you think Rachel will say?"

Kyle shook his head. "I have no clue...though it won't surprise me if she plays dumb. Based upon what I've seen, she's a damn good actress." Kyle observed a curious expression on Katelyn's face. "What's the matter?"

"Oh, I was just thinking. This whole thing could really put Don in a tough spot."

"Understood...and I'll be extra careful in that regard. Not only will I not let on that Don clued me in, but I'll give no hint that I know she's in cahoots with Clint."

Katelyn's odd look failed to disappear.

"You have a problem with how I plan to handle Rachel?"

"No...not that. I was wondering about Larson, what he might do next?"

Kyle thought for moment. "Damned if I know."

"Well, I hope he takes care of you."

"Hey, Denny is a good guy. He assured me, he had my back." Despite the confident words, trepidations gnawed.

Katelyn gave Kyle a protracted look. "Seems you're the one with the strange expression now."

Kyle shrugged. "You're quite perceptive, not to mention wise."

"Did I miss something?"

Kyle went over to his wife, put his arm over her shoulder and kissed her on the cheek. "Let's just say I'm mighty glad you had me get that fax from Denny requesting that I play along in his detective game."

The foxy farmer lays a trap. The fox, though sly, is presumably no match. And so, the trap ensnares the fox...or sometimes, the farmer.

The following morning Kyle arrived at his office just before nine. He had mapped out his strategy and rehearsed some lines he would throw at Rachel. He unlocked the door. As he stepped across the threshold, he spotted an envelope at his feet. He immediately surmised the source. The tight seal of the portal around all four edges precluded the possibility it had been slid under the door. He was the last to leave the night before, and only one other person had a key to the office. That person was Rachel. Kyle picked up the envelope and carried it through the reception area into his office where he opened it. Inside was a typewritten note that read:

> *Dear Mr. Gordon:*
> *This is to inform you that I hereby resign my position as your Administrative Assistant effective immediately. When you contacted me several months ago and lured me away from my position at Quigley and Watkins, you misled me. The opportunities and benefits that you told me about were not forthcoming. Your version of so-called ethics was worse yet. You have disappointed me greatly.*
> *Rachel C. Wallace*

"You lousy bitch!" Kyle pounded a fist on his desk. "I misled you? Bullshit! I lured you away from your job at Quigley? The hell I did! You came to me begging for a job, telling me that Clint Horstmeyer was a browbeating bastard." Kyle stared out the window. If it had been open, people in the parking lot would have heard his rant. He took another look at the note. Though it was dated that morning, he was willing to bet it had been prepared either the preceding day or perhaps earlier yet.

He sat down at his desk and stewed for several minutes before he leaned over to his computer and punched in the symbol for Solstinergy. The stock was trading at 4.87. It had tanked more than sixty percent following management's after-hours warning that the company would incur a loss, rather than an expected profit, and that guidance indicated hard times for the foreseeable future. His $40,000 investment was worth roughly $15,000. Knowing he could count on Denny Larson and the SEC to make him whole provided solace; nevertheless, concerns, ones he tried to dismiss, lurked.

His response to the turn of events, a call to Denny Larson, was obvious. But prior to dialing, he took a moment to assess Rachel's strategy. Was it not risky? An initial affirmative answer fell by the wayside once he re-evaluated the facts in light of what had occurred during the preceding twenty-four hours. She and Clint had no idea he had contacted the SEC. As far as they were concerned, he had voluntarily traded on inside information. No way would he dare complain. From their perspective, not only would he have no right to reimbursement, but if he voiced an objection, he would be acknowledging that he was guilty of a crime. Such a complaint would send him to prison. Kyle glanced again at Rachel's note. He felt his teeth grind. He could not, however, deny that Rachel and Clint's scheme was ingenious.

He reached for the telephone receiver but stopped before picking it up. Rachel had a key to the office. She could have bugged it. The thought was arguably paranoid, but he was taking no chances. He headed to a quiet area outside. Using his cell phone, he dialed Denny at the SEC.

"Hi Kyle. I know it's you from my caller ID. I assume you're alone, a place where you can talk."

"Yes. As a matter of fact, I went outside my office, just to be safe, not that Rachel will be coming in."

"God, don't tell me you fired her and, worse yet, let her in on our involvement."

"Nothing like that."

"She out sick or have the day off?"

"The bitch quit, and she left me a parting note. I'll read it to you." Kyle proceeded to read the resignation letter.

"Sounds like you were a nasty taskmaster."

"You gotta—"

"C'mon, I'm teasing."

"When it comes to jokes, you got the wrong guy on the wrong day. And just so we're clear, the twenty-five or so grand I lost on Solstinergy is on your dime."

"Absolutely."

The response eased Kyle's pique. A knot in his stomach made him conscious just how wound up he was. He took a deep breath. A voice within pressed him to apologize for the sharp tongue he had brandished a moment earlier; frustration kept the expression of regret from his lips.

"If you don't mind, I'll have my guy, Lionel Fisher—he's the one who installed the recording device under your desk—pick up the recordings."

"Fine. Just have him give me a call before he comes. That way, I'll be sure to be here."

"Will do. And before I go, I want you to know that we appreciate your cooperation. I know you weren't comfortable getting in the middle of this. But as I've said before, rest assured, we've got your back and we'll make you whole."

"Thanks." As the call concluded and Kyle put his cell phone into his pocket, he felt much better than he had two minutes earlier. The reiterated guarantee was a needed injection of valium.

CHAPTER XVI

WORD TRAVELS FAST. Sometimes those in the know are the last to know.

Over a week had passed since Kyle had spoken to Denny Larson. With Rachel gone, Kyle was putting in long hours, forced to do a multitude of additional tasks, many of which, though necessary, were mundane. A temporary employee, who was coming into the office for four hours each day, helped reduce the burden, but owing to unfamiliarity, there were numerous duties she could not perform. Add to the equation that she lacked Rachel's skills and was hardly a self-starter, and Kyle had his hands full. A couple of days earlier, Kyle had placed an advertisement in the *Republican*, Springfield's leading newspaper and the largest daily in western Massachusetts, but it would be at least several weeks, and perhaps longer, before he would be able to bring a new Administrative Assistant on board.

In the meantime, rather than go out for lunch, most days he brought a brown bag and worked through the noon hour. Such was not the case, the Friday of the first full week after Rachel's departure. Just before noon, he headed for lunch at the Kingston Inn. The stone structure still sported the original hand-hewn interior timbers that had been part of its construction two centuries earlier. Kyle loved the place, not merely for its character and its fabulous overstuffed sandwiches, each of which bore the name of a founding father, but also because he was sure to find familiar faces from the local brokerage community.

The moment he walked through the huge hickory door, one dressed on either side with a kerosene lantern, a voice off to his right calling his name drew his attention. Jack Waterson, seated in a booth along with Vic Kolsin, motioned Kyle to join them.

"How you doin'?" said Waterson, sliding over to make room for Kyle.

"Good…You fellows at the start or end of your meal?"

"Just got here two minutes ago," said Kolsin. "Haven't even ordered yet." Kolsin seemed to study Kyle.

"Something the matter?"

Kolsin's brow dipped. "You giving us the business?"

"Business? What are you talking about?"

"You mean you haven't heard the news?"

"What news?"

Kolsin shot Kyle a skeptical look. "About your buddy from Williams and that woman who works for you. It's all over town."

Kyle assumed he was referring to Clint and Rachel. As for the news, he had no idea. "Apparently, it's not quite all over town, at least not so much that it reached my ears."

Kolsin gave him another look. "You really don't know?"

Kyle shrugged. "Know what?"

"That just this morning the feds arrested Clinton Horstmeyer and…what's her name, the one who works for you."

"No, I didn't know. And if you're referring to Rachel Wallace—"

"Yeah, that's the one."

"She quit on me a week ago, and with absolutely no notice. But here, tell me about this arrest."

"There's nothing to tell," said Waterson. "All anybody knows is that a federal marshal showed up at the Quigley and Watkins' office and hauled Horstmeyer off to jail."

"Word has been spreading faster than a jackrabbit caught in a vegetable garden." Kolsin gestured at Kyle. "Given that Wallace was your employee, maybe you have some idea why the two were arrested."

Kyle had a strong suspicion, but Larson had instructed him to keep his mouth shut. He shrugged as innocently as possible.

Waterson scratched his head. "I wonder if her quitting on you had something to do with her arrest. Maybe she saw the handwriting on the wall."

Kyle endeavored to maintain a blank expression. No way was he about to allow the speculation to pry into what he knew.

Across the table, Kolsin sighed. "Like lawyers and politicians, our profession is always getting a bad rap. Folks think we're a bunch of money-grubbing hustlers. Having another broker arrested will add more fuel to that fire."

"You got that right," said Waterson. "On the bright side, none of us are members of Quigley and Watkins. Hell, having the cloud of a criminal investigation hanging over the firm will make running a marathon with an iron ball and chain seem easy. Their clients will be racing for the doors. And apart from idiots, none will be opening new accounts."

Though the assessment suffered from hyperbole, Kyle could not deny its underlying point: Quigley and Watkins was certain to face challenging headwinds. The observation provoked thoughts of Don Burns. More often than not when headwinds hit, new hires were the first victims.

Pit bulls are notoriously ill-tempered. Pose a threat, real or not, and vicious propensities are apt to unleash

.

"Disappointing...mighty disappointing," said Bill, seated across from Kyle and Eric in their favorite booth at the Irish Mist. He shook his head. "Hell, if I can fly here all the way from Fort Myers, you'd think Burns could make the trip from Springfield. It can't be much over forty miles, if it's that."

"Well, he had another commitment." The statement, by itself true, amounted to a white lie. Yes, there was a commitment, a family get-together, but it was one that Don could have skipped. Kyle knew the real reason Don had not joined his friends for Homecoming Weekend. Facing Eric and

Bill after inducing them to invest in the Silver Sky Fund was too embarrassing. Worse yet was the possibility that together Eric and Bill might gang up on him. With no defense, Don had chosen the safe road, stay at home in Springfield.

"What can I get you fellows?"

Kyle welcomed the interruption, the arrival of their server, a heavy-set woman in her forties.

"Three brews…whatever you have on tap, and…" Kyle gazed at his compatriots. "The works?" A nod and a shrug from the other two, and he continued. "An eighteen-inch pizza with sausage, pepperoni, mushrooms, onions and…damn, what's the fifth item we always get?"

"Peppers," said Eric. "And don't feel bad about the memory problem. At your age, senility is to be expected."

Kyle welcomed the jab. Old banter, their unique way of staying tight, continued to survive the passage of time.

"Anything else?" said their server.

"Just a question," said Eric. "Does Kelly still work here?"

"No, she left about six months ago. It took her the best part of a decade to get her degree, but she finally finished. I understand she's teaching. I believe it's fourth grade at a school in New Jersey. Gotta give her credit. More than I could do." She eyed the trio. "You fellows back for Homecoming Weekend? Just a guess, given that you're not among my regulars…and, if I may say without insulting, a few years older than the typical students."

"Very observant," said Bill. "Back in the day, this was our booth…except on days when squatters stole it."

"Well, welcome back." She glanced in the direction of a guy waiving a credit card. "Gotta run." She headed off.

"Whad'ya know?" said Eric. "Kelly moved on."

"Perhaps you were hoping to hit on her?"

"Hadn't thought about it, but it mighta been nice. She was a looker."

"I didn't know she was a hooker."

"Damn you, Gordon. I said looker, not—" Eric heaved a sigh. "Bill, maybe you can help our friend."

"Maybe so. Unlike his memory problems a couple minutes ago—an advanced case of dementia, if I've ever seen one—this time a hearing aid might do the trick."

Kyle cupped his hand to his ear and, in a gravelly voice, said, "Whad'ya say?"

"He said you're a sick puppy for whom there's no help." Bill sat up tall, his face bedecked with a self-satisfied grin.

Kyle reached for the brew that had just arrived. It was as if they had never left the ivy-covered Williams' campus. Common sense told him the observation was grossly inaccurate. Still it was nice to know that they could return and recapture elements of bygone days. The sight of Bill, his hand atop his head, interrupted Kyle's musing. "You checking to see if you still have hair?"

Bill shot him a quizzical look.

"The hand on your head...or has that become your normal posture?"

"Nah, I've got a little headache."

The response left Kyle kicking himself. Jocularity was great, but not when it was at the expense of his pal who was hurting.

"Hard to believe the mess that Clint Horstmeyer has gotten himself into," said Bill. "Is the jackass still in jail?"

"Nope," said Kyle. "He posted bail a few days ago. A bond of one hundred thousand dollars. According to the newspapers, he's charged with insider trading."

"Is he back at his firm, the one where Don works?" said Eric.

"You've gotta be kidding," said Kyle. "Word around Springfield is that the members of his firm have distanced themselves from him. Rumor has it, Quigley, one of the senior partners, summed it up this way: 'The bad apple won't be coming back to the barrel unless and until he proves himself completely free of worms.'"

"Maybe," said Bill, "but I wouldn't bet the cider mill on that."

Eric shot him a look.

"C'mon," said Bill. "Clint's not the type to go down without a fight. To save his ass, he'd throw his grandmother in…even if she were innocent. The guys at his firm better watch their backs. And for that matter…"

"For that matter, what?" said Kyle.

"Uh…nothing." Bill fidgeted with the handle of his mug.

"Young, you're not getting off the hook that easily. You had a thought, and we want to hear it."

Bill heaved a sigh. "Fine. You want it. I'll tell you…Clint Horstmeyer may go down in flames, but if he does, he'll drag as many others as possible into the conflagration. With both of you topping his shit list, you best be careful." Bill eyed his pals, seemingly daring them to disagree.

"So, Horstmeyer hates us," said Kyle. "Big deal. I've got my own firm with no connection to Quigley and Watkins, and Eric is even further removed, working for an insurance company in Hartford. How could Clint possibly tie us into his mess?"

"No clue," said Bill. "But the guy is the king of grudges, and when it comes to being devious, he makes the devil look like a saint."

"You're making a tree out of an acorn," said Eric.

"Maybe," said Bill, "but some acorns grow into trees, tall ones at that."

Kyle groaned.

"Fine, it's a lousy metaphor, not that I was the one who picked it. But that's not the point. All I'm saying is that you fellows should watch your backs. You can take or leave my advice. It's your choice."

Kyle felt the urge to groan again. Disturbing doubts checked the propensity. Clint had planted Rachel in his office. What he might resort to, what other insidious plan he might entertain, was hard to predict. Kyle glanced at Eric. A pensive expression hinted that perhaps he too had concerns. Kyle reached for his brew. Given his druthers, he would rather have been seated on the opposite side of the booth, his back protected by a wall.

"Prognostics do not always prove prophecies…" (Horace Walpole in a letter to Thomas Walpole, 1785).

"Gordon speaking." Ever since Rachel Wallace had quit, Kyle had been answering his own telephone. He had begun interviewing for a new Administrative Assistant but was yet to hire one. In the meantime, he continued to employ an administrative aide from the temporary agency.

"Hi Kyle. It's Denny Larson."

"What's up?"

"I want to update you on the Horstmeyer case. You deserve it after the way you worked with us. As you may have surmised, we've turned our evidence over to the United States Attorney."

"The possibility had crossed my mind, given the indictments against Horstmeyer and Wallace, and knowing that the SEC engages in civil remedies."

"Our investigation suggests that Horstmeyer was a rogue trader. At this point, there's no indication that others at Quigley and Watkins were involved. Under the circumstances, a criminal prosecution against him seems the way to go. While restitution is bound to be an issue, at least for now, there's no reason to proceed against his firm."

"What about Wallace? Did she make any insider profits?"

"Not sure, but the facts suggest they may have been a team. Though I'm not privy to the ins and outs of the U.S. Attorney's strategy, based upon past experience, I suspect the charges against her were aimed at more than her conduct. My guess, they're intended to bolster the case against Horstmeyer."

"Come again?"

"The U.S. Attorney may have gone after her as leverage, hoping she'll opt for a deal—leniency—in exchange for her testimony against Horstmeyer."

"You think she's likely to throw him under the bus? After all, they are an item."

"Your guess is better than mine, given that she worked for you."

Kyle chuckled.

"Why the laugh?"

"I'm hardly the one to predict what Rachel Wallace will do. She sold me a bill of goods when she came looking for a job. I fell hook, line and sinker for her story that Horstmeyer was an impossible boss. I had no clue they were in bed together, both figuratively and literally. That said, you care to guess what she'll do?"

"Don't know, but were the shoe on the other foot, if Horstmeyer had the chance to screw Wallace to save himself, I'd wager he'd do it in a heartbeat."

As well as Kyle knew Clint, no way would he take the other side of that bet. "Do you know whether the U.S. Attorney has contacted Wallace in an effort to negotiate a deal?"

"No…but I doubt it. She's represented by an attorney, the same one that represents Horstmeyer. I'm not a lawyer, but having seen lots of cases here at the SEC, it's my understanding that once a defendant has counsel, the U.S. Attorney has to go through him or her."

"Well, let me rephrase my question. Do you think the U.S. Attorney contacted Wallace's lawyer?"

"Don't know that either. But if so, it must have raised a red flag with the lawyer."

Kyle tried unsuccessfully to connect the dots. "You care to explain?"

"As I said, I'm not a lawyer, but it strikes me that an attorney representing both Horstmeyer and Wallace, once offered a deal for one to testify against the other, would have a conflict. What would be good for the goose would be bad for the gander, and vice versa. Presumably he couldn't represent both."

"So, the offer of a deal could be a divide and conquer strategy?"

"I hadn't thought of it that way…but I suppose so."

"What if Wallace turns the deal down? Could the lawyer represent both of them?"

Larson laughed.

"Did I miss something?"

"You're asking the wrong guy. As I said, I'm not a lawyer. Add to that, the fact I'm not privy to possible negotiations, and my speculations would be about as meaningful as a prediction what the incoming Congress will do."

"Well, that one's easy," said Kyle. "Nothing, absolutely nothing...apart from obstructing the opposing party's agenda."

"Point well taken. And on that uplifting note, I'll bid you a fond adieu."

A snake in the grass is...a snake in the grass.

"Glad you could make it," said Kyle, getting up from his seat at the Old Torch Inn where he had arranged to meet Don Burns for lunch.

They shook hands and, after sitting down, ordered a couple of Heinekens.

"We have to do this regularly, say once a month."

"Deal." Despite his assent, Kyle harbored doubts. Experience had taught him that busy schedules often defeated the best of intentions. "So, how are things at Quigley and Watkins?"

"Same old, same old."

The instinctive response pushed Kyle to make his inquiry more pointed. "You telling me that Horstmeyer's fiasco had no impact?"

"Yes and no."

"What kind of cockamamie answer is that?"

"A legitimate one."

Kyle rolled his eyes.

"Well..." Don stared at the mug of Heineken he was holding. He heaved a sigh. "Only time will tell."

The assessment was undeniably accurate. Unfortunately, it was also ambiguous, and indirect fallout was a definite possibility. Charges against one member of the firm would strap an albatross around the necks of the rest. In a sea replete with brokers, potential new clients might set sail on other ships, and those already on board might race to the lifeboats. Kyle kept the observations to himself. No need to fill his pal's plate with rancid fish.

"Word around the firm—and mind you, my information is mainly third hand—says the SEC is only after Clint. Apparently, he was acting alone and strictly to line his own pockets...at least that's the scuttlebutt at the water cooler. They're also saying that the case against Clint is as solid as Gibraltar. One thing sure, if he's convicted, he won't be coming back."

"Interesting." Tasting his brew, Kyle took a moment to ponder the assessment. "From what I know, insider trading is generally tough to prove. It's kinda like political payoffs. The only ones who know what happened are the provider of information and the recipient, and neither of them is likely to talk."

"That may be...in most cases. But from what I've heard, this is not most cases. Rumor has it the SEC had a wiretap on Clint's phone. That, plus it appears he traded in the very stocks in which our firm makes a market. If so, he's in deep doo-doo."

The information, even about the wiretap, was no surprise to Kyle. Given that the SEC had induced him to record his conversations with Rachel, the possibility of the wiretap had previously crossed his mind. He would have shared the tidbit with Don had he not assumed that the disclosure would upset Larson. "Sounds as though they have Clint by the short hairs."

"That's exactly the way Jerry Walker—I think you know him—described it the other day. And I'm pretty sure his assessment came straight from the horse's mouth."

"The SEC?"

"No, the horse's ass...Clint!"

"You mean he actually admitted they had him cold?"

"No."

Kyle would have called his pal on the glib, but illogical response, had Don not immediately clarified.

"Clint admits the government has a good hand, but he told Jerry he has a few aces up his sleeve."

"Such as?"

"He wouldn't say. But he dropped a not-so-subtle hint. He said the firm, rather than standing in his corner, had made a big mistake, distancing itself from him. He said lots of folks will regret it."

Kyle thought about his ugly past with Clint, as well as the fact that Rachel Wallace had spent several months working in his office. "You think the threats were idle?"

"Don't know. But between you, me and the wall, I've spent a few nights worrying."

Fairy tales can come true, but not all have happy endings. Lest one forgets, many were penned by authors named "Grimm."

Fresh from another wonderful day at Disneyland, Eric sat on the living-room couch of Carla Pender's Pamona, California apartment. "So, what did you like best, Ricky?"

"Big Thunder Mountain Railroad. It's gonzo!"

"You weren't scared when it whipped around the curve just before the tunnel? If it weren't for the dip, our heads would have been lopped off."

"Mom was the one who screamed. Not me." Ricky turned toward the kitchen area where his mother was drying some dishes following an evening snack.

"He has a point," said Eric. "Only one person in our car let out a yelp."

"That's because the two of you were too frightened to open your mouths."

"We were not!" Ricky slapped the floor where he sat playing with his new Mickey Mouse top." He looked over to the couch. "Isn't that right, Uncle Eric?"

"Yup!"

Carla folded her arms. "Seems you boys are ganging up on me. But what can I expect from a couple of men?" She glanced at the clock that hung on the wall beyond the dining table. "My God! It's after ten. Way past your bedtime." She gestured at Ricky. "In your pajamas, right now."

"Just a few more minutes?"

"Not one second!"

Ricky turned toward the couch.

"Don't look at me," said Eric. "You heard your mother…and I'm sure you don't want to spoil a perfect day."

Ricky sighed but then grabbed Eric's hand and led the way to his room.

"And don't forget, brush your teeth."

"I'll make sure he does," said Eric, as he lifted Ricky piggy-back style and carried him to his bedroom.

Minutes later, with teeth brushed, Ricky, decked out in red, yellow and blue *Spiderman* pajamas, said, "Read me a story, Uncle Eric. Okay?"

Knowing the delay would not sit well with Carla, Eric curbed the temptation to reach for a book. He pointed at his watch. "Not tonight."

"Just a short—"

"Oh no, you're not gonna get me in Dutch." Eric pulled back the covers.

Ricky dutifully climbed in. He reached out.

Eric bent down and embraced him.

"I love you, Uncle Eric."

"I love you too."

Carla came in. After turning on the night light, she leaned over and kissed Ricky. "Goodnight, my Lovey."

"Night, Mommy. I love you."

As Ricky turned over, Eric slipped an arm over Carla's shoulder. He pecked her on the cheek. Everything felt right. The duo shut the door behind them as they returned to the living room, where they seated themselves at the end of the couch farthest from the kitchen. Eric took Carla's hand.

"We're…we're just like a family." The utterance echoed in Eric's head, as if he were hearing the words of another.

"Yes, I'd say so."

"Really?"

Carla's brow furrowed. "You made a statement. I agreed. And what did you do? React with surprise."

"Sorry, but my reaction was anything but disagreement. I appreciated your including me."

"Well, the way I see it, you're my big brother. Ricky calls you *Uncle*, and besides lending the moral support of a brother, you help me out financially. I can't imagine a better big brother, especially for someone like me who has no other family."

The kudos aroused an already stirring impulse, one that Eric had been contemplating for months. "Maybe we should think about becoming even more of a family." He caressed Carla's hand.

"What does that mean?"

"Do I have to spell it out?"

"No, I'm pretty sure I understand. And it's a wonderful idea, one I would love to entertain…"

He waited for what was probably no more than two or three interminable seconds. "But?"

She inhaled deeply. "We had our chance…back at Williams. And mind you, it was an unforgettable fling, one I will always cherish. And rather than break up on bad terms, we parted friends, the dearest of friends. We've managed to not only maintain that friendship but enabled it to grow. Most of the credit for that lies with you…your kindness."

"It's a two-way street, but…regardless, an enduring friendship is a great foundation for an even closer relationship."

"You're absolutely right."

Her concession inveigled him to press the issue. "So, why not?"

"If…if things weren't as they are, believe me, I would love to try." She squeezed his hand as she gazed into his eyes with a yearning look.

"Things?…What things?"

She took another deep breath. "I'm glad we're having this talk. It's a good way to broach the subject. I needed to, but didn't know how."

His heart fluttered with longing; his mind, however, floundered with puzzlement.

"I have to ask a favor." She shook her head and muttered softly, "God, you do so much for me…and I ask for more."

Though he had no idea as to her request, he knew she hated to ask. Her reluctance to accept his generosity had always been apparent. Her guilt attributable to his beneficence was unmistakable.

"I have a problem." Her head hung low.

He squeezed her hand. "Tell me."

"These past few months I've been feeling more and more tired. When I finally went to the doctor, they found cancer…ovarian cancer. It's stage five…terminal. The doctors tell me I have just a few months."

Eric longed to say something…something that would mitigate the terrible news. With his brain endeavoring to contradict the message, words escaped him. His stomach knotted. Tears welled up in his eyes. He thrust his arms around Carla and held her tightly. She broke into a wail as she melted in his arms. His own sobbing grew equally uncontrollable. For one…even two full minutes, they embraced one another.

When finally Eric had regained a modicum of composure, though hardly free of crying, he said, "Are the doctors sure? Maybe they're wrong."

She leaned her head back and shook it slowly. "I've already gotten a second opinion."

He kissed her forehead and clutched her tightly again. He longed for a panacea. His yearning provoked nothing more than feelings of helplessness. He said, "Earlier you said you need a favor. Tell me…whatever."

"I went to see a lawyer. He drafted a will for me. I named you as Ricky's guardian. Before signing, I need to ask you (she looked him in the eye)—Are you willing to do it? And before you answer, know that I will understand if you say *no*. Asking you—"

"Say no more. I would be honored and privileged, and my God…" Renewed sobbing choked Eric's voice.

Carla clasped his two hands. "You're a wonderful man, a rare gem. Any woman with the chance to have you as her husband would be a fool to let you slip away…Glenna Snow fits that mold."

The comment came as a shock, but not because Carla knew about Glenna. Back when Eric was dating Glenna, Carla often asked him about his life after Williams. That included not just his job, but his love life, as well. Eric had told Carla about Glenna and that he was in love with her. But once Glenna had dumped him, her name had ceased to be part of their conversations. Several years had elapsed since her name had come up.

"I know. I should mind my own business, but that young lady from Bennington College—name not to be repeated—is a fool. A damn fool."

Eric shrugged, mainly because he had no idea what to say.

Carla leaned back and looked him in the eye. "You're still carrying a torch for her, aren't you?"

He shrugged again, knowing that the repeated reaction bore a message quite different from its predecessor. He had acknowledged that his feelings for Glenna persisted.

Curiosity is a wonderful thing. Often discretion is better yet.

With Eric to his left, Don sat on a park bench, his wife Linda on the other side and their six-month old daughter, the newest addition to their family, sleeping in her lap. Their son played in a nearby sandbox.

"After all this time, you finally made it down here to my apartment."

"C'mon, give us a break," said Don. "It's not like we're close by. After all, it's (Don did a quick mental conversion of the nearly thirty miles)...it's roughly 150,000 feet from Springfield to Hartford."

Brow deeply furrowed, Eric said, "I rest my case."

The absurdity of Don's excuse laid bare, he thought better of pressing it further.

"The gap until our next visit will be far shorter," said Linda. "That's a promise."

"I'm gonna hold you to that."

"Fair enough." Linda flipped her sunglasses up from her eyes, so they rested atop her flowing locks. "Of course, now that we've come down here, it will be your turn to come up to Springfield."

Eric chuckled briefly and then turned to Don. "So, what's the latest on our dear friend, Clint?"

"I'm not really sure. Partners at the firm have been in touch with the SEC. Sounds like they have a solid case against him. But when it comes to the criminal charges, the Justice Department handles those. Someone told me the case is a slam dunk, and maybe that's right. Still I wonder. Proof beyond a reasonable doubt is tough. And the other day, one of the guys at the firm bumped into Clint coming out of a movie theater. The fellow said Clint, cavalier as ever, dismissed the entire thing. Labeled it 'a pebble in a gravel pit.' Claimed the Mt. Holyoke women's basketball team would sooner beat the Celtics before any jury will convict him. Said he'd be back at the firm before Election Day."

"Would the firm take him back?" said Eric.

"Only if he gets a clean bill of health on all charges." Don contained the urge to add that he was rooting against that outcome. The mere thought, however, that Clint might return was revolting.

"Well, knowing Clint," said Eric, "I'd put my money on what the Feds are saying."

"That's the consensus at the firm." Don observed a funny expression on Eric's face. "Whatcha thinking?"

Eric leaned around to Linda. "Your husband doesn't miss a trick."

"I wish that were true on Pinochle night."

"I'm learning, but before Johanson gets away with a bait and switch, let's hear what he had on his mind."

Eric heaved a sigh. "I was just wondering if you think Clint might implicate others, legit or not...perhaps to get a deal."

"Wonderful question, one that I've wrestled with loads of times. The facts suggest he'd be hard pressed. But knowing Clint, I'll bet he looks for a way, and devious as he is, he's apt to find one."

Linda, who had just put their daughter into her baby carriage, said, "Why in God's grace, with all the good guys at Williams, did you fellows befriend a jerk like Clint?"

"Wait a second," said Eric. "Let's set the record straight. Clint was never our friend. An acquaintance, yes, but nothing more."

Don was glad Eric had saved him from the need to make the clarification. Regardless, with the incessant discussion about Clint at the office, he preferred something better on a Sunday afternoon. "Not to change the subject (Don ignored the look from Eric), how's your job going?"

"Really well. The transition into my supervisory role has been much easier than I expected."

"Any new women in your life?"

"No one new…"

"But if I read between the lines, perhaps an old flame has rekindled?" Don immediately thought of Glenna Snow.

Eric hesitated. "I've made several trips to California to see Carla Pender. Her son Ricky is a great kid. He's like a son to me."

"Could this be it?"

Eric bowed his head and stared at the ground. "Might have…"

"But?"

"Donald!" Linda directed a scolding look Don's way. "If Eric has something to share, fine. But otherwise keep your prying to yourself."

"That's okay," said Eric. "And yes, I did suggest that Carla, Ricky and I become a family. Unfortunately, Carla shot the idea down."

"Damn! I don't believe it," said Don. "I thought she still had a thing for you…Well, it's her misfortune."

"It's not like you think." Melancholy crept into Eric's voice. "Carla…Carla has cancer. The doctors say it's terminal."

A lump filled Don's throat. If only he had waited to learn of Carla's circumstances before going off half-cocked. "I…I'm sorry. So very sorry."

"Does Ricky know?" said Linda.

"Not yet, at least nothing except that his mom isn't feeling well." Eric gazed pensively skyward.

Don's mind forked to a long unanswered question. *Was Eric Ricky's father?* No way was Don about to ask, not with his recent miscue fresh.

"Let's not allow morbid thoughts to spoil a wonderful afternoon," said Eric. "So, tell me, what do you hear from our other two, Kyle and Bill?"

"Kyle seems to be doing fine, especially now that he has his own brokerage firm." Don steered away from mentioning the saga with Rachel Wallace. If and when Kyle wanted to share that information, he could. "As for Bill, it's been a long time since I've spoken to him."

"Well, last I did," said Eric, "he called me two…maybe three months ago—he still loved his teaching and writing and his life down in Florida. Safe bet, things haven't changed."

A curious smile appeared on Linda's face. Even before Don could inquire about her reaction, her uncanny ability to read his mind seemingly kicked in. She said, "Don't mind me. I was just thinking. The four Inseparables are all doing quite well."

Don contemplated the assessment. It had merit. He suspected a mirror, were one available, would have revealed a smile even broader than the one his wife had displayed moments before.

Years have passed since Amelia Earhart disappeared, and still the questions remain. Searches, there have been many. Evidence has provided clues. Speculations have abounded. A definitive answer?…No.

Their dinner just finished, Katelyn and Kyle sat at either end of their family-room couch watching the local news.

"This just in," said the broadcaster. "A plane believed piloted by Clinton Horstmeyer, the Springfield stock broker who is out on bail on charges of insider trading, reportedly crashed outside of St. George, Utah. According to the flight plan filed at Barnes Municipal Airport in western Massachusetts from which the plane had originally departed, Horstmeyer, along with a lone passenger, Rachel Wallace, was bound for Las Vegas. Initial observations of the crash scene indicate there were no survivors. As soon as we have more information, we'll update this breaking story."

Kyle pressed the mute button on the television remote. "God, can you believe that? Clint and Rachel…killed in a plane crash."

"Wasn't it this past spring that he took Don and Linda Burns up over the Berkshires?"

"Gosh, I had forgotten about that." The reminder had Kyle suspecting that news of the crash might have his friends thanking their lucky stars they were not on board at the wrong time.

"What with the pending charges, and Horstmeyer and his girlfriend out on bail, you think they were authorized to fly to Las Vegas?"

"Good question. I don't really know. But according to the newspaper reports—I read all the articles about the charges, sometimes more than once—the judge required them to surrender their passports. Of course, knowing Clint, rules never meant much. That's probably why he's in trouble with the law."

"Well, after the way he tried to screw you, I have no sympathy. It may be less than charitable, but a part of me says, 'good riddance.'"

Kyle gazed down to the other end of the couch where Katelyn faced him kitty-corner. Rarely could he recall her voicing such a harsh remark. He might have scolded her were he not entertaining similar feelings. He said, "Not to celebrate his misfortune, but with Clint gone, I won't need to watch my back, the way Bill Young warned me."

"Maybe."

Kyle shot Katelyn a look.

"Well…from the stories you and your pals told about Clint, you never know. Even from beyond the grave, he's not to be trusted."

"From beyond the grave? You really think so?"

Katelyn burst out laughing.

"What's so funny?"

"You—actually thinking I meant it. It'd be one thing if I were talking to your superstitious buddy Don. Having him take

251

me seriously would be no surprise. Heck, even before I said anything, he'd probably have such crazy thoughts on his own. But from you, My Dear, I'd expect something more."

Kyle shrugged. "Being gullible is better than crazy."

"Yes…And having an IQ of 40 is better than 30. But that doesn't make 40 good."

"Are you accusing me of having an IQ of 40?"

"No, only being gullible." Katelyn smiled before sliding over from the other end of the couch and pecking Kyle on the cheek.

PART II

CHAPTER XVII

FUNERALS ARE THE FOUNTAINHEAD of many emotions. All too often, guilt.

Kyle glanced at his watch—6:07—as he picked up the telephone receiver. Chances were, another of those damned telemarketers was calling at dinnertime. If so, the guy would get short shrift.

"Hi Kyle. It's Eric. Sorry, it took me so long to get back to you, but I just heard from Bill Young's mother. She gave me the details of his funeral. It's going to be held on Thursday the 12th, at two o'clock in Provo, Utah. They want to bury him near their home, rather than Fort Myers."

The information sent Kyle's brain into a tailspin. Accidents during the preceding week had taken the lives of two members of his Williams' graduating class, both of whom he knew well. The first, who had his life stolen by a plastered bastard in an SUV, was a dear friend. The second, a victim of an airplane crash only a couple days later, was a conniving jerk.

"You're going to the funeral. Right?"

"Absolutely, though I doubt that Katelyn will be able to join me. She's in the midst of a trial, a corporate lawsuit that's likely to last another week, barring a sudden settlement."

"Do you think Don will come?"

"Not sure. When I talked with him a few days ago, right after you notified me about Bill's death, he was noncommittal. Utah is a big trip."

"Fort Myers wouldn't have been so small."

254

The point was valid, but Kyle surmised that an overriding issue was at play. Ever since Don had left Kingman & Woodhill, he had minimized contact with Bill. The shame of having put his buddy into the Silver Sky Fund was the reason. With the possibility that Bill had told his family about the betrayal, facing them at Bill's funeral would not be pleasant.

"Look, tell the lunk he has to come…that we say so."

"It's not that simple. What with the Silver Sky Fund fiasco, Don's ashamed. He—"

"Hey, don't forget, he sold me the same garbage."

"I know, but you forgave him. You even told me so."

"Yeah, and to tell the truth, Bill was part of the reason."

"I take it you discussed it with him?"

"Actually, no. I didn't have to. I knew he wouldn't hold a grudge. I didn't want to be less of a sport, lest, after being screwed, I ended up feeling guilty."

Eric's strange logic somehow made sense. That Bill hadn't held a grudge was indisputable. He had proved that when, at Kyle's request, he had contacted Clint Horstmeyer and helped get Don a job at Quigley and Watkins following his layoff at Kingman & Woodhill. But Bill never let on to Don about the help. Instead Bill had forced Kyle to keep it in confidence. But with Bill gone, perhaps the time had come for Don to know the facts.

"You know as well as I that Bill would want us all at his funeral."

Everything Eric said made good sense. Whether Don would acquiesce was another matter. "I'll try to convince him."

"Fair enough…and oh, by the way, I made a reservation at the Hyatt in Provo. If need be, I can change it to a suite with two beds and a fold-out couch. That way it will work with either the two of us or three."

"Sounds good. Take care."

"You too…And press Don, until he says *yes*."

People have many items on their bucket lists. Some are accomplished; others, not. Now and then, an item gets done after one has kicked the bucket. Such is life, or so they say.

A brew in hand, Kyle sat by the telephone contemplating strategy, how to convince Don to attend Bill's funeral. Since learning of Bill's death, Kyle had shed countless tears and spent hours mourning the loss of his friend. But for the moment, such gloomy thoughts had to be put aside. He had a task to do. Logic was what his college professors would have recommended, but in the face of reluctance, he would need more. Persistence would help, but it too was likely to come up short. Then there was guilt. Kyle hated to resort to the tactic, but when all else failed, one had to do what one had to do. Like it or not, Don was going to attend the funeral.

Kyle picked up the receiver and dialed. Moments later, Don answered. Pleasantries exchanged, Kyle cut to the chase...almost. "Bill's funeral is this Thursday. It's in Provo, Utah, kinda what we suspected when we spoke several days ago." Kyle waited several seconds. "You there?"

"Yeah...just finding it hard to speak." Don's voice cracked. "I...I can't believe Bill's gone. I miss him."

"Me too...If only—" Wishful thinking, something Kyle had repeatedly done since learning of Bill's death, was futile. Kyle wiped a tear from his eye.

"Have you checked the flights?"

The question refocused Kyle on the task at hand, convincing Don to go. "American Airlines has one the day after tomorrow, Wednesday morning. Flight 1064 out of Hartford. There's a change in Chicago before going on to Salt Lake City. We'll get a rental car there. It's only forty-two miles to Provo. Five hundred twenty-nine dollars round trip." The rehearsed barrage poured from Kyle's mouth. "Eric and I have already booked it. We can all stay at his apartment the night before. With a second bedroom, plus a sleeper couch in the living room, and just a short drive to the airport, it'll be very easy."

"I...I don't know."

"What don't you know?" Kyle prepared to turn up the heat.

"After what I did to Bill, I doubt he'd want me there."

"You're wrong."

"Easy for you to say. Whether Bill would agree is another matter."

"You're wrong again." Kyle had always kept the confidence that Bill had requested. With his passing, Kyle rationalized the rein was off his tongue, especially given the circumstances. "I happen to know that after you lost your job at Kingman & Woodhill, Bill contacted Clint Horstmeyer and convinced him to go to bat for you at Quigley and Watkins. No way would Bill have done that if he held a grudge." Kyle waited a moment. "Aren't you going to say something?"

"Yeah...Bill Young was a helluva guy...a much better man than I."

Kyle swallowed hard. His disclosure, an effort to apply pressure, had been more like a knife. He said, "Besides ignoring the issue, your comment lacks merit. But I won't debate it." Resorting to the disingenuous technique, one his Williams' philosophy professor abhorred, gave Kyle pause. Even as he had claimed that he would not argue his pal's point, he had disputed and dismissed it without any justification. But Kyle had a goal, and, niceties be damned, he would not be sidetracked. "The bottom line is that Bill would want you there. He would want all three of us there."

The barely audible sound that greeted Kyle's ear gave no indication of Don's leaning. His discomfort was, however, apparent.

"Look at it this way. This is the last chance for the Inseparables to take that long-planned trip out West."

"Excuse me, but unless I've lost my marbles, our last chance evaporated the moment the drunk driver slammed into Bill's car."

The response rekindled sadness. But crying had to be left until after the call. Kyle's goal, convincing Don to attend the funeral, needed to take precedence. Kyle took a deep breath. "You're wrong again, my friend."

"Really? Then please, enlighten me."

257

"Put yourself in Bill's place. If it were your funeral, wouldn't you want your three closest friends to show up and be there with you...and for you? Doing the trip...doing it for Bill, is a testament to the bond of friendship he enjoyed in life. True, he'll be in a casket, but he'll be there. And you never know, he might just feel our presence." The instant Kyle uttered the dubious speculation, he felt the need to spin it. "And before you think of arguing the point, look at it this way. We know the trip, with all four of us, was on Bill's bucket list. It's the best we can do...so, let's not let him down." Kyle waited for a reaction. "Aren't you going to say something?"

"Yeah, you've twisted my arm." Don sighed. "Hell, having screwed Bill once, the mere possibility of doing it again, now that he's dead, would eat me up."

The distress in Don's voice induced Kyle to temper any celebration. "I'm glad you've decided to come. Eric and I plan to spend a few extra days out there, maybe go to Reno or Vegas and fly back on Sunday. Whad'ya say?"

Following several seconds of silence, an enervated voice responded. "Yeah...okay, I'll do the whole nine yards." A wet dishrag would have expressed the acquiescence with greater enthusiasm.

Spoils supposedly belonged to victors. Kyle was hardly in a festive mood. Victory had come at his friend's expense, not to mention that another had died. "If you'd like, I can make your plane reservation and email you all the details."

"Thanks. I appreciate that and look forward to seeing you guys."

All too often plans delayed are plans unfulfilled. Other times they eventuate, but not necessarily as planned.

"Can you believe it? At long last we're doing it," said Kyle, seated between Eric and Don on an American Airlines 727, the second leg of their journey, a flight from Chicago to Salt Lake City.

258

"Unfortunately, it took Bill's death to get us to make the trip," said Eric, who had been gazing out the window.

For an instant the sobering remark gave Kyle pause. He glanced upward, not that the view, the bottom of an overhead compartment, was much. "I've got a hunch that Bill is looking down on us with a big smile."

"Since when did you get religion? Young and I were always the pious ones."

"Just because I don't go to church, doesn't mean I don't have a spiritual side."

Eric rolled his eyes. "I won't debate the point, but only because I like the sentiment, the idea that Bill is with us."

Kyle turned to Don. "You're awfully quiet."

Don shrugged.

"Now there's a garrulous reaction."

"Some of us, the duo to my left both excluded, are carrying extra baggage...and I don't mean suitcases."

Kyle chided himself for having remarked about Don's silence. Failing to recognize that it was a product of guilt was insensitive. Kyle reached into his pocket. "Just before I left the house this morning, I tore out this article from the front page of today's *Springfield Republican*. It has some new details about the plane crash that killed Horstmeyer, as well as the charges against him. It says the plane went down in a remote canyon and that the severity of the crash precludes the possibility of survivors. Traces of one body, believed to be that of Rachel Wallace, were found. But the wreckage was strewn over a wide area, suggesting the plane may have struck a tree and/or exploded prior to the crash. It says that Clint, the pilot, made a mayday call just before contact was lost. The FAA examined the scene and in accordance with normal protocol plans to pursue a full investigation. The United States Attorney is expected to make a motion to dismiss the charges against both Rachel and Clint, as required by law, owing to their deaths. For the moment, however, the prosecutor is awaiting final identification of their bodies."

"I guess that's one way to escape jail," said Eric.

"What? Get yourself killed?" said Kyle.

"I didn't say it was a good way...just a way."

"Makes me a little nervous," said Don, "talking about a plane crash when we're flying."

"Here come the old superstitions." Eric glanced at his watch and then turned to Don. "It's Wednesday, the eleventh of the month. In just two days, it will be Friday, the thirteenth of October."

"I'm well aware," said Don, "but you needn't rub it in. And as a matter of fact, if the flight were two days later, I might not have made the trip. And might I suggest we change the subject."

"Why?…because talking about a plane crash could cause one?"

"I don't know, and for that matter, Johanson, you don't either. And for that reason, if you had any sense, you wouldn't tempt the hand of fate."

Eric grabbed the sides of his head and grumbled before responding in a more intelligible way. "Seems if I recall, you and Linda went flying with Clint some months back."

"Yeah, but what's that got to do with anything?"

"Well, nothing, I guess…What kind of pilot was Clint?"

"He seemed good…no crazy maneuvers…loops or dives or close encounters with mountains or trees or the like. Linda and I really enjoyed the ride over the Berkshires. I felt as comfortable as if he were driving the speed limit on an uncrowded highway with—"

"With a blindfold over his eyes on Friday the thirteenth in a car with license number 666." Eric smirked.

Kyle might have joined in the revelry, but having previously showered Don with guilt, he remained silent man in the middle.

"Go ahead. Make fun of me," said Don. He pulled the flight magazine from the pocket of the seat in front of him and began reading.

Eric turned to Kyle. "Seems someone is in a huff."

Kyle checked the urge to reinforce the observation.

"Well, I think I'll grab a few winks." Eric leaned his head against a small pillow.

With the nose of one pal buried in a magazine and the other choosing to doze, Kyle pushed his seat back and closed his eyes. A little nap could make the flight go faster.

All men think all men mortal but themselves. (Edward Young, *Night Thoughts, Night 1, Line 424*).

Dressed in a black suit, white shirt and conservative gray and black striped tie, Kyle watched as Bill Young's eldest sibling Marie ascended the altar to deliver the eulogy. It was the first time Kyle had attended a service in a Church of Latter-day Saints, and the acoustically fine edifice had heightened his senses. From the moment they had pulled into the parking lot in their rented Ford Expedition SUV, he was in awe. A long series of colorful flowerbeds led to an array of fountains fronting the Provo Temple. From a circular stone section atop an expansive rectangular base, a spire climbed toward the heavens. At its apex, a golden figurine of the angel Moroni, his arms outstretched, beckoned the Almighty. Rock Canyon, a stunning mountain backdrop, framed the magnificent tabernacle. Even Kyle, skeptic that he was, found it hard to deny that he was in God's country.

As Marie, a shapely brunette, attired in a black, knee-length dress, arrived at the lectern, she unfolded some papers she had been carrying in her hand. She drew in a deep breath in an obvious effort to gain as much composure as possible.

"Dear friends." She cleared her throat while gazing out over the eighty or so who had gathered in the pews. "Thank you all for coming today to celebrate the life of my brother, Bill. And I know that the word *celebrate* is in order. Our Mormon faith teaches that at death the soul is judged, and based upon that judgment, sent to either spirit prison or spirit paradise. In Bill's case, there can be no doubt. A better person, one could not find. A better soul is hard to imagine. No doubt he is bound for spirit paradise, and blessed with that knowledge, those of us here on Earth, much as we will miss him, can celebrate his life, each with the hope that one day our judgment will entitle us to join him in that heavenly realm.

"These past few days, while bearing the burden, but also having the privilege of formulating these remarks, I have endeavored to select those adjectives that best characterize Bill. Four, in particular, go a long way in describing him: kind, generous, honest and modest. While none of us are perfect, and it is by no means my goal to create a saintly image, not only did Bill consistently exhibit these four qualities, but he was as free of negative attributes as one can be. Yes, he was my brother, and that does make for bias, but bias or not, he was an extraordinary person. Numerous people, when expressing their condolences, have voiced this sentiment over the past few days.

"Bill was born twenty-eight years ago. An excellent student, he was always near the top of his class. A few may have been brighter, but none more dedicated and determined. From an early age, he loved to read and write. The latter became his passion, even well before he enrolled at Williams College, where he majored in English. Following graduation from that prestigious institution, he took a position teaching English at Fordison, a small private school for girls in Fort Myers, Florida. Though the job may not have been high paying, its rewards were great. I suspect that each of you recalls an extraordinary teacher who holds a special place in your heart. Bill was just such a teacher. A look through his Fordison yearbooks verifies this. Countless messages from his students confirm the manifold times and ways he made their lives better. Girls who had previously disliked school became academic enthusiasts. Others previously lacking in self-esteem and confidence blossomed. One wrote that she had recently seen an old movie, *To Sir, with Love*. In her words, Bill was a real-life *Sir*.

"Although, as I mentioned earlier, Bill's teaching did not make him financially wealthy, it made his life rich—very rich. But what people, apart from his agent and our immediate family, didn't realize was that Bill was, in fact, well on the road to financial success. His passion, writing, was responsible. Recently, he received a large advance on his first novel, *Destiny's Invention*, which is already in high demand. Modest as my brother was, he published it under the pseudonym Thurston Caldwell."

A buzz pervaded the church. Marie paused, seemingly to catch her breath or check her notes, though perhaps to allow the congregation a chance to digest the disclosure.

"Amazing," whispered Eric.

"Absolutely," said Kyle, not wanting to disclose that Bill had previously shared information about the new book with him. As to Bill's reluctance to broadcast success, that was quintessential Bill. Kyle would have voiced the sentiment were Marie not already resuming.

"Several from Fordison, including Headmaster, Dr. Vernon Longberry, have traveled from Florida for this service. Our entire family appreciates your presence, a tribute to Bill. What none of you knew was that the scholarship recently endowed at your school by Thurston Caldwell was the gift of my brother. Even as he worked long hours for the limited pay of a private school educator, Bill was silently giving funds for students in need. Such was the selfless nature of my very generous brother.

"Before concluding my remarks, I also wish to acknowledge three other individuals who have made the cross-country trip from the East Coast. Back when Bill was in college, at Williams, he developed what became a lifelong bond with three very special friends, Donald Burns, Eric Johanson and Kyle Gordon."

For Kyle, who already had been listening to every word, the mention of his name, amplified his focus. He glanced at Don. A stoic face revealed nothing. Nevertheless, Kyle was confident that Don, ambivalent about coming, was thankful he had.

"Ever since their freshman year at Williams, when the three, along with Bill, were roommates, they have been extremely close. During their four years of college, they spent thousands of hours together. They called themselves the Inseparables. Back then, Bill liked the name, but as he passed into adulthood and the hubris and invincibility of youth faded, maturity altered his view of the term. Still he valued it as a reminder of the danger of arrogance's creep. Regardless, he

263

always cherished his relationship with his three buddies. That they are here today means a great deal to our family. For much as we will remember Bill with anecdotes from his life, no doubt they will too. Memories etched in their minds and hearts, as well as others who loved Bill, will enable him to live on. Amidst pain from his passing, that knowledge is a source of solace." Marie hesitated, as she struggled to maintain composure. "Bill, my brother dear..." Marie's voice cracked. "I...I will miss you." Head bowed, she stepped away from the lectern and down from the altar.

Kyle reached for a handkerchief and dabbed his eyes. The reality that he would never again spend time with his friend had been underscored. The Inseparables had ceased to be. Kyle had been to funerals before, most notably his grandfather, his mother's father. But Papa Peter, like the others, was old. He had died at ninety-one. That Bill, not even thirty, was lying forever still in the wooden box in the center aisle was hard to comprehend. Finality had come from nowhere. Crudely capricious, death had proved it waited for no man. Kyle and his buddies had planned their trip West together. At long last, it had come to pass. But this was not how it was planned, not how it was supposed to be. And there would be no chances to rectify the deficiency. Kyle closed his eyes. In an instant, he had passed from that part of life where his years were seemingly boundless to that in which the end draws inevitably closer. His own mortality gripped him. He took a deep breath. There was much he wanted to do. Exactly what, he was not sure. The time had come to put his bucket list on paper...not just write it down, but do it. Sadly, Bill would never get the chance.

Even the great Harry Houdini could not send a message back to his wife from beyond the grave. Persuasive on the issue of post-death communication, perhaps, but not conclusive. Such is the problematic nature of proving a negative. On the other hand, maybe, just maybe, some decedents can transcend the gap that divides life and death.

Seated in a booth at the Pony Express Café in Provo, along with Eric and Don, Kyle nursed a cup of coffee. "So, which way should we go?" he said.

"Seems we've already asked that question a half-dozen times," said Eric.

"Yeah, but we still haven't arrived at an answer." The reason did not escape Kyle. Still fresh from the image of Bill's coffin being lowered into the ground, the trio lacked enthusiasm. Geography had helped them narrow the choices to either Las Vegas or Reno. They had weighed the pros and cons. Bryce Canyon and Zion National Park were on the way to Las Vegas, a trip of about 350 miles, about 200 less than the distance to Reno. But Reno had the advantage of Lake Tahoe, plus the possibility of a stop in Salt Lake City en route.

"What would Bill choose?" said Don.

"Knowing him," said Eric, "he'd probably say, 'Whatever you guys pick is fine.'"

"Damn, you're no help, Johanson," said Kyle.

"Are you suggesting I'm wrong?"

"No, but don't bother me with details." Kyle sipped his coffee, silently acknowledging the irrationality of his response.

"Suppose we take a vote?" said Eric.

"Secret ballot?" Don smirked.

"Just a sec," said Kyle. "I've got a text on my phone."

Eric threw up his hands. "God, it's tough to get anything done with you two."

Kyle winked. "Impatience will get you nowhere." He ran his finger over the screen of his cell phone and read the message.

> Hi Guys,
> As Mark Twain once said, 'The reports of my death have been greatly exaggerated.' Meet me tomorrow afternoon at four, at Cabin No. 6, at the Red Stone Cabins in Cannonville, Utah.
> I had to send this message on a borrowed cell phone. I don't have further access. Can't say

anything more until tomorrow. Please don't
disappoint. I really need your help.
Bill.

Kyle did a double take, after which he read the message aloud.

"Let me see that!" Eric grabbed the cell phone out of Kyle's hands. "What the hell?" He held the device so Don could read it too.

"A message from Bill," said Don. "Maybe he's alive." He eyed his two pals. "What's with you? You don't believe it?"

"In case you've forgotten," said Kyle, "we attended his funeral today. We watched his casket roll down the aisle, and we saw him lowered into the ground...not that I mean to bother you with details."

"I suppose you looked inside the casket and checked for his body." Don folded his arms. "And while you were at it, no doubt you checked his pulse."

"C'mon," said Eric. "You're being ridiculous. His whole family was there at the funeral. Do you think they would have gone through all that if he weren't dead?"

"Maybe it was someone else. Maybe it was a hoax...Or maybe he came back from the dead." Don turned to Kyle. "What do you think?"

He took his cell phone back from Eric and reread the message. "I don't know what to think, but I damn well don't believe that Bill's alive."

"What—you're hoping our buddy is dead?" Don banged his folded arms against his chest.

"Jesus, Burns! That's not what I said, and you know it."

"Well—"

"Well, nothing! You asked me what I thought, and I told you."

Don turned to Eric. "And I suppose you agree with Mr. Skeptic."

"I don't know, but one thing sure, I'm anything but convinced that Bill is alive."

"So, you two intend to simply ignore Bill's message, even though he says he needs us?"

"Nobody said we should ignore the message, not that I think it's from Bill. But before you get all crazy and go off half-cocked, how about we find out where (Kyle glanced at his cell phone to refresh his memory)...these Red Stone Cabins and this Cannonville place are located, assuming they exist?" He tapped his cell phone pulling up the Google Maps app. He typed in Red Stone Cabins, Cannonville, Utah. A moment later, a light bulb marking the spot appeared on a map. "The Red Stone Cabins are for real."

"What do you guys say now?" said Don.

"Big deal," said Eric. "So, the cabins exist. That hardly proves that Bill's alive."

Kyle pressed the *minus sign* on the app a couple of times to get a broader perspective. "They're located in the southern part of Utah, not all that far from Bryce Canyon."

"That means they must be close to the route to Las Vegas," said Don.

Kyle pressed the *minus sign* again to zoom out further. "I'd guess about an hour...give or take...from Interstate 15 that connects this place to Vegas."

"Earlier when we were discussing whether to go west to Reno or south to Las Vegas, either seemed okay," said Eric. "But now with the text message, I'm definitely for heading south. Mind you, that's not to suggest that I think the message came from Bill, but at the very least, it's aroused my curiosity." He turned to Kyle. "What about you, Gordon?"

"I vote for Las Vegas too. Like Eric, I have no expectation that we'll find Bill or even that he sent the message, but damn, just going to Cannonville, not knowing what we might find, will be a blast. Back in college, we always said our trip out West would be a great adventure, and now with this crazy text, it's all but guaranteed. You might say, it fits the *bill*...no pun intended."

"Sure," said Don, his brow furrowed. "Anyhow, that makes it unanimous. Cannonville, here we come." Don eyed his watch. "You think we should go this evening?"

Kyle, who had taken the opportunity to check the directions on his app, said, "It's a little under two hundred fifty miles from here...my guess, about a four or five-hour drive, with the first two-thirds on the Interstate. Seeing as how we don't need to be there until four tomorrow afternoon, I say wait. Given that we're already booked for tonight at the Hyatt, we might as well stay and enjoy the breakfast and go tomorrow."

"Makes sense," said Eric.

"Agreed," said Don.

Kyle pulled up another app on his phone, this one with the weather. "It says here that temperatures in southern Utah will hit ninety-five degrees tomorrow."

"Hey, what do you expect in the Southwest in August?" said Eric.

Don put his hand to the side of his mouth, as if to address only Kyle. "That from the guy who asked whether he should pack any shorts."

"Yeah, because at the time, I didn't know that we'd be going south after the funeral." Eric leaned back and folded his arms. "Now that our plans are settled, would you gentlemen, and I use the term advisedly, wish to make a little wager—say a sawbuck each, winner take all—on what we'll find at the Red Stone Cabins?"

"I'm in," said Kyle. "And my bet is that it won't be Bill."

"And that the message didn't come from him?" said Don.

Kyle hesitated in a moment of self-debate. "Yeah, and that the message didn't come from him."

"What about you, Don?" said Eric. "You wanna put your money where your mouth lies?"

Don sat with pursed lips.

"All your big talk about the message being from Bill, and now you're chicken to back it up with a sawbuck?" Eric's smug stare dared Don to refuse the challenge.

"Not at all...But fair is fair. If I'm gonna take the longshot, I'm entitled to some odds. So, here's the deal. If the message turns out to be from Bill, you each pay me fifty dollars. And if we find Bill at the cabins, you each cough up a C-Note."

"A hundred dollars!" Kyle nearly spilled his coffee.

"Now who's the chicken?" Don extended his elbows and flapped them. "Cluck, cluck, cluck."

"I'll take your bet," said Eric defiantly.

"Gordon, you gonna accept my odds...or your feathers caught in your throat?"

"Yeah, you've got your odds." Kyle turned to Eric. "So, Mr. Insurance man, as the guy who makes his livelihood underwriting bets—excuse me, I mean risks—what's your prediction?"

"I predict we find Gary Parker at the Red Stone Cabins."

"Parker?" Don burst out laughing. "Talk about a harebrained prognostication." He focused on Kyle. "That insurance company where Johanson works is fortunate he's not in the actuarial department."

Kyle chuckled, but only to himself, fearing that added ridicule might induce Eric, like Don, to demand odds. Kyle said, "So, what makes you think it might be Gary?"

"Well...it just so happens that three weeks ago, I punked Gary...big time. He told me he needed to have his driveway sealed. I recommended a name, but he was actually a buddy of mine at Granite, a guy who, like Gary, loves to pull pranks. Anyway, when my buddy went to Gary's house, he gave Gary a good quote and then he went into a spiel, pretending to be a Jehovah's Witness. The way my buddy described it, he had been going on for five minutes when he told Gary that as a condition of the contract, Gary would have to become a Jehovah's Witness. That's when Gary threw him out. Just before my buddy left, he said to Gary, 'By the way, I've never done a driveway. I work at Granite with Eric Johanson. And I practice Buddhism.'"

"I love it," said Don. "It serves Parker right. High time he got a taste of his own medicine."

"How did he take it?" said Kyle.

"He was a good sport. We had lunch together just last Friday. But at the time, he vowed to get even with me. He said I should expect his ultimate prank. After I told him that we'd be going to Utah for Bill's funeral, he responded with an interesting tidbit. This week he has to travel to northern Arizona for some depositions in a big Travelers' case. Said he planned to take a few vacation days, once the depositions were done."

"You son of a bitch!" said Kyle.

Eric exhibited a bewildered expression, the exaggeration of which intimated it was contrived.

"You know why I'm pissed!" said Kyle. "You sucked us into a bet when you knew all along that Gary was behind the text message."

Eric shrugged. "Look at it this way. The excitement and the debate about the text, together with the mere thought that Bill might be at the Red Stone Cabins, was worth ten dollars. If I had told you about Gary right away, you would have missed all that fun. Plus, you're getting a bonus. We have no idea what Gary has in store for us. We're in for a cool adventure."

Much as Kyle wanted to argue, he could not deny he was getting his money's worth. "Yeah, I suppose you're right, not that I like getting ripped off by a con man."

"You referring to Gary or me?" said Eric.

"If the mirror reflects your image," said Kyle, "then it must be you."

"Don't mean to interrupt a private party," said Don. "And yes, it's great that you two seers are certain that Gary sent the text message."

"What—you still think we'll find Bill at the cabins?" Eric shook his head derisively.

"Let's just say, we have a bet, and only after the proof is in, will we see who's right."

"Fine," said Eric. "You keep dreaming. In the meantime, I'm a patient man, happy to wait until four tomorrow to collect my dough." He turned to Kyle. "You still think the message might not be from Gary?"

"Not really…but I'm kinda hoping otherwise."

"What?" said Eric. "You're still hoping to win the bet? You still think the text came from someone other than Gary or Bill?"

"Nope, I wanna lose the bet, but not to you, Johanson. I want Don to win. More than anything, I'm dying to pay him a C-note."

"Damn you, Gordon," said Eric. "When you put it that way, I have to concur. Even though I know I'm gonna win,

270

nothing could make me happier than to pay Don one hundred bucks, to find Bill at the Red Stone Cabins.

CHAPTER XVIII

"I SENT MY SOUL through the Invisible,
Some letter of that After-life to spell;
And by and by my Soul return'd to me,
And answer'd 'I Myself am Heav'n and Hell."
(Fitzgerald, Edward, *The Rubáiyát of Omar Kháyyám,*
Stanza 43, referencing Milton, John, *Paradise Lost, Bk. I*).

Eric steered the silver Ford Expedition southeast along
Cottonwood Canyon Road. Only minutes before they had left a
café in the small town of Cannonville, Utah, the stop timed to
ensure their arrival at the Red Stone Cabins at four o'clock.

"GPS indicates a left turn, just a mile ahead on
Kodachrome State Park Road," said Kyle from his seat as
shotgun.

"I'm glad we got the four-wheel drive SUV," said Don,
seated behind Kyle. "Though I'm not sure we needed one as
big as this Expedition. The Explorer would have sufficed."

"Hey, you can't argue with a free upgrade." Kyle adjusted
his seat, tilting back a few more degrees. "And if we decide to
hit the back country, the big tires will help on tough terrain.
This area ain't Springfield or Hartford."

"Yeah, it's a helluva lot more impressive, especially the
red rock formations." Eric eased his foot off the gas, glancing
at the sights.

"This brochure I picked up at our last rest stop says it took
nearly two hundred million years to form the layers of rock."
Don reached forward and waved his brochure in Kyle's face.
"It says Kodachrome Basin State Park has sixty-seven

monoliths." He gazed out the window. "God, the skies are blue."

"Isn't that normally the case?" said Kyle, though he understood the point.

"Jeez, I'm talking deep blue. It's—"

"Just one tenth of a mile, and you turn left...to the north...on Kodachrome State Park Road, and then it's a little under two miles to the Red Stone Cabins."

As Eric made the turn, Kyle grew introspective. Every rational fiber of his brain precluded the possibility that Bill would be at the cabins. Wishful thinking challenged logic. He looked back over his shoulder at Don. "You still think that Bill will be there?"

"Wait a second. I never said that."

"Bullshit!" Eric threw up his hands.

"Jesus, keep your hands on the wheel!" Even before Kyle completed the utterance, Eric's hands were back in place. "Either you're senile, Burns," said Kyle, "or you're a liar. Back in Provo, you claimed we'd find Young at the cabins. That's why we came."

"No...and no!"

"No what?" said Kyle.

"Yeah," said Eric. "Let's hear you double talk your way out of this. And keep in mind, both Gordon and I heard you."

"Then no doubt you recall that I said the text message was from Bill. That's not to say he'll necessarily be there."

Kyle shook his head. "Burns, you can't get off the hook by splitting hairs."

"I'm not, goddamn it! Bill may have sent us the message. He may have even sent it from the world beyond. But that doesn't mean he'll be at the cabins."

"In case you've forgotten," said Eric, his inflection acerbic, "the message said to meet him there."

"But I never said he'd be there. He may well communicate with us again. He may be there with us in spirit. It could be his way of being part of the big trip we always planned."

The parsed explanation was better than Kyle had expected, not that he bought into it. He would have voiced an objection, but the mere possibility, even an absurd one, that they might hear from Bill was appealing, enough to let the issue be, at least until they had more facts. He turned to Eric. "So, tell us, how's your love life?"

"What prompted that? Had it come from our buddy in the back, I'd understand…a feeble attempt to change the subject."

"You didn't answer my question," said Kyle.

"Fine. It's right where it was last year…and for that matter, the year before that…and the year before that and so forth. There, you happy now."

"Have you tried any Internet dating sites?"

"Hell, I've tried everything…Internet dating, speed dating, church socials, blind dates…you name it."

"And?"

"Damn it, Gordon. You can be a pest."

"Katelyn tells me that too." Kyle flashed a quick smile. "Now that we got that settled, tell me—did you give any of these women a second call?"

From the back seat, "Nah, first date he compares them to Glenna, the mythical goddess in his favorite Renoir portrait, and then he crosses them off his list."

"That's not fair!"

"Maybe yes…and maybe no," said Don. "Regardless, you can't deny you still have Glenna on the brain."

The quip failed to draw a response. A telling silence pervaded the vehicle. They drove another half mile.

"The GPS indicates just three tenths…make that two tenths of a mile to the Red Stone Cabins." Eric pointed up ahead. "That's gotta be them, up there on the right…There's a bigger building, presumably where you check in, down at the far end. That must be where to pull in."

Eric turned off the road into the parking lot that fronted a wooden structure. Its Victorian front façade looked like something from the Old West. Four pairs of vertical timbers, each pair with a wagon wheel in the middle, supported the front overhang. The recessed upper façade was flat, but with rectangular cutouts to give it character. In the center, near the highest point, was a sign that read, "Camper Store."

"Damn, this is one cool-looking place," said Eric.

"You got that right," said Kyle. "You think we should first go into the store and see if Bill is registered?"

"If he's not," said Don, "we'd have no excuse to hang around. Telling the clerk we're looking for someone who had his funeral yesterday wouldn't cut it. If anything, he might call the cops, thinking we're some kind of nuts."

"You have to admit—he'd have a point."

Kyle chuckled. Eric's humor underscored the absurdity that surrounded their excursion. Still he could not deny that the mystery of what awaited them, the anticipation it fostered, was enticing. He glanced at his watch. "Two minutes to four. Perfect timing."

"You expected otherwise when you have the master at the helm?" Eric leaned forward close to the rearview mirror and smirked. He backed the vehicle up and headed slowly to the right, along the row of six log cabins facing the road. Each of the pine structures, stained in redwood and at least twice as deep as wide, had a porch across the front.

"This one is cabin One," said Don, pointing at a small plaque over the door. "Six must be down at the far end."

Eric continued down the line, past cabin Two, the only one with a vehicle in front. He paused alongside the last cabin. "Here it is—number Six." He turned left, so the vehicle faced the building.

"Neat little place," said Kyle.

From the back seat, Don reached between his two pals and pointed out the front windshield. "What an amazing backdrop...those buttes or mesas or whatever the hell they're called."

Kyle would have gibed his buddy had he known the term to describe the broad, flat-topped stone formations. He said, "You think all those horizontal, colored layers were formed thousands of years apart?"

"Probably more like millions," said Eric, as he turned the engine off.

Several seconds passed. No one moved.

"We just gonna sit here?" said Kyle.

"No...but..." Eric reached for the door handle and pulled it, still not opening the portal. "Damn, you've got to admit this is mighty weird, being drawn out to nowhere, responding to a purported message from a dead person."

"Doesn't seem weird to me."

Eric looked back over his shoulder. "Knowing you, Burns, that's no surprise."

Hope, albeit fatuous, kept Kyle from voicing concurrence. Regardless, rationality, a sober examination of the facts, had convinced him that Gary Parker had lured them to the remote destination. Still that begged the question: What surprise did Gary have waiting for them?

"C'mon, it's four o'clock. Let's get the show on the road." Don climbed out of the vehicle.

A moment later, Eric and Kyle did so as well.

"Wow, look over there," said Eric. He pointed across the road where, several hundred yards away, roughly a half-dozen red stone columns rose one hundred, two hundred or more feet from the desert floor. "Damn, they're even more amazing than what's on this side of the highway."

"Those are monoliths," said Don.

"You sure about that?" said Kyle.

Don pulled out his Kodachrome Basin State Park brochure from his back pocket and pointed. "See, Kodachrome Basin State Park. Right here beneath the picture, it terms the red sandstone structures you find in this area, monoliths."

"They are impressive." Kyle tried to imagine how they were formed. "They're odd, the way they stick straight up from nowhere."

Eric shot him a questioning look.

"Well...unlike mountains and valleys and gorges, where it's easy to see how a river or a glacier might have carved them, these things...look at them...some are really skinny, and they just stick up like...like big phallic symbols."

"They hardly look like big pricks," said Eric.

"Jesus, you know what I mean. And anyway, if you're so smart, you tell me how they got here."

"How should I know? Maybe a dinosaur planted monolith seeds."

"And maybe you—"

"Would you guys stop bickering?" Don pointed at Cabin Six. "In case you've forgotten, we came here for a reason."

Kyle conceded the point, though only to himself. No way would he openly knock the inane conversation, not when the chances to reprise their insouciant days at Williams had grown so infrequent. He looked back over his shoulder at Don. "I hope you were right...and Eric and I were wrong."

A puzzled expression showed on Don's face.

"About Bill...that the text really was from him...and better yet, that we find him here." Kyle silently laughed at himself. The chance that Bill had brought them to Cabin Six was nil...well, virtually nil.

The trio stepped onto the porch.

"Really well-maintained," whispered Eric.

Kyle nodded, as he tried to peak through the corner of the window to the right of the door. A drawn curtain largely blocked his view. "Someone gonna knock?" he said softly.

Eric tapped lightly on the door. Five...ten...fifteen seconds elapsed. But nothing.

"Give it another rap, a good one," whispered Don.

Eric banged the door.

"Come right in. It's unlocked."

The trio, nonplused, gazed at one another.

Eric whispered. "Damn, Parker did a decent imitation. I can't say flat out that it wasn't Bill."

"Who knows?" Don shrugged before turning the door handle. They stepped inside, just over the threshold.

"I'm in the bathroom. Be right out. Have a seat on the bed."

With the voice a bit muffled, Kyle found it hard to make a definitive judgment about the speaker's identity. As he followed Eric and Don to the bed, his brain raced. Was it possible? Might they come face to face with their pal? Could he be alive? Could he have come back from the dead? Ridiculous though the questions were, wishful thinking cajoled Kyle to entertain them.

Eric and Don seated themselves on the edge of the bed. Kyle remained standing. He eyed his two buddies. Like him, they waited in silence.

The seconds ticked, roughly a half-minute, though it seemed far longer. Still no one said a word. Finally, the bathroom door opened. Kyle jerked back. This was not among the scenarios he had contemplated.

"Nice of you fellows to come." A man stepped out with a semi-automatic rifle aimed their way. "You were expecting your pal Bill, perhaps?"

Whatever Kyle had expected, Clinton Horstmeyer was not part of it. Add the gun that was pointed in their direction, and the scene was as unpleasant as it was shocking. "What the hell is going on?"

"I'll do the talking." Clint raised the rifle several inches, pointing it more demonstratively. "Gordon, take a seat, next to your buddies."

Kyle complied with the command.

"Now that we understand one another, let me introduce myself...Shelby Horstmeyer, identical twin brother of Clinton Horstmeyer, at your service...On second thought, strike the part about *at your service*."

The disclosure helped explain a portion of the anomaly. Clint had not come back from the dead... nor had Bill. But why would Clint's twin brother lure them to a cabin and greet them with a gun? No sooner did Kyle have the thought than it was addressed.

"I suspect you're curious why I invited you here. Well, nice fellow that I am—and let me assure you, I'm a *very* nice fellow—I'm not going to tell you." He glared. "Burns, I saw that frown. And don't you dare say anything." He grew briefly pensive and then scratched his head. "You know what...I believe in democracy. So, rather than taking my word, we'll do this democratically."

Do what democratically? Kyle suppressed any facial reaction for fear it would draw ire.

"We're gonna take a vote on whether I'm a nice guy. But before we do, one minor ground rule. Anyone who raises a hand...gets shot!" Horstmeyer took a deep breath and exhaled slowly. "Okay, time to vote. Anyone who thinks I'm not a nice guy, raise your hand."

Several seconds passed. The trio remained motionless.

"Gentlemen, I have wonderful news. It's unanimous." A pleased look on his face, Horstmeyer nodded repeatedly and then murmured, "Isn't democracy wonderful?"

God, craziness runs in the genes. Thoughts about what the nut had in mind for them amplified Kyle's concern.

"You're no more Shelby Horstmeyer, than I'm Confucius!" Eric pointed, his extended arm nearly as long as the weapon that pointed back.

Kyle did a double take. What folly had possessed Eric to challenge the barrel of a gun?

"You lookin' to die now?" The aim of the weapon shifted, just enough so it was directed squarely at Eric.

"Don't antagonize him," whispered Don, putting a calming hand on Eric's shoulder.

Eric brushed the hand off his shoulder. "It's Clint…Clint Horstmeyer."

"Clint's dead." Kyle's whisper was even softer than Don's. "Clint was killed in a plane crash."

Eric shook his head. He pointed again, but this time lower. "Look at his right knee…the scar."

Kyle eyed the knee. Just below the bottom of cargo shorts, there was a scar in the shape of a capital "T." The possibility that like Clint, his twin, had torn up his knee in a manner that left the unique disfigurement was too much of a stretch. Kyle was about to voice the conclusion, but Don beat him to the punch.

"You're right. It is Clint!"

The gun-wielding antagonist displayed a smirk even broader than the bar at the top of his T-scar. "As I indicated in my gracious invitation to you gents, the rumors of my death, like those of Mark Twain, have been grossly exaggerated. But unlike Twain, in my case, the rumors are certain to persist." Clint nodded slowly, a seeming confirmation of his assessment. "You see, I'm confident that none of you will reveal my little secret."

That Clint would trust the trio to keep silent seemed dubious. Kyle's fear mounted.

Eric pointed at Clint again. "Forget about you being Shelby Horstmeyer. My money says you don't even have a twin. And for that matter, all that stuff you fed us about growing up in abusive foster homes was a lie as well."

"The hell it was!" Fire showed in Clint's eyes. "I was kicked around like a soccer ball, screamed at, belittled and whipped."

"But Eric was right," said Don. "You don't have a twin."

A second or two of silence, telling silence, ensued.

"So," said Kyle, "all that garbage about your twin getting to live with a rich uncle and never giving a crap about you was fabricated."

Clint stood briefly mute before muttering just loud enough to be audible, "Given their destiny...What the hell." He drew in a deep breath. "Yeah, I made up the shit about having a twin. I did it when I was about six. I hated my home. I hated my foster parents. I hated my life. I imagined what it might be like if I lived with a rich uncle, not that I had one. I became Shelby. He was my escape." Clint gestured with his gun. "If you bastards faced the shit that I did, you'd have done it too. So, don't judge...On second thought, go ahead, judge all you want. It'll add another reason for me to get even." His countenance appeared briefly thoughtful. "All my life, more than anything—except maybe a pro-football career—I've wanted to get even. And now that I'm dead—at least as far as the world is concerned—I'm gonna get what I want. I'm gonna get even!" One by one, he looked Eric, Don and Kyle in the eye. "And you, my little chickadees, are at the top of my list. But don't get swelled heads, thinking you're an exclusive club. There are others on my agenda. Unfortunately, one bastard, my fourth foster father—he was the meanest prick this side of Siberia—has deprived me of the pleasure. The son of a bitch, a chain smoker, died of lung cancer a few years back. I heard it was slow and painful. Helps make up for denying me the joy of doing him in."

For years Kyle had known that Clint was a louse. But the stunning harangue demonstrated the guy was worse, and, apparently, much more treacherous than previously imagined. Kyle's mind forked back to a debate he and his Inseparable buddies had shared at the Irish Mist just before they had graduated. Eric had argued that Clint was a psychopath. Bill had contended the claim was over the top. At the time, Kyle had voiced no opinion, though he had silently concurred with Bill. There at the Red Stone Cabins, gun pointed his way, Kyle re-assessed his view. Clinton Horstmeyer was, indeed, a psychopath.

"Enough of this inane banter! Time to get down to cases." Clint eased over to the cabin door, all the while keeping his gun trained on the three. He locked the door's dead bolt. "Case you thought I didn't notice, you boys arrived a couple minutes late. Tardiness is a bad habit, one you need to break."

"What's this about?" said Eric.

"I'll ask the questions...and from now on, I'll do the talking." Clint grabbed a large roll of duct tape from the window sill and a pair of children's scissors. He tossed the items over by the bed. "First things first. Gordon, cut off a piece of tape, about a yard, and wrap it tight around Burns' ankles. And then do the same with Johanson's ankles."

Kyle remained motionless.

"Perhaps your hearing ain't too good. That's a shame. 'Cause unless you get started wrapping, fifteen seconds from now I'm gonna blow Burns away. And then fifteen seconds after that, I'm gonna do the same to Johanson."

Kyle immediately reached for the duct tape, cut a piece and began wrapping it around Don's ankles.

"Tight...Pull it tight, unless you prefer I pull the trigger."

Kyle followed the instruction. Once he had completed the task on both of his friends, Clint said, "Gordon, take a seat. Back onto the bed, next to your pals."

Kyle complied.

"Johanson, tie Gordon's ankles together...and pull it tight!"

Eric struggled to get into position. He kneeled, and after reaching for the tape and scissors and cutting a piece, he bound it around Kyle's ankles.

"Good. Now have a seat alongside your buddies."

With a bit of maneuvering, they arranged themselves so they sat side by side on the edge of the bed.

"What the hell is this all about?" said Eric.

"Apparently, someone has a short memory." Clint shifted his weapon just enough that it focused on Eric. "I'm the one asking the questions...But now that you boys are comfy, perhaps it's time to fill you in on a few details. You came here hoping you might find someone back from the dead. Good news is: You found just that. Bad news: You found me, rather than Bill Young. Presumably he's resting quietly in his lovely little box, six feet under. You're probably wondering what I'm doing here...how I got here. Well, I got more good news. I'm gonna tell you. Reason though is not so good, at least for the three of you. You see, where you're headed—and I'll tell you about that in a minute—you won't be repeating the story. As a matter of fact, you won't be repeating anything." A demonic laugh punctuated Clint's message.

A knot in Kyle's stomach grew tighter. Earlier apprehensions were being confirmed.

"I did a helluva job faking my death. Hated to do it to Rachel, sweet thing that she was, but I had no choice. Either we were both headed to the slammer, or one us—her—had to be sacrificed. Needed to make it look good. And just so there were no hitches, I gave her a special cocktail while we were flying west. Spiked the thing so she was out cold. Once I reached the right spot, I parachuted out of the plane. But before I did, I poured gasoline on both seats and around the cockpit. I ran a neat little fuse from the door to the gas, lit the thing and then tally-ho. Last I saw the plane, it was still flying but starting to flame. By the time it crashed, I'll bet it was three or four miles from where I jumped. It was headed towards a tree-laden canyon. Maybe it exploded in mid-air. Don't know for certain, but one thing sure, it musta been one helluva fireball. From what I read in the newspapers, pieces were strewn everywhere. Finding or identifying anything had to be nigh on impossible. As far as the authorities are concerned, Clinton Horstmeyer, yours truly, is dead and gone. And so much for the criminal charges I was facing." Clint smirked. "You boys are behavin' very well, and since you are, I'll let you ask a few questions before I take you for a little ride."

"Why you doing this?" said Eric.

"I think you know, but if you want me to spell it out, I will. You, Johanson, ya son of a bitch, along with Gordon, you're the reason Carla Pender didn't marry me. You talked her out of it."

"Don't flatter yourself," said Eric. "Even if I had said nothing, she wouldn't have married the likes of you."

For an instant Clint appeared to bristle, but then he chuckled. "Have your little say. It will merely make my getting the last word more satisfying." He pointed his gun at Kyle. "Gordon, I'm not even gonna tell you why I'm getting even with you. Course, you know anyway."

"What have you got against Don?" Kyle gestured to his right, past Eric.

"My money says he did something to tip you off about Rachel, maybe even contacted the SEC and put me in the deep weeds."

"The SEC was investigating your insider trading even before Rachel came to work for me."

"Whatever…it doesn't matter. No way can I afford to have any of you mouthing off that I'm still alive…Hey, a guy's gotta do, what a guy's gotta do."

The remark confirmed that Clint intended to kill them. Kyle said, "When we turn up missing and the authorities discover that you were here, you're gonna have a big problem."

"So you think…Well, it just so happens, they'll never know I was here. I registered for three, all under Don's name. He and I are the same height, six feet and medium build, and with a couple items I bought at a costume store—nowhere near here—I made myself look like him. That plus I wore a big, broad-brimmed hat when I registered…Oh, and one more thing, I paid cash when I registered. They like that out here miles from anywhere." Clint smirked. "Given that the world has me marked dead, no one will be thinking that I was here. You can take that to the bank…or perhaps I should rephrase that, given your circumstances. You can take that to your graves."

"You actually intend to kill us?" said Don.

"*Kill*…that's much too strong a word. Let's just say I plan to take you for a ride on a special road…a very special road.

283

You'll love it. It has spectacular scenery. Very remote. It forks off Highway 12 not far from Boulder, and miles later links with Posey Lake Road. I gotta admit—it's a treacherous bastard, winding with sheer drop-offs everywhere. I guess that's why they call it Hell's Backbone Road. Beautiful name, don'tcha think?" Clint paused briefly, as if he were offering an opportunity for a response to what had plainly been a rhetorical question. "Far from anything, it has this great, one-lane bridge, about two hundred feet long. Talk about a scary son of a bitch. Runs fifteen hundred feet above the canyon floor. Fortunately, it has guardrails, at least on the bridge itself. Of course, once you reach the end, there are none, and the edge of the road drops straight off that fifteen-hundred-foot cliff." One by one, Clint looked the trio in the eye. "You chaps are going to find out whether that big SUV you're driving can fly. Gonna find out right at the end of Hell's Backbone Bridge. And once again, I've good news. My money says your vehicle can fly. But like the other times, I've got bad news too. Based upon what I know of gravity—mind you, I only took high school physics—my guess, an educated one, says it will only fly fifteen hundred feet, and that's straight down. According to what I read, and allowing for air resistance, I figure it oughta be going about two hundred miles per hour when it hits bottom and explodes." He pointed his weapon at Kyle. "Gordon, if I recall, you took physics at Williams. Perhaps you could run the formula and give me your best estimate. You might even want to count how many seconds it takes to hit bottom. Then you can verify your estimate." Clint scratched his head theatrically. "Of course, there is one problem. Once you hit bottom, I doubt you'll be in any condition for calculations." Clint smirked again. "We got some more work, but before we do, any other questions?"

"How did you send us the text that lured us here?" said Eric.

"Piece of cake. The Internet has easy instructions for anonymous text messaging. It enables one to send messages with an alias. And Rachel, back when she worked for Kyle, had access to his personal information, including the number to text him a message...Now, assuming your questions are done, let's move on to more important matters."

"But how did you know we were coming out here?" Kyle posed the question partly from curiosity, but also in an effort to stall.

"Damn, I give you goons an inch, and you take a mile...Well, nice guy that I am—and we already agreed on that—I'll answer this one last question, but no more. Since the plane crash, I've had lotsa time. I check the Internet every day. First I read the *Springfield Republican*. I like to see what's happening back East, and most of all, what the local police or the feds are doing about my case. Seems it's pretty much ancient history, ever since Rachel...and I...died in the crash." Clint laughed loudly. "I also check the news from our old campus, mainly to follow the Williams football team. You know you can read our old student newspaper, the *Williams Record*, as well as any alumni news, on line. That's where I found out about Bill's death. Right away I knew you boys would be coming to his funeral. Talk about a sure thing. Ain't a bet in Vegas better than that. But enough with the blab. On to more important matters. All three of you, stand up and turn around, so your backs face me."

The trio climbed off the edge of the bed where they had been sitting and followed the instruction. Owing to the duct tape around his ankles, Kyle nearly fell, but managed to keep his balance.

"Now toss your wallets and cell phones, along with the keys to the SUV, onto the floor in my general direction, and do it without turning around."

The trio complied. Clint gathered the wallets, phones and keys from the floor and stepped back toward the door.

"Good news again. Except for the key to the SUV, I'm gonna give the stuff back, complete with credit cards and whatever...So, let's see. What have we got?...Gordon, nice, some hundreds...Burns, fifty-seven dollars. A little more cash would be appreciated...Johanson, a few fifties and a bunch of twenties. Could have been better. And that said, I should probably stiff you guys, but...generous fellow that I am, I'm gonna put a little back in each wallet. Let's see.

285

Fifteen...twenty-three...and Johanson, you're the lucky one. You get to keep forty-seven. Don't want this to look like a robbery." Clint proceeded to count the money in a mumbling voice that was barely audible. Finally, he said, "A bit disappointing, only five hundred seventy-three for me. Successful guys like you shouldn't be so cheap." He tossed the wallets across the room where the three stood. "Pick 'em up and stick 'em back in your pockets, and make sure you got yours. Chances are, they won't be identifiable, but just in case, I want your little accident to look like one."

Once the three had put their wallets back into their respective pockets, Clint said, "Gordon, Johanson, turn around, back to me, and put your hands behind your back. Now Burns, you turn around and tie each of their wrists together, just the way we did with the ankles—tight! Then put duct tape around each of their mouths." When for a moment, Don seemed to hesitate, Clint raised his weapon higher. "Do it now, or I'll blow the three of you away."

Don followed the command.

Still by the door, Clint reached over to the table in front of the window and grabbed two large, rolled-up sacks. He tossed them to Don. "Put one over each of their heads."

Don again complied.

"Gordon...Johanson, both of you, on the floor, and pull your legs up into the bags...you know, into a fetal position."

While it took a minute for the bound duo to fully comply, once they did, Clint said, "Burns, pull the drawstring on each of their bags."

"Jesus, Clint...this is crazy."

"I said pull the goddamn drawstrings, and tie them."

Don did as he was ordered.

"Okay, Burns, cut a piece of duct tape about two feet long and lay it on the floor, sticky side up. Then kneel facing the bed with your hands behind your back."

Again Don complied.

Clint walked over to Don, and with the gun in one hand, took the tape in the other and wrapped it repeatedly around Don's wrists. Clint cut another piece, about the same length. "Anything you want to say before I decorate your mouth?"

286

"When they find our bodies at the bottom of the canyon in burlap bags, our hands and feet and mouths wrapped in duct tape, the authorities will know this was not an accident."

"Excellent point...almost." Clint laughed disdainfully. "Minor detail. I plan to pour gasoline inside your SUV. A match tossed in just before it goes flying, will have it up in flames. And when it hits bottom, there's gonna be one hell of an explosion. Don't suspect there will be a lot left to identify. But just in case I'm wrong, I've got more good news. Before sending the SUV over the cliff, I'm gonna remove your bags and the duct tape."

From inside his burlap bag, Kyle was attuned to every word. The moment Clint cut them loose, just before he dumped them to their deaths, would be their one chance to escape. But they would need to be quick. He wondered if Eric and Don might be entertaining similar thoughts. Clint could not cut them all free at the same time. Holding his gun on them and removing the bags and tape would be difficult. With quick, aggressive action, they might have a chance.

Clint wrapped duct tape around Don's mouth. He got a third burlap bag. He put it over Don's head. "Burns, on the floor and curl your legs up." Once Don complied, Clint pulled the open end of the bag over Don's lower extremities and yanked the cord tight.

"Oh, by the way, I forgot to mention, I have another bit of good news for you gentleman. Before launching you over the cliff, I'm gonna return your cell phones, right after I chloroform each of you. You'll be out cold. You won't feel the flames, nor the crash when your SUV smashes into Mother Earth...I realize that right now, what with your mouths taped, you may not be able to voice your thanks, even though I'm sure you'd like to. So, just wriggle your bodies, and I'll know that you appreciate my kindness." Several seconds passed. "That's awful. Not a muscle moved. Thought you boys developed good manners back at Williams. Apparently, I was mistaken...Well, on the bright side, your impudence makes my newest piece of bad news even more pleasant to deliver. The chloroform will come before I remove the duct tape from your hands or feet.

That way, there'll be no risk that you put up a fuss...try to break free."

Kyle swallowed hard. Moments before he had come up with a plan of escape. Already the strategy was out the window. Indeed, the surviving three members of the Inseparables seemed destined to join Bill. In all likelihood, they were doomed. Kyle immediately began trying to conjure a new avenue of escape. His mind drew a frustrating blank. Presumably the other two were also attempting to figure a way out. Kyle could only hope they were having more success, but given the circumstances, the prospects seemed dim.

"I want you boys to know that you've caused me great inconvenience. Out on Hell's Backbone Road, about halfway between the point where the road forks from Route 12 and the bridge—nearly ten miles from each—I left a little Suzuki hidden in the brush. I had to walk all the way to Route 12 before hitchhiking back here. And to make matters worse, after I dump you over the cliff, I'll need to walk roughly the same distance, about ten miles, to get the Suzuki. Of course, if you hadn't showed, and I had to hitchhike back to Hell's Backbone Road and walk the ten miles just to get my car back, I would have been really pissed, knowing it had all been for naught. Anyway, I hope you appreciate how I went out of my way for you. Matter of fact, I'll give you a chance to express your thanks. Since your mouths are taped, roll around a little to show your gratitude."

No way would Kyle give Clint the satisfaction. He remained still. He listened, trying to hear if the others were moving. He heard nothing.

"Unappreciative bastards!...Fine, if that's how you want to be, don't expect any compassion from me."

Kyle heard what he thought might be the sound of the door opening and closing. A couple of minutes went by.

"Apologies," said Clint. "I had to slip outside to turn the vehicle around and back it up to the porch." One by one he rolled the bagged bodies over near the door. Then he loaded them into the back of the big SUV. As he lifted the last bag, he said, "Damn it, Johanson, you musta put on a few pounds. Mighty inconsiderate, making me lift so much dead...well, almost dead…weight. Fortunately, even though my football-playing days are over, I work out. I'm still in great shape." He slammed the rear compartment of the SUV.

Moments later, Kyle heard a door open. A few seconds passed and it closed and the engine started.

"You boys enjoy the ride. And just to make sure you do, knowing that you're gonna miss the scenery, I'll put on some nice music."

Kyle felt the vehicle move. Soon after, his burlap sack bumped into the one next to him as the SUV apparently turned out onto the highway.

CHAPTER XIX

EASY IS THE DESCENT TO HELL; night and day the gates stand open; but to reclimb the slope, and escape to the outer air, this indeed is a task (Virgil, Aeneid, Book IV, Line 26).

The Expedition, which had been traveling for a while, turned left and the road grew rough and winding. From inside his burlap bag Kyle was bouncing left and right, banging into the bags which held his buddies. Even with the radio playing up front, he could hear the stones roil beneath the vehicle's big tires. Presumably they were on Hell's Backbone Road, on their way to their ill-fated destiny. The centrifugal force of what seemed like a hairpin turn sent him reeling. His head, cushioned only by the bag, banged against the floor of the vehicle.

Kyle wriggled and struggled to free his hands and feet, but only briefly. Earlier repeated efforts when they were still on a paved road with fewer curves, apparently Route 12, had proved useless. Based upon what Clint had told them, their destination, Hell's Backbone Bridge, was roughly at the halfway point of the thirty-eight-mile stretch on which Hell's Backbone Road wound away from Route 12 before rejoining it. If so, likely they had something less than twenty miles before Clint would send them plunging to their deaths. Try as he did, Kyle came up with no plan of escape. The futility of his efforts was hardly a surprise. Back when they were on a straighter and smoother road, he had been unable to come up with anything. With the twisting, rough road jouncing him about, concentration, a prerequisite to an idea, was all but impossible. The inevitability of death grew ever clearer. It crossed his mind that dozing might at least allow him to spend his waning minutes in the illusion of a dream world. He immediately dismissed the thought. He was not about to give up. In any event, he was far too panicked to sleep, especially bouncing around on a bumpy ride.

A bizarre thought popped into Kyle's head. Perhaps Gary had punked Eric and, unwittingly, all three of them. Maybe Gary wasn't really going to Arizona for depositions. Perhaps he had made up a story to that effect after learning of the trio's upcoming trip. The story may have been designed to make Eric believe the trip would be interrupted by one of Gary's stunts. If that was Gary's intent, if the story itself was a prank, Gary had been successful. But whether Gary really went to Arizona didn't matter, and Kyle preferred not to waste time on such irrelevancy. His brain, as if it had a mind of its own, didn't seem to care. It had conjured the unwelcome thought, all the while generating no solution to his dire predicament.

One by one, the nerve-racking minutes ticked. As best as Kyle could estimate, more than a half-hour had elapsed since their SUV had turned off onto the uneven terrain. He suspected that Hell's Backbone Bridge might be getting close, though all he could do was guess. Suddenly he felt something at his feet. He glanced down. A moment later, the end of his bag opened and a trace of light shined in. Down by his ankles someone was working the duct tape that bound his legs. It was Don. He had a small knife. An instant later, Kyle felt his legs come free.

"Stay down, and don't make a sound," whispered Don. "I'll explain later." Don squeezed into Kyle's bag and cut the tape that bound Kyle's wrists behind his back.

Kyle slowly pulled the duct tape that wrapped his mouth. The thrill of getting free mitigated the discomfort to his skin.

"Stay in your bag for now," said Don, maintaining a whisper. "And keep down. I'm going to cut Eric free. Then we can all figure out what to do."

Don drew himself back out of Kyle's bag. Kyle slithered his way so his head was at the open end of the bag. He peeked out and watched as Don cut Eric free. From the front of the vehicle, he could hear Clint singing loudly to the rap that was playing on the radio. Much as he wanted to steal a glance over the second row of seats, risking the possibility that Clint might see him in the rearview mirror was out of the question.

Don finished cutting Eric free and crawled back into his sack. Like the other two, Eric rotated his position so his head was at the open end of his bag. Still laying low, the trio adjusted their positions so their heads were close together.

"How the hell did you get the knife?" whispered Kyle.

"I'll tell you later. Let's focus on more important things—how we can overcome Clint."

"Should we try now?" said Eric. "He can't drive and deal with us at the same time."

"It would take us several seconds, probably more, to climb over the seats," said Don. "By that time, he might be able to hit the brakes and grab his gun. My guess, he has it on the passenger seat, right next to him."

At first blush, Kyle liked the idea of an immediate attack, but the images created by Don's comments altered his thinking. "Even if we're quick enough to grab him before he could get his gun, he'd probably lose control of the vehicle, and we all might go sailing over a cliff."

"So, what do you guys suggest—that we open the rear door and jump out?"

"Can we open it from here?" said Kyle.

"Don't know," said Don, "but I can't say I like the idea, not when he's got a gun."

Once again, Kyle imagined the scene. Might the three of them get hurt jumping out of a moving vehicle, and there was no telling what the terrain would be like. Getting away from Clint when he was armed with a semi-automatic would be difficult. Chances were, he'd get at least two of them. Kyle disliked the odds. "You think we should wait until he stops the vehicle?"

"You mean when we get to Hell's Backbone Bridge?" said Eric.

"That's my thought," said Don. "When he opens the rear compartment and tries to chloroform us, we can all jump him at once. He'll probably need to put his gun down to give us the chloroform. It'll be three on one. We can take him...I think."

"What if he has the gun in one hand and the chloroform in the other? He might just start shooting."

"That's a possibility," said Don. "Either of you have any better ideas?"

The whispers ceased for the better part of a minute. Kyle searched his brain for a better strategy. He weighed the three that had been proposed. Finally, he said, "I say we go with Don's idea and wait until the vehicle stops."

"I agree," said Eric, "but maybe we should try to get out and jump him before he comes to us."

"Minor details," said Kyle. "We're not sure we can open the rear gate, and climbing over the seats seems too slow and risky. Presumably Clint would have his gun in a second."

"Damn," said Eric. "I hate waiting until he comes to us."

Kyle silently conceded the point, but he disliked the alternatives even more. "Waiting isn't great, but it's the best we've got. I say we stay low until after the vehicle stops and Clint comes to us."

"Okay," said Eric. "But—Wait a second...We've got a weapon too."

"Don's knife? All what...maybe, two and a-half inches of it?" A mocking inflection underscored Kyle's skepticism.

"Hey, don't knock it," said Don. "It's better than nothing, and it got you free, didn't it?"

"Sorry." Kyle voiced the regret so softly that he was unsure it was audible.

"That's not what I was referring to," said Eric. He gestured downward with his finger.

Kyle had no idea what his friend was thinking.

"The tire jack. It's located in the compartment right below us. All we have to do is lift that little handle and fold back the cover. C'mon, everybody squeeze forward...just a foot or so, and we should be able to get it."

The trio quietly pulled their knees to their chests. With second efforts, they managed to get clear of the fold. With one hand Eric pulled back the cover, and with the other he reached down and grabbed the jack handle, along with the lug-nut wrench.

"I'm leaving the jack itself in the compartment. It's much too bulky. I doubt it will be of any use." He put the cover back down over the compartment. He handed Kyle the lug-nut wrench, keeping the jack handle for himself. "Now we're all armed."

"Yeah, you guys have solid iron weapons, and I, the one who got us all free, have my little knife."

"You want to trade?" said Kyle. "You can have the wrench, and I'll take your knife."

"Part with my knife? No way!"

Kyle shot Don a look. Ordinarily he would have given him the business. But fresh from regrets and with more pressing concerns, it was no time for frivolity. "So, exactly how will we handle this, once Clint stops?"

"We'll wait until he comes around and opens the tail gate to give us the chloroform," said Don. "That's when we'll all jump him."

"What if his talk about chloroform was a bluff and, rather than coming around back, he simply dumps us into the canyon?"

"Then we're screwed," said Kyle.

The Expedition hit a large bump, and the trio bounced, with Eric and Kyle nearly banging heads.

"Jesus," said Kyle, in what he thought was a subdued voice.

"Shh!" Eric put a finger to his mouth. "At some point, Clint will have to get out of the vehicle...Think about it. He's not gonna take the ride with us over the cliff."

The remark brought a measure of reassurance to Kyle. "Is there any way we could do this without staying in these lousy bags? They hardly put us in a fighting posture."

"I think we have to stay," said Don. "There's a good chance that when Clint stops, before he opens the tail gate, he'll look in the side or rear window. If we're not in the bags, he's apt to start shooting. Regardless, we'll lose the element of surprise."

Eric heaved a protracted sigh. "Yeah...I guess you're right."

Much as Kyle disliked the idea of remaining in the sacks, he silently conceded it was probably best.

"We should get back to our original positions...except with our heads by the openings of our bags." Don, who had earlier moved to the center to free his friends, maneuvered his way so his bag was again toward the passenger side of the vehicle. Kyle occupied the position in the middle, with Eric on the driver's side.

"Do we—" Kyle clipped his tongue the instant the radio music halted. He assumed the moment of destiny was at hand.

From up front, Clint called back, "Good news. GPS says we're less than two miles from the bridge. Let's see, our arrival time is four forty-seven...just seven minutes. Damn, these gravel roads are slow going. But you boys enjoy—"

The vehicle swerved.

"Shit! With you bastards distracting me, we nearly took the big dive! Enough!" Clint's voice trailed off into momentary inaudible mumbling. The radio came back on, even louder than before.

"Should we have a signal when to attack?" Kyle glanced left and right.

"Let's not get complicated," said Eric. "I say we attack the moment the tailgate goes up."

"I agree," said Don. "Given that we're getting close, I think we should take our positions and just lay low and wait."

"Sounds good, but before we do, I suggest that we all have a peep hole, just enough for one eye, at the top end of our bags. That way we'll know exactly when to spring into action."

"Good idea," said Don.

"One last thing," said Kyle. "In case we don't make it, I want you guys to know...You're the best."

"Same goes for me," said Eric.

"Unanimous," said Don. "But let's save that kind of talk for when we're sailing into the canyon. It takes some time to fly fifteen hundred feet."

"Minor detail," said Eric. "At that point we'll likely be unconscious, thanks to chloroform." Eric tucked his head back into his sack.

Kyle did so too. He arranged himself so he could peer out the end of the bag. He practiced opening the end, making certain he could leap into action in an instant. He simulated how he would swing the lug-nut wrench with his right hand. Then he pulled back into the bag and waited. His senses heightened, as he became conscious of every bump and curve in the road. Adrenaline pumped. His brain raced, repeatedly rehearsing how he would attack. Seconds slowed, as time seemingly stopped. A minute became an eternity. At long last, the SUV drew to a halt. The engine, as well as the radio, went silent.

"We're here, my friends, at Hell's Backbone Bridge. It may not be the Irish Mist, but think of it as an oasis...*your last oasis.*" Clint laughed loudly.

The perverse humor sparked rage in Kyle. He heard the car door open. He endeavored to suppress his anger, lest his focus be lessened.

"Jeez, this sucker is even scarier than I recall." Clint let out a diabolical laugh.

Several moments of silence ensued.

Was Clint still in the vehicle? Was he looking down over the cliff? Was he coming around to the back? Or...? Kyle's brain nervously raced.

"Hope you boys enjoyed the ride. No doubt you'll love your upcoming flight. As for the landing, I'm not so sure." Clint laughed again.

The car door slammed. Again, there was silence. Kyle waited, listening for any clue. What was Clint doing? Was he carrying his gun? Was he dousing the SUV with gasoline? Maybe he already had and was about to set the vehicle on fire. Perhaps he was readying his chloroform. Maybe he was peering through the window watching them. What if his plan differed from what he had told them? What if he simply sent the vehicle over the cliff without opening the tailgate? More than a minute passed. Kyle longed to steal a peek, but he dared not. He was far beyond antsy. Panic had all but eclipsed rationality. Stay calm, he told himself.

What sounded like footsteps at the rear of the vehicle drew Kyle's attention. He readied himself, poised to swing into action. Through his peep hole he could see the rear tailgate, but not high enough to see out the window. Was Clint staring in on them? Was his weapon set to blast them? A second later the tailgate started to lift. Kyle lept from his bag swinging his wrench with all his might. It crashed into Clint's side, several inches above his waist. Simultaneously Eric smashed the jack handle into the hip on the other side of Clint's body.

Clint let out a blood-curdling scream as he sank to the ground, landing on his back. A small satchel he held in one hand and keys in the other both dropped free.

Don jumped out, kneeling over Clint with his knife to Clint's throat, while Eric and Kyle stood over their antagonist, ready to smash him again.

"Don't...no, no," pleaded Clint, writhing in pain.

"Put your arms straight out to the side," bellowed Eric. "If he moves a muscle, smash him in the head, Kyle. I'll check the front seat for his gun."

"Shit, you busted my hip."

"Shut your goddamn mouth, or I'll slit your throat!" Don stuck the knife within an inch of Clint's Adam's Apple.

Seconds later, Eric returned with the semi-automatic weapon. "The damn thing is loaded." He trained it on Clint.

Kyle grabbed the sack in which he had been housed. "Let's see how you like it." He slipped the bag over Clint's head. "I doubt the pieces of duct tape he used to tie us up are any good."

"I'll cut one of the other bags into strips. We can use them to tie his feet and hands." As Don got up to get the bag, he said, "Keep the gun trained on him. Shoot the son of a bitch for all I care!"

Kyle did a double take, uncertain whether the remark was serious or bravado.

Using his knife, Don cut a sack into strips. With one piece, he tied Clint's hands behind his back. He tied two more, one just above Clint's knees, and the other around his ankles. He slid the sack covering Clint's head, down over Clint's legs and feet.

"What are you gonna do to me?" said Clint, his voice racked with pain.

"Shut your damn trap!" snarled Don. He rolled Clint over, ignoring the excruciated yelp it provoked. Don grabbed another strip and tied it around the outside of the bag, about halfway between the top and bottom. "That oughta keep the bastard."

"Should we drive him to the police or hospital now?" said Kyle.

Don put his finger to his lips and motioned the other two to follow him to the far side of the vehicle, about fifteen feet from where Clint lay bagged.

"You weren't serious before about killing him, were you?" whispered Kyle.

"Of course not," said Don. "But after what he put us through, I want him to sweat."

"What are you proposing?" said Eric.

"That we make him think we're gonna torture and kill him." He motioned them back behind the SUV. With his voice no longer subdued, Don said, "I say we dump Clint's body over the cliff. No one will miss him. As far as the authorities are concerned, he died in a plane crash."

"Please guys…give me a break."

"Horstmeyer, shut your mouth or I'll pump you full of lead." Eric smiled at his two pals.

"Maybe we should set him on fire before we throw him over the cliff." Even though the remark was purely in jest, Kyle could hardly believe it had come from his mouth. "That way he won't be identifiable."

"I don't know," said Eric. "Today with DNA, I imagine they can identify even a burned body."

"Maybe so," said Don. "But you think anyone would ever find him at the bottom of this canyon? And even if they did, they'd never make a DNA match. There's nothing to match. There'd be no reason to think it's Clint."

"I say we take him with us. We can look up tortures on the Internet and pick out the most hideous." Eric put his hand to his mouth suppressing a laugh. He motioned the others to the side of the vehicle and whispered. "Suppose we drive him back to Cannonville or, better yet, the Ranger Station in Kodachrome Basin State Park where the authorities can take custody and get him medical treatment."

Don and Kyle nodded. The trio went back around to Clint.

Eric pushed a foot against the bag holding Clint. "Horstmeyer, this must be your lucky day…'cause I've got good news. We're not gonna shoot you. Unfortunately, this good news, like yours earlier, has some bad accompaniments. You see, we're gonna take you for a little ride, after which we're gonna torture you…the more horrible, the more painful, the better. Then we're gonna kill you. But before you start to fret, there's more good news. I'm giving you dispensation to open your trap, just this once. After that, any time you do, we'll add another torture. So, what do you think? Pretty sweet deal…wouldn't you say?"

"Eric…please. I beg you. Give me a break…You're religious. Your father's a reverend. What would he say?"

"First off, my father won't ever know. So, forget him. As to the fact that I'm religious, you have a point…an excellent one."

"You…you gonna give me a break?"

"Let's just say I have more good news. God-fearing man that I am, I plan to look to the Bible. That's the good news…and, as we're both learning, good news generally travels with bad. You see, the Bible teaches an eye for an eye…and, of course, the Golden Rule says: 'Do unto others as you would have them do unto you.' Just as you planned to kill us, we're gonna kill you. And unless you're itching for some extra torture, don't open your mouth, because that special dispensation I gave you a minute ago has left town." Eric turned to Don and Kyle, both of whom were grinning. "I'd say the time has come that we take Clint for a ride."

The trio loaded him into the back of the SUV. They climbed in, Eric, as driver, and Kyle riding shotgun, with Don in the second row. Clint, tied up in the bag, occupied the rear, including the third row that remained folded down.

"Clint," said Don, "just want you to know that I'm right here. That I have your gun aimed at you. I suggest you remain very still, even when we go over those nasty bumps…because if I see you move, I'm gonna assume you're trying to wriggle free. And just to make sure that doesn't happen, I'll shoot first and ask questions later."

They drove off, back over Hell's Backbone Bridge and along Hell's Backbone Road, toward the Ranger Station.

"Damn," said Kyle, as they bounced along the treacherous road. "Traveling on this monstrosity, here in the front seat, is almost as bad as when we rode the other way inside those burlap sacks.

From the driver's seat, Eric shot him a look.

"Okay…so I exaggerated a little, but keep your damn eyes on the road!"

Ninety minutes later, they arrived at the Ranger Station at Kodachrome Basin State Park. They delivered Clinton Horstmeyer, wrapped in his burlap sack, to the authorities.

CHAPTER XX

SUPERSTITION IS THE BANE OF LOGIC, an excuse subjugating the mind, a shackle foiling knowledge and progress. But occasionally it is a candle in the darkness, a balm amidst pain, a bridge to the unknown.

With brews in hand, Eric, Don and Kyle stood alongside the three-story Grand Staircase Inn in Cannonville, Utah. A mesa with layers of pink, gray, white and red provided a magnificent backdrop to their motel. They had briefly considered a stay at the Red Stone Cabins, about nine miles east, but given their experience there with Clint, they preferred to spend the night elsewhere. An hour earlier, they had delivered Clint to the rangers at Kodachrome Basin State Park. Their stop at the Ranger Station had lasted longer than they had anticipated. They were asked to wait for the Utah State Police, who, upon their arrival, took extensive statements from them. Just before they left, a State Police investigator gave them a partial rundown of the laundry list of charges likely to be leveled against Clint. Most significant among them was murder, owing to the plane crash in which Rachel Wallace was killed. Regarding their own harrowing experience, kidnapping and attempted murder topped the list. Criminal impersonation, attributable to the text Clint had sent in Bill's name and his use of Don's name when registering at the Red Stone Cabins, were among others that were apt to be added to his prior charges of insider trading. The investigator indicated that with the testimony of three eyewitnesses, Eric, Don and Kyle, the case against Clint should be a slam dunk. Kyle questioned whether

301

Clint's admission about killing Rachel could be used in court because he hadn't been given *Miranda* warnings. The inquiry drew a chuckle from the investigator, who explained that the exclusionary rule only applies when a defendant is under arrest in police custody.

"God, this country is stunning!" Eric pointed at the mesa.

For an instant, the comment, a deviation from constant conversation about the bizarre day, jolted Kyle. But with a semblance of normalcy slowly returning, the departure was welcome.

"It says here in the brochure that—"

"Jesus, Burns, you and your damn brochures." A groan added an exclamation point to Eric's remark.

"What have you got against brochures? Or are you afraid you might learn something?"

"After the day we've had, I'm not in the mood for school."

Don turned to Kyle. "What about you?"

"It's a good change of pace, and, yeah, I'm willing to listen a little, provided we don't get a harangue."

"Well, as I started to say before my philistine friend interrupted, it says that these escarpments are two hundred million years old."

"And just how do they know that?" Eric laced the question with sarcasm.

"How should I know? I'm not a geologist. I'm merely telling you what it says here."

"Perhaps the layers contain dinosaur bones, the kind that roamed the earth way back then." Impressed with his surmise, Kyle took a bow, one that his two pals ignored.

"It says here that the gray layer, largely shale, contains sharks' teeth and seashells, suggesting there was once an ocean here."

"That's kinda like what I was saying." Kyle shot Eric a look.

The lanky blond made an imaginary mark in the air. "Could it be? Do we have a first? Kyle Gordon makes a valid point."

"It's one more than you ever made." Kyle smirked.

"Enough with your back and forth," said Don.

Eric frowned.

"What's the matter now?" said Don.

"That should have been Bill's line. If ever we had a peacemaker, he was it."

The remark struck a banter-silencing chord. Like his buddies, Kyle turned mute. It was as if the realty of their pal's death had just sunk in. Never again would the Inseparables be together. Yes, they could have a threesome; they could exchange affectionate repartee; they could return to the Williams campus for future reunions; and yes, they could and would retell old war stories, not the least of which would be their capture of Clint. But never...ever...would the four of them be together again. Bill, their good buddy, was gone.

"You...you guys think he's in Heaven?" said Kyle.

"Of course," said Eric. "You couldn't name a more deserving candidate."

The point was valid. Unfortunately, it begged the question. Was there a Heaven? Kyle already knew Eric's answer. "Burns, what do you think? Is Bill in Heaven?"

"Uh...I don't know." He lowered his head, perhaps to contemplate the issue, more likely in a defensive posture. Finally, he said, "Like Eric, Bill believed. For his sake, I'm gonna set my usual opinions aside and believe with him." Don gazed skyward. "Bill is up there...somewhere, looking down on us from Heaven."

Kyle stole a glance at the firmament. "You're right," he said, preferring to allow wishful thinking to supersede his normal demands for well-reasoned logic. He eyed the colorful escarpment that stood before them. Within the seemingly lifeless rock, no doubt there were literally millions and millions of stories of lives come and gone. Giant reptiles that roamed the Earth; colorful fish that filled the oceans; and tiny whatever had all left their marks. But if there were no souls, no Heaven, then they were nothing more than bones and fossils...and debris long since decayed. The ruminations, Bill's absence, once again confronted Kyle with his own mortality. It also forced him to acknowledge his insignificance.

"Not to interrupt this rare moment of quiet," said Eric, "but Burns, how the hell did you escape from your sack, the one that Clint put you in?"

"Whad'ya mean? I used my lucky Swiss knife, the one I always carry."

"Yeah, I understand, but how did you get it...all tied up? Where did you have it?"

"Tucked in the side of my sock."

"But how did you get it out, what with your hands and feet tied?"

"That was easy. Clint made us curl up in a fetal position so we fit into the bags. My hands were near my feet. The hard part was opening the knife. While trying, I dropped it inside the bag. It took me five minutes...maybe more...to get hold of it again. When I finally got it back, I made sure to hold it tightly in one hand while I worked at opening the blade with my other thumb...And while we're on the subject of my knife, it's high time you boys apologize."

"Pardon me," said Kyle, the words no sooner spoken than he suspected the reason for the demand.

"If it weren't for that good luck charm, the one you guys repeatedly ridiculed back at Williams, the three of us would be dead and fried, fifteen hundred feet below Hell's Backbone Bridge. As a matter of fact, on the way out here, I took it on the plane in my carry-on, rolled up in a T-shirt."

"You what?" said Eric.

"You heard me. I brought it in my carry-on. I like to have it with me all the time."

"You realize the trouble you could have caused us?"

"Frankly, I wasn't all that worried."

"Why—because it's a lucky knife?" Kyle laced the question with all the sarcasm he could muster.

"No, because random tests have shown that the TSA only picks up a tiny percent of contraband. And do I look the dangerous type?"

"Damn it, Burns. You're off the wall!" said Eric.

"Would you be happier if I kept my knife in my big suitcase? Maybe you'd prefer that I had it there when we were stuffed into those damn sacks?"

"Uh…when you put it that way," said Eric, *"Mea culpa."*

Don looked at Kyle.

"That goes for me too." Kyle broke eye contact, his brain conjuring a chilling image. He pictured himself, bagged and unconscious in a Ford Expedition, hurtling through space to certain death.

"Anybody know what today is?" said Eric.

"Unfortunately, yeah." Don gestured at Kyle. "You know what he's referring to?"

"Uh…not really."

"It's goddamn Friday the 13th. Knowing that we'd be out here on unlucky Friday, I made sure I carried my lucky knife all the time. Maybe now, at long last, you lunkheads will stop making fun of me and finally take paraskavedekatriphobia seriously?"

Kyle's gut urged that he argue the illogic of the fatuous superstition. Judgment counseled he keep his mouth shut. Whatever validity or lack thereof the concept bore, it had led Don to carry his lucky knife. It had saved their lives. Kyle swallowed pride and stilled his tongue. He found it hard to believe that just minutes after allowing an argument for life after death to go unchallenged, he was doing the same when confronted with an illogical superstition. Still he had to admit that apart from his own beliefs, he had no proof the arguments were wrong. He glanced at Eric. That his friend had also chosen silence, rather than balk, was far more understandable.

"It's after nine," said Don, eyeing his watch. "After a day this long, rather than looking for a restaurant, I say we grab a decaf in the lobby, along with something from the vending machines that we can stick into the microwave."

The trio headed to the far end of the building that housed the office. Once there, Eric and Don went directly to the large carafes at the rear of the room. Kyle paused alongside a table with two piles of books, each pile about a half-dozen. Between them, taped to the table, was a sign: "Borrow and Return…Or Take One, and Leave One of Your Own."

Kyle shuffled through the first pile. Nothing struck his fancy, not that he actually planned to read anything. He looked through the second. There, at the bottom, he spotted a copy of *Destiny's Invention.* "Hey guys, take a gander at this."

"You found a book to read?" said Eric.

"Not just any book." He headed over to the coffee. "One by Thurston Caldwell."

"Who?" said Eric.

"Jeez, what planet are you from?" Don jabbed Eric, nearly causing him to spill his coffee. "Thurston Caldwell. It's Bill's book...What do you two say now?"

"About what?" said Kyle.

"Damn, do I have to spell it out for you? No wonder you're a skeptic." Don turned and eyed Eric. "God, not you too?"

Eric shrugged.

"It's a sign...a sign from Bill. He's here with us."

Kyle rolled his eyes.

"C'mon, what's the probability we'd walk in here and find his novel? What are there, maybe ten books?"

"More like a dozen," said Kyle.

"Fine, make it a dozen...or even fifteen. What's the chance we'd find his book here? And don't tell me it's a coincidence."

That was exactly the word Kyle would have used had Don not already rejected it. "Look, *Destiny's Invention* is a big seller. Finding it among a bunch of books is no great surprise."

Don threw up his hands. "Bill's twin could walk through the door right now, and you'd dismiss it as nothing."

"He doesn't have a twin, no more than Clint."

"Damn it, Gordon. I know that. But the point is—that if he did, and his twin walked in here, you'd still treat it as nothing." Don turned to Eric. "I suppose you agree with your cynical buddy."

"It just so happens you're wrong. Since there's no way to be certain, I choose to believe it's a sign from Bill."

Whether Eric was merely appeasing his superstitious friend, Kyle was unsure. Still it set him to thinking. He had no proof it was not a sign. Why argue with Don, especially when his claim, however unlikely, if by chance true, was extremely appealing. "You know what—unmitigated skeptic that I am, on this occasion, you've sold me." Kyle held up the book. "I believe it's a sign from Bill. And I believe he is here with us."

CHAPTER XXI

LIFE, NAY BUT A CANDLE,
A spirit vibrant, bright,
Alas, a gust, capricious,
A flicker, dark, good night.

It was midday when Eric pulled the big Ford Expedition into the parking lot outside the apartment complex where Carla Pender lived. With his flight reservations back to Hartford already re-arranged, earlier that morning he had dropped Don and Kyle off at McCarran International Airport in Las Vegas and driven roughly 240 miles to Carla's place in Pamona, California. Following the harrowing day in which Clint had tried to dump them into the canyon below Hell's Backbone Bridge, the three pals had headed southeast about thirty miles, where they had spent a day at Bryce Canyon National Park and then another, roughly seventy miles further southeast, at Zion National Park. They had continued to Las Vegas where, during a two-night stay, they had caught an Elvis impersonator at the Bellagio, walked six miles up and down the Strip checking out the lavish hotels and, of course, gambling. All three had lost, though none more than fifty dollars. Just before they left the Luxor where they were staying, Don stuffed a last quarter into a slot machine. "This one's for Bill," he said. His effort yielded nothing. He dumped another Washington into the one-arm bandit, repeating the same mantra. An instant later, eight quarters, all of two dollars, came jangling out of the machine. "There...you see?" The comment drew a "See What?" from

Kyle, prompting Don to throw up his hands and say: "Nothing will convince you non-believers."

Meaningless though the occurrence may have been, Eric deemed it a fitting end to what had been a remarkable trip. So long planned and so long postponed, it had finally come to fruition. Much as the glitz of Las Vegas, the spires of Bryce and the massive cliffs of Zion had lived up to expectations, those experiences paled when compared with the time spent crossing swords with Clint. Without doubt those hours were the worst of the trip. And without doubt they were by far the best. And equally certain, those hours were sure to be replayed whenever the three got together. College war stories, they had many, but none came close to the sojourn over Hell's Backbone Road.

As he climbed out of the SUV, Eric glanced at his watch, not for the time, but the date—Thursday, the 19th. He had three days to spend in Pamona before he headed back to Hartford on Sunday. He had spoken regularly with Carla in recent months. She had sounded upbeat. He had begun to hope she might lick the cancer. She had taken Ricky to a children's museum; walked a short trail with him at Big Bear Lake in San Bernardino; and even joined in activities at the Fast Flume Water Park. Perhaps her doomsday prognosis had been erroneous.

Eric climbed the stairs to her second-floor garden apartment and rang the bell. A moment later, Carla opened the door. Even before he could get a word out, Ricky wrapped his arms around him.

"Uncle Eric, Uncle Eric, come see my new bike!"

"Slow down," said Carla. "Let him through the doorway, so we can all say hello."

Ricky gave his mother a dissatisfied eye but reluctantly stepped back.

"I can't wait to see your bike," said Eric. He stepped forward and hugged Carla. "How are you doing?"

"As well as can be expected." Her tone bore a disheartened hint. Her face appeared drawn, and she had lost weight.

Eric gave her a questioning look.

"I'm doing pretty well, but...we'll talk about it in a few minutes. In the meantime, come in."

"Can I show Uncle Eric my bike now?"

An exasperated expression showed on Carla's face. "All right...I guess." She turned to Eric.

"It's fine. He's excited."

Ricky grabbed Eric's hand and tugged him back out the door and down the stairs where, chained to a rack, a red and blue Schwinn, with streamers coming from the ends of the handlebars, was locked onto a bike rack.

"It's even got a bell!" Ricky rang it repeatedly.

"Cool," said Eric. "Can you ride it?"

"Yup." Moments later, after Carla arrived and unlocked the chain, Ricky took off down the sidewalk with bell ringing again. A minute later he returned and hopped off.

"I'm impressed," said Eric. "I was eight before I could ride a bike."

Ricky beamed. "Can we go to Polar Cone for ice cream?" He looked at Eric. "They have swings and a jungle gym there." He refocused on his mother.

Carla hesitated.

"Sounds good to me," said Eric, "provided your mom gives the okay."

"Looks like I'm outvoted again." Carla gestured to her late model Corolla. "We can take my car. It has Ricky's car seat."

Little more than ten minutes later, the three were seated at a picnic table beneath a red umbrella licking their cones. Ricky, normally a slow eater, finished first. While his ice cream was the smallest, the attraction of the play area may have explained his speed.

"I'm going to the swings. Okay?" Even before Carla had voiced her approval, he was on his way.

"I'm glad you came." The gravity of Carla's voice suggested her comment was more than small talk.

"I'm glad I did too...How you doing?"

"Fair to midland. But we'll get to me in a moment. How was your trip with the guys? Obviously, it was not what you had planned, having to attend Bill's funeral, rather than having him with you."

Eric shrugged. "It was certainly different." He recounted their experiences, most of them briefly, the lone exception their encounter with Clint.

"God, you guys are lucky to be alive." She looked off into space and shook her head slowly.

"Whatcha thinking?"

"I probably should feel sorry for him."

"Sorry…Why?"

"Well, he is the father of my child."

The comment bore information that Eric knew well. Nevertheless, it struck like a hammer. "Just because he got you pregnant, doesn't make him a father, not in any real sense. Did he ever provide a penny of support?"

"No."

"And more important, did he ever show Ricky the slightest interest…let alone love?"

"No…though I preferred it that way." She gazed off into space again. "I've never told this to anybody." She hesitated. "What the hell. With time short, I might as well."

Curiosity's antenna up, Eric tried to imagine what secret Carla was about to reveal.

"The one time I slept with Clint…he got me drunk—me who rarely had more than a single glass of beer. I can't say he raped me…but I can't say it was consensual. I really don't recall …Well, that's not altogether true. I remember earlier that evening thinking that I was allowing myself to be taken advantage of. Stupid me!"

That Carla blamed herself was intolerable. Eric longed to jump in, squelching the unacceptable notion. But the moment was wrong. She had more to say. She was digging deep into her soul, and a patient ear, not counsel, was what she needed.

A smile, a pensive camber, accompanied her brief hiatus. "Funny…that inauspicious night with Clint turned out to be the best mistake of my life." She gestured toward the swings. "Without it, I wouldn't have Ricky."

The irony, that a huge error could be the progenitor of one's greatest windfall, left Eric speechless…well, for a matter of seconds. "Bottom line, Clint's an asshole."

"You got that right. Unlike me, whom he got pregnant, he nearly killed you guys…and speaking of death, it's really sad about Bill Young. He was such a nice guy."

"That he was." Eric's mind forked back to the funeral. Images of the stunning church and the casket being wheeled down the aisle popped into his head. He pictured the Inseparable*s* seated at their favorite table at the Irish Mist. It was all in the past. Never again would they share such times, at least not the entire group. Wistful emotions forced him to pause before speaking, lest sadness choke his words. Finally, he said, "Now, tell me, how are things with you?"

"Not so good." She nibbled at the remainder of her cone.

Eric was anxious for an explanation, but sensing she preferred to respond in her own time, again he waited patiently.

She nibbled some more, until finally her cone was gone. "According to the doctors, I'm nearing the end, not that they needed to tell me. My strength is waning. An hour or two of activity—and I don't mean vigorous exercise—and I'm pretty much wiped out."

Eric found himself at a loss for words. Still well short of thirty, and already two of his four closest college friends, Bill and Carla, fifty percent, had reached the end. It wasn't supposed to be that way. They should all be in the prime of life. He gestured, albeit weakly, toward Ricky, who was swinging with carefree abandon through the air. "Does…does he know?"

Carla nodded halfheartedly. "Well, sorta…He knows I'm very sick and that at some point I won't be here anymore, but he doesn't know how soon that will be. The concept of death is still something foreign that I'm sure he doesn't understand…not that I do either. I've told him that I'll be looking down from Heaven and watching him. That even though he won't be able to see me or hear my voice, he'll be able to talk to me…I don't know why, but lately I've been feeling guilty. It's as if I'm abandoning him when he needs me most." Carla began sobbing.

Tears dripped from Eric's eyes. He got up from his seat and went around to the other side of the table, squeezed onto the bench and put his arms around Carla. "God, don't blame yourself. You're a wonderful mother."

"I...I don't know what I'd do if it weren't for you. With no family, I can't imagine Ricky with..." Her crying halted her words.

The better part of a minute elapsed before she finally said, "I'm sorry. Lately I find myself crying all too—"

"Don't apologize...You have absolutely no reason to."

"I know...I guess, but..."

Eric longed to say something that would alleviate her pain and, even more so, cure her. But magic words, he had none. He simply maintained his embrace.

A chic, new pair of shoes may be stylish, but when embarking on a lengthy walk, a tried and true, comfortable pair, like a good friend, is the best fit.

"Glad you could make it for lunch." Kyle got up from his booth at The Hungry Hollow. He shook the hand of Don, who had just arrived at the trendy Springfield, Massachusetts eatery.

"Hope you haven't been waiting long." Don seated himself across from Kyle.

"Nope, just arrived a minute ago." He glanced at his watch. "Anyway, you're two minutes early."

"Did you hear the latest about Clint?"

The last Kyle had heard went back more than a month when a Utah grand jury had indicted Clint. Chances were that was not the latest. "I doubt it. What's happened?"

"He was—"

"Can I get you gentlemen something to drink?"

Kyle looked across the table. "Share a half-carafe of the house wine?" With a nod from Don, he gave the server their order.

"As I started to say, I understand the District Attorney in Utah has decided to seek the death penalty."

"The death penalty?" Even with the mountain of charges, including murder, kidnapping and attempted murder, along with a laundry list of other felonies, Kyle had not anticipated the ultimate punishment. "Damn, I wouldn't have expected that."

"Well, the fellow who told me said that a lawyer he knows thought it might be a ploy to get Clint to take a deal...one with a long, long sentence, maybe even life without parole."

The image of Clint spending the rest of his life, perhaps a half-century or more, triggered a surprising pang of sympathy. After killing Rachel and attempting to do the same to Eric and Don and, for that matter, Kyle, there was no reason to feel sorry for Clint.

"No reaction?"

Kyle shrugged. "I...I guess he's got it coming, but..." *On second thought, there was no "but," not for an unremorseful killer. Time spent with Clint at Williams, rarely a pleasure, was irrelevant.* "Have you heard anything from Eric since our trip?"

"I talked with him just a few days ago. As you know, once he dropped us off at the airport in Las Vegas, he drove to Carla's place in Pamona. Her cancer has apparently taken a turn for the worse. He plans to go back out there soon."

"You think he has any thoughts of marrying her?"

"My guess is no. Add what he told us back in Utah to the most recent update on her health, and it's hard to imagine them tying the knot."

"Yeah...I guess you're right. For that matter, the decision was probably made years ago at Williams when they traded their romantic relationship for friendship...though I have to admit her son is a strong link."

"I assume you mean *their* son." Don studied Kyle. "You don't still have doubts on that issue, do you?"

The clarification sparked a moment of silent debate. Eric had never confirmed or denied that he was Ricky's father. All Kyle knew was that over the years Eric had been sending money to Carla. Then again, that seemed reason enough to conclude Eric was the father. "No, I didn't mean to resurrect that old paternity debate. Still, it's strange. Eric has never told me that he is Ricky's father. Did he ever tell you?"

"No, but I long considered it a safe assumption, not that I ever asked."

"Me neither. It just didn't seem appropriate." Kyle reached for the carafe that had arrived a moment before. After pouring some for Don, he filled his own wine glass. He swirled it several times in a moment of contemplation. The night before, he had decided to present Don with a proposition, and the time to do so seemed right. "I have a proposal for you…I was wondering if you might be interested in joining my firm?"

"You serious?"

"Very."

Don studied him for a moment. "This isn't something you're doing out of charity."

"On the contrary, I was expecting that you'd turn me down. A one-man firm growing to two is a far cry from Quigley and Watkins."

"Maybe yes, and maybe no." Don chuckled.

"Fill me in on the humor."

"Ever since Clint was charged with insider trading, the firm has gotten loads of bad press. Rumors, not that they were valid, that other members of the firm might be implicated, have clients racing for the exits, transferring their accounts elsewhere. Speculations about possible downsizing are rampant, and with me the newest hire, I'm apt to be the first to go. Even if they keep me, I'm expecting a pay cut. Between you, me and the wall, I've dusted off my résumé and begun looking. I imagine—" Don halted midstream, displaying a puzzled look.

"What's the matter?"

"Before we get ahead of ourselves, I have to ask—if not charity, why the offer?"

Having anticipated the question, Kyle was well prepared. "By the time Larry Rockland retired, I had built a decent following, but nowhere the size of his. Much to my surprise, most of his clients have stayed with me. Bottom line, I've got far more than I can handle. Ergo, I need a partner."

"Why me?"

Unlike its predecessor, the question caught Kyle by surprise. The answer, however, a legitimate one, was easy. "Put yourself in my shoes. Wouldn't you much rather hire a friend, someone you know and trust, rather than some stranger. And don't get a swelled head, but you're bright and great with people."

"How about trust?"

For an instant, the inquiry was another surprise, but just as quickly Kyle realized what prompted it. "What about it?"

"I'm the guy who got Bill and Eric into the Silver Sky Fund."

"And yes, that was a mistake, but one that was occasioned by pressure from higher-ups."

"That doesn't excuse it."

"True, but you've regretted it ever since. You still feel guilty. Unlike a creep who is sorry, but only because he got caught, you're truly sorry. Along the way in life, we all make mistakes. What matters is whether we move forward in a positive way, so we don't repeat them. I know you well...very well. I've got confidence in you. No way would you repeat Silver Sky, not that Linda would let you."

"You sure this isn't charity?" Don looked Kyle in the eye.

"I thought we went over that already."

"Maybe so, but..." A pensive countenance accompanied an extended pause. "When I got the job at Quigley, unbeknownst to me at the time, Bill went to bat for me, despite how I had treated him."

"That's what friends are for."

"And that's my point. What Bill did for me was charity."

"Big deal. Let's assume it was. There's nothing wrong with charity among friends. Hell, if you can give to strangers, why not friends? That said—Let's get it straight. Plain and simple, this is *not* charity. It's not like you approached me looking for a job. I'm the one who came asking. For all I knew you were doing great and would have no interest."

"You didn't by any chance talk to Linda?"

"No, I didn't talk to Linda." Kyle swallowed hard. His response was accurate. On the other hand, it was hardly forthcoming. Katelyn had spoken to Linda, or, more precisely, Linda had spoken to Katelyn. Kyle knew Don's situation. Regardless, he reasoned, maybe rationalized, this was not charity. He needed a partner, and he was far happier hiring his buddy Don than a stranger. He held out his wine glass. "A toast to our future together."

The unknown breeds fear. At times the fear is justified; others, not. Occasionally, that which is feared turns out to be a blessing; now and then, it's a disaster, worse than the advance trepidation. One never knows. Such is the unknown.

Eric headed down the hallway on the top floor of the Granite Insurance Building to the office of his boss, Executive Vice-president Steven Powell. Eric had no idea why the high-ranking officer wanted to see him. Nothing dramatic had transpired in recent weeks, nor were any earth-shattering events on the immediate horizon. The face-to-face meeting might provide a perfect opportunity to ask for a month off to return to California to be with Carla and Ricky. During his time at Granite, Eric had always taken less vacation than his annual allotments. His accumulations amounted to over eleven weeks. But perhaps it was premature to think about asking for time off. Perhaps his boss, a man who was distant from underlings and hard to read, had a bone to pick. Eric slowed what had been a rapid stride, as he tried to relax. He grabbed a quick drink at the water fountain before entering the outer sanctum of Powell's corner office.

"Go right in. Mr. Powell is waiting for you," said Thelma Stottlemyer, the executive's very efficient and imperious gatekeeper.

Eric glanced up at the clock on the far wall, confirming he was a minute early for the ten o'clock appointment. He had made sure to start down the hallway so as to arrive just before the appointed time. Rumor had it that Powell abhorred tardiness. But rumor also had it that one who could afford to arrive early had time to waste. When and how these rumors had begun, no one seemed to know. Whether they had merit was equally a mystery. Regardless, few, if any, of Powell's subordinates chanced ignoring them; certainly not Eric.

"Good morning, Eric." Powell got up from his sumptuous leather chair and reached across his handsomely carved walnut desk and extended his right hand.

"Good morning, Mr. Powell." Eric shook the boss's hand. It had been nearly a year since Eric had been in the bigwig's office. Most times any contact was in a meeting room, along with many others.

As Powell re-seated himself, he gestured at the chairs that stood across his desk.

Eric took the one to his left. "You wanted to see me, Sir?"

"Yes." He flipped open a manila folder.

Eric's fingers tightened on the arms of his chair. He should have spent more time analyzing the reason for the meeting. Even if he could not identify the precise issue that had occasioned it, he might have narrowed it down to several and prepared for them.

"Relax. I'm not going to bite."

I'm sure that's true. On the other hand, whatever you have in store for me may be far worse.

"I've been watching you these past couple of years."

The remark was disconcerting. Eric thought he had managed to go about his business unobtrusively. Rumor also had it that Powell preferred it that way; that the enigmatic boss noticed squeaks, and rather than oil, the *boot* was his way of dealing with them.

"Recently I reviewed the performance of our claims adjusters. On comparable pre-litigation claims, your pay-outs were nearly five percent over the mean."

A knot formed in Eric's stomach. His worst fears were being realized. "I know it looks bad, but I...I try to be fair to our policy holders. Chiseling folks who faithfully pay their premiums, just because they're unlikely to sue, doesn't seem right." The explanation, one that had crossed Eric's mind many times before, echoed hauntingly. When sitting alone at his desk, his conscience loved it. Granite's executives, Powell included, interested in the company's bottom line, would have no use for it.

"I also looked at broader statistics."

Eric held his breath, preparing for the next dose of bad news.

"Your cases end up in litigation roughly ten percent less than average. Litigation…goddamn litigation is expensive, not to mention that it leads to animosity. The numbers indicate that when we factor in litigation, on average your cases cost Granite six percent less than the mean. As a matter of fact, you have the second lowest cost."

Hands that had been clinging to the arms of his chair eased. Good sense, and perhaps modesty, prompted Eric to embrace the good news without comment.

"We recently did another study." Powell flipped to a different sheet. "We surveyed our policy holders who settled claims. You should be pleased to know that you had the highest customer satisfaction rating of any adjuster, along with the fewest policy holders who left Granite for another company within six months after resolving a claim…Bottom line: You're doing things right."

"Gee…Thank you, Mr. Powell. That's really nice to hear."

"You've earned it…and that brings me to the reason I called you in today."

For the first time, curiosity, rather than fear, was foremost in Eric's mind.

"We are creating a new position here in our home office. The title is Chief Claims Adjuster, and we have chosen you for that position."

"Wow…Thank you."

"And one more thing, it will come with a $20,000 raise, plus a new office, almost twice the size of your current quarters."

"Thank you again, Mr. Powell."

"As I said, you've earned it. And about that Mr. Powell stuff, I think it would be better if you call me Steve from now on."

"Uh…yes Sir…uh." Eric wasn't quite ready to call the Executive Vice-president by his first name. He started to get up.

"Oh, one more thing. Seems I said that before," mumbled Powell, just loud enough to be audible. "Anyway, I've noticed that you've accumulated lots of vacation. Perhaps you might want to take a couple of weeks off before you embark on your new position."

The suggestion triggered thoughts of the subject that, amidst the excitement of his good fortune, had slipped Eric's mind. Trepidations, though insignificant to what he had felt earlier, materialized. "I...uh...know that this may sound presumptuous, but I...uh...have this dear friend in California, a single mother, who is dying of cancer. She asked me to be the guardian of her only child, and I...I wondered if I might take four weeks to help them deal with their situation."

"Say no more. Take the time that's needed...And congratulations on your very well-deserved promotion." Powell got up. After shaking Eric's hand, he put an arm over Eric's shoulder and ushered him out the door.

Eric headed back down the hall. Rapid steps that had propelled him down the passageway earlier were again present. But this time, their genesis, not angst...strictly joy.

Beckoning death ushers her from her pew. Down the aisle of life, she inexorably marches, nearing her pastoral earthy retreat. Yesterday's hopes and dreams evanesce, drowned out by wistful supplications...a prayer begging a legacy transcending granite etchings.

Eric had arrived in California only three days before. Until then he had still held out hope, albeit faint, that Carla might beat her illness. Even in moments when he had acknowledged the remoteness of his wishful thinking, his brain had refused to process how soon the end lay. It was a Chamber of Commerce day when, with Carla visibly weak, they decided to go to Beppo's Playland. Ricky had asked for Disneyland, but the huge amusement park was way beyond what Carla could manage. The truth be known, Beppo's, with just five rides and a playground, plus a burger and ice cream stand, tested her capacity. But knowing there would likely be no second chances, Carla insisted they do the outing.

Eric dropped Carla and Ricky off just a few feet from a bench that adjoined the rides. He parked the car and purchased a book of tickets, while mother and son waited on the bench.

"Let's go on the Merry-Go-Round," said Ricky.

"You boys go. I'll wait here."

Ordinarily, Eric would have twisted Carla's arm to join them, but aware that the mere trip from her apartment to Beppo's was a huge challenge, he grabbed Ricky's hand. "Which horse do you want?"

"The green and blue one."

"Fine. I'll take the one next to it." He turned to Carla. "You okay here?"

"Absolutely."

Despite knowing her bravado was feigned, he followed behind Ricky's tugging hand to the Carousel, where they boarded their respective horses. Soon enough they were prancing up and down in great circles to the calliope's rendition of the *William Tell Overture*. Eric stole a glance at Carla as he passed her by. Her broad smile and wave validated the decision to come. Another three hundred sixty degrees, and this time he waved at her, his other hand remaining tightly wrapped around the pole.

Soon the Carousel drew to a halt. As the duo climbed down from their horses, Ricky said, "Let's go on the Tilt-a-Whirl."

"Suppose you do that one yourself, and I'll sit with your mom." Eric tore out two tickets, the number needed for the Tilt-a-Whirl, and handed them to Ricky."

Ricky charged toward the ride, a mere twenty feet away and in easy eye shot of the bench.

Eric went over to Carla. "Okay if he goes alone?"

"Sure. It makes him feel like a big shot...all grown up."

"How are you doing?"

"Fine."

He gave Carla a look as he seated himself.

"No...really, I'm okay."

Much as Eric doubted her words, he checked the urge to press his skepticism. With what little time she had, she was entitled to enjoy it as she saw fit. He gestured in the direction of the Tilt-a-Whirl. "You've raised a great kid. He's wise, way beyond his years."

"Thanks." She stared at Ricky for several seconds and then lowered her head. When she finally looked up, she said, "I...I need to ask for another favor."

Eric waited, anticipating she would voice it. Finally, he said, "C'mon, just ask."

She drew in a deep breath. "Make sure he...he remembers me."

"Of course." Eric choked on the words. "He could never forget you. But I'll make sure. I...I promise."

She leaned her head onto his shoulder. "Ricky loves you."

"And I love Ricky." Eric watched the Tilt-a-Whirl spin. An instant later, Ricky came into view. Just as quickly, he disappeared. "Does he know who his father is?"

"Uh...not really."

"I'm not sure what you're saying."

"No, he doesn't know. I didn't have the heart to tell him that his father wanted nothing to do with him. I told him his father died shortly before he was born; that he had hoped to be a professional football player."

Back at Williams, Clint had aspired to playing in the National Football League, not that the goal was realistic. By the time Ricky was born, Clint's fantasy had evaporated, but dead Clint wasn't, not for another six years. And even that was a mere illusion, one supplanted by a shameful saga. Eric's gut begged to ask what he should say when Ricky was older and wanted more information about his father. But Carla hardly needed the additional burden of dealing with the issue. Eric took hold of Carla's hand. Down the road when the question arose, he would find an answer. For the moment, the sleeping dog could rest undisturbed.

"Did you see me?" said Ricky, as he raced their way. "I rode one-handed." He waved one arm high above his head. "Can I go on the bumper cars now?"

"Well, if the man there says it's okay."

Ricky started to run away.

"You'll need two tickets." Eric ripped them from the book and gave them to Ricky.

He raced off, only to return a minute later. "The man made me stand next to a measuring thing. He said I didn't come up to the red line. He said I'd have to come back next year."

Eric felt the jab of Carla's elbow in his side. No doubt she knew in advance that Ricky wouldn't qualify for the bumper cars, but rather than saying *no*, she allowed someone else to be the bad guy. Eric made a mental note. He had a lot to learn about being a father, especially starting with a six-year-old. He said, "Would anyone like ice cream?"

"Me...Me!"

Even before Carla voiced her wishes, Eric said, "You're out-voted."

"What makes you think I would have voted *no*?"

"I was not about to take any chances." Eric grabbed Ricky's hand. "You and I will get the ice cream and bring it back to your mom." He glanced at Carla. "What flavor would you like?"

"Surprise me."

Minutes later they returned with Ricky enthusiastically licking a chocolate ice cream cone topped with rainbow sprinkles, while Eric carried one with peppermint stick ice cream for Carla and mocha chip for himself. Eric handed Carla her cone.

"How did you know?"

"See! I told you, Uncle Eric."

"You sure did." He seated himself on the bench next to Carla, with Ricky on his other side.

The three quietly savored their cones, each in their own thoughts. For a moment, the world was perfect...at least for a brief instant. All too soon, sublimity yielded to less appealing thoughts, the ravage of disease. Eric's eyes filled with tears. He struggled not to choke on his cone, and even more so, the maudlin musings that were consuming him. He took a deep breath. His thoughts, however, got the best of him. His crying became audible.

"What's wrong Uncle Eric?"

"I think it's the onion ice cream. You know how Mommy cries when she slices onions?"

"You got mocha chip. That doesn't have onions. And anyway, they don't make onion ice cream…do they?"

Eric shrugged. The offbeat conversation distracted him enough to regain a modicum of composure. "I'll bet they make it somewhere." He looked at Carla.

"Don't ask me."

The sight of her, knowing she recognized the source of his curious behavior, re-kindled his melancholy reflections. He immediately went back to licking his cone, lest fickle emotions face renewed scrutiny.

CHAPTER XXII

NOT EVERY CHILD BECOMES A PARENT, but every parent was once a child.

Five weeks had passed since Carla had died. Ricky had been living with Eric in his apartment outside Hartford and, all things considered, he was adjusting well to the situation. He was enrolled in the first grade and seemed to like his new elementary school. A week earlier at his first parent-teacher conference, his teacher had indicated that he was among the brightest in his class and showed skills in both reading and mathematics above his grade level. Homecoming at Williams was on the doorstep, and despite pressure from both Kyle and Don, Eric had declined to attend. It was the Thursday before Homecoming when Eric, having finished work, picked up Ricky at his after-school day care at 4:30, the regularly appointed time.

As Ricky rushed over, even before he had given Eric his usual hug, he said, "Kenny Michaels invited me to stay over at his house on Saturday night. Can I? Can I?"

The proposal caught Eric by surprise. Kenny had been over to Eric's apartment one afternoon a couple of weeks before to play with Ricky, and Eric had meet Kenny's parents at school conference night. They were very nice. But a sleepover? That was unfamiliar territory. "I...I don't know."

"Gee, all the kids stay over at their friends' houses."

The retort reminded Eric of his own childhood. Back then, he had used the identical argument numerous times. Occasionally it had worked, but more often than not, it had evoked a familiar response. Eric drew upon that experience, the reaction his mother had frequently given him. He said, "Just because other parents let their kids ride on the roof of a freight train with no clothes in the dead of winter doesn't mean that I will."

"But I don't want to ride on a freight train with no clothes."

"That's not the—" Eric clipped his tongue. The absurdity of Ricky's reply, though nothing more than an echo of Eric's own words, laid bare the folly of Eric's point. But in alien terrain, with no source of guidance, it was the best Eric could muster. "Okay, let's take this slowly. Was this Kenny's idea? Have his parents okayed it?"

Ricky reached into his backpack. He handed Eric a note. "Kenny's mom gave me this when she picked him up after school."

Eric read the note.

> *Dear Mr. Johanson,*
> *We would like to invite Ricky to stay over at our house on Saturday night. We'd pick him up Saturday evening at seven and bring him back to your home around seven o'clock Sunday evening. I will call you tonight to make sure this is okay*
> *Sincerely,*
> *Mary Michaels*

"So, can I go?...Please."

Eric thought for a moment. What at first was new and a bit overwhelming had grown less complicated. There was no compelling reason to say *no*. On the contrary, most anything that helped Ricky acclimate to the drastic change in his life was positive. "Since it's okay with Kenny's parents, and I've met them, I see no reason why not."

"Yippee!" Ricky jumped up and down before giving Eric a hug.

Hand in hand, they walked to the car. More precisely, Ricky bounded there, his steps predominated by skips and leaps.

Once they reached Eric's Toyota Camry, Ricky climbed into the back and buckled himself into his car seat. Eric simply watched, making certain everything was latched tight. Already he had learned to allow Ricky as much independence as safety permitted.

As Ricky closed the final hook, he said, "Uncle Eric, I was wondering...all the other kids in school..."

Oh no, thought Eric, another *all the other kids*.

"...they have fathers, and they call them *Dad*. I...I was wondering. Would it be okay if I called you *Dad*?"

The request hit far harder than the earlier one for a sleepover. "I would love that." Eric leaned over and hugged Ricky. "I love you, Son."

An enigmatic, impressionistic portrait reveals that which isn't there. But now and then, that which isn't there, chimera on an impressionistic canvas, metamorphoses into reality.

With Ricky at his sleepover, shortly after breakfast on Sunday morning, Eric headed for Williamstown. Once the plans for the sleepover had been firmed up, he contacted Kyle and arranged to meet him, along with Don, at one o'clock on Sunday for lunch at the Irish Mist. Although he had to forego the Saturday Homecoming football game, he welcomed the opportunity to join his pals, albeit briefly.

The one-hundred-mile trip from Hartford to Williamstown took about two hours. As expected, the Sunday traffic was light, and Eric arrived at the Irish Mist about 12:45. After a quick visit to the restroom, he took a seat in the corner booth, the Inseparables' old favorite. He was there no more than a couple of minutes when he spotted Kyle and Don coming through the door. He waved to them.

"Glad you could make it," said Don.

"Me too," said Eric.

"Three of us together, even if it's only for a couple of hours, is better than two," said Kyle. He slid into the booth alongside Don who had taken his spot seconds before. "Of course, it's still not the same without Bill."

Eric anticipated Don would suggest that Bill was there in spirit, looking down on them from above. When Don failed to make the point, Eric felt a pang of disappointment. Much as he would have doubted the claim, he would have kept his skepticism to himself. Even a cynic could occasionally yield to a rosy delusion. The hypocrisy of the rumination did not escape Eric.

"So, how are you making out with Ricky?" said Kyle.

"Really well. He's even started calling me *Dad*." Eric could all but see his own face beaming.

Kyle poked Don. "See, I told you all along that Eric was the father."

"I didn't say that."

"Not exactly," said Kyle, "but given that he's calling you *Dad*, I thought…"

"Well, you—" Eric pressed his lips together. Why let people know that Clint was the father. If Carla had wanted it that way, she would have told people long ago. Apart from Ricky and himself, it was nobody's business, not even his dearest friends. When the time was right, he could give the details to Ricky, who could maintain his privacy, if he preferred. "As I said, Ricky calls me *Dad*, and I call him *Son*, and I prefer to leave it at that."

"Sorry," said Kyle, "I should not—"

"No need to apologize. It's just that I'd rather not go there. Like Carla, the matter should rest peacefully."

"Gotcha." Kyle reached for his brew, one of three large mugs their server had just delivered.

"Not to change the subject," said Don, "but after lunch Kyle and I plan to head north to Manchester to meet our wives at the outlets. Care to join us?"

"I would, not that shopping is my thing, but I need to be back home by six. Shortly after that, Ricky is due back from a sleepover. If I went with you up to Manchester, no sooner would we arrive than I'd have to turn around and head for home. Heck, the drive from there down to Hartford must be close to three hours."

"Well, we're glad you could at least make it for lunch today," said Kyle. "Having only two of us here just isn't like old times."

Once again, Eric felt tempted to point out that anything less than four wasn't the same, but why harp on a depressing redundancy, not that discretion would free them of the sad reality. Regardless, enough had already been said that Don and Kyle were probably entertaining the disheartening thought. The magic the Inseparables had known during their four years at Williams was never to be recaptured. The observation, though hardly new, was still hard to digest. An image of the four of them playing tennis popped into Eric's head. Unlike the hotly contested, trash-talking doubles matches they had enjoyed in the past, the best they could do was play two-against-one, Canadian style, constantly rotating who played alone. The score, as well as the competition, would be of no consequence. More important, the camaraderie would not be the same. "How's your new partnership working out?"

"Really well. What with all of Larry Rockland's clients, plus my own following, I had more than I could handle. Having Don step in, rather than hooking up with some unknown quantity, was a boon. Believe it or not, we're even talking about bringing in a new associate. It's hard to believe the way the business is growing, not that I'm complaining…How are things at Granite?" Kyle turned to Don. "You're aware that our buddy is now the Chief Claims Adjuster."

"So, I heard. He's got forty or fifty claims adjusters under—"

"Try sixteen…and let me tell you, that's quite enough. And to answer Kyle's question, things are good. These past few years, several of my cohorts told me I was making a huge mistake, going out of my way to be fair with our insureds. They insisted that despite the rhetoric, the top brass favored minimal pay-outs. Turns out they were wrong. My approach, giving our insureds an even break, has paid off in the long run. Besides the promotion, I can look myself in the mirror without feeling like a chiseler. And there's another bonus. I now know

329

that those who judge my performance and have my future in their hands approve of my methods."

"Seems you've proved Leo Derocher wrong," said Don.

Eric consciously contorted his face. "Leo who?"

"Leo Durocher, the manager of the New York Giants who—"

"You mean *coach*, don't you?" said Eric.

"No, *manager*. I'm referring to the New York Giants baseball team."

"Baseball team? You gotta be kidding. It must be a half-century since the Giants abandoned New York in favor of San Francisco."

"Actually a few more than that, but who's counting? Anyway, my grandfather—he grew up in the Bronx, right near the old Polo Grounds—was an avid New York Giants fan. He loved to quote Leo Durocher."

"Enough with all the ancient history," said Kyle. "What the hell did this Durocher fellow say?"

"That 'nice guys finish last.'" Don shook his head. "From what I know, Durocher was a successful manager, but he was also a mean son of a bitch. Anyway, my grandfather often invoked the Lip's quote—that's what they called Durocher—and I took the quote to heart." Don bowed his head. When he finally looked up, he said, "Not to make excuses, but that wonderful quote, what it represented, helped me sell the Silver Sky Fund to my friends." He looked Eric in the eye. "I never adequately apologized to you and Bill for that fiasco. In Bill's case, I'm too late. As for you (Don continued to look Eric in the eye), I'm late, but hopefully, late is better than never…not that words are adequate."

"Forget it," said Eric. "It's water over the dam, far downstream and forgotten. And as for Bill, I know for a fact he didn't hold it against you. Proof of the pudding is that he went to bat for you after you lost your job at Kingman & Woodhill. No way would he have done that if he held a grudge."

"That's because Bill, like you, was a nice guy."

Eric drew back histrionically. "So, what you're saying is—I *was* a nice guy, but now—"

"Give me a break. You know that's not what I meant. I was—"

"Relax, I know what you were saying. And for the record, you're a nice guy too."

"Thanks. That's more than I deserve."

"You two...particularly you, Burns, enough!" Kyle directed a stern look at Don. "You've beaten yourself up too many times. And just to be clear, I would not have asked you to be my partner if I didn't consider you a straight arrow. No way would you make the same mistake again. And God forbid you even thought about it, Linda would have your head."

"You got that right. In the six years that we've been married, never was she angrier or, for that matter, more disappointed with me than with the Silver Sky fiasco. When I look back, it's easy to see what happened. I was ambitious. My firm, especially my boss, was far more interested in our bottom line than our clients' well-being. They pushed me to compromise my values, and eager as I was to get ahead, I did their bidding. It's a chapter of my life I'd rather forget, but it's important that I don't, lest I make the same mistake again."

"I can give you three reasons why you won't," said Kyle. "Linda makes one, I make two, and you'll find the most important, when you look into the mirror. You learned your lesson. Screwing your clients just to make a buck is not who you are."

"I appreciate that," said Don. He breathed a deep sigh and then lifted his mug. "Let's drink this one to Bill."

"To Bill," said Kyle.

"To Bill," echoed Eric, as the big vessels clinked. "If only he were here and..." Eric's words trailed off. Without Bill, without all four, it just wasn't the same. They were no longer college kids. Those days were in the past. They could reminisce, relive old war stories, but the years had moved on. There was no going back. Eric took a healthy swig of his brew. A part of him longed for time travel, the ability to relive those carefree college days. But the truth be known, deep down he preferred to move forward. Yes, it was fun to get together and laugh and joke about bygone days, but given the choice to turn the clock back or head forward into the future, he would choose the latter. He gazed across the table at his two friends. No need to ask their views on the subject. He had no doubt that they too would opt for the future, and understandably so. They had a successful partnership, and Don had Linda and two beautiful children, and Kyle had Katelyn. Several months earlier the thoughts might have triggered a pang of jealousy. No longer. Eric had found his niche in the working world, and, better yet, he had Ricky. The reflection sparked thoughts of Carla. Her misfortune was the font of his gain. A few months back, the same notion had kindled moments of guilt. Time, the relationship he had built with Ricky, had modulated such emotions. He was making sure to preserve Ricky's memories of his mom. Ricky was thriving. Indeed, Eric was fulfilling Carla's last wish, and he was doing so admirably.

Kyle glanced at his watch. "Unfortunately, it's getting to be that time. We need to be on our way up to Manchester. We promised Linda and Katelyn we'd meet them at the Ralph Lauren outlet at two, not that they'd mind if we were late." He directed his attention to Eric. "You sure you can't join us?"

"Much as I'd love to, it's not in the cards. As I said earlier, I'd no sooner get there than I'd have to turn around and head back south. But I might make a quick stop at the Clark."

"Sure," said Don. "You've got time for a museum, but not your buddies."

"C'mon, you know that's not it. I've only got—"

"Jeez, after all these years, you can't tell when I'm teasing?"

Eric shrugged sheepishly.

"We'll have to do this again soon," said Kyle.

Eric had doubts, but he was not about to voice them.

"Matter of fact, Katelyn plans to invite both of you, along with Linda, and, of course, your kids, for a barbeque some Saturday soon."

Eric's pessimism evaporated. The chance Katelyn would follow through was far more likely than the three procrastinators.

The trio paid their bill, exchanged goodbyes and headed to their cars, Kyle and Don to the rear lot, and Eric, a few doors down the street where his was parked. A few minutes later,

Eric arrived at the Clark Institute. He went inside and, after paying his admission, checked the clock on the wall. A forty-five-minute stay, a pleasant hiatus, though hardly sufficient to do the wonderful gallery justice, would leave more than enough time to be home for Ricky. He moved rapidly through the familiar galleries. He paused briefly to study some Winslow Homer seascapes, several with foreboding seas and waves crashing against huge rocks. He moved on to another room, taking in a quintessential Stuart portrait of George Washington. He negotiated another hall where he flitted aimlessly, allowing for a brief stop at Frederick Remington's masterful bronze carving of the *Wounded Bunkie*. For one who had long appreciated the brilliance of the Clark's collection, the haphazard wandering was anomalous, more like a visit by a disinterested philistine. But Eric knew otherwise. A method to his seeming madness lurked in the back of his mind.

Finally, he slowed his pace as he entered the bright white hall which housed a formidable collection of the works of Pierre Auguste Renoir. He took a moment to view the *Bridge at Chatou*, the *Sleeping Girl*, and the *Child with a Bird*. Still none of these held his attention for more than a few moments. They were but preludes in preparation for the one painting he wanted to see. Much as the museum's many magnificent masterpieces merited great attention, with limited time, he was determined to devote himself to the one work he most adored. Slowly he approached Renoir's *Woman with a Fan*. Even from more than twenty feet, the demure face of the French beauty was captivating. Eric drew closer, the sight of her blue eyes beckoning him. Nearer yet, he felt an urge, albeit absurd, to remove the pink, blue and white pastel-flower-bedecked straw hat adorning her head in order that he might caress her silky, red hair. He inched back to a familiar bench less than ten feet from the amazing portrait and seated himself.

Amidst a palpable silence, he stared at the masterpiece. The stunning beauty, her face turned directly over her left shoulder, stared back. In her left hand, a fan, trimmed with Japanese adornments, added an element of mystery to the goddess. Eric closed his eyes. The after image of the painting he knew so well remained.

"May I join you?" The voice was soft, no more than a whisper.

Lost in his own world, for an instant Eric questioned whether he had imagined the painting talking to him. He opened his eyes and slowly turned to his right. Glenna Snow stood alongside.

"Sorry, I didn't mean to interrupt your musing."

"No…it's…it's nice to see you." Eric started to stand up.

"Mind if I join you on the bench?"

"Please do." He slid a bit to his left making room for her. "I was just looking at—" He clipped his tongue before adding *you*. "…at my favorite painting."

She smiled.

"What brings you here?"

"I have a girlfriend who lives in Williamstown. We arranged to meet this weekend. That, plus I was hoping to speak to you…in person. It being Homecoming, I suspected you and your buddies would come. You might say the trip gave me a chance to kill two birds with one stone."

You killed one of those birds several years ago when you broke his heart. Eric kept the thought to himself.

"Anyway, I figured if you were in town, you were bound to hit the Clark, and, of course, the Irish Mist. I caught Don and Kyle in the parking lot, just as they were leaving the latter. They told me I'd find you here."

"I'm really glad you came by." Eric pointed at Renoir's masterpiece. "She's as beautiful as ever, and…" Eric hesitated. Common sense counseled he not say more. Emotions overruled. "It must be nice to come here and gaze at such an exquisite painting and feel as though you're looking into a mirror."

Glenna blushed, her rosy cheeks a complement to her shimmering red hair.

Eric tilted his head, as he endeavored to project a whimsical mien. "Though I must say, for someone who's roughly a century and one-half old, you're extraordinarily well preserved."

"Gee, thanks."

"So, what brings you to the Clark?"

"Can't a person come to a nice museum without an explanation?" A sigh punctuated a brief dip in Glenna's gaze. "But that's not exactly why I came. As I said earlier, I…uh…wanted to see you. Uh…how can I put this?" She briefly muttered aloud, though incomprehensibly, and then reached into her purse, pulling out a piece of paper. "Here, maybe this will…uh…help to explain."

Eric unfolded the paper. He quickly scanned it, noting that it bore Carla Pender's signature at the bottom. He proceeded to read the correspondence.

Dear Glenna,

For the past few years, I have considered writing to you but have procrastinated. I worried that to do so could cause me to lose my dearest friend, Eric Johanson. Perhaps I even held out hope that at some point he might marry me. Now that inoperable cancer has me on death's door, the issues that kept me from sending you this no longer apply.

Even though Eric is not the father of Ricky, my son, Eric has provided me with financial and moral support. Never have I known a kinder or more generous person. He has been like a father to Ricky, and in fact, I have named him as Ricky's guardian, once I die.

While there is no way I will be able to repay Eric for his incredible kindness, I want him to enjoy the happiness he so richly deserves. Back when you and he dated, he referred to you as the love of his life. I don't know the circumstances that caused you to break off your relationship with him, but I believe you made a grave mistake. You will never find a finer man. He is honest, caring, giving, hardworking and faithful. He also happens to be hot.

In the past, I have debated with myself whether I should simply mind my own business. The ambiguity was sufficient to enable me to

335

procrastinate. Now that my days have all but expired, I no longer enjoy the luxury of delay. Apart from Ricky's wellbeing, nothing could please me more than for Eric to enjoy the happiness he deserves. I hope that you will take this to heart.
Sincerely,
Carla Pender

Even after Eric finished reading the letter, he continued to stare at the paper. The appreciation it voiced warmed his heart. But having Glenna know that after so much, he still might harbor feelings for her was embarrassing. "I appreciate your showing me the letter. Carla was an extraordinary person."

"I thought you'd want to see it." She looked away, focusing her gaze on the *Woman with a Fan*. Finally, she said, "There's another reason I came here today. I…I owe you an apology."

"Apology?" Eric searched his brain. Other than spurning him, and she had done that without rancor, she had never done anything that would require her to beg forgiveness…at least nothing he was aware of.

"I misjudged you. I…I thought you weren't honest with me."

The disclosure left him more confused than before.

"Several years ago, back when we were still dating, I bumped into Clinton Horstmeyer on the Bennington campus. At the time he acted as if he had come to the campus for another reason and that our paths had crossed strictly by chance. After I got Carla's letter, I did a little investigating and now suspect that it was not a chance meeting; that Clint had come to Bennington looking for me in order that he could drive a wedge between us, get even with you for encouraging Carla to dump him. Clint told me you were giving money to Carla for the support of her son. When I was skeptical, he suggested I contact Carla's friend Mary Denson. He said that Mary could confirm the payments; that she had been told of them by Carla herself. Clint also asked if I was familiar with the awful things you had done in your sordid past. He referred to you as Jekyll and Hyde."

"That lousy—"

"I know, but don't waste your breath on the creep. Anyway, I asked him what he meant by awful things and Jekyll and Hyde, and right away he clammed up. He said, 'Far be it from me to air the dirty laundry of a fellow Williams' alumnus.' Stupid me...I fell for Clint's act...Well, not completely. Unfortunately, it was enough to plant a seed in my head. I kept waiting for you to tell me about the payments and your connection to Carla's son and things you had done before we had met. I even dropped hints, but all I ever heard were stories of a happy childhood...a minister's son who had followed the straight and narrow."

Glenna's comments triggered recollections of the day they had hiked from the Bennington campus to the Silk Road Covered Bridge, when, as she had done before, Glenna had curiously pressed him about skeletons from his earlier days.

"I repeatedly told myself that you're a wonderful person and I should trust you. My heart wanted to, but my brain spawned concerns. After much self-debate, I decided to contact Mary Denson. I was certain she would put the matter to rest. Much to my chagrin, she confirmed that you were giving money to Carla. Naturally, I assumed that you were the father of her child. Understand—that was not a problem. Not one bit! But what did trouble me was that you didn't tell me you had a son. Add to that, the broader hint that Clint had dropped, and I could only wonder what else you were hiding from me. Very simply, I doubted I could trust you. Long ago, my mother told me, 'Any man you can't trust, is a man you don't want.' Her advice was great...in theory. It got me to thinking, enough so that I took the matter to my two dearest friends at Bennington. I assumed they would tell me to go with my heart, rather than my brain. They didn't. Both urged me to break off the relationship before it went further. And so, with all that wonderful counsel, I broke up with you."

Eric felt his jaw tighten. He had done a good deed, provided support and love for Ricky. His good deed had been misconstrued, and it had cost him the love of his life. On the other hand, he had far more than a small consolation. His good deed had given him an incredible largess. He had Ricky, a wonderful son. He said, "I appreciate your coming today."

Glenna heaved a beleaguered sigh.

"What's the matter?"

"Well…getting my comeuppance, even if it was expected, isn't easy."

"Comeuppance?"

"I…I came here today—it took all the courage I could muster— hoping you would forgive me."

"No problem. There are no hard feelings. I forgive. I want us to be friends."

She sighed again. "That's the problem."

"Excuse me…What problem?"

"Now that I know the facts, I realize that the guy I loved, rather than being dishonest, was even better than the fabulous man I believed him to be. I came here today with faint hopes that you might give me another shot, not that I blame you for rejecting me."

"You…you want us to get back together?"

She nodded sheepishly.

Eric gazed at the *Woman with a Fan*. Could it be? Was she…was the real…did Glenna Snow want him back? His brain, almost as if terrified to hear bad news, struggled to process the shock. He gestured at Glenna and then himself. "You and me…us…together again?"

She nodded once more. "Ever since I received Carla's letter a couple of months ago, I've been kicking myself, knowing that I let the best thing that ever happened to me slip away. A part of me may have known it all along. These past four years, I've compared every guy I dated to you. None of them came close."

"Sounds familiar." Eric's words precipitated a glorious irony. That he had put Glenna on a pedestal, so long a burden, had suddenly become a blessing. It had saved him from settling for someone less. He gazed into Glenna's eyes and whispered, "I never stopped loving you." The rapture painting her face mirrored what he felt. He leaned forward and pressed his lips to hers. He closed his eyes but only briefly, opening them again to make sure that Glenna was there before him. He put his arms around her and locked her in a tight embrace. Seconds...the most magnificent of seconds ticked. When finally their lips parted, he opened his eyes. Her amorous smile, more articulate than words, echoed the ecstasy he felt. The backdrop, the Clark, was perfect. It had long been his oasis. The thought reminded him of a comment Bill Young had made in one of the Inseparables' countless bull sessions. He had claimed that there were oases and *there were oases*. At the time the observation had seemed vapid. Suddenly, the nicety had merit. The Clark may have been an oasis, but next to Glenna's embrace, it paled. Her arms were his oasis. Eric looked to the Heavens, not that he could see beyond the white paint of the ceiling.

"Whatcha thinking?" said Glenna.

"Oh, just enjoying Heaven." The spontaneous utterance reverberated in Eric's brain. He savored the earthly Eden into which he had voyaged. He was close to the Mormon spirit paradise housing Bill Young's soul. Their worlds were inexorably linked, seemingly one and the same. Bill Young was there with him in spirit.

Eric stole a glance at his favorite painting, before turning back to Glenna. He closed his eyes and kissed her once again. The after image of Renoir's masterpiece, yet to vanish, persisted. Denying its magnificence was impossible. Arguably, it was perfection. But next to Glenna Snow, the *Woman with a Fan* was nothing.

www.ingramcontent.com/pod-product-compliance
Lightning Source LLC
Chambersburg PA
CBHW020213260626
47156CB00002B/352